BRIGHT LIGHTS,
BIG BANG . . .

I looked back at the professor, and waved a final goodnight. They got into their car.

I turned my attention to the problem of a cab. I was peering intently down Madison Avenue when it happened. A hellish, blue-white light, a ghastly parody of daylight, burst upon my retina for a duration of somewhere between one to twenty seconds. A cityscape seared my brain, like an image burned into a videocon tube. Ginny gripped my arm. The report followed, ricocheting off the surrounding buildings, milliseconds after the fire-ball. Then came the merry sound of glass tinkling on the concrete.

The Subaru lay on its belly on the asphalt. The car was junk. So were the people inside, the funny little professor and his busty wife . . .

SWINDLE

GEORGE ADAMS

POCKET BOOKS

New York   London   Toronto   Sydney   Tokyo

For Mary Walsh, an original edition,
and Samuel Adams, a first edition.

———————

An *Original* Publication of POCKET BOOKS

POCKET BOOKS, a division of Simon & Schuster Inc.
1230 Avenue of the Americas, New York, NY 10020

ISBN: 0-671-65958-8

First Pocket Books printing February 1989

10 9 8 7 6 5 4 3 2 1

POCKET and colophon are trademarks of
Simon & Schuster Inc.

Printed in the U.S.A.

Chapter 1

Maybe it started when the cashier at the coffee shop ordered me to "Have a nice day!"

Nice day? I'll have any kind of day I want. "You, too," I said, and paid for my bacon and eggs.

Later on, my assistant Tito said, "Hey, man, chill out."

Good advice, and I took it. I changed into shorts, Nikes, and a polo shirt, and hoisted the Lejeune off the ceiling hooks in the storage room. Before hitting the sour city streets, I checked the air pressure in the tires. So far this had not been an especially nice day.

Five minutes later I was in Central Park, fitted into a pack of cyclists breezing past the entrance to the Great Mall. The pace was easy and we stayed bunched to the Boathouse. The hill behind the Metropolitan Museum scattered the pack. A young guy on a graphite-frame bike, several pounds lighter than the Lejeune, took the lead. I used the stirrups and upstroked, keeping a constant interval between us without shifting. A good way to lose your torque, and a punishing way to ride. We crested the hill side by side, stayed parallel up the East Side and past the Reservoir. We were flying under a lemon-yellow sky on the long downhill to Harlem.

The West Side is a series of killer hills as you head back downtown, and it was on the first of them that the kid shifted gears, stood up in the stirrups, and dusted me. I refused to shift. A mistake. Hello, pain. The pack regrouped around me. A young black rode a Panasonic on my left. A guy about my own age, thirty-seven, rode a Motobecane on my right. We sneaked glances at each other from time to time, keeping tabs on our positions. At the Delacorte Theatre the Motobecane popped out in front, while the black kid fumbled shifting and fell off the pace. We were level now and I had my torque back. The Lejeune blew by the Motobecane at the Boating Pond, and I could see the graphite kid ahead of me, loafing along near the Tavern On The Green. I could catch him.

He turned when he heard the clicking of my chain, and grinned. Then he began to pump. And I began to pump. We sprinted around to the East Side. At the turnoff to Bethesda Fountain I lost him. Or, I should say, he lost me. And I lost it. What gave me the idea I could hang with a guy fifteen years my junior anyway? He turned and grinned a "have a nice day" grin, as he dusted me for the second time.

I was flannelmouthed and panting for air. Every pore in my body was leaking water. Like trapped animals, my lungs were clawing their way out of my chest. My heart banged like a two-stroke engine about to throw a rod. Smugly, I began to make my way back to the studio, gritty with caked sweat and city crud, anticipating a scalding hot, self-righteous shower, and reminding myself to lighten up on the sauce and the salt.

As I rolled the bike off the elevator on its rear wheel, I was startled to find Ginny Rowen, the prime reason for the need to chill out, parked outside my door.

"Hi, Charlie!" She jumped up to greet me with a rueful smile. "How was your ride?" She'd been sitting on the floor, reading a copy of *Vanity Fair*.

"Good. But what are you doing here? I wasn't supposed to see you until Friday."

"Yes, I know, but . . . well, I thought I'd take a chance. You were so understanding and . . ." Her voice trailed off.

"Been here long?"

"Not long. I called first and got the machine, so I had a glass of wine across the street." She collected her magazine, and a canvas bag large enough to stuff a horse in, and followed me into the studio. "Had dinner yet?"

"Not yet. I was going to shower first, then make an omelette."

"Oh good. I'm starved." She dropped the bag and maga-zine on the couch, and yanked her baggy T-shirt over her head. Her small breasts shimmied as she shucked a pair of equally baggy jersey pants and bikini bottoms in a single

8

easy motion. "Well?" she exulted, hands on hips, naked except for a pair of old espadrilles.

Unprepared, I gazed at her with obviously foolish pleasure. "I'm stunned," I murmured.

"Sure you are." She laughed. "Come on, you scrub me and I'll scrub you." Before I could answer, she spun and marched off to the bathroom, as perfect a picture going as coming.

Even though this was not how I had imagined this scene, I didn't need a second invitation. My shorts and polo shirt discarded quicker than yesterday's newspapers, I stumbled after her in my sneakers. "Have a nice day!" I thought and ducked into the steamy bathroom.

It was only much later, while we were watching Letterman, that I remembered she had a problem. I got out of bed and threw on a terrycloth robe.

"Going somewhere?" Ginny asked.

"Just to look something up. Be right back."

"Hmm . . ." she said sleepily.

I pulled *The Player's Guide* from the bookshelf above my desk, and took it to the couch. I thumbed the *M's* until I came to Marshall, replaying, as I did, my mental tape of the conversation we had had that afternoon.

"I blew it, Charlie," were her first words.

"Big time" was what I thought, but I kept my mouth shut.

She dumped herself on the couch and messed her hair over her face, hiding behind it in embarrassment, like a schoolgirl. Her hands were fine-boned, tanned, and freckled. She began apologizing in that fluted voice that constantly threatened to take a skid on the chromatic scale. "Don't say anything, Charlie. It was a mess today, I know. I made you look bad."

That was no lie. I had nearly ten grand riding on that shooting. A magazine ad for a health club. And no little chrome barbells. The kind the client wanted. Two models were sitting around talking shop at better than two hundred and fifty bucks an hour, and the client was steaming.

Ginny Rowen had been propping and styling for me for more than a year now, on a freelance basis. She had never failed me before. Along with her good taste and resourcefulness, she had always been thorough and dependable, the indispensable qualities of a good photostylist. So why this suddenly? Forgetting a lousy barbell, and having to run out of the studio in the middle of a shooting, while the meter's running?

She shook her copper-colored hair out of her face and gazed mournfully at me with a pair of bottle-green eyes. "I owe you an explanation," she said.

"Go ahead," I said.

She flicked her tongue across her teeth. "I've done a dumb thing," she said. She had a slight overbite, a disposition that was ordinarily sunny, and an easy, lopsided smile. She was, all in all, a sexy, fine-looking woman in her late twenties.

"Oh?" I said, waiting in suspense. Sexy, fine-looking women always get a chance to explain themselves.

She hesitated. "I haven't told this to anyone yet."

A secret. I felt flattered. "Sure you want me to be the first to know?"

"I've got to talk to someone."

"Right," I said, feeling less special.

"You know how it is in this business."

"How is it?"

"I mean how you meet people on a shoot and you're instant pals, but then when the job's over, everyone goes their own way."

"Yeah . . ."

"Well, last year, while I was styling for a television commercial, I meet this actress, a principal in the commercial. We were just like that." She held up her hand with her index and middle fingers together. "Instantly," she said. "We just seemed to hit it off. We promised to stay in touch when the job was over, and we did. Rare in this business, no?"

"Rare," I agreed.

"We exchanged phone numbers, and when the shoot was wrapped, she said something like, oh, by the way, my boyfriend and I are having a few people in Friday night. If you're free, why don't you drop by?"

"Does this actress have a name?"

"Sloane, Sloane Marshall, but that can't be her real name," she said quickly. "It's too perfect, too Park Avenue."

Sounded like a hooker's name to me. "And how was the party?" I asked.

"Sloane made it sound so casual. A few people? There were nearly a hundred people there. She had an open bar, and the food was out of this world. It was a great party." Then she added wistfully, "I had a wonderful time."

"No problem so far."

"No," she agreed. "I asked Sloane who all the people were, and she said they were friends . . . and clients."

"Clients?"

"That's what I said, and she said yes. Richard, that's the boyfriend, is a financial planner, she explained, and more than a few of the guests were clients of his."

"Ah, this dumb thing that you did . . . Did it have something to do with money?"

"Yes." She messed her hair again.

"You gave this guy, Richard, money?"

"Yes," she murmured.

"How much money?"

"At first, twenty thousand . . ."

"And then?"

She lowered her eyes. "Thirty."

"Total?"

"Fifty thousand dollars," she whispered.

The photostyling business must be good, I thought.

"It was my share from the sale of the house when I got my divorce," she explained.

"And now you'd like to have your money back but Richard won't give it to you. Is that it?"

"Something like that. How did you know?"

"What else could it be? But why did you give him the money in the first place?"

"Because Sloane did a number on me. She starts bragging about how much money Richard has made for this one and that one, pointing out various people in the crowd. Richard's far too modest to toot his own horn, she says, but when it comes to money, he's a genius, and if I have any to invest, I'd do well to let Richard handle it for me. He's never done less than twenty percent, and some of his clients have made as much as fifty percent on their money in less than a year, thanks to Richard, she tells me."

"And you believed her?"

"I wasn't the only one, Charlie. The room was full of believers. Sloane tells me Richard's got all the clients he can

11

handle at the moment, but if I'm interested, she thinks she can get him to take me on."

"And you were, and you got took."

"I gave him the first check last April."

"Didn't Sloane's claims sound fishy to you?"

"Fifty percent sounded too good to be true, sure. But what did I know? I never had any money before, let alone money to invest. Maybe it was Sloane, she was so persuasive. Maybe it was my own greed, but something made me want to believe that the clients were making twenty percent."

I didn't say anything.

"Anyway, in July, Richard gave me a check for a thousand dollars. A dividend check, he called it. Meanwhile there were more parties and dinners . . ."

"And by now Sloane and Richard were your pals."

"We were very chummy. They seemed to have it all, Charlie, looks, style, and plenty of money."

"And you hoped some of it would rub off on you."

She blinked angrily. "I feel like such a fool."

"Don't worry about it," I said inanely. "So, you gave him twenty thousand, he gave you back a thousand, then what happened?"

"I gave him another thirty thousand . . . because of the dividend check."

"Your own money. Now you're out forty-nine thousand." I shook my head. "That's a lot of money."

"All the money I had," she said.

"But you've asked him to give you your money back, right?"

"I've tried."

"What do you mean, you've tried?"

"If I call his office, he's always in a meeting, he'll get right back to me."

"And he never does."

"That's right. And if I call Sloane, she tells me how busy he's been, but he's gonna sit down and go over my account with me the first chance he gets. But in the meantime there's another party, or dinner, and Richard will be putting another dividend check in the mail soon. Then she signs off by reminding me how lucky I am to have Richard as my financial counselor. She has a way of making you feel like

12

they're doing you a favor. What's my measly fifty thousand dollars to a man like Richard, who handles millions of dollars a day? Nothing, a drop in the bucket." She waved her hand airily.

"Then just tell her you want Richard to give you back your measly fifty grand."

"I finally did, yesterday."

"And what happened?"

"She reminded me that there's a penalty clause in our contract for withdrawing the money prematurely. I signed up, in July, for a year."

"So you've got eight months to go."

"Yes, but she said that she'd speak to Richard. Meanwhile, there's a party Friday evening. No hard feelings, and why didn't I come."

"What did you say?"

"I said, we'll see. She said, well you're always welcome, and she thought she'd heard Richard mention something about a dividend check this week."

"It's the crying baby that gets fed. Maybe you should take your losses and get out, Ginny."

"I feel like such a jerk. I don't know what to do."

"Okay, wait and see if you get another check, then if you're still uncomfortable with the situation, put him on notice. You want your money when the year's up."

Suddenly, her eyes brimmed over. "I'm so furious with myself I can hardly think straight. Eight months is a long time. I feel like I let myself get sucked into a get-rich-quick scheme. It's no excuse, I know, but lately I've been so worried about the money that I just plain forgot that damn barbell."

"Well, don't worry about it. I'll eat the extra time on the models if the client complains."

"I can't let you do that, Charlie. Take it out of my fee. It's only fair."

"We'll see. I'll tell you what, if you decide to pull out and take your losses, I'll go with you to Richard's office and we'll demand your money, on the spot."

"Oh, would you, Charlie? That's wonderful." She smiled radiantly. "Sloane did ask me to turn my photographer friends on to Richard." She laughed.

"So much for the myth of a full client list."

She laughed again. "Do you think I should go to the party Friday night?"

"Why not? It's your money that's paying for it."

Her eyes dropped, searching the carpet momentarily, then she leveled them on me with a skeptical, lopsided grin. "But I need a date . . ." She paused. "How about it, Charlie, wanna go to a party?"

It was my turn to grin. "You didn't need to hand me a hard-luck story just to get a date, Ginny."

"Is that a yes?"

"That's a yes."

"That's wonderful!" She beamed, more like her old self.

I beamed too. I'd always had the sneaker for her, but until now, it had seemed wiser to keep the relationship on a strictly professional basis. Photostylists of her caliber are not a dime a dozen.

I had no trouble finding Sloane Marshall in *The Player's Guide* in my office. A two-inch cut from a theatrical glossy showed a pretty blonde with a worldly, professional smile. Model, actress, spokesperson, it said. Her age was listed at an optimistic twenty-seven. Height, five eight; dress size, eight; thirty-four, twenty-three, thirty-four; shoe size, seven and a half; standard model measurements. I had never seen her in a commercial, nor had I ever seen her picture in print before, not that that meant anything.

"Charlie . . ."

I looked up. Ginny was standing in the doorway, wearing my shirt. I closed *The Player's Guide* and returned it to the shelf.

"Letterman's finished," she said with a lopsided grin. "I hope the live entertainment isn't over."

Chapter 2

We were up early enough for a rerun of the evening's live entertainment, with time to spare for coffee and croissants. Under a cloudless blue sky, we walked east to Madison and Thirty-eighth for breakfast at Chez Laurence. It was wonderful just to be alive. On an Indian summer day like this one, Fun City seemed like Shangri-La to me.

I put Ginny in a cab after breakfast; she pulled me in with her and we kissed hotly before she let me go. Watching the cab carry her away, I wondered whether last night had been a mistake. Don't know what it is with me—Celtic pessimism maybe—but no sooner does something as sublime as last night happen to me than I find myself speculating how it will end. As if it made a difference. Anyway, if the night before had been a mistake, I was bound to make the same mistake Friday night. At least I knew what I had to look forward to. Never mind the Celtic gloom, pal, lighten up and have a nice day.

As a matter of fact, I not only had a nice day, I had a terrific day. First I ran to the lab and checked the test rolls from yesterday's shoot. They were perfect, on the money. Good exposure, good color. And the shot looked good too, the design, lighting, and props were all perfect. No reshoot. The photographs would sell themselves. And don't think that didn't help make this photographer's day. Old-timers will tell you, no matter how long you've been in the business, you never get over the sense of relief that comes with looking at a perfect test roll. I instructed the lab technician to run the balances normal, as tested. Before returning to the studio, I went by a newstand and picked up a copy of *The New York Times*.

Though it is only twelve stories up, paltry by New York standards, I like to think of the studio as my aerie. It is a rear duplex on Thirty-eighth Street, between Fifth and Sixth. My space, which totals twenty-one hundred square feet, rents for fourteen dollars a square foot. But the monthly bill is never the same two months in succession, and never less than twenty-seven hundred, thanks to those little extras like fuel oil, water, labor, and taxes. When it comes to creative billing, you can't beat a New York landlord.

The loft was raw space when I signed the lease. Tito, my assistant, and I built the place ourselves. We studded, wired, plumbed, and sheetrocked. We installed a full kitchen and bath, taped, spackled, and painted. It was like building a house inside a building, and it cost nearly as much.

A bank of north-light windows, a skylight, white paint and blond wood trim throughout give the place an airy, spacious feeling. On the first floor are the reception area, kitchen, shooting area, client lounge, bathroom, and storage. Upstairs are the dressing room, office, and my bedroom. There's no darkroom because I don't make money in the darkroom, I'm a shooter. The lease expires in March, at which time the landlord will demand twenty-eight dollars a square foot, or a base rent, as he calls it, of forty-nine hundred bucks a month.

Tito poured me a cup of coffee with a sly smile. "Had a guest last night, huh?"

"What makes you say that?"

"I found these," he said, grinning a broad Cheshire Cat grin and brandishing a pair of bikini panties, "in the dressing room. Who's the lucky lady, boss?"

"None of your business."

He shrugged. I had few secrets from him. "Wouldn't be the stylist, would it?" he leered.

Tito is a wiry, street-wise, you-need-it-I-can-get-it sort of guy. I acquired him, as it were, almost four years ago, along with several battered Nikon camera bodies and half a dozen lenses, as collateral on a loan to a down-on-his-luck photojournalist buddy. I sold the equipment for what I could get—much less than the loan—but kept Tito. He had a soothing presence, was cool-headed and diligent; he had long since proven himself the best part of the bargain.

"I said, it was none of your business."

Before working for my friend, Tito had been in Nam and sold pot for a living. Since coming to work for me and getting a regular paycheck, he had married, become a family man, and a taxpayer, none of which prevented him from finding vicarious pleasure in my sex life. "It's not right for a man to live alone, Charlie," he informed me, shaking an index finger in my face.

"I'll have to remember that, Tito. But don't you have anything else to do besides handing out lonelyheart's advice?"

"I see, touchy today, aren't we? That's good. Means this one must be serious. But you're right, of course, I've got a family to support, so I suggest you get on the horn and find out what the clients are up to."

"Right, wiseguy."

"Here, take these." Grinning, he tossed me the panties and moved off to busy himself in the shooting area. I topped my coffee off, and with the *Times,* removed myself to the office. Between phone calls, I sipped coffee and worked on the crossword puzzle.

My calls got results. A client I hadn't heard from in a while had some work for me. "No one does skin like you, Charlie," he said, thinking he was paying me a compliment, and making me feel like a sleaze. He had three paperback book covers to shoot. Girls and lingerie, easy stuff, if not all that well paying. Downtime is like death to a freelancer, and these jobs would keep us busy until something better came along. I finished the puzzle, an event for me, but it was that kind of day, and I was about to throw the answering machine on and go to lunch with Tito at the Greek's, when I thought of one last call I wanted to make.

The phone rang twice before a voice, lower than the bottom of a barrel, answered. "P.C. Strunk here."

"It's Charlie Byrne, P.C., remember me?" *P* was for Percy, *C* was for Calvin, and he answered either to P.C., my choice, or just plain Strunk. And that was all he answered to, unless you didn't need two good legs.

"Of course I remember you, Byrne. What do you want?" He called me Byrne, and I felt flattered.

"I want to buy you lunch," I said. We had spoken on the phone a couple of times since Pakistan, once when I saw his name in the paper, and another time when he found my

17

picture credit in a national magazine. We promised we'd get together for lunch, but never did.

"'Bout time," he said. "When?"

"Monday?" I suggested. "An Indian or Pakistani place, maybe?"

"You like Szechuan?"

"What?"

"Szechuan. Chinese food? Do you like it?"

The appeal of Chinese food had always eluded me, but I said, "Oh, that Szechuan, sure, love it."

"You said you're paying, right?"

"That's right."

"Well, you're in luck. I know a place. Hasn't been discovered yet. It's still cheap, and Monday's fine with me."

"All right, where do you want to meet?"

"Riverside, southeast corner entrance to the World Trade Center, at noon."

"Your office there?"

"The State's the anchor tenant."

"It's been a while, P.C., will I recognize you?" I asked, smiling at the memory, from another lifetime, it seemed, of a skinny kid marine, an embassy guard who liked his rice.

"Good question, Byrne. I don't wear dress blue anymore. The uniform's a three-piece suit these days. And I'm older, heavier . . . and hell, I look like a cop!" He laughed. "What about you, still taking pictures?"

"Yeah."

"Okay, we'll see if we look like what we are. I'll see you Monday, Byrne." He hung up.

It was still daylight, the sky a wash of salmon pink, Friday evening when I climbed the stoop of Ginny Rowen's Chelsea brownstone and rang the bell. She buzzed me in and waited at the head of the first flight of stairs. I loped up them two at a time, trailing Givenchy aftershave lotion in my wake. She said hi, greeted me with a luminous smile, and led me through a tiny foyer into the apartment.

When she turned to face me, I was dumbstruck. I'd never seen her so dressed up before. To be honest, I'd never even seen her in a dress before. This one was a little black sheath, cut straight across the top, and held up by a pair of spaghetti straps. The hemline kissed her knees; and so could have I. After all, you've got to start somewhere. Her hair was pulled off her face and worn up, piled on top of the head, accenting an expanse of bare, dappled skin that was her neck and shoulders. She was a knockout.

She smiled. "You look very soigné tonight, Charlie," she said. "I've never seen you in a suit before."

The suit was a Brooksgate, medium weight, charcoal grey; the only suit I owned. Uncertain what "soigné" meant, I thanked her anyway, and told her that I thought she looked swell, too.

"Would you like a drink?" she asked, moving to an antique sideboard that served as a bar.

"Please, bourbon and ice, if you've got it." I knew she bought and sold antiques and memorabilia from her home, so I wasn't totally unprepared, but still my eyes roamed the room in amazement and admiration. Ferns, mimosa, climbing plants, cacti, and orchids competed for available space with an eclectic collection of kitsch and antiques. I recognized an armoire, a wingback chair, a small Tiffany lamp, a bentwood coatrack, even some turn-of-the-century theatrical posters, all items I had rented from her, at one time or another, as props.

"Well, what do you think of the place?" she asked, handing me my drink with an amused smile, after I'd taken it all in.

"It's an awful lot to look at. I mean . . . it's fascinating." She laughed. "It's all for sale."

"Actually, I like it. It's cozy."

She laughed again. "It's cluttered, you mean. But if you don't like it, wait. It changes by the week. It's the price one pays for living in the store."

We sat at opposite ends of an Art Deco green-velvet sofa, and twisted to face one another. The ice in our glasses made a friendly clinking sound in the momentarily awkward silence. It seemed to come in a rush, the awareness that our condition was changed, that we were in strange, uncharted country. She sipped her drink and gazed at me with a grave, inquisitive face.

"How about some music?" she said and stood up.

I put my glass down, intercepting her. For a beat we were

19

face to face, then we kissed. She fitted her body neatly into mine. She tasted like vanilla, and smelled like scrubbed cotton.

"We don't have to go to Sloane's," she said.

I liked that, just like that, but tonight I was in no hurry. And tomorrow was Saturday. We could sleep late. "Let's go. I'm curious about your friends, Richard and Sloane."

"Yesterday I got a check for a thousand dollars," she said.

"Every little bit helps."

We sat down again. She swirled the ice in her glass a moment before looking up at me. "God, Charlie, what a load I dumped on you the other day."

"What are friends for?"

"I feel much better after getting that check. But I want you to know I appreciate your offering to help. I may take you up on it yet."

"Anytime."

"Anyway, tonight I want to forget about all of that. I feel good." She gave me the lopsided grin. "Tonight we are going to party."

We touched glasses, and I repeated, "Tonight we're going to party."

On the way out, she paused to freshen her lipstick in the foyer mirror, while I inspected a collection of photographs that hung on the wall. In one picture she was sitting next to a smiling man in a nightclub or disco. She was wearing the same dress she had on tonight. I couldn't blame the guy for smiling. But I sure as hell resented it.

I nodded at the photograph. "Nice picture. Always wanted a girl who looked like that."

"You've got one," she said.

I hesitated, thinking the party could wait, then slipped a proprietary arm around her waist as we went out the door.

At Sloane Marshall's building, red brick with an Italianate facade, fourteen stories high just off Park Avenue on Seventy-fifth Street, the doorman directed us to an elevator that sported matching rosewood panels freshly lemon-oiled. We rode up in silence with several other possible revelers. A scattered young woman, in for the night, I assumed, received us at the door and ushered us through a stark hallway. She deposited us in a large, graciously proportioned living room, and abandoned us. People milled about in uncertainty, the party not quite in full swing yet.

My eye was caught, quicker than it takes a trout to whack a mayfly, by a large black-and-white photomural that was the centerpiece of the room. Lit by a single spot and mounted and framed under glass, it was a nude of our hostess, Sloane Marshall. She was posed against a painted canvas backdrop, an electric fan (out of picture) blew her hair, and shrunk her nipples. Her arms reached for the skies, out of frame and above her head. Good for the breasts. Uplifting. One thigh coyly crossed the other, and her eyes gazed resolutely off into the ether, disdaining the voyeur's lens. It was an arty, pretentious photograph, like a fashion magazine nude.

"Nice tits," I murmured.

"They're okay," Ginny said.

This was not a room meant for living in, I noticed as I checked out the rest of the place. There was no comfortable chair, no wonderful end table, no family heirloom nor sentimental old piece from Grandma's house. Everything looked new, bought yesterday, and without history. It was like a display, as tricked up as a Bloomingdale room set, designed to make only one statement: expensive. It was a hard, brittle room of metal and glass. Reflected lighting and an off-white paint job helped compensate a little for the lack of fabric and wood and flattered the skin at the same time.

A young man in a white jacket drifted by with champagne in plastic stemware on a silver tray. We helped ourselves, and sipping champagne, turned our attention to the other guests.

"Could all these people be clients?" I asked.

"Not all," said Ginny. "Sloane's a clever one. She likes to salt the crowd with her fashion and show business friends. Although I'm sure even some of them must be clients."

"I see. Let the hoi polloi have a chance to rub elbows with the beautiful people. That is clever."

"Exactly," she said, with a sour little smile.

"Ginny, Ginny Rowen, there you are, I'm so glad you could come." Sloane Marshall, herself, glided up to us. She was modestly but elegantly dressed in a high-necked, long-sleeved, white cocktail dress, on loan, no doubt, from some designer who was probably part of the crowd. Her hair was cropped shorter than in the photomural, and her accessories were simple: a single strand of pearls with matching earrings. Her makeup was flawlessly understated, too. She was better than her photographs, a brown-eyed blonde with skin like butter.

"Hello, Sloane," said Ginny. Sloane glanced from me to Ginny, and back again. "Sloane, this is Charles Byrne. Charles, Sloane Marshall," she recited dutifully.

"I'm pleased to meet you, Charles." She offered me her hand. "Ginny's been hiding you from us," she purred, assessing me with a practiced eye.

"A pleasure meeting you, Sloane," I said.

"And what do you do, Charles?"

Whatever happened to "how do you do"? I wondered. Ginny answered for me, "He's a photographer."

"A photographer?" The sculptured eyebrows rose in mock surprise. "But you don't look like a photographer," she said, laughing with her eyes. She was a practiced flirt, a helpful knack, no doubt, for cadging an occasional modeling job, but it meant nothing.

"It's the suit." I smiled politely.

A distinguished-looking man in his mid-forties materialized beside her. "Darling," Sloane said, "I'd like you to meet Charles Byrne, a photographer friend of Ginny's."

He smiled thinly and gave me a mild handshake. "How do you do," he said, "Richard Hungerford." His voice was both resonant and tentative.

"Nice to meet you," I said amiably.

His suit was not off the rack. He was tall, six two or three, darkly handsome, with bland, patrician features. The jawline was still firm, but the temples were streaked with grey. Sloane, with her gilded perfection, and Hungerford, impeccable and suave, together were an art director's wet dream of what "upscale" should be. They were the couple in the cognac ad.

"Richard has quite a few photographer clients, don't you, darling?"

"Several, yes," he admitted.

"Oh?" I said innocently. "And what do you do, Richard?"

"Richard's a financial planner," said Sloane. "But surely Ginny must have told you that."

22

"No, I don't think so," I said, feigning a mixture of ignorance and surprise in Ginny's direction.

"Shame on you, Ginny." Sloane grinned.

"That must be an interesting field, financial planning," I said. "All anyone talks about these days is money."

"That's the truth," Sloane agreed. "And that's why it's so important, if you have a little money, that you get sound advice on how to deal with it. If you're a self-employed person *particularly.*"

Hungerford cleared his throat. "Darling, remember, we said no shop talk tonight."

"But I'd like to hear more," I persisted. "It sounds interesting."

"Oh, don't worry, you will," Sloane promised. "And Richard's the best."

"Sloane, darling," Hungerford protested.

"He's so modest," Sloane said, slipping behind a professional smile, and turning to Richard. "I know, darling, we should circulate. Enjoy yourselves, Charles Byrne. And Ginny." And they got themselves back into circulation.

"Slut-bitch," Ginny murmured when they were out of earshot.

I glanced at her.

She smiled back sweetly. "Always hustling. Did you have to encourage her?"

"Just wanted to hear the pitch. If she can close as well as she canvasses, she's all right."

"You can believe it. That's why we're all here."

Ginny wasn't exaggerating when she said the food at these parties was out of this world. For openers, there was Irish salmon, flown in fresh from the Old Sod that very day. The roast beef was tender enough to cut with a fork. Assortments of crudités, pâtés, esoteric goat cheeses, tortellini, asparagus stalks and Hollandaise sauce, and fresh morel mushrooms at thirty dollars a pound were but a few of the eats that I could identify. And there was also real whipped cream and fresh strawberry shortcake from Dumas.

We loaded our hard plastic plates with goodies, and began eating on the hoof. Beside us, munching blissfully, was a small man with a receding hairline.

"Pretty good grub, huh?" I managed between mouthfuls.

"Uh-huh," he answered. Next to him stood a petite blonde with a pouter-pigeon chest. She agreed, she nodded.

I introduced Ginny and myself. He said his name was Louis Leveau, and that the top-heavy lady was his wife, Marie.

"You look familiar." Ginny smiled. "Have I seen you here before?"

"It's possible," he said. "We've been to enough of these soirées." He nodded at Ginny. "Does she look familiar, Marie?"

"Yes, dear," said his wife.

"I thought so . . ."

"How are you folks getting on?" It was Hungerford, the solicitous host. "I see you've met the professor." He smiled at me.

"Richard," said the little man, "I've been trying to get hold of you for over a week."

"Yes, yes, I know, Professor."

"I'd like to have a word with you."

"Yes, but not tonight, my friend. I'll call you Monday night, at home. Enjoy the food now." He left us with a smile, continuing to work the room.

"Hard to pin Richard down," Ginny observed.

"That man has more moves than Walter Payton," said the little man.

"What do you profess?" I asked Louis.

"I teach French in the City University of New York, the CUNY system," grinned Louis.

Marie glared at him.

"French?" I repeated.

"That's right. You could say I'm a CUNY linguist." His eyes twinkled.

Marie glanced nervously at Ginny. Ginny giggled.

"What's your racket?" he asked.

"I'm a photographer."

"Funny, you don't look like one."

"I know." I sighed.

He glanced at Ginny, who merely smiled. "What kind of photography? I understand there are specialties."

"Advertising, primarily, still-life and illustration, but anything for a dollar."

"Do you do nudes?" he asked with a leer.

"Occasionally."

"Ah, I think I'd like that," he said dreamily.

Marie gave him a poke with her elbow that shimmied the cantileverage and nearly caused him to drop his plate. "Louis," she snapped, and then to Ginny and me she explained, "Louis is a dirty old middle-aged man."

"Sweetheart, my little honeypot," he protested, "the man is a professional. Here's an opportunity to get a few tips from the top. Think of how much better our Polaroids will be."

Marie shook her head, and rolled her eyes to the heavens. The man was obviously incorrigible. Ginny smiled sympathetically. Then, suddenly thoughtful, Marie asked Ginny, "Are you a client?"

"Of Richard's, you mean?" said Ginny.

"Yes."

With a forkful of food suspended in midair between face and plate, the professor waited for her answer.

"Yes, I am," said Ginny.

"And are you a happy client?" asked the professor.

Ginny hesitated. "Well, mostly," she said finally.

"What's that supposed to mean?" the professor demanded.

"Well, I've had my anxious moments," she confessed.

He turned to his wife. "You see, sweetheart, we're not the only ones."

"But why?" I asked. "Haven't you been making money?"

He moved closer, his eyes darting around the room. "Sure, we've made a few dollars. There have been several interest checks, but it's our principal we're worried about. All we've got to show for it is a computerized statement, and what's that? I'll tell you what that is, it's bullshit."

"I guess I feel the same way," said Ginny.

"And lately," the professor continued, "Sloane's been after us to give Richard more money. She's gotten real aggressive, even to the point of suggesting it's a matter of loyalty. I don't like it." He grinned. "Hell, if I could ever pin the guy down, I'd like to get some of the money back, and put it into something nice and safe, like Washington Public Power bonds, or swamp land in Florida." He laughed at his own joke. "Know what a 'Ponzi' scheme is?" He was staring at me.

25

"I think so," I said.

"Then you know why I'm so nervous."

"Have you spoken to any of the others about this?" I asked, glancing around.

"You gotta be kidding," was the answer. "Sloane and Richard have this crowd so snowed they think he's the best thing since doggy bags. And besides, if Richard is running a Ponzi scheme, the last thing I'd want to do is tell the others."

I could see his point.

The music was turned up, and people began to dance. Ginny excused us, and slipping her arm through mine, led me to the dance floor. "We were going to party tonight, remember?" she said.

We began to move gently to a Salsa tempo, my left hand resting where her waist flared out at the hip, our right hands clasped palm to palm. I inhaled the smell of her; scrubbed cotton and vanilla. For that moment it was as though we were the only two people in the universe.

When the music stopped, Sloane approached, arms open, hips swaying. "May I steal a dance with your handsome friend," she asked Ginny, in mock humility, with a false smile.

That seemed to be a sleek, dark middle-aged man's cue. Flashing a mouthful of well-kept enamel, he stepped up and asked Ginny to dance. "Anthony!" she exclaimed. The timing was too perfect. We were being double-teamed, I thought.

"Where has our little Ginny been hiding you, Charles Byrne?" said Sloane, moving gracefully into my arms, and working her thick eyelashes.

No one ever called me handsome, except when they meant it in the sense that all women are beautiful, and therefore all men are handsome. For one thing, my nose wanders over my face like a meandering stream, a memento of two dozen amateur fights when I was a kid. For another, I'm not tall enough. I'm shy of six feet, and chunky at a hundred and ninety pounds. But I've got two of everything I'm supposed to have two of, and one of all the rest. My hair is still dark and curly, and my eyes are still blue, which makes me an average-looking guy, I guess. Sloane seemed to like what she saw. Her eyes shone with approval, like I was baby beef.

"You do head shots, don't you?" she said. We were slow dancing, and her thigh slipped momentarily between mine.

Over her shoulder, I watched Ginny and Anthony. He was my size, with a carriage that hinted at coiled strength, big cat power. He was a very good dancer, much better than me. Ginny seemed to enjoy dancing with him, and I felt a pang of envy. "Yes, I do head shots, occasionally," I said. "Why do you ask?"

"My pictures are all so dated."

I glanced at the photomural. "Yes, but some pictures are timeless."

"Oh that." She laughed, pleased I'd mentioned it. "I won't tell you how long ago that was taken."

That seemed like a good idea, although I could guess.

"Richard's crazy about it, though," she went on. "He's the one who insisted we should hang it. But as you can see, my look has changed since then."

I could see, and I could see Hungerford standing on the edge of the dance floor, watchful and morose. I sensed he didn't have her dance card filled, not by any means. "Well, whenever you're ready," I said, "you can call me. I'm in the book."

"I don't call men." She laughed, showing two even rows of feral teeth. "And I'm not in the book." She plucked at my lapel, then she slipped a card into the breast pocket of my jacket. "Why don't you give me a ring whenever you feel like it." She patted my pocket.

Then she dropped her hands to her sides, and we were no longer touch dancing. She snapped her fingers in time with the music, and rolled her shoulders, teasing me with her breasts, and throwing her head back to show off her long, white neck. People drew back and stared, expecting her to solo, maybe. Instead, she flashed the gathering audience an apologetic smile, and took my hand again, the impromptu performance mercurially over before it had begun.

"I love to dance," she explained.

"That was wild," I said. "Too bad I'm not Fred Astaire."

"Yes," she replied. "Don't you ever feel like letting go, just busting loose?"

A fat man, in a three-piece suit and too much jewelry, cut in before I could answer. "Don't forget, give me a call," she said over her shoulder as he took her off.

27

I watched the other dancers for a moment. Ginny was dancing with the professor, and laughing at something he said. Anthony, I noticed, was now dancing with Marie. He was very animated, smiling a lot. Marie seemed to be having none of it. When she smiled in return, it was only half-heartedly, for mostly she seemed skeptical of whatever it was he was saying.

I decided to see what the rest of the apartment was like, and went exploring. In the bedroom I found some of the beautiful people passing small, brown vials back and forth, and making trips to the bathroom in twos and threes. No one offered me a toot, so I made my way back to the living room.

I repossessed Ginny from the randy little professor, and we danced.

"Look at Richard," she said. "Why doesn't he ask someone to dance?"

Hungerford, a wallflower at his own party, stared gloomily at Sloane and Anthony as they danced.

"No one could be as hot as Sloane pretends to be," Ginny said. "What do you guys see in those ice queens, anyway?"

"I wouldn't know," I said. "But who is this Anthony guy? Doesn't he have a last name?"

"Oh, he's Anthony Pesce. Marvelous dancer, isn't he? He's at all these parties. Sort of the extra man."

"You sure?" It was easy to see that Sloane and Anthony, from the way they were enjoying themselves, had danced together before. They were good, they were very good, almost professional, and yet it was eerie watching them. "We know that Friday nights are Richard's," I said. "How many other nights a week are his, do you suppose?"

"Charlie!"—she laughed—"you're a cynic."

"Yeah."

"Do you really think there's something between Sloane and Anthony?"

"If not him, someone else then."

"But Anthony's such a different type, from Richard, I mean."

"Maybe she doesn't go for type, or she likes a change now and then. Like out of the sauna, and into the snowbank. Know what I mean?"

"I think so. Like sweet and sour."

We were hardly moving. "Like wet and dry," I said.

"Mmm, like rough and . . ."

"Smooth." I pulled her closer.

"Like hard?" She giggled.

"And soft. Good is what you like. And what I'd like is to jump your bones."

"Oh, you're so glib. Let's get outta here."

We rode down in the elevator with the professor and his wife, and together the four of us walked to the corner of Madison and Seventy-fifth.

"Can we drop you somewhere?" the professor offered.

"Thanks, but we'll grab a cab," I said.

"Well, see you at the next shareholder's meeting," he joked.

"You never know." I laughed. "Goodnight now."

"Goodnight," they called, starting across the avenue.

The avenue was empty, no traffic. Ginny and I huddled together for warmth, waiting for the light to change, and a possible cab. I waved futilely at two cabs that went by with their off-duty signs on, and regretted turning down the professor's offer. When I looked across the street again, I saw the professor fumbling in his pockets for his keys. At the same time, a figure caught my eye as it emerged, mid-block on the avenue, from the shadows of a doorway. A shopkeeper, working late, I thought. I remember being amused at the prospect of such a big man climbing into the low-slung Datsun 280Z, but he managed it swiftly, without a hitch. I looked back at the professor, and waved a final goodnight. He and Marie both waved back, and they got into their car.

I turned my attention again to the problem of a cab. I was peering intently down Madison Avenue when a hellish blue-white light, a ghastly parody of daylight, burst upon my retina. A cityscape seared my brain, like an image burned into a videcon tube. Ginny gripped my arm in terror. The report followed, ricocheting off the surrounding buildings, milliseconds after the fireball. Then came the merry sound of window glass tinkling on the concrete.

The guy in the Datsun must have thought WW III had broken out because, rear end fishtailing, tires screeching, he peeled out, up Madison, and was gone. At least that was my first thought.

Ginny buried her face in my chest and clung to me. "Oh, my God, no," she cried.

A column of greasy smoke ascended lazily into the black sky, from where the Subaru lay on its belly on the asphalt. The car was junk. So were the people inside, the funny little professor and his busty wife.

Lights went on, up and down the street, all along the avenue. Windows were thrown open, and heads appeared. Slowly, the street began to fill with people, people in pajamas and bathrobes, people in raincoats, people in evening clothes, people in warm-up suits, people in every kind of getup. Sirens wailed. First the firemen came, then the cops.

Ginny and I held on fiercely to each other. She was trembling so hard I worried that she might be in shock.

"Here, take these, miss," a man said. He was in bathrobe and slippers, carrying a black bag.

She stared at him, eyes glazed.

"It's all right, I'm a doctor. They're Valium." His eyes went to the wreck. He shook his head. "Nothing I can do here," he said, and shuffled off into an apartment building.

The plainclothes cop that took our statements was a no-nonsense middleweight, sandy-haired and rough-complected. We told him all we knew, and what we'd seen, which didn't amount to much. I told him about the Datsun Z, and he asked if I'd got the plate number. I said no. He asked me what color it was, and I had to tell him I thought it was dark green, but I couldn't be sure. He glanced at me with a pair of hard, cold eyes. I explained that the light was lousy, it was late, I wasn't at my best.

"Thank you for your help," he said politely, if ambiguously, and snapped shut a leather notebook. "If we have any further questions, we'll be in touch."

Her place or mine, either one was fine with me. Instead, Ginny dropped me off at the studio and kept the cab, a single unspoken thought between us. We could have been in that Subaru. As numb and exhausted as I was, I felt an urgent need to reaffirm the fact that we were still among the quick. But celebrating the life force seemed the farthest thing from her mind. She wished to withdraw, become uncommunicative. I wanted to comfort her, and to be comforted by her, but I didn't press.

We weren't going to party tonight; we had brushed too close to death.

Chapter 3

I was at the southeast corner of the World Trade Center at noon on the dot. A chrome metal sun beat down from directly overhead, scattering shards of refracted light off the glass-sheathed twin towers and stabbing me in the eyes.

It had been almost a dozen years since I'd seen him last, but I had no difficulty recognizing him, in spite of the harsh light that made me squint, and his new silhouette. Uncomfortable and hot in the three-piece suit, he glanced impatiently at his watch before looking up and spotting me.

"That you, Byrne?"

"The same." I still had to look up to him, and when I did, I saw the same determined expression of the kid marine I used to know. His skin, in the bright light, shone like a burnished horse chestnut. He'd be thirty-one or -two now, and the nappy black hair was beginning to recede, as well as showing flecks of grey. I tried to imagine that skinny kid trapped inside this huge body.

He looked me over. "Shit, never did think you looked like a photographer."

I seemed doomed to be a disappointment. If I owned a denim or leather jacket, I would have worn it, instead of the blazer, shirt, and necktie I had on. "I get a lot of that lately," I said. "But you sure as hell look like some kind of cop, P.C."

He chuckled. "Come on, my car's over here. Can't take a long lunch, I'm expecting a call from a snitch."

He led the way briskly to a construction divider on the West Side Highway, where a brown Plymouth Fury was illegally parked. The legend "Govt. Vehicle" was displayed on the windshield.

"Don't have to worry about being towed, huh, P.C.?"

"Not when you're a public servant."

He unlocked the car and eased himself behind the wheel. Leaning over, he opened my door, and I climbed in. He wheeled the car around in a U-turn, and we headed for Chinatown via Battery Park, and the FDR Drive.

"It's been a few years, P.C.," I said.

"And you're showing 'em, Byrne."

"You don't look so gung ho yourself."

"Still with the Company?" he challenged me with a grin.

Knowing, no matter what I said, he wouldn't believe me, I smiled. "Retired," I said.

"Expected you'd say something like that. Shit, I may have been a dumb nineteen-year-old kid marine . . ."

"Don't be so hard on yourself," I interrupted him.

"But even back then, I knew a spook when I saw one."

"Spook, P.C.?"

He chuckled. "You know what I mean. I thought you were slick. Wanted to be just like you when I grew up. You were my idol, Byrne."

"I had no idea. I'm flattered, P.C." Back then, as he called it, I was globe-trotting as a freelance photojournalist. I had used the kid marine, through his embassy contacts, to help me get a shot of Ali Bhutto, which I sold to *Newsweek* for a cover story. Then Ali Bhutto was assassinated, and somehow P.C. Strunk became convinced that the CIA had a hand in his assassination, and that I had a hand in the CIA. I no longer bothered to try and dissuade him that I was nothing more than I appeared, a photojournalist bum. And it didn't help my case any that I made a lot of money on that picture.

"It's a fact," he said. "I even applied, when my hitch was up. But they turned me down. Big, black ex-marines just ain't their style."

"Too conspicuous for them?"

"That, or not devious enough for the bastards."

I wasn't too sure about that. "You must be a good cop, you're suspicious enough."

"I am a good cop. That's why I don't understand what they saw in you that they didn't see in me?"

"You're asking the wrong guy. But I wouldn't eat my heart out if I were you, P.C. Call it anything you like, intelligence, tradecraft, spook-work, what it comes down to is deviousness, and betrayal elevated to the status of a profession. Life is lousy enough with both on the amateur level; who needs to make a career out of them?"

"Listen to the guy," he sneered. "You're missing the point, Byrne."

"Yeah, what's that?"

"Someone's got to do it." He wheeled the car into a no-parking zone, and pulled down the "Govt. Vehicle" sign. We had a short walk to an unpromising-looking dark hole painted landlord green with a lone plastic potted palm that was wilting. It was slightly past noon, and the place was empty. This seemed to please Strunk. "No one knows about this place yet," he bragged.

Or maybe they didn't live to tell about it. The joint was only a little larger than a phone booth, and had ten tables jammed into it. We seated ourselves in the aisle chairs of a table for four. It was the kind of place where you ate with strangers when they had a full house. A sallow, hollow-chested survivor of the Burma Death March approached with cups of tea and menus in hand.

"Sort of a no-frills theme restaurant, huh?" I said. "Why don't you go ahead and order for both of us."

"Okay," he said happily. "You like hot?"

"Sure," I said recklessly. What I liked was half a canteloupe and some cottage cheese.

"Hungry?"

In a spirit of containment, I answered, "So-so."

"Love this stuff," he said ardently.

"No kidding," I said.

"You noticed." He smiled. The waiter spoke no English, naturally, and Strunk proceeded to order by pointing to the number. The waiter wagged his head affirmatively each time, then pronounced the item in Chinese.

From seemingly nowhere, a gang of boisterous Chinese

kids clamored in and crowded around a couple of tables they pushed together. A few businessmen from Wall Street drifted in after them, and filled the few remaining tables.

"Got here just in time," Strunk observed gloomily. "Looks like I'm not the only one who knows about the place. Now watch the prices jump. The good news is, joints like this are popping up all the time, like bean sprouts."

The food came immediately. Chinese dumplings, two kinds of lo mein, a chicken and a pork, and a sautéed eggplant dish. We shared.

Strunk munched contentedly on his lo mein while I worked up courage to try a mouthful. He raised his eyes from his bowl, and ordered me, "Eat! It's good."

I tried some, and found it wasn't bad.

Between shoveling in mouthfuls of food, he said, "Okay, Byrne, you got me here, now what's this all about?"

"What do you know about so-called money managers, or financial planners?"

"Only that half of them used to sell co-op apartments, and that it's a license to steal, if they're so inclined."

"Ever bust any of them?"

"Not yet. Why?"

"Well, I've got a friend." And I told him Ginny's story.

"Your friend should have walked the minute she heard the claims they were paying those kind of interest rates," he said, when I finished telling him Ginny's story.

"She admits it, she was seeing dollar signs."

"They always do."

"You don't seem particularly interested. What's the matter, is it small potatoes?"

"It isn't that. It's just not the type of case I get involved with."

"I would have thought it was right up your alley."

"I'm State Police, I'm with the Attorney General's office. I'm an investigator with the securities division. If anything, you want the District Attorney's office. For me to become involved there'd have to be solicitation through the mails or by phone. Or there would have to be phony paper involved, stocks, bonds, that sort of thing. If he was moving money internationally, money that the taxes hadn't been paid on, then he'd have me on his case. But from what you tell me, I don't even see that there's been a crime committed yet. The guy's been paying her dividends."

"Yeah. I thought you might say something like that. But no harm checking."

"Sorry, Byrne. I'd like to help."

"I know, P.C."

"My cases are fairly routine. Mostly I'm setting up snitches to run stings on bucket-shop and boiler-room operators. We bust 'em one week, they're back in business at a new location the next."

"Well, are you having any fun?"

"It's never dull, and once in a while we get a real winner. I have a case now, you'd know the name, the guy's a famous realtor. He's broke, on-the-balls-of-his-ass broke. But he's got a foundation that he funds. Named after himself, of course. The law says he's not allowed to touch that money because he hasn't paid any tax on it. But he's been getting it out of the country, funneling it through a bank in Israel. They charge a fee and send the money on to Zurich for him, where he gets it back in the form of an interest-free loan. Slick, huh? It's not the CIA, just the next best thing. But getting back to your problem, know what a 'Ponzi' is?"

"There are no investments. The money collected from one person is used to pay interest, or dividends to another."

"In a nutshell." He smiled thinly. "They named it after a guy who was running a multimillion-dollar scam like that in '29, when the stock market crashed."

"That's exactly what my friend is afraid of, that she's caught up in a Ponzi-type scam."

Strunk hesitated. "There's another possibility," he said, thinking out loud. "They're buying drugs with the money. That's the reason they can offer those high rates."

Sloane Marshall and her pal Hungerford, coke smugglers. That was food for thought. "Think so?"

"You never know. Just had a case, some guys in Florida were selling gold certificates through the mails. It was just a scam to raise money for drug deals. We had dozens of complaints about them from disgruntled investors. To save her own skin, the bookkeeper blew the whistle on them to the Feds. They got a search warrant and broke into the warehouse where the bullion was supposed to be stored. Lo and behold, no gold."

35

"How much money did they raise?"

"About thirty million."

"Jesus, with that kind of money they could have gone legit, I'd think."

"Not quite. The reason people bought the gold certificates was because they were drastically underselling the gold market."

"I see. So when the Feds busted them, where did that leave the people with the certificates?"

"Up the proverbial creek. But don't waste any sympathy on them, you can bet they bought them with black money."

"What's black money?"

"Money they were hiding from the IRS. Wanna know who the biggest suckers for these scams are?"

"Who?"

"Doctors," he beamed. "They've always got lots of cash to hide, and they're the dumbest when it comes to hiding it."

"And now the lawyers get the doctors' money."

"And so it goes. But getting back to cases, there are several possibilities you and your friend might think about."

"Such as . . ."

"That there's nothing to worry about. This Hungerford guy's a straight arrow and sharper than Ivan Boesky," he laughed.

"Oh sure."

"Why not? He's as good as advertised, and pays off at a better rate than your friend can get elsewhere."

"Anything's possible in this best of all possible worlds."

Strunk grinned. "I see you're skeptical. Okay, how about this one? Hungerford's not a crook, he's just dumb or unlucky. He's invested and lost your friend's money."

"That scenario stinks, but it's plausible. I still like the Ponzi or coke-dealer scenarios."

"I don't blame you," Strunk agreed. "The problem with them is that by the time you know for sure it's one or the other, it's too late. As I've said, Byrne, unless there's solicitation through the mails or by phone, or there's phony securities, or money moving from country to country, by wire, I can't help you. At best, what you've got is the kind of white-collar crime that belongs in the District Attorney's office. And the hitch is, if you file a complaint with the D.A., the crooks will run. Or, if they don't run, they'll sit on the money until legal matters run their course. Chances are slim to none, even if they indict and convict this guy Hungerford, they'll ever recover any money." The dumplings and lo mein polished off, he dabbed at his mouth with a paper napkin.

"What you're saying is, unless Hungerford's honest, the money's lost. Chalk it up to experience."

"That's pretty much it. As Grandma Strunk used to say, 'P.C., he who has cattle, has trouble.' Thank you for the lunch, Byrne. We must do this again soon, in the next decade. I might even treat."

"It was my pleasure, P.C." The check came to eleven and change. It cost more than thirty bucks to take a client out for a couple of hamburgers and drinks uptown. Not a bad deal, and the food wasn't so bad either.

Strunk pushed back his chair. "There is one more thing, P.C.," I said.

"Make it quick. I told you, I'm expecting a call from a snitch."

"I didn't mention that my friend and I went to a party Friday night at Sloane Marshall's house."

"Yeah, and . . . ?"

"While we were waiting to hail a cab home, we saw a couple get blown up by a car bomb."

He raised his eyebrows. "Was that the one on the news all day Saturday?"

"I don't know. How many car bombings were there Friday night?"

"Don't be cute, Byrne. Get to the point."

"The point is, they were at the party. We talked to them. They were worried about their money. They wanted to pull out."

"They were about to blow the whistle on Hungerford, so he had them car-bombed. Is that where you're coming from?"

"Something wrong with that?"

"Car bombings usually are the calling cards of wiseguys and terrorists. You ought to know that. I doubt a guy like Hungerford would go in for car bombing. Why compound fraud with murder?"

"If the professor was about to spoil a good thing for him, why not?"

37

He sighed. "Look, anything's possible. But if there's a connection between Hungerford and the car bombings, the cops are on the case. Believe me, they'll find it."

"Maybe. But that won't help my friend."

"That's true," said Strunk. He glanced at his watch and got to his feet. "It's getting late. I've got to bolt. It's been great seeing you again, Byrne."

I got up with him. "Good seeing you, P.C., and thanks for the information." We parted on the sidewalk. I hopped the "A" train uptown.

Strunk called the next day. "Been thinking about your friend's problem, Byrne."

Me too, almost constantly. And what I thought was that Ginny had lost fifty thousand dollars. And she wasn't going to get it back by asking politely for it. Hungerford didn't seem the rough type, but someone had dealt awfully rough with the professor and his wife.

"If you're up for lunch Friday," Strunk went on, "I'd like you to meet someone. He may be able to help your friend."

"Tell me where and when."

I agreed to meet him at another Szechuan restaurant. Szechuan food twice in one week came under the heading of wretched excess in my book, but I felt it was the least I could do if Strunk was willing to extend himself on my behalf.

Ginny and I went to a movie that night, and had sushi later at Akasaka. A change from Szechuan. We sat at the bar and the chef fed us by the piece.

"Try some uni, Charlie," she dared me.

"What is it?"

She offered me a glutinous, orange blob from her chopsticks. "Raw sea urchin," she said, laughing at the look on my face. She seemed to be over her funk, her usual sunny self again.

I shook my head. "I'll stick with the tuna, thanks."

"A real steak and potatoes guy, huh?" she scoffed. Showing off, she slurped down the glutinous mass with a smack of her lips. "Mmm, good." She grinned. "You don't know what you're missing, Charlie."

"That good, huh?"

"The best. Still hot to jump my bones?"

"Do I have to eat uni first?"

"If you want to jump these bones."

"Pass the uni."

"Say please." She had a wicked gleam in her eye.

"Please pass the uni, please."

"Good boy. Chef, another uni, if you please." Beaming with delight, she fed me the thing. It slid down like a raw egg. She put her lips to my ear, and whispered, "Uni wanna party?"

"My place or uni place?"

"Uni party at my place."

Hailing the cab, I prayed for no car bombings between the restaurant and her place. The uni party started in the backseat of the cab. I chased her up the stairs of the brownstone. We were tearing the clothes off each other before she had the key in the door. We laid a trail of ready-to-wear from the foyer to her canopied bed, where a life-and-death tussle for each other's jockey shorts ensued. She had all the right moves. She could fight dirty, or fight clean. She could be shifty, or come straight at you. One minute she was tender and composed, the next minute she was nuts. She was a worthy opponent. The contest ended in a draw, with further engagements the rest of the night. When I left her, early in the morning, I could have kissed the sanitation worker.

Chapter 4

Friday, I met Strunk at the latest Szechuan find. The place was empty. Strunk told the waiter that there'd be three of us. "Take any table," the waiter said.

We nursed a beer, and reminisced about "back then" while we waited for the mystery guest to show.

Presently, we were joined by a small man, wafer-thin,

mid-forties, dressed in a conservative brown tweed suit, blue oxford-cloth shirt, and red tie.

He paused, glanced around the empty restaurant, sighed, and said, "Jesus, Strunk, another roach ranch." He pulled out a chair, and sat down opposite me.

"Byrne!" Strunk beamed, as though he were presenting the governor himself. "Meet Henry Stein, S.T.S.—swindler, thief, and snitch."

"Unindicted co-conspirator would do, Strunk," Stein said with an amiable grin.

"Henry Stein, meet Charlie Byrne, S.P.S., spook, photographer, and sucker for some babe's hard-luck story."

"Nicely done, P.C.," I said. Stein and I exchanged nods, and continued to gaze at each other in mild curiosity while Strunk went ahead and ordered lunch.

He had the kind of face that was easy to trust, an asset for a con man. The mouth was broad and relaxed. His eyes were a clear grey and evenly spaced. He wore an expression of perpetual, unequivocal bemusement, as though he had figured out the punchline of the joke you were telling. His suit, and the expanse of dome, topped with thinning, salt-and-pepper hair cut in Fifties whiffle style, lent him the air of a raffish academic.

"Well, Charlie, let's hear how your honey got skinned." He smiled, holding my gaze.

"Skipping the amenities, are we, Henry?"

"If you'd like, we could talk about the weather, the Mets, or the New York Giants Superbowl chances, but it won't put any money in either of our pockets." He smiled.

I glanced at Strunk, who simply gazed back at me expectantly. I wondered if our minds were running in similar channels. Our food came, and as we ate, I repeated my story for Henry Stein. When I finished, he gave me a dry smile and said, "Sounds like a Ponzi, doesn't it, Strunk?"

"If this Hungerford guy's a crook, it does."

"Only a crook offers those kind of rates," Stein said. He shifted his gaze from me to Strunk, and back again. "But you sports didn't invite me to this sumptuous repast merely to chat about Ponzi schemes?"

Strunk grinned. He pushed back his chair, and got to his feet. "Just remembered, got to make a phone call."

"Ask her if she's got a sister," said Stein.

Strunk spoke briefly with the waiter, then disappeared into the kitchen. Stein's sober grey eyes searched mine. "Alone at last," he said.

I got the message. It was camel-trading time. "Strunk wasn't very encouraging when I told him this story," I said.

"I can see why."

"Then I remember him mentioning that he ran stings, that he set up boiler room operators, and the like, with . . . ," I hesitated, "ah, with the help of people like yourself."

The mask of tolerant bemusement seemed to slip, and I thought I detected, beneath it, the man's innate hubris. He didn't respond, so I continued. "P.C. and I must have had the same idea, I guess. The best chance my friend has to recover her money is to run a sting on Hungerford. At least that was my thought. What do you think? Can it be done?"

His eyes were focused on the middle distance, the ingenuous smile gone. "I'm not a free counseling service," he answered finally.

"Ah-ha, I get your drift. What are we talking about?"

"Fifty percent of whatever I recover."

"That means you think Hungerford can be stung?"

"Probably. Consider this, though: if you expect to net fifty grand, and allowing for interest, he'll have to be stung for better than a hundred thousand dollars."

"As long as I net the fifty, with interest, that's fine with me."

"There'll be some start-up costs."

"How much?"

"Thirty grand ought to do it."

"I've got twenty." And that was all I had. I felt giddy pledging it.

He gave me a pitying smile. "She must be quite a piece."

"She does it for me, Henry."

"She must, if you'll put your money where your mouth is." Then with a genuine smile, he added, "The things we do for love, huh?"

I grinned ruefully. "We'll factor the start-up costs into the sting, Henry. I'll expect the same rate as a T bill."

Stein gazed at me thoughtfully. "You know, Charlie, you don't look like a photographer." He smiled.

"Appearances are deceiving."

"I should hope so, and no offense intended," he said mildly. "I myself never judge a book by its cover."

Strunk returned to the table. Towering over us, he eyed us speculatively. "How you fellows getting on?"

"Famously," said Stein.

"Glad to hear it." He beamed. "As I always say, it takes a thief to catch a thief."

"That's because there are only two things a cop can catch, a nap and a cold," Stein complained.

I grinned.

"I'm gonna dash," said Strunk. "Thanks again for lunch, Charlie. If this thing with you and Henry goes well, I'll let you buy next time, too." He jostled his way through a throng of hungry suits, and before making his exit, he turned and tossed us a disgusted look.

Stein took a sip of tea.

"Where do we go from here, Henry?"

"You said the broad gave you her number? So give her a call. Tell her you want to take her picture."

"And then what?"

"Then we'll find out how gullible she is. And even more important, how greedy she is."

The waiter placed the check face down on the table. Stein ignored it. I turned it over. Less than thirty dollars, not bad. I put three tens and a five on it, considering them part of the start-up costs. We stood up together. There were people standing in line for the table. "Come again," the waiter called happily to our backs.

The noon sun exploded in my face like a strobe, and a monosodium glutamate rush pounded in my temples as I staggered out of the restaurant.

"The sooner you have the money, the sooner we get the show on the road," said Stein, squinting.

"Ten now, and ten in two weeks," I said.

"That'll be fine," he said.

"I'm still unclear about what happens next, Henry."

"So am I, pal. But don't worry, we'll take it a step at a time. The first thing we want to do is give the Marshall broad some of your twenty grand." He beamed and squinted, rocking on his heels. "If you want to remove a spot, Charlie, the best solvent is the thing itself." He gave me a pat on the back and a conspiratorial wink, and strolled off.

I headed for the nearest subway, wondering about this penchant for aphorisms that Strunk and Stein seemed to share, and wondering also whether Stein's family had ever been in the dry cleaning business.

Chapter 5

A few years back, after a big score on a cigarette ad campaign, one of the smarter things I did with the money was put a down payment on fifty acres upstate, in Delaware County, near a town called Hobart. I had thirty acres of woodlot and pasture, twenty acres of tillable land, a dilapidated Greek Revival farmhouse, and a mortgage. I leased the land to a dairy farmer, and in between the hunting, skiing, and fishing seasons, I puttered around my handyman's special in dilatory fashion.

Periodic lean times at the studio had forced me to list the place with a real estate agent, but, fortunately for me, the photography career always revived itself before a buyer was found, and I managed to hang on to the property.

Saturday was the opening of grouse season. Ginny and I had been together every chance we got since Sloane's party, and I saw no reason now to forgo one for the other. So Friday afternoon we tossed our overnight bags in the back of a rented Toyota Celica, and took off for Hobart with Ginny at the wheel. She had a heavy foot, but she obeyed the law and was a surprisingly good driver.

We drove for about an hour without saying much, content to listen to a Van Morrison retrospective on FM radio. It was a warm, sunny day and the trees along the Thruway were showing their first traces of scarlet and gold. I glanced over at Ginny's almost comically earnest profile; she was serious about her driving. I relaxed and enjoyed the ride, letting my mind wander over the events of the past week. I hadn't mentioned to Ginny what I was up to. Since the party, in fact, the subject had never come up. It was as though she'd shut the potential loss of fifty thousand dollars totally out of her mind. I didn't see any need to remind her. And I didn't want to get her hopes up only to have the scheme collapse, in which case I'd have thrown good money after bad.

Stein had called it right, I admitted ruefully to myself, I was looking to be a hero. And if we could pull it off, I would be a hero.

We turned off the Thruway at the Kingston exit and headed west on 28. Ginny shifted smoothly and the Celica performed for her like a Porsche. There was a fluid precision to the way she handled the car. I shut off the radio.

"You like to drive, huh?"

"Yeah, I do," she admitted.

"Where did you learn to drive this way?"

"Guess I picked it up from my brothers. They were into sports cars and road racing." She shot me a rakish grin. "I can strip a motor down and put it back together, if I have to," she bragged.

Strangely enough, I couldn't remember her having mentioned her family before. "How many brothers do you have?" I asked.

"Three, and three sisters."

"That's a big family, seven kids. Must be nice."

"It's all right. How about you, got any brothers or sisters?"

"No brothers or sisters."

"An only child, huh?"

"That's right."

"Are your parents still around?"

"I don't really know," I said. My family history was pretty sketchy, and talking about it always made me slightly defensive.

"You mean you don't know whether or not your parents are alive?"

"My mother died when I was a kid. I don't know about my father. He may still be alive. He went out for cigarettes not long after I was born and forgot to come back. That's the story I got anyway."

"Charlie, you're an orphan!"

"Maybe. Tell me about your folks," I said, curious as always about family life and happy to shift the subject from myself.

"They own a furniture store out in the mall on route 50, Hillsboro, Ohio. Dad's a big, affable guy with a good line of patter, a salesman. He played guard for Ohio State in the Fifties. Since then, life's been an anticlimax. Those were his best years. He keeps a photo of himself, in uniform, on his desk at the store. You know the kind, charging like a bull, making a ferocious face, like a bulldog. He's living in the past."

"But he's a good salesman," I said encouragingly.

"He's okay," she said.

"And your mother, what's she like?"

"You mean the boss?"

"Is that what you call her?"

She laughed. "That's what Dad calls her. She runs the store. She knows what sells in Hillsboro. We use to do all the displays and room sets together, Mom and me. All of us kids worked in the store when we were growing up. That's where I got my training."

"At your mother's knee."

"Yeah, you could say that. But who raised you, Charlie?" she asked, tossing the ball back to me.

"An aunt, my mother's sister, and her husband."

"So they're your family."

"More like guardians. They didn't have any kids of their own, and that was the way they liked it. So I was packed off to boarding school."

"Poor baby, you had no luck at all."

"Oh, it wasn't so bad. Who do you look like, your mom or your dad?"

"Like both, I think. The coloring's Dad's, and so is this dumb chin, but I've got Mom's hands." She displayed one proudly. "Birdlike, huh? And I've got Mom's legs, luckily. She was pretty when she was young, did the whole beauty

45

queen, cheerleader number. She's still a pretty good-looking woman for her age, and she's not hung up on the past, like Dad."

"Are they still in love?"

"You are a romantic, Charlie," she chuckled cynically. "After thirty years and six kids?"

"You never know."

"I know."

"But they're still together."

"If that's what you call it. Oh, I shouldn't say that. They get along okay, I guess, when they're not on the booze."

"Drink a lot, huh?"

"They love to party. Always did. There wasn't a week that went by, when I was a kid, that they didn't have a party to go to."

"And when they drink what happens?"

"Oh, Mom starts mouthing off about leaving Dad. Dad complains that she won't sleep with him. Mom makes passes at her daughters' boyfriends. Dad gets belligerent. Stuff like that."

She painted a laconic and unsentimental portrait of family life. "I guess orphans miss the good, but they don't miss the bad," I said.

"Big families aren't all they're cracked up to be," she agreed.

"What were you like as a little girl? I bet the boys were crazy about you."

"I wish!" She laughed. "I was a mess, skinny, gawky, freckles, and braces. When I was fourteen, some of my girlfriends were already sleeping with boys. And I hadn't even had my period yet."

"What a shame I didn't know you then." I winked.

"When I was fourteen?"

"Yeah."

"How old would you have been then?"

"You're how old?"

"Twenty-seven."

"When you were fourteen, I would have been twenty-four. I was just starting to sell my pictures to an international news agency."

"It's better we waited. What would you have done with a gawky, flat-chested fourteen-year-old, with braces?"

46

"Ravished you," I leered.

She glanced at me and snickered. "There are laws against ravishing fourteen-year-olds, Byrne. Although I might have enjoyed being ravished by an older man," she said thoughtfully. "Anyway, overnight it seemed, I got my period and my tits. I was still gawky and had braces, but this was a definite improvement. Things started looking up. The boys started taking notice."

"The pigs."

"I got my first real boyfriend when the braces came off. His name was Billy Hunt."

We were in the mountains now. You could feel the drop of several degrees in the air temperature. The hills closed in around us, pinching the road, the trees yellow, green, and crimson. Ginny was impatient, stuck behind a pickup truck doing fifty.

"Wasn't Hunt your married name?"

She didn't answer. Instead, she floored the Celica and we blew past the pickup. "That was Billy," she said cheerfully, the maneuver completed and the Celica in the proper lane. "His dad sold farm machinery and was president of the bank. That was society around Hillsboro."

"So you married your childhood sweetheart."

"Sounds corny, huh?"

"Not at all. Sounds . . . uh, all American. Billy was the first, I take it?"

"Nope." She grinned.

"No?"

"Steve Markham was the first," she said, curling her tongue ruefully over her teeth momentarily, her gaze steady on the road.

I hated Steve Markham.

"He worked at the store, on the truck. He was eighteen. We were fooling around one day in the back of the delivery van. He was teasing me about it. I was curious, so I let him do it." The memory made her giggle. "I guess you could say I seduced him. Afterward, he was funny, so serious and embarrassed. I couldn't figure it out. It didn't seem like a big deal to me. The next time was with Billy. We were out at his folks' cottage on the lake. He was clumsy, but enthusiastic. And I still couldn't figure out what the big deal about sex was. But all that summer, every chance we got we practiced, and by September I was getting pretty good at it."

"God, I'm jealous."

"You asked."

"I know. How old were you then?"

"Sixteen. How old were you when you had your first girl?"

"Eighteen."

"Who was the lucky girl?"

"The big sister of a friend of mine from school. He had invited me to spend Christmas at his house, and the night before we went back to school she snuck into my room and got into bed with me."

"Sounds like the kind of story you'd read in a sex magazine." She laughed. "Horny adolescent's wet dream comes true."

"Yeah, all these stories sound like that. Anyhow, I was clumsy and enthusiastic too, I suppose. But I knew one thing—sex was a big deal."

"Think so?"

"Sure, don't you?"

"I don't know. It just seems like one of those things you stumble through as best you can—a rite of passage, that's all."

"If that was all, how come you got married?"

"Because I was a jerk. I thought that if I slept with Billy I must be in love with him. I thought that was what we were supposed to do, get married."

"Did Billy want to get married?"

"Not right away, of course, but, yes, he wanted to get married. It was more or less understood that we were engaged. I made Billy promise, though, when we were married, we wouldn't hang around Hillsboro."

"Why? Was Billy a homeboy?"

"You could say that." She giggled. "But he kept his promise, even if his heart wasn't in it. We got married in Billy's senior year at Ohio State, and moved to New York right after graduation. His father pulled strings and got Billy a job with a commodities firm. I tried modeling for a while and hated it. But I did discover there was such a thing as a photostylist. And it was pretty much what Mom and I used to do back in Hillsboro. I can do that, I said to myself. I put together a portfolio of some of the stuff I'd done back home and got a couple of jobs. Soon I was working all the time, for dozens of photographers."

"Well, barbells notwithstanding, you're good."

"Thank you. I like the work. And maybe, so far as Billy was concerned, that was the problem. I wasn't paying much attention to him. I was always busy. I had guys coming on to me all the time on the job, but I never did anything about it. That is, until I found out Billy was fooling around with a woman broker. Couldn't really blame him, but the next guy that came on to me that I *liked,* I slept with. After that, Billy and I came unglued fast. The divorce was civil, polite."

"And no big deal," I finished.

She glanced at me. "Nope," she said.

"What happened to Billy?"

"He went back to Hillsboro and married Peggy Babcock. She always did have the hots for him. I get a card from them at Christmas, and Mom says they ask about me whenever they're in the store. But you've never been married, have you, Charlie?"

"No, I haven't gotten around to that one yet."

"How come?"

"I don't know, just haven't felt ready. When I was doing the journalist bit, I was traveling too much. And now, well, the studio takes all of my time."

"Oh sure," she scoffed. "With all those beautiful models that hang around your studio, who *needs* marriage? Why buy a cow when milk's so cheap, right?"

"Every business has its perquisites," I admitted. "But I'd like to get married someday. Who knows, maybe soon. Turn left at that light," I said, nodding. We had just passed through Stamford and were turning off 23 on to route 10, so we'd be at the house in twenty minutes. She reached over and flicked on the radio. Van Morrison was singing about a brown-eyed woman.

Saturday was a brilliant, lazy Indian summer day. In the afternoon I outfitted Ginny with a faded, red-checked cotton flannel shirt of mine, a favorite, and a feed store cap—the kind with the plastic adjustable band in the back. It said *Goldkist* above the visor. She tucked her hair up in it and grinned lopsidedly. She was coltish and boyish in the too large shirt, the red cap, heavy cord pants and hiking

49

boots. An old side-by-side twenty-gauge that I kept for guests completed her outfit. I carried a twelve-gauge Remington Wingmaster pump.

We hiked a leisurely half mile up the hill in the pasture behind the house, to where the thorn apple trees melded into the first tenuous stands of ironwood, ash, oak, and maple about to ignite with color. Dry weather made every step sound like Chinese New Year. Grouse flushed regularly, like rolling thunder. But always too early and well out of range. Ten yards apart, stopping and starting, periodically changing pace, we worked the tree line for about a mile up the valley. We put up dozens of birds without firing a shot. The sun beat down hot and soothing on our backs. I sweated freely: the muscles in my neck and back were fluid and loose when I swung the shotgun into place and sighted. Reactions and reflexes were both fine. I needed an obliging grouse to hold longer, flush later and within range. Ginny tromped along, toting her gun, enjoying the outing, not bothering even to shoulder her gun as the birds flushed.

We stopped for a breather in a sun-dazzled clearing bordered by paper birch and hemlock. Ginny wore a transparent mustache of tiny beads of perspiration on her upper lip. Rubber-legged, she collapsed in the knee-high dried grass.

She tossed the cap on the ground beside her. Her hair tumbled down. Beaming, she shook out her hair and laid back in the grass. "Phew, what a workout."

I stretched out next to her. "Feels good though, doesn't it?"

"Mmm . . ." she sighed, eyes closed. Her hand found mine and squeezed it.

Turning on my side, I undid a button on her shirt and slid my hand in. Her breast was warm and damp.

She lifted her head, shielding her eyes from the strong light, and cocked an eyebrow. "Is this what you meant when you said, how about a little bird shooting?"

I took that for a rhetorical question and continued exploring.

First one breast flushed from the old flannel shirt, then the other, just like grouse from cover. "Hmm, the sight of the speckled bird in tall growth. What a powerful aphrodisiacal effect it has on my libido!" I laughed and dove for her.

"It gives you an erection, too," she squealed, struggling to escape *and* to be caught. And grabbing me. "Careful, Charlie, or you'll get a mouthful of feathers."

The shadow of a hemlock crept across the meadow and touched us like a long, cold finger. We dressed quickly and started back down the valley for home. The grouse, beginning to roost for the night, flushed much closer, but my concentration and reflexes were lost somewhere in the tall grass of that sun-dazzled meadow. Halfheartedly, I shot at a couple of birds, but I was late and off the mark. Ginny cheered the birds on. We turned downhill for the pasture. A doe, white tail flagging danger, bounded from a stand of hemlock dead ahead. To our left, a grouse exploded from a clump of blueberry bushes and was gone before I could swing the twelve-gauge into position. A second grouse spluttered into the air and fell back to earth. I dashed to the spot. The bird was running downhill, dragging its wing. I chased after it and Ginny chased after me. The bird scurried into a thicket of brambles and froze, hugging the ground, the broken wing extended. I reached and grabbed it. The wing was smashed by birdshot. The grouse's heart thumped stoutly in the palm of my hand. I wrung the bird's neck. Ginny turned her face from me. The bird's heart continued to beat—then it stuttered to a stop. I dropped the grouse in my canvas gamebag.

When we got back to the house, I cleaned the grouse and put it in the freezer. Ginny and I ate chili from a can for supper that night.

Sunday was another glorious Indian summer day. We spent it lazing around the house with the Sunday *Times*, eating, drinking, and making love. After dark, we hit the road again, back to the Big Apple.

Chapter 6

Monday morning I found a check in the mail, always a pleasant way to start the week. It was for a job that had been in accounts receivable for over ninety days, and with fee and expenses it totaled thirteen sixty-five. For the time being, it meant I wouldn't have to tap my savings for the first half of Stein's twenty grand start-up costs. It also meant a serious gap in my cash flow—or, as they say on Wall Street, my liquidity. Which in turn meant that the factors got ten percent of the next piece of business in the house. I bit the bullet and wrote Stein a check for ten thousand, postdating it a couple of days to allow the deposit check to clear. Then I bolted for the bank, dropping Stein's check in the mail on the way.

A week later, Stein called. "Got the rest of the money, Charlie?"

"I've got it." In my savings account.

"Good. See you tomorrow then, the Chrysler Building, sixty-third floor. And bring along your dough. I'll show you how I've been squandering your money. Look for a brass sign with my name on it," he said cheerfully, and hung up.

Tuesday afternoon I stepped off the elevator at the sixty-third floor of the Chrysler Building, and found myself in a small vestibule facing a pair of matching dark walnut doors. The door on the left bore a brass plaque, reading: "Financial Futures Services, Inc." An identical, but newer and shinier plaque on the righthand side read: "Strunk, Stein & Mulligan, Inc." "SS&M." Catchy, but I wondered who the hell Mulligan was.

A champagne-blond receptionist, not long out of her teens

and as adorable as an unclipped poodle puppy, greeted me. I gave her my name, and said that I was there to see Henry Stein. She pressed Stein's line with a lacquered nail, and breathed his name into the phone as if she were talking to her pillow. She beamed at me, I beamed back.

I glanced around. The place looked the way I'd imagined a palimony lawyer's office would look. The walls were ecru suede; the floors were done in dark chocolate tile. The furnishings were tubular chrome, nubby wool, leather, and glass. A palm in a floor planter was behind the blonde's desk. The operational part of the office was concealed behind more walnut at either end of the room.

Stein had mentioned that Financial Futures, whoever that was, was an old friend. They had an arrangement for the use of the hall. I wondered about Stein's friend's clients. Old money wouldn't feel cozy in this setting. Had to be go-go and yuppie money, money made ten minutes ago.

"Mr. Stein will be with you in a minute. Please have a seat, Mr. Byrne." The blonde nodded at the couch.

I sat down dutifully, and picked up a copy of *Forbes* magazine from the table. It was the issue devoted to the four hundred richest Americans. I browsed the list of names without spotting anyone I knew.

"Charlie." Stein motioned to me from the doorway. He was in shirtsleeves, the picture of the working executive. The little blonde seemed to wag her tail as I passed her desk. I followed Stein through a hallway padded—walls, floor, and ceiling—with a brown industrial carpet. He opened another walnut door and stepped aside.

It was like stepping up to the edge of a cliff, the view of lower Manhattan and the East River was so spectacular. When I recovered from the view, I noticed that the office was bare except for a desk and a phone.

"Furniture comes tomorrow. A rental," grinned Stein.

"I wouldn't be able to do anything but stare out the window all day, if I worked here."

"Great view, huh? But you get used to it," said Stein. He dealt me a business card from the deck near the phone. "My card." He smiled.

It was tastefully designed and expensively printed on high-quality, two-ply rag.

"Who's Mulligan?" I asked.

"My loan officer at Chase," he said with a laugh. "Three names sound more substantial, don't you think? Makes for a nicer logo, too, 'SS&M.'"

"If you're in the surrogate sex business."

"You have to pay attention to details, Charlie. I'm a stickler for them. Did you bring the money?"

I reached in the pocket of my suede windbreaker, took out the envelope, and slid it across the desk. With this payment went all the cushion I had against a slow month. I was gambling, and I knew it, but I had no qualms. Ginny Rowen was worth much more than twenty grand to me.

"Filthy stuff." Stein sniffed the envelope, pretending it smelt bad. He peered in at the two cashier checks for five thousand dollars each. "Okay, we're rolling. By the way, I like the jacket. Makes you look more like a photographer, Charlie. Which reminds me, have you called the Marshall broad yet?"

"Not yet."

"Got the number?"

"In my wallet."

"Well, get on it. Here, use my phone."

Stein gazed out the window, hands in his pockets, rocking on the balls of his feet, while I dialed. On the second ring, a man's voice answered, "Hello."

"Sloane Marshall, please."

"Who's calling?"

"Charles Byrne."

"Just a moment." I heard him say, "It's for you."

Sloane came on the line with her soporific contralto. "Well, hello, Charles Byrne. How are you?"

"I'm fine."

"So you finally called," she said triumphantly, "and here I was, just thinking of you."

"You were? What a coincidence."

"Yes." She laughed. "I meant what I said at the party, Charles. I'm a lady in distress. I'm desperate for new pictures. That is why you called, isn't it?"

"Yes, it is."

"Well, perfect timing. Tell me when's convenient for you, and I'll be there with bells on."

"How does five o'clock Thursday sound?"

"Wonderful. I'm really looking forward to working with you, Charles."

"It will be my pleasure, I'm sure."

"I'll see you then," she said sweetly, and hung up.

"That was easy enough," said Stein.

"Yeah."

"And now the games begin," he said, rubbing his hands in glee. "You're gonna get a real kick out of this, Charlie," he promised. The little man's exuberance was infectious. I did feel something akin to butterflies in the stomach, or maybe it was just anxiety—a reasonable enough response if you've just handed over your last twenty grand to a known con artist.

"You think so, Henry."

"I guarantee it."

"I'm happy to hear you say that. Perhaps you'd be good enough to put it in writing."

"Put what in writing? This is a scam. You expect a guarantee that a scam will work?"

"Don't get defensive, Henry. I wouldn't expect you to be able to guarantee the scam will work. Just give me a receipt for the twenty grand."

"I hope you're not expecting a refund."

"I'm going into this eyes wide open. It's a gamble, and I know it. But if it goes down the toilet, maybe I can write it off against taxes."

"I'll give you a bill for services rendered on SS&M's letterhead, how's that?"

"It will have to do."

"Good, now that that's settled, I've got a few calls to make. If you'll excuse me, Charlie," he said, dismissing me. "You can find your way out yourself, can't you?"

"Sure. One thing, though, before I go—how much have you dented the petty cash for so far, Henry?" Not to mention the dent in my incipient excitement about the scam.

He considered the question a moment, the gaze of his clear grey eyes resting on me while he did some rapid calculation. "So far? Four grand. But don't worry, I'll blow it all before I'm through."

"Swell."

He waved me a cheerful goodbye.

Chapter 7

Thursday rolled around, and so did my date with Sloane Marshall. We swapped pleasantries as I escorted her into the studio, and her eyes roamed with curiosity, inspecting the premises. Tito stood by, and his eyes roamed with curiosity as well. I introduced them, and she conferred on him a polite smile; the one reserved for the little people. He asked if she'd like something to drink, reciting the beverage list. She settled for Perrier. Tito took her bag and escorted her to the dressing room.

Now, sitting in front of the makeup mirror, she seemed oddly sexless. "We're going to do a mailing to all the agency casting people," she said, methodically laying out her hot curler and makeup gear. She was wearing black leather pants, and a strapless, flesh-colored bra: "My agent says I've got a hot commercial look, very now. What we want is a straight, squeaky-clean headshot, Charles."

I returned her reflected gaze solemnly, reminding myself that it was not what she wanted, but what *I* wanted that was the purpose of this exercise. "I think we can manage that," I replied.

"Afterward, if we have time, we can do some pictures for ourselves . . . more glamorous, sexier, perhaps." She gave me a promising smile.

"That'll be great," I said. I could hardly wait.

She peered into the mirror, eyes narrowing, and began to apply base with a sponge. "Which blouse shall we start with?"

I fingered a white silk number on the clothes rack. "This would be a good one to start with."

The up-from-under look ricocheted off the mirror. She wrinkled her nose; no. She wasn't as cute as she thought. "Let's start with the green one. The high collar is more demure," she said.

She could wear burlap, for all I cared. I'd still make her look good. "Okay, let's go with that one," I said amiably.

I left her to finish her makeup, and went downstairs. Tito was at the camera caddy, loading the Nikons. He grinned knowingly, and made a rude gesture toward the dressing room, the implication of which was that he'd happily hose the bitch.

"Are we ready?" I asked.

"You're all set."

"Good. Do me a favor, stick around until a Mr. Stein shows. Then you can go home. Okay?"

"Okay, boss."

Waiting for her, I killed time with the crossword puzzle in the lounge.

"Ta-da . . ." Sloane sang, making her entrance.

When I glanced up from the puzzle, she cracked a winning, self-deprecating grin; mocking her own perishable beauty. She seemed so vulnerable at that moment, I couldn't help liking her. I felt a twinge of guilt. Did I really intend to sting this charmer?

"How about some music?" I asked.

"That would be nice. Have you any jazz? Something quiet?"

Tito put on Wes Montgomery. Sloane smiled her approval and danced to the waiting stool.

"Here we go," I said.

Tito handed me the Hasselblad. Sloane squinted into the light, and I snapped a Polaroid.

"Hey, I wasn't ready," she protested.

"That was only for exposure," I said. Wes Montgomery soloed through a long minute of silence while we waited for the Polaroid to develop. I peeled off the paper negative, and stared at the image.

"Let me see it," she demanded.

The exposure was fine, so was the lighting, but Sloane's face was lifeless. I chucked it into the wastebasket.

"Bad exposure," I lied. "Let's make another one."

She collected herself and posed. I snapped the picture. Wes Montgomery filled the break in the action while the second "Roid" cooked.

"Better." I passed her the Polaroid.

She studied it several seconds, raised her eyes to me, and nodded, okay.

I swapped the Hasselblad for the Nikon with Tito, and focused, staring at her through a 105mm lens. She made the same face she had for the Polaroid. I took the picture. She was obviously tense and guarded, carefully editing herself. We ran through a series of poses—businesslike, concerned, thoughtful, friendly, amused—manufactured moods she had practiced in front of her mirror. She was showing me the faces she wanted me to see. Makeup, hair, and my lighting would be the only differences between these pictures, and other photographs of her. Or, as she had put it, her "very now look." I had to remind myself again of the real reason for this session.

I shot out the roll, and passed the camera to Tito. "Shall I change?" she asked.

"Why not. It'll give us more to choose from."

She strolled off the set. I returned to the crossword puzzle. Tito busied himself at the camera caddy.

She reappeared wearing the blouse I'd originally suggested. We silently took our places again. I made another Polaroid, and she beamed with pleasure when I showed it to her.

"Very flattering," she said.

"We try." I smiled.

"I love your lighting, Charlie."

Suddenly, I was Charlie. "Yeah, it's good."

"We're going to get wonderful pictures, I just know it," she beamed.

Tito chimed in, "Charlie's the best."

It was my turn to slip her the oil. "You're beautiful, Sloane," I said, straightfaced. "Makes you easy to photograph." If I've learned anything in this business, it's this; just because they're beautiful, and know it, that doesn't mean they don't like to hear it.

"Thank you, kind sir," she said, accepting my small paean with her self-deprecating grin.

I lifted the Nikon to my eye, signaling we were about to begin.

This time, as we worked, I began to chat her up. "I like that . . . oh, yes . . . hold that . . . again . . . more . . . yes, good . . . more to the left now . . . right . . . wait for me . . . hold it . . . now come back again . . . slow, slower . . . good . . . don't move now . . . freeze . . . that's great, Sloane . . . just great . . . yes, yes . . ."

She was still in control. She'd never give that up. But there was more energy and animation in her poses now. She was getting into it.

The buzzer sounded.

Sloane collapsed like a soufflé. Photo-coitus interruptus. We swapped glances of mutual annoyance that dissolved instantly into rueful grins.

Tito went to the door.

Henry Stein bounded into the studio, dapper in a well-cut, dark blue suit that made him look as if he owned a bank.

"Henry," I sighed.

"Bad timing?" he said, smiling hopefully at Sloane.

She ignored him.

"Could be better," I said.

"Sorry, Charlie, but this one just wouldn't keep. Tomorrow, and it would be too late. I should have called first, but since I was in the neighborhood, I thought I'd take a chance, and drop by and pick up a check. Is that okay?"

"Yeah, it's okay, Henry."

"Good. He who hesitates is lost. Double your money in thirty days, or less. This is a hot one, Charlie."

Sloane's eyes flickered with interest.

He smiled deferentially at Sloane. "Excuse me, miss, but you know how these artist types are, easy come, easy go. If someone doesn't look out for this guy, he'll be eating dog food in his old age."

"Sloane, this money grubber is Henry Stein. Henry, the lady's name is Sloane Marshall," I said.

Her eyes narrowed in automatic appraisal, a reflexive action whenever she was introduced to a man. "Hello, Henry Stein," she smiled, offering her hand.

He took it, and for a moment I thought he would kiss it, but he merely held it in both of his. "Hello yourself, Sloane

59

Marshall, and don't photographers have all the fun," he replied, hanging on to her hand an extra beat or two.

"Henry, have a drink, why don't you. When we finish shooting, I'll get you a check," I said.

Stein consulted a Rolex, beamed at Sloane, and said, "I have time. Why not? I'll have a scotch."

"How about you, Sloane? Can I interest you in something more than Perrier?" I asked.

"All right, a white wine."

"Tito, would you? And I'll have a beer." Tito nodded and withdrew to the kitchen.

Stein grinned fatuously at Sloane, and bounced on the balls of his feet. "Would it be all right if I lurked in the background and watched? I find photography fascinating. And business, I'm afraid, is so dull by comparison. The appeal of the marketplace pales next to the charms of a beautiful woman."

I cringed. This farce was hopeless. Surely, Sloane would see through Stein, and his cheesy compliments. I consoled myself with the thought that I'd only be out four grand if I pulled the plug on the scam here and now.

"I don't mind, if Charlie doesn't," she answered, with a throaty laugh.

"Wonderful," Stein beamed.

Tito served the drinks, reminding me with a glance that I'd promised he could leave when Stein arrived.

"If you're going to lurk, Henry, I'm going to press you into service," I said. "Can you load a Nikon?"

"I think so."

"Good. You can fill in for Tito. He's got to go."

"What's the job pay?" he asked.

"Rice and beans, and a little extra," Tito cracked. There were polite chuckles all around, and Tito said goodnight.

Sloane took advantage of the break to dash to the dressing room for a quick touch-up of her makeup and hair.

Stein rubbed his palms in satisfaction. "I think we're making an impression, Charlie," he said.

"I certainly hope so."

"Trust me."

"We all know what that translates to, Henry."

He chuckled. "Seriously, though, I have an instinct for

these things." He rolled his eyes impishly in the direction of the dressing room. "She's quite a piece."

Sloane sashayed back to the stool, seated herself, and took a sip of wine. "Ready when you are, gentlemen." A fresh audience, another performance, and she was up for it.

Stein handed me a Nikon, and I shot a roll of film as Sloane went through her paces. "That was amazing, absolutely amazing how you do that," Stein said, when I handed the camera back to him.

"Do what?" Sloane asked innocently.

"You know what you do . . . those looks . . . and the moods they convey."

Stein had no shame. He was piling it on thick, and I felt that sinking feeling again. But then Sloane tossed her head, and laughed, displaying those small feral teeth. Obviously, she was pleased with her new slave; but then, horseshit does make strawberries grow.

"Henry," I said.

"Yes?"

"How much are we talking about this time?" It was a clumsy attempt to refocus Stein's attention from sex back to money, the point of this comedy.

"Entirely up to you, my friend," he replied grandly. "The minimum is five thou, your usual."

Sloane stirred perceptibly. Beneath her languid exterior, the interest was palpable. The smell of money, vulgar money, was in the air. She rested her gaze on Stein.

"Remember, double your money in thirty days, or less," he beamed. He unloaded and reloaded the Nikon as he spoke, snapping shut the back with a flourish, and handing me the camera with the aplomb of a full-time assistant. "But we'll discuss it later, after the shooting," he said. He and Sloane were groping each other with their eyes. I half expected him to toss me ten bucks, and tell me to go to the movies.

I raised the Nikon and focused. Sloane posed, and I snapped. Midway to the next pose, she balked.

"I think we've done enough of these, Charlie," she announced. She sipped her wine, and smiled at Stein. "What exactly is it that you do, Henry?" she purred.

"You could say that I see to it that parties with similar

interests are properly introduced," he answered with a cryptic smile.

"Oh?" she said.

"Yes," Stein continued. "Like investor and entrepreneur, money and business . . ."

"Like an investment banker?" said Sloane happily.

Stein smiled modestly. If that's what she wanted to believe.

"Sloane, what would you like to do now?" I asked.

Reluctantly, she switched her gaze to me. "Whatever you'd like to do," she said amiably.

What I'd like to do was pack it in for the day, and go have dinner with Ginny. Instead, I said: "Let's go for a more fashion look. More *outré* . . . hotter, know what I mean?" Hell, I hardly knew myself what I meant, but if that's what she was buying, I could be as big a cornball as Stein.

Sloane, the little narcissist, clapped her hands with delight. "I love it," she exclaimed.

"Mess up your hair," I said. "And heavy up the makeup. The lips should be blood-red. I'm gonna light you harsher, bolder. We'll shoot you bare-shouldered." I was almost mincing.

Stein rocked on his heels and grinned benignly.

Sloane jumped up from the stool. "I love it," she repeated herself. Hairbrush and wineglass in hand, she ran off to the dressing room.

"While Sloane's changing, I'll get your check, Henry," I said.

Sloane stopped cold in her tracks. "You're not leaving, Henry?"

"Not as long as Charlie needs an assistant."

She smiled and hurried to the dressing room.

Stein gave me a playful poke on the shoulder with his knuckles. "May I use the phone, big guy?"

"Go ahead." As I adjusted the lighting, I overheard Stein telling someone to meet him downstairs in an hour.

"Help me with this towel, someone." Sloane cocked an insolent hip, and assumed a stance. A bitch-goddess in black leather pants, naked from the waist up, breasts challenging and enticing. Her eyes mascaraed, her lips blood-red, the close-cropped hair tousled and spiky, all lent her an androgynous charm. She was *outré* all right.

A gelid, insular smile played on her lips. She gazed at us with unflinching eyes. Double your pleasure, double your fun, cocktease two guys at a time instead of just one.

I gave Stein the nod. He pounced on her like a puppy on a Liversnap. Sloane held the towel across her chest with one hand, and tossed him the clips with the other. She pirouetted, turning her back on us. Stein smirked at me, joined the towel behind her back with a clip, and escorted her back to the stool.

I shot a sequence of pictures of her gazing into the lens, eyes at half mast; the ready-for-bed look. Then I asked her to look off in one direction, or another, and began murmuring encouragement to her. Stein joined in with a litany of his own. She shifted her somnolent gaze to him, and smiled. It sounded as if we were chanting to her. I clammed up. Stein soloed. She was exuding a free and easy carnality now, her chief talent, perhaps her essence. These pictures would be much better than our earlier efforts.

In less than ten minutes, I exposed three rolls of K36.

"That was marvelous, Sloane, really marvelous," I gushed. "I think we've got it. It's a wrap. *Fini.*"

"Mmm, I know we got some good pictures," she said. "That felt good."

"It was fantastic," I assured her.

"I'd like to have a print of one of those last ones, if I might," said Stein.

"Why Henry, how sweet," Sloane purred. "Would you like me to sign it for you?"

"Sure. I'll hang it in the office," he said, with an aw-shucks grin, bashfully scuffing the floor with his toe. "I could never explain it to the wife."

Sloane giggled.

It was a bravura performance. Sloane was digging it. I felt a surge of confidence. I realized Stein knew what he was doing. The sting might work after all.

"Can I drop you somewhere, Sloane?" he asked. "I have a car and driver waiting."

"Just give me a minute to get my things together." She beamed.

Friday morning we were up early. After coffee and juice, Ginny dashed off for a nine o'clock call at another studio. I climbed on the bike for a trip to the lab to pick up the pictures of Sloane.

The night before, as soon as Sloane and Stein had left, and I had locked the cameras in the safe, I biked to the lab with the film, then I cruised over to Ginny's place in Chelsea. I hauled the Lejeune upstairs with me and left it in her place while we went out, bought a bottle of red wine, and had dinner in a neighborhood restaurant. The cuisine was Argentine; it was plentiful, tasty, and cheap. The ambience was blue-collar. Ginny had a saffron rice and lamb dish. I had a beef stew. It seemed best not to mention photographing Sloane, or that we were planning a sting. I had no idea if Stein could deliver as promised, so why get her hopes up? Also, any mention of the name Sloane, or Hungerford, was sure to taint an otherwise certifiable blissful evening.

I always feel as though I'm doing myself a favor when I ride the Lejeune. The cardiovascular benefits are obvious, but more than that there's the thrill of matching wits with the traffic and pedestrians. It helps if you have the reflexes of a downhill ski racer. On the practical side, there's the ease of moving swiftly around a congested, gridlocked city, and the fact that although I paid fifteen hundred dollars for it, the Lejeune has paid for itself more than ten times over in cab fares and messenger fees.

I was busy congratulating myself on my love affair with the Lejeune, and waiting for the light to change at Thirty-fourth and Madison, when a voice said: "Where you been, sport?"

I looked, and he was gone. He was threading his way through the two-way traffic, against the light. It was my friend from the Park, with a messenger's pack on his back. The graphite kid, except his street bike was assembled from parts, single speed, clincher tires, and one handbrake on the front wheel. He rode day and night. It was no wonder the kid was so good.

Henry Stein showed up at the studio at nine-thirty. I was halfway through the *Times* crossword, which was as far as I was going with it, and working on my second cup of coffee. He accepted a mug of coffee from Tito, and peeked over my shoulder. "Stuck, huh?"

"Got five letters for 'Tantara'?" I asked.

"Mantra . . . maybe? No, that's six letters. Hmm, try

'dredge' for four down, Panama Canal site. Fifty down, Izaak Walton? That's 'angler.' That ought to help get you going again."

It did. I might even finish the puzzle later.

"Well, interested in hearing how I made out with her nibs last night?" he grinned.

"What do you think? First we'll put her pictures up in the projector, and we can look at them while you give me all the lurid details."

"Got 'em back already? That was fast."

"It only takes a couple of hours."

"Just like the amateurs."

Coffee mugs in hand, we moved to the lounge. Tito loaded the projector, and adjusted the screen. We settled into the sofa, and Tito dimmed the lights and left us. I punched the forward button on the remote. A life-size Sloane Marshall blazed onto the screen before us.

Stein gave a low whistle. "She certainly is a piece," he commented. In Stein's lexicon women seemed to be either "a piece," or "a broad."

"Well, you gonna keep me in suspense, or are you gonna tell me what happened last night?"

"You want it blow by blow?"

"Just tell me what happened, Henry."

"Okay. Well, as soon as we're in the limo, she wants to know if what I said in the studio was true. Could I really double your money in thirty days?" He paused, distracted by the image on the screen.

"And what did you say?" I coaxed him.

"I said yes. And then she said, 'Can anyone get in on it?' No, not just anyone, I tell her. She says she understands. Besides, I tell her, there's always a certain amount of risk." He paused again. "May I see that slide again?"

"Sure." I pulled the slide from the stackloader, and projected it again.

"That's a good one. I like that one." He sounded like an art director. "We're thigh to thigh now, and that's the look she gives me. Like in that picture. 'But Henry,'" he said in falsetto, "'you'd give me a chance to double my money . . . wouldn't you?'"

The accuracy of his imitation made us both laugh. "I'll mark that chrome," I said.

"I play it coy," Stein continued. "These deals don't always work the way they're supposed to, I say. I wouldn't want you to be disappointed. 'Not to worry,' she says. She likes to gamble occasionally, and she likes to win, she tells me, but if she lost five K it wouldn't be the end of the world for her. Apparently five K means nothing to her."

"Not when it's someone else's money."

"Yeah. Well, anyway I tell her it's against my better judgment, and she gives me another one of those looks, like I'm supposed to turn to cheese dip. So I melt a little, I say, well . . . maybe, Sloane . . . as long as you understand it's not one hundred percent sure." He switched to the falsetto again. " 'Oh, I understand, Henry, I really do.' "

We chuckled.

"Finally, I cave in. Aw, all right, I say. She squeezes my hand, and gives my cheek a peck. 'Done,' she says. And I shouldn't worry. If the deal sours, she won't blame me. When we get to her place, she says, 'Come up for a drink, and I'll write you a check.' "

"And did you?"

"Of course. We'll have to make it quick, I tell her, I have another appointment. That broad lives well. Quite a place she's got there."

"Yeah, she does. Was there anyone else there, like Hungerford, maybe? A tall, distinguished-looking guy."

"There was a guy there, as a matter of fact. He was on his way out as we were coming in. I thought that was strange. This guy wasn't that tall, though. He was tanned, well-kept, and well-dressed, built like a truck, and about as pleasant as a head cold. Oh, and she called him Anthony, but she didn't introduce us. Any idea who that can be?"

I thought immediately of the "dancer" at the party, who fit the description. "Probably one of her punches. Hungerford doesn't seem to own the franchise. There was a guy at the party named Anthony, could be him."

"Would she give the guy keys to her place? This guy, Anthony, had wiseguy written all over him."

I hadn't thought of Anthony that way, at least not up till now. "Who knows, maybe it's a key club. But you didn't meet Hungerford."

"No. As she's writing the check, she says, 'Double my money, Henry, and we'll have dinner.' It's a date, I say."

"Henry, suppose she waits the thirty days, pockets my money, and passes on the rest?"

"Getting cold feet?"

"I've had a few anxious moments. Counting petty cash, I'll be out nine grand."

"What do you think of that picture, Charlie?"

"It's a good one."

"Yeah, I like it too. We should have asked her to drop the towel for some. Too bad, huh? Now, how about prints?"

"You didn't answer my question." I snapped the lamp on cool and turned up the lights.

"Want some advice, Charlie?"

It looked like I was about to get some advice whether I wanted it or not. "Speak, sage of swindle."

He regarded me momentarily with his clear grey eyes, then the broad mouth broke into a generous smile. "That's very good, Charlie. You're an amusing guy, but forget about the money . . ."

"Easy for you to say."

"Yes, it is. But you should think of the money as spent, gone," he lectured me. "There are two human frailties that make swindle possible, and they are greed and gullibility. All marks are gullible. All marks are greedy." He paused to let it sink in. A con man's catechism. "All marks believe there's something for nothing. In other words, they're gullible. All marks want something for nothing. In other words, they're greedy. My money—well, actually your money—says that Sloane Marshall has both of these frailties, and therefore is the ideal mark. Believe me, I know a mark when I see one."

I believed him, but it did little to ease my anxiety. "I'm sure you do, Henry."

"You've got nothing to worry about. Your five grand's bait, and Sloane's gonna take it," he said, getting to his feet. "And when she does, we'll set the hook, and play her like a fish. You know why it's called a con game, don't you, Charlie?"

"Yeah, con for confidence."

"That's right, it's con for confidence. We've got to get the mark's confidence, and we've got to have confidence in ourselves. Luckily, I've got enough confidence for both of us." He grinned and rocked on his heels.

Stein's pedantry was less than inspirational, but his hubris was awe-inspiring. "Yes, professor."

"You've got a lot to learn."

"No doubt. Tell me, is Henry Stein your real name?"

He gave me that bemused look. "That's what Strunk calls me."

"Yeah, but what does your wife call you?"

"Darling, of course."

"And always safe. But what I'm getting at is how do folks react when they realize they've been stung for a hundred thousand dollars?"

"I don't plan on being around for that. But mad as hell, usually."

"That doesn't worry you?"

"Oh sure, there are death threats, cheap talk like that, if that's what you're getting at," he replied coolly.

"That's what I'm getting at."

"They calm right down after a while. Why compound one bad mistake with something worse, like mayhem and murder? If you're looking for something to worry about, just pray we don't get nailed for fraud, pal."

"Strunk said just about the same thing, when I mentioned to him that an investor and his wife were killed by a car bomb right after leaving Sloane's party."

He picked up his mug and drained the cold coffee in one gulp. Leveling his solemn, grey eyes on me, he said, "These are perilous times in which we live, my friend. There are a lot of nuts out there."

"Okay 8x10's on the prints?"

"Sounds fine. Good coffee, Charlie."

Stein didn't wait thirty days. Two weeks later, the nineteenth of October, Black Monday, Roman numeral II, when the Dow sank lower than the *Titanic,* and that's on the bottom of the ocean, Stein, blithe spirit that he was, strolled into the studio in the late afternoon without an apparent care in the world.

"Smells good in here," he said. The place smelled like a brewery.

"Want a beer?" Tito asked.

"Don't mind if I do. I hear people who drink a glass a day

of the stuff live longer than the rest of us." Tito poured him a mug. "To your health," he said, raising the mug to his lips.

"One more exposure, Henry," I said. "We've been pouring beer all day, looking for the perfect head."

"I understand, a perfectionist."

Tito sprayed sweat on the beauty bottle and a clean mug with an atomizer filled with a mixture of glycerin and water. He positioned them in front of the 8x10 Deardorff camera. With the lens open, to me the image appeared inverted on the ground glass. Under my dark cloth, I studied the still-life image at the back of the camera, asking Tito to twist the bottle and the mug to the left or the right.

Stein inspected the setup. "Ah, so that's how it's done. You put bits of mirror behind the bottle and the mug to get that glow. I've often wondered why my brew never looks the way it does in the photograph."

"Tricks of the trade," I said. "Speaking of which, how'd you make out in the market today, Henry?"

"I was outta the market weeks ago."

"Yeah? I heard Donald Trump said the same thing."

"You positioned and focused?" asked Tito.

"What else was he gonna say?" grinned Stein.

"Looks good," I told Tito. "Stop 'er down." I slid a filmholder into the camera back and removed the slide.

"Pour?"

"Pour."

Tito poured slowly from a chilled quart of Budweiser. The head formed nicely, small, tight bubbles. Carefully, Tito raised the level in the mug, bringing the head to the top, and then some, without letting it spill over. I waited for the effervescence to clear, then I pressed the cable release.

"That was perfect. Quick, let's get one more," I said.

Quickly, Tito recocked the lens, and I reversed the filmholder. The shutter clicked, the strobe popped, and we had a second exposure a moment before the head collapsed.

"That one was a hero," I said.

"I notice Tito's been pouring Bud," said Stein, "but the bottle in front of the camera is Stroh's."

"Could you tell the difference in a photograph?" I said.

"I doubt it."

"What's real anyway, huh?"

Tito poured us each a mug of beer, and freshened Stein's glass. "Charlie thinks Bud gives better head," he said.

"So much for truth in advertising. All is sham. Life's a swindle." Stein shook his head sadly.

"Life's a bowl of cherries, a joke, a cabaret, ol' chum," I grinned.

"That, too," a bemused Stein agreed.

"I'll clean up, Charlie," Tito said.

Stein and I removed ourselves to the lounge. I produced the prints of Sloane from the chest of flatbed drawers while he folded himself onto the sofa, mug in hand, adjusting the crease in his trousers. I sat opposite him in a director's chair, and he studied the two prints silently.

"Very good, Charlie," he said finally. "You do nice work, they'll be just fine." He glanced up at me. "Ever been to La Côte Basque?"

"No. I don't have a rich photographer for a client."

He smiled. "Well, we had our dinner date there, Sloane and I, last night."

"How much did the tab come to?"

"Don't ask." The broad mouth spread into a grin. "It'll only make you crazy, but you ought to go there sometime. The food is out of this world."

"And so were the prices, I'll bet."

"True, but you only live once. Believe me, it was worth it. I'd never been there before, but she had, of course. Broads like Sloane get around, you know."

"You bastard, Stein."

"The lady had just doubled her five grand in two weeks, Charlie. I think that calls for a celebration, don't you?"

"Right, and now she's a lady, huh?"

"I stand corrected," he grinned. "The broad."

"A five-grand piece of ass."

"Pricey, I'll admit, but Sloane likes to show her gratitude."

"I'm sure she does."

"You know, Charlie, I think you're jealous."

"Shit."

"Listen, my friend, if it'll make you feel any better, she wasn't that great. You know the type? Here I am, on my back, doing you a favor."

70

I don't know why I flared up like that. Stein was doing what he had to do; he wasn't out of line. And I wasn't jealous. How could I be when I had Ginny? I only wished it was someone else's money, not mine, that he was playing with. "All right, Henry, enjoy the licky face. But don't forget what you're there for."

"I'll try not to." He smiled. "But you should be excited that we've got her attention . . . and that she thinks she's got mine. We're on base, Charlie. That's what we wanted. Now we steal second, and bingo! we're in scoring position." He held up the palms of his hands deferentially, and smiled broadly. "An unfortunate choice of words, and no pun intended. But I assure you, if Sloane and her playmate have a hundred K, I'll get it. Remember, Charlie, the name of the game is confidence."

I nursed my beer, and listened to the assurances of a con artist.

"I'll give her a rest for a couple of weeks," he went on, "then I'll start setting her up for the next stage. She's hot, Charlie. When she hears the next proposition, she'll be all ears. 'When another opportunity like this comes up,' she says to me, 'I have access to larger sums of money.' What more could we ask for, huh?"

Chapter 8

Two weeks later, the end of the month, I was back in Stein's office, staring out the window. The Twin Towers were a pair of gold ingots in the sun sinking slowly into the Jersey swamps euphemistically known as the Meadowlands. I was so dumbstruck by the view that it took real willpower to turn my back on it.

I refocused my attention on the office, a changed place since my last visit. I didn't have to wonder how much was left of my twenty grand, or where it had gone. Zilch was left. A Bokhara rug lined the parquet, and an eighteenth-century cleric's standup desk leaned against the wall. Neat conversation pieces; the sort of touches I'd expect from Ginny. Stein had style. Sloane's portrait hung on the wall, a splash of glamour among a collection of forgettable faces: local TV personalities, state and city politicians, and a couple of hockey players. She looked like the winner of a Catherine Deneuve lookalike contest, if you squinted.

Stein pointed to a low-slung beige couch, and I planted myself in it. He pulled up a straight-backed chair, and straddled it. The normally cool grey eyes glistened, kilowatts of energy crackled around him. He rubbed his palms together, and in rapid-fire delivery, began: "I know a broker who has, on the sly, been buying up the outstanding shares of a small mining company in Edmonton, Canada. Out in the boonies. Eighty percent of this company's stock is held by family, company execs, and employees. This guy has managed to corner most of the remaining twenty percent of stock that is publicly traded. He and his broker pals are about to start boosting the stock. Their scam's gonna establish, beyond a shadow of a doubt, my bona fides with her nibs. And there's a chance here for you to make a few bucks for yourself at the same time. Interested?"

"There's a catch, right?"

"No catch."

"No risk?"

"No risk, no profit, Charlie. Shall I continue?"

"I'm listening."

"Good. I'll put you in touch with one of these brokers. He'll recommend the stock to you, naturally. This is what he's gonna say. If you buy one hundred shares of the stock, and it doesn't go up at least one point by the end of the week, then you don't have to pay for the stock. But if it goes up a point or more, then a messenger will pick up a check from you Friday, before the banks close. These guys will be selling their asses off, all over town, all week long. Come Friday, and you've seen the stock start to move, he's gonna offer you the same deal again. Buy another hundred shares now, and pay later. And then, only if the stock moves a point or better. And, of course, he'll want his check again that Friday, before the banks close."

"And they'll repeat the pattern until they've unloaded all the shares they're holding."

"You got it."

"At which point the suckers and their money are parted, and the stock goes in the tank."

"Exactly."

"How much do these brokers stand to make?"

"Figure they've got fifty to a hundred thousand shares to sell, and the stock is selling for ten dollars a share, if they can bump it up fourteen or fifteen points, you're talking in the range of one to two hundred thousand dollars a man."

"Sounds tempting, Henry."

"Is that all you've got to say? Sounds tempting?"

"What do you want me to say, sounds crooked?"

"Crooked? What the hell are you talking about? Sounds crooked."

"Take it easy. It's just that I'd like to steer clear of anything shady, that's all."

"Shady? Listen, schmuck, we are scheming to clip some guy for a hundred K so you can be a hero to your girlfriend, and now you tell me you don't want to get involved in anything shady. I've got to know now, are you prepared to do what has to be done, or not? What's it gonna be? Make up your mind."

"All right, calm down, Henry. I'm with you."

"Look, if it'll make you feel any better, think of it this way—it's like betting against a bookie, knowing your line is superior to his, that's all."

I wished that was all. "Okay, you'll tip Sloane and me when to sell?" I said, with the sinking feeling that I was wading into quicksand.

"Of course. I'll tell Sloane which broker to buy from, how much to buy, when to sell, and which broker should sell her shares. The only thing I won't tell her is that these guys are running a scam."

"What if she gets nervous, or decides she knows best, and sells either too soon, or too late?"

"Sloane's gonna be a good little girl, and do as I say. But let's suppose she does sell too soon, she'll still make money, and kick herself for not following orders, and making all she might have. On the other hand, if she's greedy, and hangs on too long, she'll learn a painful lesson: Follow orders. Either way, after this little number, Sloane, bless her mercenary heart, will be convinced, beyond a shadow of a doubt, that I have access to insider information." He rested his cool grey eyes on me, a confident, smug grin on his broad mouth.

The following day I opened a trading account with the broker he recommended.

Wednesday, as Stein predicted, the broker, named Lundy, was on the phone to me.

"I'm gonna make you rich, Byrne. I've got a stock, Edmonton Engineering & Minerals, Ltd., that's all set to bust loose . . ."

Lundy and his pals boosted the stock for nearly two months, but I dropped out after the first month. Lundy was furious. "What's the matter with you, Byrne? The goddamn stock's still going up. You can't sell now," he yelled at me over the phone.

"Hey, pal, you don't want to sell the stock? I'll get another broker to sell it for me."

"You can't do that."

"Who says I can't?"

"All right, sell, and fuck you, asshole." He slammed down the receiver in my ear. He sold the stock, though, and took his commission.

I came out seventy-four hundred dollars ahead, and feeling pretty pleased with myself.

Stein's estimate of the broker's take turned out to be conservative. They boosted the price of E.E.&M., Ltd., stock up thirty-one points, and seven of them split better than two and a half million dollars.

Sloane had been a pussycat, was the way Stein put it. She sold at thirty-eight, following orders to the letter. What's more, she wasn't lying when she said she had access to larger sums of money. In six weeks she doubled forty grand.

I didn't ask Stein what he made on the deal. But shortly after that, there was an item on page one of *The New York Times* that read: "Special Investigator P. C. Strunk of the Securities Bureau of the Attorney General's office announced today the arrests and indictments of seven stockbrokers on charges of fraudulently manipulating the stock of Edmonton Engineering & Minerals, Ltd. Investigator Strunk said that his office acted after an anonymous tip alerted them to the possibility of fraud involving the unusual activity of E.E.&M., Ltd.'s stock in recent days."

It didn't take a rocket scientist to figure out who Strunk's anonymous tipster might be.

I suggested to Ginny that it would be a good idea to give Hungerford a call, he might have a check for her. And it was a good idea—she got a check for a thousand dollars. I still hadn't let her in on the sting. What I hoped to do was present her with a check, and say that I'd persuaded Hungerford to return the money, and let it go at that. I didn't want her involved in any of Stein's shady business.

The last two weeks of the year are a good time to get out of town. There's too much partying all along the corporate ecosystem for any real work to get done in the ad game. Flushed with ill-gotten gains from the E.E.&M., Ltd., stock-boosting scam, I could afford to get out of town, so I did.

Now, on a bitter cold evening early in January, I was tripping through some Kodachromes on the projector, of Ginny and me—the camera on self-time, horsing around, in the buff, on a deserted beach. I was busy warming myself with a bourbon and the memories of four sublimely sybaritic days in the Bahamas together with Ginny, when Stein called.

"Fit and tanned, pal?" he inquired cheerfully.

"Both, thanks to you. What's happening in the murky world of financial chicanery?"

"We're about to go for the gold."

"You are?"

"Yep, and I could use a little help from you. You will be interested to know, since we last spoke, Sloane and I have enjoyed more than one tête-à-tête."

"At all the best places, I'm sure."

"Hey, Charlie, if I were twenty-one, and a Greek god, I'd take her out for Szechuan; of course all the best places. Suffice to say, as a result of these rendezvous her nibs is fairly wetting her pants to make some more money."

"You lead some life, Henry. Dining out at the best eateries, Sloane Marshall on your arm. Maybe I should consider a career change."

"Don't do it. You don't have the disposition or aptitude for this life. Stick to what you know, pal. Getting back to cases, I've finally met our friend, Hungerford."

"Oh yeah?"

"Yeah. Sloane introduced us. We're a regular threesome, out on the town several times now."

"Sounds sordid to me. Who picks up the tab for these escapades?"

"You're not I.R.S., Charlie, are you? I picked up the first check, Richard's picked up the rest."

"Richard?"

"That's progress, pal. Yeah, it's Richard, Sloane, and Henry now. We're all pals. At least we are until Sloane gets me alone. Then it's Richard's a wimp. Richard's cheap. Richard can't get it up."

"Must be flattering for you, Henry. Does Richard know about you and Sloane?"

"I'm sure he does. The guy's not stupid. But hell, I keep bumping into that wiseguy Anthony, and then there's another guy, Philolius, a lawyer, for christsake. I haven't been at her place once that he hasn't called or dropped by. As for Hungerford, poor bastard, he pays all the broad's bills, and what does he get for it? She shtupps the Seventh Fleet, and parades them under his nose. That's how she shows her appreciation. But it all comes down to money, my friend. Hungerford's cool—if there's money to be made, he can look the other way."

"Money talks, bullshit walks."

"Crudely put, but accurate."

"And I thought I was being earthy. You said you needed my help."

"I need an actor. You do casting, don't you?"

"All the time."

"I thought so. I'm looking for a substantial type in his mid-sixties. He should convey the notion that he's an important man. That he's big. Big physically, big mentally, and big financially. Got the idea?"

"I think so. You want Mr. Big, right?"

"That's right, Mr. Big, exactly."

"Anything else?"

"No, that's all. Just give me a call when you've got it set up."

"I'll do better than that. I'll videotape them, and save you time."

"Fine. In that case, have them say a few lines. Improvise, like they're George Bush, or Edwin Meese, someone like that, a regular plutocrat, know what I mean?"

"Yes, and no."

He chuckled. "Make sure I've got plenty of bodies to pick from."

"You want a cattle call."

"Absolutely. This is the big one, Charlie. We're going for the gold." He hung up, and I went back to my bourbon and Kodachromes, and tried to imagine how it would be when I handed Ginny her check.

Tito and I spent two days casting nattering nabobs, and when we were done, I called Stein and told him I was bringing the tape to his office.

"Wanna tell me what this is all about?" I asked, after Stein had studied the candidates for Mr. Big on tape.

Stein bounced on the balls of his feet and smiled. "It's about appearance and reality, and the window of vulnerability between them."

"Glad I asked. That certainly clears that up."

"Play back the last five or six guys. I think I like the guy with glasses, near the end of the tape."

I reversed the tape, stopped it, then pressed the forward button.

"That's the guy," Stein said, motioning at the first head with glasses. "Looks like a cross between Robert McNamara and William Simon. What do you think—like him?"

"Did McNamara wear glasses?"

"Doesn't matter. Always thought those two guys were really the same person. Notice how you never saw the two of them together?"

"How come, if we're looking for a double for McNamara or Simon, we have them doing impersonations of Bush and Meese?"

"We're casting for a Washington plutocrat, a sort of generic cabinet member, say from . . . oh, any administration before Carter's. How many of Nixon's or Ford's cabinet members can you name?"

"McNamara was Secretary of Defense, but I'm not sure

what administration. Simon was in Nixon's administration, and maybe Ford's. He was Secretary of Defense, and I think Treasury. Name some names, I can probably tell you whose administration, and the job."

"Let me see the guy with the glasses one more time."

"Sure." I replayed the tape.

"Yeah," he mused, thinking out loud more than speaking to me. "He'll do. He'll do fine. He looks the part; self-important, a regular stuffed shirt. I'd judge you to be better with politicians' names than most. Sloane, certainly no better than you. Hard to tell about that enigma, Hungerford, though. He seems like a pretty bright guy. I'll have to be careful."

Feeling like a dimwit, I consulted the casting sheet. "The guy's name is Warren Ulrick."

"Good for him. What's he gonna cost?"

"How do I describe the job to his agent?"

"I don't know. Make up some bullshit. Tell 'em it's public relations work. Show a little ingenuity, pal. We'll need him for an afternoon."

"We can probably get him for fifteen hundred dollars."

"Fifteen hundred! I don't wanna sleep with the guy, for christsake. I just want to take his picture, and have him shake a few hands if necessary."

"Three hours, with agent's commission? It'll be a grand, at least."

"That's what's wrong with this country, with the world—people have gone money-mad. Don't they realize, it's only paper? Hondle with them, see what you can do," he sighed. He rummaged in a leather case until he found a manila envelope, which he passed along to me. "Here, take a look at these. We'll need Warren's mug on one of these bodies. A Republican, I think."

The envelope contained a series of 8x10 glossies of Stein with various politicians, past and present, Republican and Democrat, mayors, councilmen, governors and senators.

"Had no idea you were so well connected, Henry."

"You kidding, these guys would pose with a corpse for a vote." He laughed. "Believe me, it's been known to happen. What do you have to do, photocompose the picture?"

"I'll take a black-and-white Polaroid of Warren, cut it out, and paste it over D'Amato's face. Tito will make a copy negative, and print it. We'll clean up the edges with spot tone."

"That simple?"

"That simple."

"If it's that simple, give me an alternate."

"Okay."

"I'm having dinner tonight with our fun couple at a place called Canastel's."

"The new spot on Park Avenue South?"

"Right. It was Sloane's idea. Ever been there?"

"No. Trendy spot, though."

"That's what I hear. You've got to get out more, Charlie. Anyway, tonight, for an appetizer, I'll pique their interest with a deal I'm concocting."

"A legit deal?"

He gazed at me with a patient smile. "This deal, I'll explain, is legal, borderline legal, and just shady enough to be very lucrative."

"Sloane ought to like that."

"Hungerford, too, I hope. I'll tell them I've been approached by a Washington powerhouse, a former cabinet member, to find investors for a syndicate he's forming."

"Ah-ha, this is where Warren Ulrick comes in."

"A cameo part, but yes. The syndicate, I'll tell them, is about to buy from a conglomerate, at distressed prices, a company that's been leaking red ink, but is real estate rich. There's a new management team in place, and the company's about to turn around. But the company's stock is outrageously undervalued."

I interrupted him. "But why would the conglomerate want to sell a company with assets, a company that was about to turn around?"

"A good question." Stein beamed. "Now we're talking main course. My guy, I'll say, has a couple of pals on the board of the conglomerate, and one hand washes the other. In other words, the answer to your question is—collusion."

"You're a devious bastard, Henry. The insider's insider. I like that. And I think Sloane will, too. In fact, I think she'll be wetting her pants."

"I think so, too. Now, for dessert," he chuckled. "I'm

gonna tease them a bit. I'll tell them I'm fully subscribed, but if anyone should drop out, the minimum participation starts at a hundred K. I'll say it may take as long as six months before the syndicate can take the company public— the stock is all held privately by the conglomerate—but when they do, the investors will be paid off in the newly issued stock at the rate of ten dollars a share. The plan is to float the issue at sixty dollars a share . . ."

"Are you saying that for one hundred thousand dollars, they'd get six hundred thousand dollars' worth of stock?"

"That's what I'm saying. Not quite as good as hitting Lotto for a buck, but it should happen to us."

"Suppose Hungerford doesn't go for it?"

"He is the enigma, but I think he'll go for it. He's not wasting time being polite to me for nothing. Besides, Sloane will make him go for it."

"What good is stock to them? They're gonna want cash."

"We don't know that, but if that's the case, then cash is what they'll think they're gonna get. This is the way it works. Participation is according to the amount invested, which translates into shares. The syndicate then uses the investors' money as collateral to borrow from larger, institutional lenders, like Westinghouse, for instance, to finance the actual purchase. The lenders will be agreeable to such a highly leveraged deal because of the company's real estate assets. Once the syndicate gets its paws on the company, it strips it of its assets—the real estate—and sells them off. The syndicate rapes the company, in other words."

"Sloane ought to like that image."

"Yeah. Then I tell them, when the cabinet member takes the company public, the investors will receive two-thirds of their shares in cash, and one-third in stock."

"Which is now outrageously overvalued."

Stein grinned. "Now it's coffee and brandy, and the fox is in the henhouse. Our cabinet member, I will explain, has foisted off on an unsuspecting public the stock of a company he has damn near put into receivership. The investors will dump their shares immediately, of course, before the public gets wise, and the stock nosedives."

"Phew, that's a complicated scenario."

"The more complex, the more plausible. At this point

Sloane should be so excited she's sitting in a puddle of her own barbecue sauce, or we're back to square one. She would swallow a simpler line, but for Hungerford? . . . He's the enigma. He may know his way around this kind of stuff. Great pokerface that guy's got."

"I'm in awe, Henry."

"In awe of what?"

"You, your imagination, I guess."

"Imagination?" he scoffed, getting to his feet. "What imagination, I picked it up whole from *The Wall Street Journal*. That's the way business is done these days. The most respectable people are always the biggest crooks. Don't you know that?"

"More of the pithy sayings of Chairman Stein," I said, accompanying him to the door.

"Just be ready to roll, my friend," he cautioned me, and departed with a mocking smile.

Dinner at Canastel's was evidently a success. "This is it, pal," Stein said, a few days later, when he summoned me to his office. "We're going for it. Bring along your equipment. There's a part for a photographer in this sketch. You ought to be able to handle that."

The three of us were sitting around Stein's office. Sloane was expected in half an hour. Stein had just finished hanging the doctored photograph on the wall. And Warren Ulrick, the old fart, was having second thoughts about taking the job.

"I don't think I care to do this."

"What do you mean, you don't care to do this?" I demanded.

"This is not the job I contracted to do, gentlemen." He sat, legs crossed, on the couch, polishing his spectacles with a linen handkerchief.

"You . . . ," I started.

"I'll handle this, Charlie." Stein gestured for me to remain seated.

Warren held his spectacles to the light, and examined them for dust.

"Now, Warren," Stein said genially. "Of course this is the job you contracted to do. It's exactly the job. You were

81

contracted to pretend that you're a former cabinet member."

"You're asking me to impersonate someone."

Stein had decided generic wouldn't do, we had to have a brand name.

"That's true, and you do a great William Simon," said Stein.

"But I've never laid eyes on the man."

"All the more remarkable."

"And another thing, there is no such company as the Inspirational Word Press and Bible Publishers, Inc., is there?"

"Au contraire, Warren." Stein smiled. He punched a couple of keys on a modem, and pointed to a video terminal. "Check it out for yourself."

Nice touch, the computer, I thought. Henry Stein, high-tech flimflam man.

Warren didn't budge.

I wanted to strangle the dopey bastard. "It's a joke. We're playing a practical joke, Warren," I said.

"I'm an actor, not a comedian," he replied.

I made him out to be a "walker," a paid escort, at best. If he'd ever appeared in anything more than dinner theaters or industrial films, I'd eat my Hasselblad.

"We're all actors, Warren," sighed Stein. He produced his billfold from inside his jacket pocket, and counted out ten crisp one-hundred-dollar bills.

Warren blinked and stared at the money.

Stein stepped up to him, and casually stuffed five of the bills in Warren's breast pocket. "That's for you, Warren. Don't tell your agent about it." He snapped the remaining bills under Warren's nose, and returned them quickly to the billfold. "They're yours, too, Warren. Just do a good job."

Warren Ulrick drew himself up to his full six foot two, patted his breast pocket, and smoothed out the apron of his jacket. Beaming down on the diminutive Stein, he announced, in a fruity baritone, "Magic time!"

"Fuck up, Warren," Stein warned, "and it's your ass." He turned his back on him and walked away. As he passed me, he muttered under his breath, "What a putz." He turned to Warren again. "Pay attention, Warren. I want this dog and pony show to go smoothly. The lady will be here any minute. I assume you can improvise?"

"With the best of them."

"Good, because we're playing this by ear. I may introduce you, or I may not. If I introduce you, it will be as William Simon, since you'll have to have a name. If you are introduced, by all means, stroke her. My guess is she'll have eyes for you anyway."

"How delightful," said Warren. "As it happens, Mr. Stein, I have some experience in these matters. Few members of the opposite gender can resist the Warren Ulrick charm when it's turned on full power."

"No doubt," said Stein, "however, since this whole business is supposed to be hush-hush, it isn't really necessary you be introduced." He considered Warren momentarily. "It may even be counterproductive. What I might do is just let her have a quick glimpse of you. Flash you at her, you know, like you're the big cheese."

"I shall pray for the former, but in either contingency you may depend on Warren Ulrick to play his part brilliantly."

"See that you do, Warren," Stein deadpanned, "or before you know it you'll be four foot two, instead of six two, and there'll be no more magic time, understand?"

"Warren Ulrick does not give shoddy performances."

Stein shot him a baleful glance. "Charlie, I want you and your equipment in the reception room when she arrives. Warren, you come with me. Remember, guys, take your cues from me and everything will be all right."

The champagne-blond receptionist closed a copy of *People* magazine and smiled brightly at me. Her name was Traci. "So, you're a photographer?"

"That's right."

"Hmm . . . it must be interesting, being a photographer, I mean."

"Keeps me on my toes."

"Do you take a lot of pictures of models?"

"Quite a lot." She seemed to have no preconceived idea of what a photographer should look like. I found that refreshing.

"You'd be amazed how often people tell me I should model."

83

"Not at all." I smiled.

She blushed and squirmed with pleasure. "I'd really like to try it, but I don't have the foggiest idea . . ."

The door opened, and in sauntered Sloane, looking smart in a business suit of tweed and earth colors.

"Oh, hello, Miss Marshall," Traci stammered. "You, you must want Mr. Stein."

"Please," Sloane said, standing at the desk, her back to me.

"Hello, Sloane," I said.

She turned. She was slow to rearrange her expression from imperious to mild. "Charles? What are you doing here?"

"I was about to ask you the same question."

"You startled me. What a surprise finding you sitting there. I'm here to see Henry."

"That's a coincidence." I smiled. "So am I. He wants me to do some P.R. photography for him."

Traci breathed into the intercom: "Miss Marshall to see you, Mr. Stein."

"My new pictures are a great success, Charlie. Everyone loves them."

"That's wonderful."

"Yes. What do you drink, scotch or bourbon?"

Since it appeared I wasn't going to get a dinner for my efforts, Krystal was the thing to say. I said: "Moussy."

She tossed her head and laughed. "We'll have to think of something else then."

Stein arrived. "Ah, Sloane."

"Henry."

They rushed to buss the air beside each other's cheeks. "You've caught me at an awkward time. Would you mind waiting a few minutes in my office?" He gave her a knowing look. "I'm right in the midst of a meeting with the Washington connection."

"I understand, Henry. Don't let me interrupt anything. I can do some shopping, and drop back later if you like," she volunteered sweetly.

"No, no, that won't be necessary. We'll only be another ten minutes or so, and besides, I may have some good news for you."

Traci made a face at Sloane behind her back, then giggled at me.

Stein pretended to see me for the first time. "Ah, Charlie, why don't you bring your equipment and follow us. We're in the conference room." He stepped aside and waved Sloane through the door. I brought up the rear of the procession, toting two camera cases.

We paused at the entrance to the conference room. The door was slightly ajar, affording Sloane an easy view of Warren, who seemed to be poring intently over a slew of documents. Stein gestured for me to go in before guiding Sloane on to his office.

"So that's our pigeon," said Warren. "Very attractive."

I gave him a skeptical look and busied myself unpacking gear. This guy was big physically, but mentally and financially he was a Pygmy.

Stein reappeared. "Her nibs is settling down with a glass of Perrier. Let's give her ten minutes or so. Meanwhile, you guys make like you're taking pictures." He disappeared again, leaving the door ajar.

Warren struck a convincing chief executive officer pose. "I could use a good boardroom scene for my composite."

"Easy, Warren. This is just a goof, remember?"

"No, no, Charlie, I want to pay for it." He pulled one of Stein's bills from his pocket and pushed it across the table at me.

Maybe I'd misjudged Warren. Maybe he directed dinner-theater shows and industrial films, because he knew how to put the motivation into my part. I grinned, pocketed the bill, and put a roll of film into the camera.

Two rolls of Tri-X later, Warren and I were both suddenly aware of Sloane and Stein watching us from the corridor.

"Think we've got it?" said Warren.

"I think so. Thank you for your time, Mr. Simon," I said.

"Not at all, my good fellow." He slapped me on the back and laughed. "If I like them, and I'm sure I will, I'll order three sets of prints, one for mom, one for the wife, and one for the girlfriend. Why, Henry Stein, you old rascal," he beamed, "and here I thought all you were interested in was the bottom line." Warren brushed past me as Stein steered a pliant Sloane toward him.

"Ah-ha, and who is this dazzler that can distract the diligent Henry Stein from his precious bottom line?" gushed Warren.

Sloane flushed with pleasure.

"Bill, I'd like you to meet a very dear friend of mine, Sloane Marshall," Stein intoned. "Sloane, this is William Simon."

"How do you do, Mr. Simon," said Sloane, for all the world like daddy's little girl.

"Very nicely, thank you," he beamed. "And how do you do yourself, Sloane Marshall. But please, call me Bill."

Sloane batted her eyes, and smiled demurely. "I'm fine, thank you . . . Bill."

"Isn't it reassuring to know that Henry is a mere mortal," Warren continued to spout. "That he's no more impervious to the charms of a beautiful woman than any other man."

Stein cleared his throat. "Yes, well, I'd suggest a quick drink at Smith & Wollensky's . . ."

"Oh," Sloane exclaimed, "what a marvelous idea."

"Yes," Stein continued hurriedly, heading disaster off at the pass, "but unfortunately we're on a tight schedule. Bill and I have work to catch up on before he dashes for the six o'clock shuttle back to Washington." He turned and glared at Warren.

Disappointed, Sloane made a moue.

"Ah, sad, but true, dear lady." Warren smiled graciously. "But you will arrange it for another time, won't you, Henry?"

"Of course," Stein replied.

"And not to worry, I'm in town frequently," Warren assured her.

"We'll do it next time," said Stein.

"Promise?" said Sloane.

"Yes, you promise, Henry?" grinned Warren.

"I promise," Stein said, making it a quorum. He took her by the elbow. "Let me walk you to the elevator, Sloane."

She waved bye-bye to a beaming Warren Ulrick, and I began packing up my gear. "I think that went well," Warren said, with a smug smile.

"I think Henry will be the judge of that," I warned him.

He polished his spectacles nervously, placed them back on his nose, and gazed at me with a sober face.

Stein returned a minute later looking grim. He marched straight up to a quivering Warren Ulrick. "That did it, you asshole," he said. Warren trembled on the verge of tears. Stein smiled broadly. "That was an Academy Award–winning performance, Warren," he said, and he counted out five crisp companion bills to the five hundred dollars Warren had already received. He stuffed the money into the breast pocket of Warren's jacket, as before. "Yessiree, Warren," he announced, "you deserve an Oscar for that performance."

A look of relief flooded across Warren's puss. "Well, thank you, Henry," he murmured, touching his breast pocket. "Kind of you to say that."

"Yeah, yeah, you're real good. Now get outta here." Stein grinned, dismissing him with a wave of his hand.

"Thanks again," said Warren, backing out of the room with a bow. "Thanks again."

"Real sure of himself, that guy," Stein grinned after Warren had gone. "I have some time to kill before my train. I'll buy you a drink."

"Okay."

"Gimme a minute to call home."

"Go ahead."

I stared out the window, downtown, into darkness, while I waited for him to make his call. The city lights, mostly yellow, but some red, seemed punched out of black velvet and disconnected. Stein spoke in a voice I hadn't heard before, soft and affectionate, telling his wife to hold supper, he'd be on the six-thirty train. It was something of a revelation to discover Stein had a house in the suburbs with a wife and kids. The con man lived a normal family life. I felt a twinge of jealousy. As soon as Stein hung up, I asked if I could use the phone. I called Ginny and got her machine. I told the machine that it was me, and asked it to have its mistress give me a call, I'd like to see her tonight.

Stein offered me a hand with my camera cases, but I said I felt balanced carrying one in each hand. We found Traci closing up shop in the reception room. "Charlie wants to take your picture, Traci," Stein teased.

"Mr. Stein!" She blushed furiously.

"No kidding, Traci. Isn't that right, Charlie?"

"Sure." I smiled.

"I told him what a great body you have, Traci."

She gave him a playful shove. "Goodnight, Mr. Stein."

"Nice kid," said Stein, pushing the elevator button.

We threaded our way through traffic on Lexington Avenue and into the Graybar Building, and from there made our way to the Grand Central Bar, overlooking the terminal. Commuters stood three deep at the bar, getting faced on the mortgage money. We managed to get a couple of Heinekens, and find a spot to roost.

"Well, judging from what you said to Warren, it went pretty smoothly," I said.

"Yeah," he agreed, gazing at me with that bemused expression.

"That was cold, the way you jerked Warren around."

"It was a payback for holding us up for more money."

"I thought he was convincing."

"He was, but he's still a putz."

"Sloane thought she'd made another conquest."

"Sloane's sold. Now she's got to sell the enigma."

"God, it was all so quick. She only had about a minute and a half with him."

"Believers want to believe."

"Yeah, and we have nothing to fear et cetera, et cetra."

"And don't forget, less is more." He rocked on his heels, the glint of hubris in the clear grey eyes. "Remember, my friend, her nibs has already made a few bucks on my tips. It may have been a brief encounter, but she saw the photograph of Warren and me, and she met the face in the picture. When I stepped out of the office, she saw the bogus letters, and the documents with Simon's signature on them that I left on the desk. Also, I showed her how I.W.P.& B.P., Inc.'s stock was doing on the computer. It was doing nothing. Remember, too, Sloane thought this was just a social call. Slip ol' Henry the oil. She wasn't prepared for any of this."

"What a manipulator."

"I'll take that as a compliment." He grinned. "Just before I introduced Sloane to the Washington connection, I told her that one of my original investors was feeling the heat from the SEC for allegations of possible insider trading, and, as a result, thought it wiser to drop out of the deal. They hated having to do that, but it's an ill wind that blows no good. There was a spot open now for her and Richard, if they were interested. She assured me they were, and to prove it she kissed me. Charlie, she stuck her tongue so far down my throat I damn near choked. Anyway, I told her she had to hustle, I couldn't keep the spot open long. I said, you have ten business days to get all your ducks in a row."

"What did she say?"

"She said she understood, and that she thought Richard could handle that."

"That's fantastic."

"I don't know about that," he said, with uncharacteristic modesty. "But I'm happy with the way it went. I think it went well."

"That's what Warren said."

"Warren." He laughed and drained his mug. "Talented, but still a putz. Gotta catch a train, pal."

Tito was long gone when I got back to the studio. I played back my machine. I only had one message. Ginny, in a cheery voice, telling me she was busy tonight and would call tomorrow. I brooded awhile in splendid isolation, then I pulled the Lejeune off its hooks and took it out for a spin.

Chapter 9

It was a strike day for Tito and me. We were cleaning up from a two-day video shoot for a feminine hygiene product, that first week in February, when I heard from Stein again. He wanted to know if I could come see him after lunch.

"Sure. What's up, Henry?" It was no problem breaking away for an hour.

"The eagle shit," he said succinctly.

"Say no more, Sultan of Swindle, I'll see you at two-thirty."

"Fine," he said.

It was a blustery, pewter-grey day, the kind of day that made you glad to stay indoors, and it took me less than five minutes to trot over to the Chrysler Building from Fifth and Thirty-eighth. Traci was frisky and friendly, as usual, and buzzed me in with a happy face.

I found Stein hunched over the computer. He looked up, a neutral expression on his face. "Hello, Charlie."

"Hello," I answered. I nodded at the computer. "Is that thing for real, or are you programming another scam? You looked so grim just now, when I came in, Henry."

"It's for real. I was following the market," he said, smiling thinly. He got to his feet, fetched a couple of envelopes from the cleric's desk, and passed them to me. "The Dow's off two hundred points already and the day's not even finished. The sell programs on the computers have kicked in, and the market's undergoing a correction. Better keep an eye on your stocks."

"Only stock I have is in my own ass. Hope you didn't lose any money."

"Not me, pal, I was out weeks ago."

For his sake, I hoped that was true, but it sounded like something a plunger would say. He rocked on his heels, waiting while I tore open the first envelope. It contained a cashier's check, in the amount of eighteen thousand dollars, drawn on a bank in Altoona, Pennsylvania.

"Your twenty K, less Warren," he explained. "And you made money at stage two. Remember?"

I remembered money well spent on blue skies, emerald-green water, blazing white sands, and Ginny Rowen alfresco. And it warmed me to the bone to see most of my twenty grand again.

I tore open the second envelope. It contained another cashier's check drawn on the same bank in the amount of fifty-two thousand and change. Ginny's principal, intact, with some interest. Good enough. I wasn't about to question Stein's math.

"This is great," I cried. "You did it. You really did it, Henry. Congratulations."

"Yeah, my pleasure. I've enjoyed our collaboration, Charlie."

"You did it all, Henry."

"Nearly," he admitted.

"Thank you very much. This is terrific." It sounded inadequate and inane, like a winning contestant on a quiz show, but it was all I could think to say.

"You're welcome."

"How about a drink? To celebrate."

"Another time, perhaps, Charlie. I've got to get back to the computer, and keep an eye on what's happening downtown." He gently guided me to the door.

"Henry, how can I show my appreciation?"

"You don't have to do a thing. There was a recovery fee. Remember?"

"That's right. You made yourself fifty or sixty grand, huh?"

"Somewhere around there."

I nodded at the computer again. "Too busy to count it, is that it?"

"They keep me jumping. Listen, tell your girlfriend she was lucky this time. I only did this as a favor, because you're a friend of Strunk's." He gazed at me with eyes bleaker than the weather. "I'm gonna keep the office for another week or so. If you need to reach me after that, Strunk will know where to find me."

"That's it then. This thing's been going on now for nearly six months—and suddenly, bingo, it's all over. There's gonna be a void in my life, Henry."

"You're gonna miss me, huh? I'm touched, but every sting must end." He offered me his hand.

"It was fun while it lasted," I said, shaking hands. "Take care of yourself."

"I always do," he said dryly. He gave me a glimpse of the perpetually bemused face, and added: "The women are the life, Charlie."

I mulled over our parting as I strolled back to the studio. The whole scene couldn't have taken more than five minutes —another brief encounter. I wondered if, like Sloane, I had seen only what he wanted me to see, and not what I should have seen. There was none of his usual hubris today. He was different from the Henry Stein I knew. His personality was flat and greyer than his eyes. He seemed almost furtive. I wondered if the checks were good. And rejected that thought immediately.

Either he was having a bad day in the stock market—and that would certainly explain the strange mood—or, as I've found it to be with photography, a sting, like a shoot, is far more compelling while it's happening than when it's finished. You can't help but come alive when you're into it, doing it. Alive in the now. And that feeling intensifies as you crank up for the finish. But when it's over and done with, the finished thing is a dead thing. At the end of a job, I'm never in the best of moods. I'm happiest when the picture's slightly out of reach, shimmering alluringly in my mind's eye. When it's taken, and fixed on acetate, it's not unusual to find myself slipping into a mild funk until the next job comes along. It's as though the action is more important than the result. Maybe it's like that with Stein. This sting is history. Maybe that's what's bugging him.

I felt the twin envelopes nestled snugly inside my jacket pocket. Two good reasons for me not to continue pursuing this morbid line of thought. The sting wasn't quite history for me yet. For me, the best was yet to come. I was Lochinvar.

"What are we celebrating tonight? Did you get a cigarette account?"

"Nothing like that, but something almost as good." I smiled. This was my hour to shine, and I wanted to do it right. So here we were, going for French, me in my suit, Ginny, drop-dead beautiful, in a black chiffon number below the armpits and over the knees.

"Must be good, if sushi at Akasaka wouldn't do."

"Not tonight," I beamed.

"Dinner at Le Perigord?" She gazed at me quizzically over the menu. "Are you going to keep me guessing?"

I smiled mysteriously, withdrew the envelope from inside my jacket, and presented it to her.

Her eyes searched mine momentarily. Then she opened the envelope. "What's this, Charlie?" she gasped.

"I don't know," I said, almost giddy with pleasure. "What does it look like to you?"

"Money of some kind. Treasury bills, to be exact."

"Oh good, that's what I thought."

"There's fifty thousand dollars' worth here."

"Better yet, all present and accounted for."

"But I don't understand. Whose are they?"

"They're yours, darling." I smiled. "They belong to you. It's the fifty thousand you gave Hungerford."

She glanced at me apprehensively as the waiter approached, and stuffed the T bills back into their envelope, as if they were a hot potato. We ordered. She had the rack of lamb, and I had the poached trout. I ordered a bottle of Bordeaux, vintage '76.

"But you're having fish," she said.

"Rules are made to be broken. And besides, you're having meat."

Her eyes narrowed skeptically. The waiter smiled tartly and departed. She leaned across the table. "Charlie, where did you get fifty thousand dollars?" she demanded.

I didn't like the tone of that question. It sounded as though she thought I might have stolen the money. "I merely asked Hungerford," I explained patiently, "if he'd be kind enough to write me a check, made out to cash, and to certify it. He'd be happy to, he said. Nice man, Hungerford. Then I bought the T bills for you with the money."

She frowned. "Bullshit," she said.

What could I say? In my imagination, reuniting Ginny with her money had always loomed as an occasion of unqualified joy. But then, I never did have much luck with good deeds. Once I offered a blind man my seat in the subway, and he yelled, at the top of his lungs, in a car full of people, "Whatta ya! A fuckin' hero?"

"All right, Charlie, what's the real story? Where did you get the money?"

I gave her the real story.

She avoided my eyes while the waiter displayed the wine label. I nodded, dumbly. He poured, I tasted, and nodded dumbly again. He poured again and withdrew.

"Suddenly you're very quiet," I observed.

Her tongue curled briefly over her teeth. "I don't know what to say."

I raised my glass. "Don't say anything then. Here's to happy endings."

She wasn't with me. "Charlie . . . I don't mean to seem ungrateful . . ."

"But! Ah, but we do have something to say. Let's have it."

"Well, I'm stunned that you would take it upon yourself to do this."

"Check me if I'm wrong, but I seem to remember you bawling to me that you'd done something dumb, that you'd lost your last fifty grand, all the money you had in the world."

"But you might have said something about what you intended doing."

"I had no idea whether we'd succeed or not. I didn't want to get your hopes up."

"Okay, but for five months? You never said a word. And all this time I've been getting interest from Richard. Every time I call, I get a check."

"Three thousand dollars, that I know of, and you still have to call."

"There was another check—for a thousand dollars that I didn't mention."

"Four thousand dollars then," I scoffed. "Hardly the fantastic return that was promised."

"They haven't had the money a whole year yet."

"Three more months and it'll be a year, right?"

"Yes."

"Ginny, why this change of heart?"

"I'm keeping even with C.D. and T bill rates. Richard may deliver, as promised. It's only three months more, why not wait and see?"

"I'll tell you why not wait and see. Because if your pal, Richard, is running a Ponzi, sooner or later, there'll be no more interest, or dividends, or fifty thousand bucks, for that matter. And that can happen anytime, tonight, tomorrow, or next week. Three months is plenty of time to lose it all."

"The only one that I know who's run a Ponzi is you, Charlie," she snapped.

"You've got me there," I admitted ruefully. "And I'm sorry if I've upset you, Ginny. But this isn't such a big deal. Hungerford hasn't a clue yet that he's been had. As far as he's concerned, you've still got your account with him. Why don't you hang on to the T bills for now, and let's see what happens. If Hungerford proves to be for real, we can always do the right thing and return the money, discreetly, of course. On the other hand, if it turns out he's a crook, then your money is safe."

With downcast eyes and moodily twirling the wine in her glass, she tacitly agreed to the wisdom of my proposal. For some reason, I thought of Stein watching our little scene with his gaze of perpetual bemusement, and I felt like Lochinvar with egg on his face. What the hell was going on? First Stein, now Ginny, everyone seemed to be sprouting multiple personalities. "Call Hungerford tomorrow," I said, relieving the stone silence. "Ask him for another check. Maybe you'll get lucky."

We manufactured polite, desultory conversation until the check came, but a pall had settled over our evening. She insisted we split the tab. She had an early call, or so she said, so I dropped her first and kept the cab, returning to the studio feeling like I was under indictment.

I called first thing the following morning, and got her machine. It was nearly seven in the evening when she returned the call. She was going out of town on a job, she told me, and would call next week as soon as she got back. She didn't call, I did. And I didn't see her again until the week after that.

When we finally connected, she was in high spirits. Her jaw jutted off at an arrogant angle as we leaned into the wind off the East River walking across town. She was full of news, and full of herself. Or was this another personality? She was going on about a new job; an interior design job, model apartments for a twilight-zone village in Florida. It would keep her busy for some time.

I was happy for her, of course, glad the career was going well. But I hadn't seen much of her lately, and if she was going to be shuttling back and forth to Florida a couple of times a month, I wondered when she'd have time for me? The less time she had for me, the more for someone else. Was there, could there be, more in Florida than model apartments, I wondered? The more she carried on about the new job, the more my own spirits sank deeper than a Florida sinkhole.

We sat at the sushi bar at Akasaka, and the chef fed us by the piece. "Try some uni, Charlie," she said. "It's got lots of zinc in it. It's good for your you-know-what."

"No thanks, I'll stick to tuna." My you-know-what had a mind of its own, and I could feel its mind was changing.

She shrugged, and made a show of slurping uni. "Mmm, good!" She grinned lopsidedly.

"Good is what you like, I guess. Did you call Hungerford?" I asked.

"Uh-huh."

"And?"

"I got a check, two hundred and fifty dollars."

"Less than usual, but something, I suppose."

"I don't want to talk about it, Charlie."

"Fine."

We went back to her place after dinner, and straight to bed. We both had early calls in the morning. The lovemaking was decorous and perfunctory, and when we were done, she patted my thigh lightly and declared, "We're used to each other now, Charlie."

"What's that supposed to mean?"

"Nothing," she murmured.

"The thrill is gone?"

"Don't be silly. I only meant we're familiar with each other."

"Yeah, that's what you said."

"Go to sleep." She yawned complacently. She rolled on her side, letting me have her back, and was asleep in minutes.

I lay awake staring at the ceiling.

Chapter 10

Bold as brass, Sloane Marshall blew into the studio with the winds of March, trailing the chill of winter after her. Full steam ahead, she barged into the shooting area, where we were busy with a jewelry catalog. Tito, following her, shrugged and raised his eyebrows helplessly.

"Sloane!" I said affably. "This is a surprise."

"Hope I'm not disturbing you, Charlie," she said, her eyes darting around the studio. "When I found myself in the neighborhood, I decided to take a chance, and drop in and say hello."

"Not at all. Glad you did," I said disingenuously. "How about a drink?" She looked as though she could use one.

"Please," she said without hesitation. Tito helped her off with her mink. She was dressed for business in a flannel skirt, matching blazer, silk blouse, and leather boots.

We needed to test a film emulsion that night, so Tito went back to work on the still-life. I propelled Sloane to the lounge. "Now, what'll it be?" I asked.

"Brrr, it's awfully cold out there." She hugged herself and shivered. It was a hollow attempt at gaiety. "Do you have any brandy or cognac?"

She did need a drink. I had a bottle of Martell's, and I poured us both a glass. She had seated herself on the couch and was arranging her legs when I handed her the glass. She flashed the professional smile briefly and said, "Thanks."

I lowered myself into a director's chair. "To the weather," I smiled, and raised my glass.

"It's beastly," she said. She sloshed her glass, nodded, and knocked back a fast slug.

"Well." I smiled noncommittally. She hadn't fallen in for the pleasure of my company or my brandy. I wondered how long it would take for her to get around to the purpose of the visit.

She gazed at me speculatively a moment, then jumped to her feet. "I feel like a cigarette. Do you smoke?"

"I don't," I said, standing. "Let me see if Tito has any."

When I returned, she was clutching her brandy and pacing. She stopped dead in her tracks and plucked a cigarette with her fingernails from Tito's pack when I offered them.

"Did you ever smoke?" she asked.

"Never."

"Aren't you lucky, you never had to give them up. I've given them up . . . but sometimes there's nothing like a cigarette." She inhaled deeply with satisfaction, gave me her right profile, and exhaled slowly.

"So I'm told," I said.

She forced a smile, sat back down, crossing her legs and arranging her skirt carefully around her knees. It took another swallow of brandy and another puff on the cigarette before she was composed and languid.

"How have the new photos been doing for you?" I asked, redepositing myself in my chair.

"Didn't I tell you? Everyone likes them. We got an excellent response from the mailing. I'm up for the TV spokesperson job for a supermarket chain."

"That's great. Happy to hear."

"Yes," she said, letting her eyelashes droop seductively. "If I get it, I'll take you out to dinner," she promised with a husky voice.

I seemed to have some upward mobility in Sloane's ratings. The last time this subject came up I was worth a bottle of booze, and now I was worth a dinner. "You don't have to do that," I demurred, playing Mr. Nice Guy. If she really wanted to do something, I thought, why doesn't she just pay me for the photos?

"Oh, but I'd like to. It could be interesting." She held my gaze. "No?"

"It could?" I grinned.

She answered with a smile, and a significant pause. "Have

you seen your friend Henry Stein lately?" she managed finally.

There it was, as black as sin, the true purpose of this chat, the hundred-thousand-dollar question. "No, not lately," I lied. "You were there the last time I saw Henry Stein. It was in the Chrysler Building, remember?"

She stared at me. "Yes, I remember."

I might have asked her why she asked, but I thought I knew the answer, and besides, I didn't think she needed to be led. Instead, I said, "You never know, though, with Henry, when he'll turn up, or where he'll turn up."

"Really," she said with a cocked eyebrow. She took another nervous puff from the butt, then fiercely ground it out. Unconsciously, her eyes hardened. "Did you take part in that deal he was putting together?"

"Which deal was that?"

"The one he was talking about here, in the studio, when we were taking the pictures."

"Oh, that one. Yes, I did. I gave him a check, don't you remember?"

"So you did. Did you do any other deals with him?"

"There was another one, some brokers were boosting a stock, as I recall . . ."

She seemed momentarily confused, then she said, "Oh yes, that one. I made some money on that one."

"Whoa, what is this?" I asked amiably. "I feel like I'm getting the third degree."

"I'm sorry." She hurried to apologize. "It's just that your friend Henry Stein made quite an impression on me. He, well, he was very astute . . . financially, that is."

"He is that," I agreed.

"And—well, it pays to stay in touch with a person like that, don't you think?" Her eyes narrowed.

"It couldn't hurt."

"Yes, and now that he's no longer in the Chrysler Building, I seem to have lost track of him. I thought perhaps you might still be in touch with him." She studied me, her eyes like slits.

"He travels quite a bit, I know that. I have a Post Office box number and an answering service, if you'd like to have them."

"Give them to me."

"Certainly, excuse me a moment."

Tito stopped me on my way upstairs. "We're all set to make the test, Charlie."

"Okay, go ahead and pop it. Let's get the film in the lab."

"Right, boss."

I jotted down the P.O. box number I had for Stein, although I doubted the number was still operative. Strunk's number was the answering service. I jotted that down also.

She was up and pacing again when I returned. I gave her the slip of paper, and she stashed it in her bag without a glance. "If he should turn up unexpectedly," she said, "please tell him I'm dying to get in touch with him. Will you do that?"

"Of course."

She picked up her brandy glass and drained it. "Mmm, that was good." She put the glass down and glanced around. "You know, you really have a very nice studio, Charlie," she said.

"It needs work, but I like it."

"Are you still seeing that little stylist . . . what's her name?"

"Ginny, yes, occasionally."

She laughed down in her throat. "A nonexclusive relationship, is that it?"

"Something like that."

"She's a sweet girl," she said, dismissing Ginny. "Thank you for the info. Sorry to barge in on you like this, Charlie. You've been most kind. I've got to run. Richard and I are having dinner with the Philoliuses tonight. You might have met them. They were at the party."

Stein had mentioned a Phil Philolius, and I remembered a fat guy with a lot of gold jewelry at the party that fitted the description, but I played dumb. "I don't think so. I wouldn't forget a name like that."

She laughed. "He's a lawyer. He's one of Richard's biggest investors. They're such a boring couple, but I have to be polite to them for Richard's sake." She hesitated. "I think he invests so much money with Richard because he wants to sleep with me." She tossed her head and laughed mockingly, as though that was the most outrageous idea in the world.

I liked the lawyer's chances.

"Men." She grinned.

"Yeah." I grinned.

I walked her to the door. "Let me," I offered, helping her slip into the mink.

"Don't be a stranger, Charlie. You have my number."

I did indeed.

The forecast called for flurries, but what we got was a blizzard, wailing out of the west and dumping two feet of white stuff on the Tri-State area in the middle of March. A cold snap dogged the heels of the gale and Manhattan became one vast meat locker.

My career nosedived with the thermometer. I bid on five jobs, and came up cold five times. One agency was shopping price. I was awarded one job, and then it was canceled. A change of strategy, the art director explained. I was the low bid on another job when the agency lost the account. The fourth job went to a notorious lowball artist, and the art director's brother-in-law was awarded the fifth job on a rigged bid.

Then the phone stopped ringing altogether, and I was colder than a frozen fish fillet.

I had been paying fourteen dollars a square foot for the studio. The lease was up at the end of the month. The agent, a prince among men, magnanimously offered to let me renew at twenty-eight dollars a square foot. That was the best he could do, he claimed with a shrug. Take it or leave it. I took it.

I watched anxiously as the accounts receivable folder got slimmer, and the accounts payable folder got fatter. I'd have to sell some equipment if the situation didn't improve soon.

In the middle of that miserable week, Ginny invited me for a late supper. She whipped together what she jokingly called a career woman's dinner—store-bought tortellini and an endive salad. My contribution was a cheap table wine to wash it down with. For dessert, we had a soft goat cheese, a baguette, and fruit. "Simple, easy, and good," she boasted. It was fine.

As we ate, she prattled on about how pleased she was with herself and her life these days. The architect who hired her for the Florida project was ecstatic with the way the model apartments were shaping up, I was thrilled to learn. And then there was the possibility of doing the home furnishings section for a new publication targeted at upscale working women. The graphic designer was a close friend. Busy, busy, busy.

She tore a piece off the baguette and smeared it with cheese. "I'm lucky to have such good friends," she said, lifting her eyes to mine. "Like you, Charlie." She conferred the demotion on me with a condescending smile, and took a bite of bread and cheese.

"Onward and upward."

"That's right." She took a swallow of wine and gazed at me solemnly. "I can hardly wait to get to work in the morning." She paused. "We've got to get on with our lives, Charlie." She watched to see how that went down.

Something inside me lurched, as though the ground had been cut out from under me. I tore off a piece of baguette, and chewed it with a forced smile. "True," I responded calmly, feeling myself in emotional free-fall.

She rewarded me with a lopsided grin, at once triumphantly cynical and optimistic. Her eyes were large and moist with provocation.

I raised my wine glass. "To getting on."

"I'll drink to that," she said happily. She stood, and began clearing the table. "Would you like a brandy?"

"Yes." Just put the bottle on the table, I thought.

She put two snifters on the table, and poured. She glanced at me apprehensively. "Any work?" she asked, sitting down again.

"Got a fistful of purchase orders. Busy all day long. It never ends. Did the sales tax today. That took five minutes. Mopped the floor, combed the cats, changed a light bulb, and worked on the crossword puzzle."

"You've had these spells before. I wouldn't worry about it. How did you do with the puzzle?"

"Nearly finished it."

"Lemme see it?"

I got the paper.

She furrowed her brow in concentration, and jiffy quick, filled in the dozen or so blanks that I'd left. "Ah-ha, an easy one," she crowed, handing the paper back to me.

The phone rang. She frowned. "Who could be calling at this hour?"

102

I could think of a couple of guys.

"Hello, yes, this is Ginny Rowen." She glanced at me with a questioning look. "We've met at Sloane's? Bruce who? If you say so. What can I do for you, Bruce? Why no, I hadn't heard. Richard Hungerford's disappeared, you say? But . . ."

"Let me talk to him." I took the phone from her. "Hello, this is Charles Byrne," I said.

"Who're you? You an investor?" demanded a Queens accent.

"Yes."

There was a pause. "Byrne? No Byrne on my list. Guess it don't make no difference," he said finally.

"Who are you?"

"Bruce Linhardt. I'm an investor. I'm calling around to let people know that that bastard, Hungerford, has split."

"What do you mean, he's split?"

"S'what I said. He's taken off, booked. He's gone," he spluttered angrily.

"When? How long?"

"It's been more'n a week since anyone's seen 'im."

"Maybe something's happened to him. Maybe he had an accident."

"Like he's in Bellevue? You mean like that?"

"Yeah."

"Forget about it. That angle's been checked out. He got lost because there's a warrant out for his arrest."

"What about Sloane? Where's she?"

"She's holed up like a rat in her apartment. The phone's off the hook, she ain't talkin' to no one."

I exchanged an anxious glance with Ginny. "The investors have been calling, huh?"

"Whadda ya think?" he blustered. "You bet your ass the investors been callin'. They're in an uproar."

I thought of how frantic Sloane had seemed the week before, when she dropped by the studio looking to get in touch with Stein. "Have they threatened her?"

"Hey, right now, people are jus' plain scared. They want some answers. They wanna know what's been goin' on with their money. I heard of one guy who's out half a mil. She's gonna hear all kindsa threats if we don't get some answers, and I mean soon."

103

"Assuming he's taken a powder, what's the damage? How much money's missing?"

"All kindsa numbers are being kicked around. Ya know Tony Pesce?"

Anthony, "the dancer" at Sloane's party, Stein mentioned bumping into him the first time he went to her apartment.
"Yes, I know who he is," I said cautiously.

"Well, he says it's fifteen mil."

"Never steal anything small," I murmured. "How did he come up with that figure? What makes him the expert?"

"I dunno, maybe he got it from her. He was a lot tighter with them than any of the rest of us."

"I see."

"The reason I'm callin', Mr. Byrne, is Tony thinks we oughta get together an' hire a private detective an' see if we can't find Hungerford before it's too late. I was wonderin' if we could count on you and Miss Rowen?"

"How did you get this number?" I asked, dodging the question.

"Tony's got the investor list."

"And was it also his idea to swear out a complaint?"

"Nah, that was our idea. He wanted no part of it, but he hadda go along with it 'cause the rest of us insisted that's what we were gonna do. That's when he came up with the private detective angle."

"Why wouldn't he want to swear out a complaint? Isn't he an investor too?"

"He says Hungerford's got a hundred grand belongs to him."

"Where does the money come from? What's he do for a living?"

"Search me, but whatever it is, it must pay good. You seen how he dresses."

"I noticed. But if Pesce's out a hundred grand, wouldn't he want to swear out a complaint against Hungerford?"

"Good question. I was wonderin' myself. What he said was, he preferred to handle the matter himself." There was a pause, then he said, "If you ask me, though, I think the sucker's lookin' out for Sloane, for whatever reason."

"He has a thing for her, you mean?"

"You seen 'em dancin'?"

"Yes, I have," I said, still stuck on the phrase "he

104

preferred to handle the matter himself." Even allowing for the lurid bent to my imagination, it had an ominous ring to it, as though he meant to break Hungerford's legs. And hadn't Stein pegged him for a wiseguy?

"Well, whadda ya think?"

"Why do you say he's looking out for her?"

"'Cause we wanna go after her, attach her property, get a lien on her bank account, and Tony don't wanna hear it. It ain't her fault, he says. She didn't do nothin' wrong. She ain't the one who's missin'. She was ripped off too. How could she know the guy was a crook? Aw, he's got a million excuses for her. And he's a kinda spooky guy, ya know. Nobody really wants a hassle with him. But hey, she hadda know what was goin' on with Hungerford, she was livin' with the guy."

I wasn't so sure about his last statement. "Maybe she knows where he is, maybe she'll join him when things cool off."

"We thought of that. That's jus' another reason we should be lookin' to attach any property of hers we can get our hands on."

"I doubt you'll have any luck with that."

"Whadda we got to lose? Anyway, whadda ya say, Mr. Byrne, are you with us, or what?"

"Why don't you call me Charlie?" I said. "How about the other investors, Bruce—are they all willing to kick in for the private detective?"

"Okay, Charlie," he replied. "No, not all of them. I've had some refusals. You gotta wonder, huh, why not everyone's hot to see this guy caught?"

"Well, if it was black money they were hiding, money they hadn't paid taxes on, then they'd probably just as soon forget about the whole thing."

"Black money? Whadda I know from black money. I'm jus' a workin' stiff, all money's green to me." He hesitated. "Ya think Tony Pesce's money's black money?" He chuckled at the idea. "Whadda ya say, Charlie? Can we count on ya?"

My eyes met Ginny's fleetingly. She was shaking her head no. She had heard every word. Linhardt's voice carried; he could broadcast without a transmitter. "Suppose you find him, what then?" I stalled.

"We turn 'im over to the authorities, an' start gettin' this mess straightened out. What else? Well, Charlie, what's it gonna be?"

"Okay, you can count on us, Bruce," I said reluctantly. I shrugged sheepishly. Ginny banged her forehead with the heel of her hand and groaned, her eyes rolling upward.

"That's great," Bruce boomed. "Good talkin' to ya, Charlie. Gotta lotta calls to make, gotta go now. Tell Miss Rowen I'll be in touch."

Ginny sighed in resignation.

"Keep me posted too, will you, Bruce?" I gave him the studio number.

"You got it. So long, Charlie." He hung up.

"Why did you tell him he could count on us?" Ginny demanded immediately.

"Look, Ginny, if I said no, then you'd be conspicuous among the absent, those not so hot to see Hungerford caught."

She mulled that over a moment, her features clouded. "What's wrong with that?" she asked finally.

"Only that there's a connection from Stein to me to you. Until this thing resolves itself, why draw attention to yourself? There's safety in numbers."

"Yes," she snapped, "and if you'd left well enough alone, I'd still be getting my checks and be out of this thing in three months."

"Don't kid yourself. Stein took the guy for a hundred thousand dollars—typewriter ribbon and paperclip money —chump change to a finagler like Hungerford. Hardly enough to burst his bubble, you'd think. You heard Bruce, there's millions missing, fifteen million maybe. That oughta clue you the guy was running a Ponzi."

She avoided my gaze, tugging sullenly on a strand of hair. She had no comeback for me. I wasn't any happier with this turn of events than she was. But what could I do? Unwittingly, Bruce had cornered me between a brick and a firm place. It had never seemed simple, but if we got the money that should have been the end of it. Apparently not, it seemed.

"Ginny, I had to say yes," I said softly. "We've got to stick with the crowd. But the good news is the sting worked. Those T bills are yours now."

She moved mechanically into my arms and buried her

face in my shoulder. "I sound like an ungrateful bitch," she murmured. "Forgive me, Charlie."

I held her and whispered, "It's all right, darling, I understand."

There was some relief in the fact that she seemed mollified. But there was plenty to remain uneasy about. Pesce's emergence as the ringleader of the investors' posse worried me. And I couldn't forget that two people were already dead, and if Stein was any judge of character, there was a possibility of a link between Tony "the dancer" Pesce and the dead professor and his wife. A chilling thought, and not one I wanted to alarm Ginny with. Maybe she was right, maybe I should have left well enough alone and minded my own business. But it was too late now, and someone was playing hardball.

My personal recession ended with the month of March. A client I hadn't heard from in over two years was pitching an orange juice account. He needed a presentation shot in a hurry. He'd have layouts in the morning. Could I come see him then? You bet!

It was a raw, grim day outside, the last storm of the season blowing itself out. Inside, however, things suddenly became nice and cozy. Tito and I settled into the familiar prep routine: checking to be sure there was enough of each film emulsion number to complete a shooting, cleaning camera equipment and replacing batteries where needed, firing strobe heads and checking sync cords to be sure the lighting and electronic equipment was in good working order, ordering replacements for the most commonly used seamless paper backdrops, white, black, and four variations of grey, and the rest of the small tasks that need to be done before you can shoot.

While we were at these chores the phone rang again. It was another client, recovering from a spell of amnesia, and waking up with my name on his lips. The business is like that, you're either hot, or you're not. He wanted to know if I was available to shoot a print campaign; newspaper ads for a major city bank. You bet your T-square I am, I told him. I'd worry later how I would fit him into the schedule—juggle my time between him and the O.J. art director. I had one more significant call that day.

"Ya asked me to keep ya posted, Charlie," Bruce Linhardt's big voice boomed. "They found Hungerford. Traced 'im through his credit cards."

"Where was he?"

"A town called Oneonta, upstate. Ever hear of the place?"

"I've heard of it. He didn't get far."

"Yeah, he made it easy. Tony Pesce sent some muscle in a rented car to go get 'im."

"Muscle?"

"Yeah, a coupla investors," he chuckled. "One guy's a cop, the other guy's a fireman. They snatched Hungerford right outta the parkin' lot of the Holiday Inn."

"Where's he now?"

"Tony Pesce's got 'im. There's gonna be a meetin' of the investors at his place. Can you an' Miss Rowen make it?"

"Where's that?"

"Tony's got a laundromat." He chuckled again. "Whadda ya thinka that? Anyway, it's in Long Island City. Twenty minutes across the Fifty-ninth Street Bridge." He gave me the address.

Chapter 11

Surprise! surprise! Ginny wanted to pass on Tony Pesce's Wash an' Dri party. It took some arm-twisting to persuade her it was in her own interest to put in an appearance. But then I hadn't expected her to be an easy sell.

"Who needs it?" she demanded at first.

"Not you," I said.

"That's right."

"And not Hungerford," I continued, "and certainly not me."

"Then why go?" she protested.

Let me count the whys, I thought. I hung on the line and said nothing. "Charlie?" she inquired in a softer tone. "Are you still there?"

"I'm still here."

"Don't you see," she pleaded, "this doesn't concern me any longer . . . thanks to you, Charlie."

She had her money, she could care less about Hungerford, Sloane, Pesce, and the rest of them. In that sense she was right. But in every other sense she was wrong. And could be dead wrong. They all had an interest in how she happened to get her money. So it made sense she should be concerned, we should be concerned. "It's not that simple, Ginny," I said patiently. "How do you think it would go down with your fellow investors if it were to get out that you got your money? Never mind explaining to them *how* you got your money."

"How would they find out?"

"Someone, anyone, Sloane, for instance, or Hungerford, or maybe even the dancer, Tony Pesce, could start connecting the dots, and a picture would emerge. They'd connect you to me to Stein, or vice versa." I paused to let the weight of that idea sink in.

"Christ," she moaned. "What have you gotten me into?"

I know a rhetorical question when I hear one. There was no need to terrorize her with a worst-case scenario, like fraud, and possibly several more violent things, which was the honest answer to what we had gotten into. "Ginny, I haven't gotten you into anything," I lied as smoothly as I could manage. "I've been trying to keep you out of something, and that's trouble. And the best way to avoid trouble now, and arousing suspicion, as I see it, is to show our faces at this thing, and splash around in the big pool with the rest of the losers, even if it is a pain in the ass." I wanted her to see what the losers looked like. Maybe it would humble her. But I felt mean, too, like I was punishing her for being ungrateful.

There was a long pause on her end of the line. "All right, I'll come," she conceded grudgingly.

It was a chilly night, temperature in the low forties. Clouds, like cheese curds, scudded across a hazy heavens playing now-you-see-them, now-you-don't with the stars. As Linhardt promised, the ride from Manhattan to Long Island City took twenty minutes. The cab dropped us on Thirty-seventh Avenue, and we walked around the corner to Twenty-first Street. The laundromat was a storefront in a tenement building.

A hulking figure detached itself from the shadows of the doorway and barred our passage. By the streetlight, I made out a towhead blond, a good-looking kid in his early twenties. His hair was cut in a "flattop do." His slacks were pleated and baggy. His sports jacket was baggy, too, and a different shade of charcoal from the slacks. The draped look was back with a vengeance, and on this guy, that meant a lot of yard goods. He wore a black turtleneck sweater and flaunted twin gold hoops in the rim of his ear above the lobe, demonstrating either that he was pretty sure of his masculinity at least, or he was a regular swashbuckler, really secure in his masculinity. On his face he wore a scowl, and he had that hard look of a guy in better shape than anyone needed to be in. I wasn't about to broach the topic of the earrings with him.

"Gee," I said, turning to Ginny, "just like a disco." I swung back to the golden boy. "Hungerford," I said, as Linhardt had instructed me to say. That was the password.

I wondered if he knew me from somewhere. He gave me the dull-eyed bad stare for seemingly an eternity, and I had an uncanny feeling I'd seen him before. Finally, he pushed open the door with the palm of his hand, and we got a blast of foul air in our faces. We swapped anxious glances and slid past golden boy into the laundromat. The air was rank with cheap cologne and deodorant, alcohol, sweat, and more esoteric bodily odors. The haze of cigarette smoke made it tangible. Our ears were assaulted with a malevolent din, like a hive of angry bees.

I scanned the hall for a familiar face. I recognized a few people from Sloane's "do." "Always the same old faces at these affairs," I joked.

Ginny was not amused.

Noticeably absent were the beautiful people. This crowd was strictly the hoi polloi—the crowd you could fool all the time. But one of the faces I recognized in the crowd

110

belonged to the fat man in the three-piece suit and the gold jewelry, the guy who had cut in when I was dancing with Sloane. A fat woman, with too much jewelry and a forlorn expression, clung like a barnacle to his arm. He must be Philolius, I thought, the lawyer Sloane mentioned. Working their way to us through the throng was another couple, whose faces were familiar, if not their names.

"Hi, I'm Bruce," he announced in that big voice that contrasted strangely with his gaunt, desiccated frame. "I recognized Miss Rowen from Sloane's. You must be Charlie Byrne."

I admitted to that.

"This is my wife, Barbara," he said, presenting a woman who was little more than a stick figure.

We all nodded and smiled.

"Well, this seems like a fun idea for a party." I smiled.

Linhardt's eyes darted furtively around the room. "Yeah, a lynch party. I never imagined anythin' like this when I asked ya to kick in for the detective, Charlie. Like I said, I thought we were gonna catch the guy and hand 'im over to the cops, but . . ."

"But now they want to hold his feet to the fire first, is that it?" I asked.

"Yeah, that's right," he said, massaging his balding scalp with a worried hand. Barbara concurred with a gloomy nod of her wiry, black-and-tan Airedale mane. "They wanna put the squeeze on 'im, make 'im cough up some dough."

"Suppose he doesn't have any money?" Ginny asked in alarm.

"That's what's worryin' me," he said. "If this situation gets any hairier, hey, we ain't sticking around here, know what I mean?"

"I think so," I said. "I guess you can't blame them, though, for wanting a pound of flesh if they can't get their money back."

Not the most soothing thing I might have said. Bruce and Barbara gaped at me popeyed with fright. "Don't get me wrong, Hungerford deserves all that's comin' to 'im," said Bruce. "But we don't want no part of any rough stuff. If it comes to that, we're clearing out."

"Don't blame you," I said. "Where's Hungerford? What's

111

everyone waiting for, Cuomo to run?" A glance at Ginny told me that she refused to be amused.

"We're waiting for Tony Pesce," Barbara answered.

"He's got Hungerford," said Bruce. "He's on his way here with 'im now."

More people had filtered in after us. There must have been nearly two hundred people in the store. The place was packed tighter than a hamper with two weeks' worth of dirty duds. The decibel level had reached maddening proportions, the crowd fairly quaking in anticipation.

The door blew open. The throng roared, and the building rocked. A gust of clean, cold air smacked us in the face. Hungerford's disheveled form, gagged and blindfolded, hands bound behind his back, was propelled into the room. A grinning bozo stuck out his foot, and the mob roared with delight when Hungerford stumbled, tripped, and fell on his face. The dancer, Tony Pesce, leaped into the store immediately behind the fallen man. He was nattily clad in a dark blue two-piece suit, tailored perfectly to his sleek, solid body, a white shirt, red club tie and matching handkerchief. He beamed in all directions at once, like a politician on the hustings. At his heels was the jolly, golden giant from the front door. Pesce plucked Hungerford off the floor as effortlessly as a dropped shoe. No mean feat, since Hungerford was a big man. Pesce held him up by the scruff of the neck for the crowd to see. Hungerford, being the taller of the two, and unsteady on his feet, gave the illusion of dangling in space.

"My God," Ginny mumbled. "How awful."

"People! People!" Pesce shouted in a voice the texture of cement and olive oil. "Take a good look at him!" He ripped the blindfold from Hungerford's face. "Take a good look at the thief who stole your hard-earned money!"

Blindfolded and gagged, Hungerford had seemed more of an enigma than ever. But now his eyes gave him away. A hollow man, filled with a single sensation. Sheer terror.

Pesce, his head on a swivel, basked in the crowd's adulation, as they took up chanting, Tony, Tony. Hungerford blinked. Pesce scornfully shoved Hungerford into the crowd. Laughing, they pummeled him and chucked him back like a medicine ball. Pesce laughed with them and caught Hungerford. At his signal, two men grabbed Hungerford by the arms and dragged him off to the basement. The mob cheered themselves and Pesce, and jeered Hungerford as he passed.

Hands raised above his head, flashing a foot of cuffs, Pesce called for quiet. "Settle down, people, settle down. Find a seat, if you can. This meeting is about to come to order."

A rustle went through the crowd as it busily made itself comfortable. A few people found seats on the fluorescent, plastic stack chairs scattered around; others sat on the tops of the washing machines. Most had to remain standing. We stood in the rear of the long narrow room.

A hush fell over the crowd.

Pesce, eyes closed as though in prayer, made them wait. When he opened his eyes, he gazed at them a moment longer, then he began. "We all know why we're here," he said, only to pause dramatically, then toss the crowd a conspiratorial grin.

This drew appreciative laughs and chuckles.

". . . And so I'll make this brief. First, let me thank you all for your support and cooperation in the matter of apprehending our friend, Mr. Hungerford." Pause.

The crowd applauded itself.

"The question before us at the moment is, do we hand Mr. Hungerford over to the police, or do we hold him forty-eight hours, and see what we can get out of him?"

"Hang the bastard," yelled one man. This was followed by laughter.

"Hold the bastard. Work 'im over," yelled another man, who was cheered.

But another voice shouted: "Turn him over to the cops." Hisses and catcalls greeted this suggestion.

"In a pig's ass," screamed a middle-aged woman. She got a round of cheers.

Pesce beamed, relishing the raw emotion of the mob. Then he raised hands again in a calming motion. "All right, all right, quiet down, people," he chided. "Quiet down."

They quieted down.

"This is a democracy, right?" he shouted.

"Right!" came the answer.

"Then we'll do this the democratic way," he continued. "Let's see a show of hands for those in favor of handing Hungerford over to the police."

Half a dozen hands rose tentatively amid boos and hisses. Even more tentatively, another half a dozen hands joined them. I raised mine, along with Ginny, Bruce, and Barbara, even though I wasn't a registered voter. We were a very small minority in this crowd.

Pesce made a pretense of counting. "Now, let me have a show of hands of all those in favor of holding . . ."

Pandemonium broke out before he could finish. A sea of hands, many in a fist, affirmed the motion.

"Those in favor of holding Mr. Hungerford have it," Pesce grinned. "No contest."

"Hey, Tony," one of the rabble called. "Let's vote an' see who's in favor of hangin' 'im if we don't get our money." The crowd cheered this idea merrily.

"Mr. Pesce! Mr. Pesce!" a voice shouted above the noise.

Pesce waved the mob quiet. "The gentleman over there," he said, acknowledging and indicating a fiftyish man in a glen plaid blazer. Not a beautiful person perhaps, but a cut above the crowd.

"I, for one, want no part of what you are doing here," he declared. "This is entirely outside the law."

The rabble jeered and booed the man soundly. Pesce looked on with tolerant amusement.

I glanced at Ginny. Her jaw was slack, her face ashen.

"Jesus," Bruce muttered. His eyes were damp and sick with fear.

Pesce quieted the crowd again. "Ah, I believe the gentleman is concerned that some harm may come to Mr. Hungerford, is that not so?"

The audience snickered.

"That is so," said the man.

"Well, let me assure the gentleman," Pesce said patronizingly, "that no harm will come to Mr. Hungerford while he is in our care."

The crowd booed Pesce and that idea good-naturedly.

Grinning, Pesce went on. "Surely you are aware," he said to the man, "that if psychological pressure is not applied now, while we have the opportunity, we'll have about a snowball's chance in hell of recovering our money.

"We all know what will happen once Mr. Hungerford is turned over to the police. The law will give him a slap on the wrist. Twenty-four months in a country club prison, that's all. And then he'll be free to prey on others. Well, I say let's make the most of this chance. Let's teach Mr. Hungerford a lesson. Let's teach him that decent, hard-working people don't have to be victims."

It was a moving speech, and the rabble roared their approval. I wondered if Pesce was practicing on them. He sounded as if he was planning to run for office.

The man in the glen plaid jacket remained unmoved, however. "I want no part of this," he announced. "This is where I exit." He began working his way through the throng toward the door. Grudgingly, people who probably could not as easily sustain their losses as he, gave way to him.

Pesce, a mordant smile on his face, rushed for the door himself. The mob yielded, clearing a path for him, and he reached the door first. "All right, everyone, calm down," he called out. "The meeting's not adjourned yet. All those who fear harm may come to Mr. Hungerford, and wish to leave, may do so now with a clear conscience," he offered magnanimously.

"Okay, we're outta here," Bruce muttered. "Come on, honey."

I began steering Ginny toward the door along with the rest of the slim pro-police faction.

"Shawn, get the door," Pesce ordered the blond giant.

Shawn jumped to it.

"Thank you for coming. And you have my word that Hungerford will be turned over to the police, unharmed, in forty-eight hours," Pesce assured the departing investors individually, pumping their hands.

"The photographer, huh?" he said, eyeing me warily as we shuffled up to the exit.

"Right." I smiled.

"You're not an investor."

"Just tagging along with the lady," I said.

"I see." He thrust his hand at me. I took it unwillingly. Our eyes locked. We tested grips. His was like a mangle. "Good to see you again," he said without conviction and released my hand.

Shawn slammed the door shut after us. "Good riddance,"

one of the rabble shouted, and the mob howled with pleasure.

Confused and rejected, the dissenters milled around in disarray.

"Shouldn't we call the cops?" asked a woman, wistfully eyeing a police cruiser rolling by.

We clustered around the original lone dissenter, our natural leader. "I don't think that'll be necessary," he said.

"But what if they kill him," said Bruce.

"What if they do?" He thumbed in the direction of the laundromat. "It's on their heads then. We're out of it. Besides, who knows, Pesce might actually accomplish something in there. Let's give him the forty-eight hours. There'll be time enough later, if Hungerford's not in custody, to call the cops."

I wasn't as sure as the original dissenter that, if harm came to Hungerford, we'd be in the clear, but I kept my mouth shut. He planned to have it both ways. He was going to keep his own hands clean while Pesce did the dirty work for him. So much for the moral high ground.

I noticed Philolius the lawyer was not among our group. Either he believed Pesce, that no harm would come to Hungerford, or the kind of law he practiced saw nothing wrong in holding a man against his will.

I gave Ginny a tug. "Come on, let's go."

We said goodnight to Bruce and Barbara.

We rode in silence, until, cautiously, Ginny said, "Poor Hungerford."

"Yeah," I agreed.

But it was a limited subject, and we seemed to have no heart for it. We lapsed back into silence, withdrawing into the recesses of our own thoughts. We felt no need to manufacture patter. As the cab pulled over to the curb in front of her brownstone, Ginny asked, "Would you like to come up for a drink?"

"Another time, thanks."

She glanced at me anxiously. "Charlie, I'm going to call the police," she said.

"Lady," said the cabbie, "could I have my fare first?"

I paid him, and we tumbled out of the cab onto the sidewalk. "Come up for a drink," she repeated.

"Not tonight, Ginny. Listen, don't call the cops yet." I

glanced at my watch. "It's eleven now. If you don't hear from me in eight hours, call the cops. Okay?"

"What are you gonna do?"

"I'm gonna get Hungerford out of there."

"How?"

"Never mind how. Just call the cops if you don't hear from me by seven o'clock tomorrow morning."

She frowned, gazing at me skeptically. "I hope you're not planning to do anything foolish."

"No, I'm not gonna do anything foolish," I promised. "Now go on upstairs, I'll call you in the morning."

The bottle-green eyes remained skeptical several seconds after the frown dissolved. She pulled me to her and kissed me. "I'll be waiting for your call," she said. "Goodnight, Charlie."

"Goodnight," I said.

I watched her trot up the stoop and fumble in her bag for her keys. Before she went in, she turned and with a polite smile waved goodbye. I walked to the avenue and hailed a cab.

I thought about Hungerford. He had never done me any harm. In fact it was just the opposite. I owed him one. I had to get him out of that laundromat. True, I'd rather he didn't talk to Pesce, but truer still was the fact that I didn't want any further harm coming to him on my account. When this nightmare was over, I wanted to be able to live with myself.

As soon as they heard my keys in the lock, the cats came to the door. It's been said that petting a cat or dog can actually lower your blood pressure. I wouldn't hazard a guess what mine read at that moment, but I felt it was going through the roof. I'm not cool and calm under pressure. I took time to rumple and stroke the cats. They seemed to enjoy it, but it did nothing to soothe me.

Three fingers of Early Times over ice was more helpful. I climbed the stairs and flopped on my bed. I flicked on the TV with the remote, and ran through the channels. There was nothing on worth watching. I flicked the set off, sipped bourbon, and read. Two-thirty in the morning the radio alarm roused me from a light sleep. I set water to boil, then showered and shaved. I brewed a pot of El Pico. It was strong coffee. I swilled down four thousand mg's of vitamin C with a glass of Tropicana.

I padded back upstairs with a mug of coffee, and dressed quickly in jeans, a grey sweatshirt, and a pair of Nikes. Then I grabbed the snub-nosed .32 caliber Harrington and Richardson revolver that was stashed in the humidor on my night table.

Downstairs, I stuffed a pair of boltcutters, a hacksaw, some tinshears, and nylon stockings into a Channel Thirteen tote bag. I slipped on a navy blue windbreaker, jammed the gun in the pocket, and slung the tote bag over my shoulder. I hesitated before locking up. Did I have everything? I couldn't think of anything else.

Thirty-eighth and Fifth is a desolate part of town at three in the morning. Nothing moved. The night was eerily still. To find a cab, I had to walk to Park Avenue, where four Japanese businessmen, returning from a night on the town, were piling out of one and tacking into the Hotel Kitano.

"Three-seven-avenue, and two-one-street Long Island City," I said to the Haitian driver, wishing this was an errand for the bike. "Go five-nine street bridge."

He floored it, plastering me against the back seat, and careened across the intersection. The driver was wasted, and the cab reeked of grass. It was going to be a wild ride. No wonder the Japs could barely walk.

I thought about Strunk, and how he would deal with a situation like this, as the mad Haitian tossed me around the back seat of his cab. Strunk couldn't help me now, but I figured I did have a couple of things going for me. Surprise and adrenaline.

The Haitian dropped me on the empty street and sped off. My trembling fingers groped in the tote bag for the nylons. My heart beat wildly and erratically.

"Charlie," called a voice.

I started, and whirled. "Goddammit, Ginny, what are you doing here?"

"I might ask you the same question, cowboy." She was dressed in black sneakers, jeans, and a bulky sweater, charcoal grey and almost to her knees. She looked like a second-story person.

"I'm gonna get Hungerford."

"Nothing foolish, huh?" she scoffed. "You thought I was gonna sit and wait for your call while you were off playing Rambo?"

"Man," I groaned, "this is all I need. How'd you get here, anyway?"

She gave me the lopsided grin and pointed. A black limo was standing halfway down the block. "It just happened by . . . But you took your sweet time getting here," she said. "What took you so long?"

"Shit. Okay, so you're here. Look, I'm going in there."

"Me too."

"Yeah," I sighed. "Here, take this." I handed her a nylon stocking.

"Anyone I know?" she said, fingering it.

"Ha, ha," I said, unamused. "Get in the doorway and stay out of sight. I'll give you a sign if it's safe to follow. Pull the stocking over your face before you enter. If there's no sign, and I'm not out of there in ten minutes, call the cops."

"Okay," she said solemnly.

I pulled the stocking mask down over my face, and strode up to the door of the laundromat. I began beating on the door with the butt of the gun, and rattling the doorknob with my free hand, making a helluva racket.

I heard someone rumbling to the door, cursing. I stepped back. The door swung open. The blond giant emerged, hair rumpled, half awake, and half angry.

I grabbed him by the lapels, and yanked him to me with all my might.

He grunted. "Whadda fuck?" he mumbled.

I brought my knee up to his groin. He doubled up. I brought my knee up again and his head snapped back. He went down in twin agony, curled in the fetal position. He wasn't unconscious, but he wasn't alert either. He was neutral.

I felt a surging sense of invincibility. Coldcocking a man was fun, a novel experience for me. I could get to like it. I bent over Shawn and patted him down. I imagined that this was the way Strunk would do it. I was feeling loose and easy now. The worst was over, I hoped. I relieved Shawn of a long-barreled .22 caliber pistol, and a gravity blade.

I gave Ginny the high sign. With Shawn out of the way, it would be safer to trespass. She crept out of the dark and joined me. She looked down at Shawn, writhing and moaning softly, and then she turned to me, her features a blur under the stocking mask. Afraid she might speak my name, I quickly put a finger to my lips. A nod told me she understood. The store appeared empty, and it was dark, except for a shaft of light in the rear, coming from the basement.

We made our way silently to the head of the stairs, Ginny behind me, her hand on the small of my back. I pulled up, revolver braced in both hands, and peered around the corner, down the stairs. The way I'd seen the cops do it on TV.

A flight of well-worn wooden stairs led down into a dim, dank basement that smelled of mildew, cats, and detergent. Hungerford, head slumped on his chest, sat on a straight-backed, chrome kitchen chair, beneath a bare sixty-watt light bulb. He was still gagged. His mouth was stuffed with something about the size of a squashball, and duct tape, strapped around his head, held it in place. He wasn't blindfolded though. His hands were bound behind him, and probably to the chair. He was duct-taped at the ankles to the legs of the chair.

We watched for several seconds, and I could hear the sound of heavy breathing. I presumed it was Hungerford until a wiry, diminutive figure darted into the light, and proceeded, with amazing force and agility, to viciously beat the wincing Hungerford about the head and shoulders with a tightly rolled newspaper.

"Bastard!" she hissed. "What happened to my money?" Whack! she unloaded with the newspaper. "You're gonna tell us what you did with the money, or we're gonna feed your balls to you," she cackled. "Do you hear me, sonny?" She cackled again, and whacked him another one for good measure before melding back into the shadows of the empty detergent drums that lined the walls.

"Oh, my God," Ginny murmured, with a shudder. "She must be over seventy."

"I've got a feeling she's not alone," I whispered.

As if on cue, an obese woman in her thirties waddled out of another part of the gloom with a piece of machine belt in her hand.

"Go on, honey, whip him good," Grandma urged. "Give it to him across the shins."

Obediently, the fat lady lashed out at Hungerford's legs. His head jerked with each stroke. Panting from her exertions, she stopped, stuck her face in his, and shouted:

"Pussy!" Then she spat at him, turned away, and waddled back to her spot, her buttocks churning under the waistband of her polyester slacks.

Hungerford the enemy, captured by the braves, and handed over to the squaws to be tortured. That seemed to be the situation. A profound sense of the primitive swept over me.

There was no telling who, or how many of them might be down there. I had to make a move. Shawn wouldn't stay down forever. I had to take a chance.

"I hope Pesce's not down there," I whispered to Ginny. "But it looks like it's just the Junior League, softening him up. I'm going down. Stay here. If you see I'm in trouble, get to a phone."

She nodded, her face like an unpainted mannequin.

A middle-aged housewife with a broomstick in her hand was starting to work Hungerford over. I let out what I hoped was a terrifying yell—Haiieee!—and bounded down the stairs, bowling the housewife over. Unfazed by my surprise attack, Grandma leaped on my back and went for my eyes. She wasn't quick enough. The fat lady was advancing, the machine belt cutting the air with a wicked snicker as she twirled it. I heaved Grandma at her. The fat lady staggered back. Grandma yelped when the machine belt hit her. They tumbled into a pile of drums and cartons. I heard footsteps behind me. I whirled and saw Ginny clip a fourth woman in the head with a bleach bottle. The woman dropped, and Ginny dropped the bottle and dusted off her hands.

Brandishing the revolver, I did a three-sixty, scanning the nooks and crannies of the basement. Four, that seemed to be all of them.

I motioned Ginny to me. "Make a false move, girls," I said, passing the gun to Ginny, "and my associate's gonna put a slug in you. Behave like ladies, and no one will get hurt."

"Easy, pal," I said, turning to Hungerford. "I'm not gonna hurt you." His eyes were wide with fright.

I set to work freeing him. He was handcuffed to the back of the chair. I snipped the links with the boltcutters. Then I knelt and cut the duct tape from his legs with Shawn's gravity blade.

He worked himself free of the gag, spitting out a

squashball, and massaging his cheeks and jaw. His mouth moved soundlessly. He struggled to his feet and limped to the dingy washbasin under the stairs. He stuck his head under the tap, and gulped great draughts of water.

"Hurry it up," I said.

He straightened up carefully, as if afraid he might break. He wiped his mouth on his sleeve. "Who are you?" he asked, his voice raspy.

"Never mind. Come on, let's get out of here." I pushed him toward the stairs.

He was stiff and brittle from being too long in the same position. He moved like a crab. I pushed him ahead of me. Ginny brought up the rear, climbing the stairs backwards, and keeping the gun trained on the squaws. At the head of the stairs, I took the gun back. I kicked the door shut and bolted it. Shawn was on his feet, his back against the door. We moved forward slowly, me in the lead, Ginny supporting Hungerford.

Closer inspection told me Shawn was harmless. I kicked his legs out from under him, and clipped him with the gun butt as he went down.

As fast as Hungerford's legs would carry him, we scurried down the block to where Ginny's limo stood waiting. Hungerford came suddenly to a halt. "Not so fast." He gasped for breath. "I can't keep up."

"It's not much farther. To the limo, see?" Ginny urged.

Hungerford blinked and focused his eyes. "Oh, the limo, yes, I see." He began shuffling for the big black car.

Traffic was sparse, there were no cabs, I noticed. "Good thinking, Rowen," I said with an appreciative nod at the limo. "We'd have been up the creek for a cab at this hour."

"Thank you, Byrne. Someone has to pay attention to details," she said.

As we hustled along, I pulled off the stocking mask, and Ginny did likewise, shaking out her auburn hair. The limo was rolling in reverse to meet us. The curbside window slid down. I heard the door click. "It's open," the driver called.

"Right," I said and yanked. Hungerford glanced from me to Ginny.

"Ah, Rowen . . . and the photographer," he said laconically.

"Go on, get in," I said, giving him a shove. I glanced down the block and saw Shawn lurch into view. "You too," I snapped at Ginny, giving her a shove and piling in behind her. He hadn't seen our faces, I was sure of it.

"Where to?" asked the driver.

"The city," said Ginny.

We leaned back in the plush seats, the driver aimed the limo at the bridge, and Manhattan loomed glowing before us like Pleasure Island. The big car ate up potholes and cobblestones smoothly as it glided toward the white lights.

"Where should we drop you, Richard?" I asked.

There was no answer. His head lolled, as if too heavy for his neck. He gazed at me with a blank, disoriented stare. "Penn Station . . ." he said finally. "Would you drop me at Penn Station?"

"Don't you want to go to Sloane's?" said Ginny.

The lethargy and fog induced by his captivity seemed to be lifting rapidly now. He shook his head, smiling faintly. "No," he said, "I'm all through there."

"Why Penn Station?" I asked.

"My family, they live on the island."

"A wife and kids?"

"Yes, I'd like to see them."

Ginny and I exchanged glances. There's always a wife and kids. "Then what?" I asked, moving to the jumpseat so I could face him.

He turned his gaze toward the window, away from us. "Get a lawyer, turn myself in, I guess."

"Maybe that's the first thing you should do. It's not safe for you to walk the streets."

"I'll have to take that chance," he said airily.

"What happened, Richard? You were supposed to be doing good. How did a smart guy like you get into such a mess?"

He smiled out the window.

"A guy like you can always make a good living," I went on. "You didn't need to run a Ponzi."

He turned to me with genuine curiosity. "What's a Ponzi?" he asked.

I glanced at Ginny, who gave me a smug look. I explained briefly what a Ponzi scheme was.

"A Ponzi, huh?" he mused. "So that's what it's called, a Ponzi." He said it like he was assimilating the word-for-the-day. "But it wasn't like that at all."

Ginny gave me a disgusted look.

"You mean it didn't start out as a Ponzi?" I asked.

"That's right."

"They seldom do, as I understand it. How did it start?"

He dropped his eyes to the manacles on his wrists, and exhaled in resignation.

"Here, let me clip those for you." I got out the boltcutter and went to work. They were off in a matter of seconds.

He rubbed his wrists thoughtfully, collecting himself. Ginny and I gazed at him expectantly, waiting for what had to be the first of many tellings of this story. He raised his eyes to mine a moment, shifted them to Ginny, then came back to me with a steady gaze. He was an actor, I thought, and could probably lie without blinking. "I was playing the market," he began and shifted his gaze from mine. "Only for myself, you understand." He paused. "And I was doing pretty well at it . . . yes, pretty well at it," he mused. "That was how it all started."

"Were you lucky, smart, or what?" I asked.

"Or what," he said with an empty smile. "I had an edge, putting it in a gambler's vernacular. I'm in the public relations business. Two of my clients, a computor software company and a pharmaceutical company, had projects in the hopper that, when the news got out, would make their respective stocks take off."

"You had insider information," I said.

"That's what they call it. That was my edge. Anyway, the timing of these news releases was part of my job as the press liaison for these companies. It was easy really to parlay this information into a few extra dollars."

"Doesn't the SEC frown on that sort of thing?" I said.

"Sure, but everyone does it."

"So, you were doing pretty well at it, and then what happened?"

"Yes, things were going along just fine. That is until the software outfit needed a spokesperson for a trade show."

"Hello, Sloane," Ginny grinned.

"Exactly," said Hungerford, with a rueful smile. He

124

leveled his eyes on me. "You know the routine, I'm sure. We went to bed. She got the job."

Ginny smirked, while I acknowledged, manfully, that I did indeed know the routine.

"It wasn't that cut and dried, of course," Hungerford said.

"Of course not," Ginny smiled.

"We kept up a pretense of the one having nothing to do with the other, and well, I guess I lost my head. I was afraid that when the job was over, that would be the last I'd see of her. I was desperate. I needed to find some way to keep her around. I needed to get her attention, to impress her."

"Some women can't be bribed by love, huh, Richard?" I said.

Hungerford tittered at that. I glanced at Ginny. She had discovered the view from her window, and found it more compelling than anything I had said.

Hungerford resumed his cautionary tale. "I persuaded her," he said, "to give me five thousand dollars. Part of her fee, actually, and thanks to some information I had at the time about a new drug, I doubled her money."

"I bet that got her attention," I said.

"Better than I could have hoped for. Before I knew it, I was her friend, Richard, the stock market genius, and people started coming out of the woodwork with money to invest."

"Nice," I said. "Now you could afford to keep Sloane hanging around."

He cleared his throat. "At the time, I was pleasantly surprised," he said.

"And you and Sloane were in business."

"More or less," he allowed. "Sloane steered a lot of people my way. Things were going very smoothly. The money was rolling in. Sloane thought it would help if we entertained, and I agreed. But she was living in a walk-up, a railroad flat on Seventy-sixth and Second, at the time. It would never do. You have to look as if you could care less about money, if you expect to make money. So I bought her the co-op. And we began to entertain, lavishly."

"I had the pleasure," I reminded him. "The food was superb. I probably owe you a dinner."

"I'm glad you enjoyed it." He smiled. "Sloane was right. It was good for business. It made for a congenial atmosphere. The investors were bringing in investors."

125

"Even more money rolling in."

"That's right. Everyone was happy. The investors were making money. They were happy. Sloane had a co-op, she was living well. She was happy. And me . . . well, I thought I was happy."

"Sounds perfect."

"It was."

"What went wrong?"

"Lots of things." He sighed. "Everything."

"Take them one at a time," I suggested.

Ginny turned to face him, her expression somber.

Hungerford avoided our eyes. He stared at the floor. "Well, I realized I wasn't the financial whiz Sloane billed me as, but I thought I knew what I was doing. I was fooling around in the market as it was . . . and this was the biggest bull market in history . . ." He shrugged helplessly. "And I got hooked."

"Look out," I murmured.

"I started fooling around with stocks I knew nothing about, and then with futures and commodities as well. I lost some money, but it wasn't that bad. I mean, they were saying there was no end in sight to this market. I could make it up. I didn't want to miss the Great Bull Market, so I went out on margin."

"Wish I'd thought of that," I said. "I missed the Great Bull Market."

He gave me a sour look. "Then, unexpectedly, the software people decided they wanted a bigger outfit handling their business, and I lost the account."

"Goodbye, insider information," I said.

"Uh-huh, and there were more problems."

The limo eased off the bridge onto Second Avenue. "Where to, pal?" the driver asked over the intercom.

"First stop, Penn Station," I answered. "What problems?" I asked Hungerford.

"Anthony Pesce," he said simply.

"A.k.a., Mr. Fish?" Ginny giggled.

"A.k.a., Mr. Shark," said Hungerford.

"What's the problem? A triangle?" I asked.

"That's what everyone thinks, isn't it?" he snorted.

"Not true?" I said, thinking like everyone.

126

"No, it's not true."

"Oh, they're just a dance team, is that it?"

Ginny giggled some more.

"Yeah, they're a dance team all right." He smiled feebly.

"That doesn't sound like much of a problem to me," I said.

He gazed at me momentarily, like I was retarded. "Pesce's gay," he said finally, with a sanguine smile.

"You're kidding," I said, wondering how I'd missed that.

He shook his head.

"Well, I'll be damned," I mumbled. A glance at Ginny told me this was news to her, too. "How do you know that?"

"What do you think that linthead, Shawn, is all about? The two of them keep house."

It seemed more improbable as he went along, and yet why not? "Well, consenting adults, and all that," I said. "But what's the problem with Pesce? How does he fit into the picture?"

"The problem with Pesce is the same problem I was having with other investors, only more so. They're always there with their hands out, looking for their return. Worrying about their money." He paused and glanced Ginny's way. "Talk about pressure. What with my shortages in the market, and the hondling from investors, I was in need of large injections of cash almost daily. The brokers were calling, the investors were calling. I was taking from this one, and pay that one. I was a one-man agency for the redistribution of the wealth."

I couldn't resist smirking at Ginny. "That's called a Ponzi, Richard," I said.

"Yeah, well, that's what I was running. And Pesce was one of my biggest headaches. He was the most aggressive of the investors. He thought of his money as a personal loan, not an investment. The bastard didn't want interest, he wanted vigorish."

"Was he someone Sloane steered to you?"

"The first, and it wouldn't surprise me if he cut her in for a percentage. He's made his money back several times over."

"Why didn't you just tell him to fuck off?"

"I tried that once," he said, with his empty smile.

"And?"

"And he said I had a real cute fifteen-year-old daughter. Shawn could dig fucking her in the ass."

Ginny whimpered softly in disgust and hugged herself.

"So really you had two partners, Sloane and Pesce."

"Yes, Pesce being a silent partner."

"And you and Sloane entertained and cultivated the suckers continually, and over a period of time . . ."

"Pretending to offer friendship, financial advice, and a wild return on their money," Ginny interjected hotly, "while knowingly defrauding them."

"What could I do?" He shrugged. "Look, I'm not proud of what I did. But I was caught in a bind. I did it under duress."

"You ripped them off, Richard," I taunted him, hoping to hit a nerve, hoping to find a twinge of remorse. "Some of them lost all the money they had in the world."

"I suppose I did. But they were a bunch of greedy bastards, you know," he replied with a scornful, vile little laugh. "They made it easy. Pesce had a name for them. He called them 'ducks.' "

Ginny turned from him and looked out the window again. There was no remorse for the "ducks." Hungerford leaned back and massaged his face. He didn't seem much of an enigma at the moment, and I caught myself wondering about his past, before Sloane and Pesce. What shortcuts had he taken then, what lies had he told looking into someone's eyes? And then I wondered about a pair of sitting "ducks."

"The professor and his wife, were they hassling you for money, too?"

He flicked an anxious glance at me. "Yes, he was a regular pain in the ass. He was constantly hassling me for money. But car bombings and murder are way out of my league."

Ginny was staring at him again, with gimlet eyes. I knew we were both thinking that car bombings and murder weren't out of Pesce's league. I remembered the large shadow climbing into the Datsun. I remembered where I'd seen Shawn before. And probably she did, too. It had to be him. Suddenly, I felt like I had to pee.

"You said Pesce called the investors 'ducks'?"

"That's what he called them."

"Does that mean that he and Sloane were in on it? The Ponzi, I mean?"

"I see what you're asking," he said, and considered his answer a moment. "No, they weren't. Oh, they may have suspected something near the end, but even with my stock losses, the software account, their preferential interest rates, not to mention the fancy commissions they took for steering the 'ducks,' I managed to tread water, keep up a good front. Sloane still thought I was the reincarnation of Jay Gould, the second coming of Bernard Baruch."

"Sounds grim."

"It was. But then, just when things looked their bleakest," he said with a gelid smile, "they got bleaker."

"Hard to imagine."

"Ah, but wait. Listen, first Sloane starts babbling about some guy she's met. Says she met him at your place. Henry Stein?" He frisked me with his eyes, never quite making eye contact.

"Oh, Henry, sure, I know him."

"The man's a swindler," he said vehemently, unaware of the irony.

"That's being a little harsh, isn't it?" I said mildly.

He made a sound of derision.

"He's probably pulled a shady deal or two in his time," I said. "But I've loaned him money. He's always paid it back, with interest. I've never had a problem with him."

"There's a problem with him now," he assured me. "Anyway, Sloane tells me she's already made some money off him, and she's convinced he's an insider." He stopped to massage his face again. "He's got deals going all the time, she tells me. She'll get me in on the next one. I prayed to God that Stein was the real thing, because on October nineteenth, Black Monday, the Great Bull Market of '87 turned to bullshit, and my luck with it. The brokers were all over me. I was being creamed on margin. Of course, I did what the big boys did, I bragged that I got out on top in September." He paused, dropped his head into his hands, and rubbed his temples.

"Go on," I urged.

"Well, then Sloane tells me Stein's got a deal going. The one about the broker's boosting the stock? Didn't you hear about that one?"

"No," I lied.

"I went in on it with Sloane," he continued. "The brokers

129

boosted the stock thirty-one points in six weeks. Stein tipped us when to sell, and we were out with a nice profit."

"And convinced Stein was a real insider."

"Yes, I could barely wait for his next deal. I realized, of course, he was sleeping with Sloane, and . . ."

"You didn't care?" asked Ginny.

He smiled faintly and patronizingly at her. "Sloane was always available. Always looking to trade up. And I was fed up. No, I didn't care." He paused, correcting himself. "No, that's not right. I did care. I wanted him to sleep with her. I wanted out. And Henry Stein was my way out. It made no difference to Sloane who picked up the tab, just as long as it got picked up. Stein was perfect."

We exchanged glances. His was sly and evasive.

"For the first time in a long while I had some hope. I saw a way out," he said. "With Stein's help, I could play catch up with the 'ducks.' All I needed was to make a killing on one of his deals, the next one, if possible. Then I could pay off the 'ducks' and be clean again. Once that was done, I'd confront Sloane, I'd accuse her of sleeping with Stein. We'd have a big scene. I'd sulk, play the injured party for a day or two, and then clear the hell out. She'd be Stein's headache after that."

I smiled.

"Did I say something funny?" he asked.

"No, it wasn't what you said. I was just thinking that you were counting pretty heavily on Stein finding Sloane as irresistible as you did."

"I admit I was grasping at straws." He grinned ruefully. "But he seemed to have what it takes. He was the new whiz of finance. They were sleeping with each other . . ."

"Yes, and because she had made a sucker out of you, you figured she could make a sucker out of any man."

"I was wrong." He shrugged. "It wasn't the wildest idea, though. It could have happened . . . he might have gone with her." He paused, wistfully, as if to mull that idea over once more. Then he dismissed it with a laugh. "But never mind about that, Stein had another deal on the fire. I don't suppose you heard about this one either?"

"What one was that?"

"Oh, a lot of cockamamie crap about an ex–cabinet member and a syndicate of high rollers taking over a solid company, stripping the assets, and floating a stock issue at an inflated price."

"No, missed that one, too."

"You didn't miss much," he scoffed. "Anyway, when I heard about that one, I said to myself, this is my ticket out."

"And you plunged."

"Yes, I plunged."

"How much did you lose, Richard?"

"All told, or to Stein?"

"Both."

"Hmm, let's see," he said thoughtfully. "I needed seven million to get even. That was the total. Stein was promising six for one on the syndicate deal—that meant he took me for a million three," he said calmly.

I wanted to cry for the guy, but I couldn't, he'd given me too much to think about. Too much to worry about. It didn't make any difference to me how much Hungerford lost. But it made a big difference to me how much Stein took him for.

"I heard you lost fifteen million, total," I said.

"You heard wrong."

"That's what Pesce's saying."

"He's exaggerating. How would he know?"

That was a comforting piece of news. If true, and I didn't see what Hungerford had to gain by lying, it meant that Pesce didn't know how much Stein took him for either. "I'll say one thing for you, Richard, you're right up there with the big-time losers. How much of the million three you lost to Stein was Sloane's money?"

"Not a cent of it."

"She wasn't in on the deal?"

"I didn't say that. She was in on it on her own. That's how sure of it she was. She probably lost about a quarter of a million, I'd guess."

"Was Pesce in on the deal?"

"He was in for the minimum, a hundred thousand."

In for a dime, in for a dollar, he was still in it. I doubt Pesce would have bothered heading up an investors' posse and hunting Hungerford down, if it were only a matter of the Ponzi's collapse. Pesce made his money back several times over, Hungerford said. Between them, Pesce and Sloane were out three hundred thousand to Stein. That was

131

enough to get anyone pissed. That was why he wanted Hungerford. And that was why he'd want Stein next.

"So that brings us up to date," I said. "When the bottom fell out, you ran."

"Stein finished me. What else could I do?" He threw his head back against the seat, drained. His eyes were closed, his mouth open.

I had no answer for him. He was finished before Stein. He just couldn't quit. I glanced at Ginny. She was staring at me with a half smile. I wondered what was going on in her head. There was no question now that she had her money because of the sting. Hungerford had admitted he was running a Ponzi. The only question now was how much the final tab would come to.

We turned west onto Thirty-fourth Street, and the slanting rays of the rising sun flooded through the rear window of the limo and hurt my eyes. I switched seats again. The warmth of the sun felt good on the back of my neck and made me sleepy.

The limo glided to a halt in front of the Madison Square Garden marquee on Seventh Avenue. The marquee boasted that Ringling Brothers' Circus was back in town. So were the Rangers. Who'd have guessed they'd make it to the playoffs. Mercifully, there was no mention of the Knicks.

It was an effort to climb out of the limo. I was exhausted, I realized. I extended a hand to Hungerford, but he waved me off and crept out under his own steam.

A garbage truck, and a maintenance man, working an industrial vacuum cleaner near the entrance to the arcade, played a mock symphony, modern in its dissonance. The untouchables were having their breakfast in Calcutta-on-the-Hudson. Flocks of homeless scratched with the pigeons for the choicest bits of fast-food detritus.

I remembered seeing the circus in the old Madison Square Garden, when I was a kid. Now the developers wanted to tear this Madison Square Garden down; it was obsolete. Like the street people scrounging their daily bread in the environs. I wondered why they kept insisting on calling it Madison Square Garden? It had to be sixty years, maybe more, since Madison Square Garden had been on Madison Square.

I glanced at Hungerford. His face was covered with grey

stubble. The elegant suit hung on him like it had seen him through a three-day drunk. Underneath it he'd be black and blue. He coughed, cleared his throat tentatively, and blinked. His eyes watered in the harsh morning light. "Tell me something?" he said.

"Just a minute," I said. I pulled two twenties from my wallet and poked my head into the backseat. "I'll walk home from here," I said to Ginny. "This ought to do it."

She took the money reluctantly. "As you wish," she said. She reached for me and pulled me to her. It was a friendly kiss. "Call me, Charlie?" she said.

"I promise," I said. The limo pulled away, and she waved. I turned to Hungerford. "What were you saying, Richard?"

"Why did you put yourself out for me?" he said, his gaze steady.

"Because they would have killed you."

"I doubt the 'ducks' would have gone that far," he said, rubbing his wrists.

"Tough guy, huh? I should have left you there. But it wasn't the 'ducks' I was thinking of."

He smiled bleakly. "You could have called the cops, and let it go at that."

"And you'd be sitting in the slammer now."

"You were in on it with Henry Stein, weren't you?" he said, looking me in the eye.

"No one is in on it with Henry Stein," I said. I didn't blink. That was no lie, I'd discovered.

"You arranged for Sloane to meet Stein."

"They met at my place, but accidentally."

His gaze turned skeptical. "Of course, at this point, it's no longer important what I think. From now on, what's important is what Pesce thinks. But I'm afraid he's going to think what I think, and that's that you were in on it with Henry Stein."

"Thanks for sharing that with me, Richard. I'll see you around, I hope." I turned to go.

"Er, just a minute, Charles . . . ," he said, clearing his throat.

"What is it?"

He made a feeble attempt at a smile. "Could you loan me a few dollars for the train ticket?"

A loan? Was he kidding? For all I knew, the guy had a

C.D. worth a quarter of a million, or more, stashed away in a bank in Podunk. I plucked two twenties from my wallet, silently said goodbye to them, and handed them to him. Forty bucks wouldn't get him very far.

"Thank you," he said gravely, stuffing the bills into the side pocket of the suit jacket.

"And Richard . . ."

"Yes?"

"Be careful."

"I will," he assured me. He gave me a parting smile completely devoid of warmth and shambled off.

I stood and watched a moment until he vanished down the terminal steps. Hungerford hadn't told me everything, I was sure, but he had told me enough. So where were we now? Ginny would be all right, she was safe, I reasoned. Pesce had nothing to connect her to Stein. And all he really had on me, I rationalized, was that I knew Stein. And in my present mood, if I knew where Stein was, I might give him to Pesce. Stein was the guy he really wanted. He shouldn't have stung Hungerford for a million three.

I grinned at the absurdity of that notion, and at my own naïveté. Why did Willie Sutton rob banks? Because, Sutton said, "That's where the money is."

That was one way to look at the situation, and the optimistic way at that. But if Hungerford was right, if Pesce believed I was in on it with Stein, then no one, not even Ginny, was safe. She was a lever he could use on me.

I was hungry and felt dirty. I wanted to sleep. I turned and trudged back to the studio.

Chapter 12

It wasn't so rare as a day in June, the first Monday in April, but it was as nice a day as you could hope for. The forecast called for blue skies, the temperature would crowd sixty. A breeze rambled around the asphalt jungle, bringing a breath of fresh air with it.

There was an anomaly in the weather, however. My patch of real estate experienced a squall at noon, when Hurricane Sloane, and company, blew in for a brief visit.

Grim, but smartly dressed—as always—in a rust-colored woolen skirt and blazer, with matching pumps and a buff cashmere sweater, Sloane, leading the parade, marched past Tito as though he were a wooden Indian. Tony Pesce, equally well-dressed—like a real estate agent with a forty-dollar-a-square-foot space to hustle—in a dark blue two-piece suit, trucked in behind her. He acclimated himself swiftly, exploring the premises with alert and curious eyes. Shawn brought up the rear, surprisingly light on his feet for such a big guy, and for a guy who only forty-eight hours before had been kicked in the nuts. The young have amazing powers of recuperation, though. I detected no bulges in the drape of his stylish threads, but I was certain there was a gravity blade, and a long-barreled .22 automatic in there with him somewhere. He wore a faint scowl on his face, which I took to be a badge of his youthful callowness.

Tito and I stared helplessly at the procession.

Wasting no time on amenities, Sloane said, "You've met Anthony Pesce, I believe?"

"I believe I have."

"How are you, Charlie?" he said with a disarming smile.

"Fine."

Shawn fidgeted, jiggling his knee inside the baggy trousers.

"Have you met Shawn?" Pesce asked, a glitter in his eye.

"At the laundromat, right?" I replied, bland-faced. "Everything come out all right in the wash?" I tried, unsuccessfully, to picture the two of them in bed.

"Witty," Pesce said and smiled.

"Well, now that you're in," I said, "how about a cup of coffee?"

"Thank you, no," Sloane said coldly.

Shawn was wired already. He shook his head no.

I glanced at Pesce. "Why not," he said amiably.

I nodded to Tito, and indicated they should follow me.

"Nice place you've got here," Pesce observed.

Shawn gawked, slack-jawed. He was a mouth breather, I noticed. I mumbled something about photographers needing high ceilings as I led them to the lounge.

Sloane plunked herself down sullenly on the couch, and went into a leg-arranging routine. Pesce slid in alongside her with feline grace. Shawn slouched in a deckchair, sitting on his tailbone, his long legs stretched out and crossed in front of him. Intermittently, he pulled at his nose with his thumb and index finger. Bad.

Tito placed a mug of coffee in front of Pesce, and I pulled up a deckchair opposite him.

Eyeing me over the rim of the mug, Pesce sipped his coffee. "Someone broke into the laundromat Saturday morning," he said finally, placing the mug on the table without breaking his stare.

"Oh?" I said.

"Yes," he said. "They clocked Shawn," he said, switching his gaze to the kid. The golden boy seemed to flush. Pesce turned his gaze back to me. "They let our friend Richard go," he said.

"That's wild," I said. "Who'd want to do something like that?"

"That's what I've been wondering," he said as we eye-wrestled.

"Were you able to get anything out of Hungerford while you had him?"

"No."

"Too bad," I sympathized.

"Yes, too bad. And he's in custody now. He turned himself in this morning."

"That was sensible. For him, I mean."

"The investors are very disappointed."

"I imagine." He hadn't called them "ducks," I noticed.

"Oh, he'll keep," Pesce said cheerfully. "You know what Joe Louis said, don't you?"

"What did he say?"

"'You can run, but you sure can't hide,'" He chuckled. "Richard's made a lot of enemies. Many of those people lost their life savings, you know."

"I'm sure."

"Our friend Richard is gonna be looking over his shoulder for the rest of his life." He chuckled again.

"I suppose so," I said.

Looking at them sitting side by side, I found myself studying Pesce and Sloane, and speculating about their relationship. Well-groomed, well-dressed, and, in his case, well-fed, they appeared on the surface to be nothing more than an innocuous, affluent suburban couple. The planes and angles were still visible under the fleshy sleekness of his face. Like her, he had good bone structure, but at forty-plus, half a dozen years older than she, if he didn't start watching the pasta, that sleekness would turn to lard. Sloane would never get fat, though. She'd spend the time and money on dance classes at Luigi's. She'd burn off unwanted pounds. Middle age would find her crisp and slim as straw. And then there was the silky, eerie way they moved. What should I make of that? Maybe Hungerford was lying about Pesce and Shawn.

"Joe Louis was a hilarious guy," I said warily. "But you didn't come here to talk about Joe Louis. What can I do for you, Anthony?"

"You're right, Charlie, I didn't come here to talk about Joe Louis. I came here to talk about Henry Stein." He stared at me with hooded eyes.

"What about Stein?"

"How do I get in touch with him?"

"Sloane was here the other day. I told her then, all I have is a Post Office box number, and an answering service number."

"He's lying," she hissed.

"Let me do the talking, please," he said, with a gentle smile.

She fumbled in her bag for a cigarette.

I nodded at Sloane. "What's the matter with her?"

"She's been through a lot lately," he said, gazing at me with impassive, somnolent eyes as he stroked her knee with a manicured hand. "She's stressed, poor kid."

"Oh," I said. I was feeling a little stressed myself.

She jammed a cigarette in her mouth, and Shawn pounced on her, butane lighter in hand. I watched her inhale and nod to him. He resumed his seat. It amused me to think, maybe Pesce and Shawn made a threesome with her on the mattress. Anything was possible. My eye picked up, peripherally, Tito's soundless move for the stairs.

"Yes, Sloane has been stressed lately," said Pesce, continuing to stroke her knee. "And Henry Stein's the cause of her stress."

Impatiently, Sloane blew smoke.

"And quite frankly, Henry Stein has caused me no small amount of stress," he added.

"But I thought Hungerford was the problem. What's Stein done?" I said, playing dense.

"Hungerford's one problem," he said, smiling tolerantly. "Henry Stein's another problem."

"I see. You've lost money on one of his deals, is that it?"

"That's it." He smiled, but his eyes didn't.

"A lot of money?"

"A lot of money."

"How much money?"

"Almost half a million."

"That's a lot of money," I said. Hungerford said they'd lost three hundred fifty thousand. You could call that "almost half a million," I suppose.

"Yes, that is a lot of money," he agreed. "And it would be one thing if we lost the money, but that was not the case. Henry Stein stole the money. The deal was nothing but a swindle."

"Bad luck, and coming on the heels of the Hungerford fiasco as it did, I can understand your being stressed," I said, hoping to sound sympathetic.

"Yes."

138

"You filed a complaint with the proper authorities, of course."

Shawn giggled nervously. Pesce silenced him with a reproachful glance. "I prefer to keep this matter private," he said.

"I see," I said.

"I'm glad you do, Charlie," he said with a malignant smile.

"I see that you got taken by Stein and, for whatever reason, you intend to deal with the matter privately," I said inanely, filling in an awkward silence.

He beamed at Sloane. "You see, Charlie's beginning to understand our distress."

She coolly smiled her tacit approval of his continuing in this vein.

His sardonic eyes switched their gaze to me momentarily. "And because I believe you are beginning to understand, I'm gonna try again, Charlie. Where is Henry Stein?" he said patiently.

There was nothing I could give him, but more stress, or distress, whichever he preferred. "And I'm gonna tell you again, Anthony. I don't know."

"Charlie, please." He sighed.

"Look, Anthony, I'm sorry if Stein took you and Sloane for a lot of money," I said, attempting to mollify him.

"I'm sure you are."

"But what's it got to do with me?"

"Just this, Charlie, if Sloane hadn't met Henry Stein, right here in your studio, Henry Stein would not have conned us out of all that money."

"It wouldn't have mattered where Stein met Sloane, he would have conned her."

Sloane puffed and fumed.

"Shit," muttered Shawn, and he drew his gums back in a canine grin, displaying a yard of gums and a mile of enamel.

Tito's shadow moved on the balcony, boosting my confidence. This encounter, at least, would end in a standoff.

"Don't be a wiseguy, Charlie. I don't like wiseguys." He stared at me blandly, casually crossing his legs. "And another thing I don't like is being conned, understand?"

I got to my feet. "And I don't like being threatened, Anthony. This interview is over."

139

Shawn leaped to his feet. I ignored him. I stared at Pesce. Pesce and Sloane didn't budge. Sloane smiled nervously.

Shawn began prowling. "Hey, Tony," Shawn called from across the shooting area. "Lookit this." He was holding a Hasselblad with a 150mm lens. "What's this?"

"It's called a camera, Shawn."

"A camera?"

"Yes, a camera."

Sloane's eyes glittered.

"Nice camera," said Shawn, as though he were talking to the dog. "Cameras cost a lot a dough, huh, Tony?"

"Uh-huh, cameras are very expensive, Shawn," he said, smiling in my face.

I glared at Pesce and felt the first jolt of adrenaline, my heart thumping. "Tell him to put it down, Anthony."

Pesce rose to his feet in one fluid motion and went bumper to bumper with me, his eyes speculative and hard. He didn't look like a guy who liked to mix it up. But he looked like a guy who liked to hit. And he looked like a guy who could hit, hit you with a sucker punch, or hit you while you were being held. I clenched my fists. He could take a punch, I thought, anywhere but in the face. I needed more room to throw a shot to the head.

"Tell him yourself," he said.

"Yo, homeboy, you heard the man."

Pesce whirled.

Tito grinned down on him from the balcony, the revolver in both hands and aimed at Pesce's broad chest. "Tell dickhead to put the camera down," he said.

Pesce gave Shawn the nod.

Shawn lowered the camera slowly, until it was an inch or so from the surface of the camera caddy. He held it momentarily, then dropped it. The Hasselblad clunked to the countertop with the slam of a car door.

"Time for you and your boyfriend to go collect the quarters from the washing machines, Anthony," I said.

That crack hit a button. He shot me a look, his face a mask of rage. He caught himself, dismissed it with a laugh, and swiftly rearranged his features. He gazed at me with an impassive, almost pleasant expression, only the malevolence in his eyes gave him away. "Tough guys, huh?" He smiled, then turned to Sloane. "The man wants us to leave, let's go. I think we've made our point."

Sloane bounced off the couch like a cheerleader, her eyes shiny with the excitement of imminent violence. She took Pesce's outstretched hand.

Tito descended the stairs, the gun held chest high and trained on Pesce. I let them pass, and we followed them to the door.

Shawn, grinning, both hands over his head in mock surrender, led the way. He did a disco step into the hall, pressed the elevator button, and pulled at his nose, his face blank. Pesce stood aside to let Sloane pass, turned, and smiled amicably, his hand in the shape of an imaginary gun. He cocked his thumb, and pointed his index finger at me. "We'll see you again, if need be," he said. "Meanwhile, when you speak to Henry Stein, be sure and tell him what Joe Louis said. Hungerford found out it's true. And Stein's gonna find it out, too." His middle finger pulled the trigger of the imaginary gun. "Hope you don't have to find it out, Mr. Photographer."

I evidently didn't have an image problem with Anthony Pesce. Sloane wiggled her fingers gaily in goodbye, like the schoolyard bully had just come to her defense, and ducked into the elevator while Shawn held the door for her. Pesce followed her. Before stepping into the elevator, Shawn balled his fist into an imaginary gun, cocked it, and pulled the trigger. "Bang! bang!" he said.

I shut the door. Tito held the .32 at the side of his leg. I held out my hand, and with a solemn face he handed me the gun. "Homeboy? Dickhead?" I said. "That's pretty gaudy patter."

"It's how assholes talk," he said.

"Thanks for the backup."

"You're welcome. You'll get a card in the mail with my bodyguard rates, and a bill." He grinned. "Want some advice?"

"What's that?"

"If you expect that crowd to drop by again, get yourself an Ithaca 12-gauge pump."

"Not a bad idea," I said. My legs felt rubbery. I was shaken, and Tito noticed.

"You look like you could use a drink," he said.

"Yeah, I could."

"Go sit down, I'll bring you one."

I went to the office, sat at my desk, and stared at the wall until Tito appeared with some Early Times and ice. I drained half the glass in one swallow. "Tito, have a look at the camera," I said, feeling the warmth of the bourbon. "See if the dickhead did any damage."

He grinned. "Okay," he said.

I flipped through the Rolodex, found the number, and dialed. "Hello, P. C. Strunk? Yeah, it's Charlie Byrne . . ."

"How's your ass, Byrne?" his big baritone came back loud and clear.

"My ass is okay, for the moment."

"Good, what can I do for you?"

"It's about the deal . . ."

"With Stein?"

"That's right."

"I told you, I don't want to know about it."

"Yeah, but Stein might. He said to get in touch through you."

"This is urgent?"

"I think so. I just had a visit from the Marshall woman, and a couple of her playmates . . ."

"Want some advice, Byrne?"

"I don't think so, but I'm gonna get it anyway."

He chuckled. "Relax, it'll blow over. There's always a lot of cheap talk after something like this. Give 'em a few days to get used to the idea that they were had, and they'll calm down, you'll see."

"Yeah, that's what Stein said. I like my assistant's advice better."

"What's that?"

"Get an Ithaca 12-gauge pump. Look, P.C., Stein made one of these guys for a wiseguy. I figure he oughta know one when he sees one."

"What's his name?"

"Anthony Pesce. He travels with a sidekick, a prettyboy named Shawn. The kid looks like he's coked out of his brains half the time."

"Not remarkable, these days."

"Maybe not, but what's remarkable is that this kid's six

three or four, goes about two-forty, and built like a linebacker. And I've got reason to believe he carries a piece."

"Jus' a lil' fella, huh? He got a last name?"

"Must have. I just know him as Shawn."

"What's the woman's name again?"

"Sloane Marshall."

"I'll punch up Anthony Pesce and the woman on the computer, and see if either one of them has a sheet," he said.

"Good idea, P.C., do it. These are a couple of scary guys, and Stein ought to know it."

"You gonna be at this number awhile?"

"I'll be here."

"Where'd you say that laundromat was again?"

I gave him the address.

"Okay, I'll get back to you, Byrne, as soon as I have something." He hung up.

I finished off the bourbon, and went downstairs. Tito was peering through the back of the Hasselblad, holding the lens toward the light and firing the camera at different combinations of f-stops and shutter speeds. Not a very scientific method of determining malfunction, but the most practical until we ran a test roll of film through it. "It got a bump," he said, "but it seems to be okay." That about summed up my own condition, I thought.

Tito left at six, and I still hadn't heard from Strunk. I waited another half hour, then pulled on my warm-ups and Nikes—not what the serious biker wore—and hoisted the Lejeune off the rack. I needed to blow off steam, still edgy with unspent adrenalin from Sloane and Pesce's visit. A few laps in Central Park were the ticket. Just what I needed to soothe my ragged nerves.

The nice weather had people out in droves, and to my disgust the bike paths were clogged with hordes of fair-weather joggers. Cyclists and joggers are natural antagonists, and motorists are the natural antagonists of them both. If cars go too fast, joggers go too slow. Opting for speed, I rode in traffic with the rest of the demon bikers. It was easier keeping up with the cars than bucking the joggers. In half an hour they'd close the Park to traffic anyway and, bikers and joggers, we'd have it all to ourselves.

For cyclists, the two most popular ways to do laps in the Park are either to do the long one, which runs the perimeter of the Park, about eight miles, or do the short one, which runs from Fifty-ninth to Seventy-second Street, a kidney shape of about four miles, and the one better cyclists favor.

I chose the long route first and took no special notice of a green sports car that seemed to want to play tag with me up to Ninety-sixth Street, until there it was again for the downtown trip. As I said, motorists and cyclists are natural antagonists. There are drivers who take a perverse pleasure in veering at you and boxing you in between themselves and another car, or pinching you up against the curb and driving you onto the sidewalk. This was one of those guys.

I was doing thirty, downhill, and he gave me a blast of horn from five feet away. It was like a touch from an electric cattle prod. He pulled alongside and leaned on me. The rims of my wheels scraped the curb. I saw sparks. I braced myself with a hand on the roof of the car. He spurted away from me and was gone. I didn't see his face, he kept me too busy and the windows were tinted, but it was a Datsun 280Z. I pumped furiously, in a rage, in a vain attempt to catch up, but it was futile.

When I reached the Sheep Meadow, I found a gang of bikers hanging out on the benches, waiting for the Park to close to traffic before getting down to some serious laps. There were twenty of them, perhaps, dressed in spandex pants, jersey sweaters with patch pockets front and back, leather riding shoes, gloves, and helmets. Even in the failing light, the splashes of raw color, yellow, orange, red, green, and blue, reminded one of jockeys. And they were, I suppose, bike jockeys. Coasting onto the footpath and dismounting, I took a seat and joined them.

One of them, in red, detached himself from the crowd. "Yo, hey sport, where you been?" he said. "Yo" was rapidly slipping into the vernacular, I was sorry to hear.

When he drew nearer, I recognized him, and the graphite frame bike. He was a dirty blond in his early twenties. His features were regular and unremarkable. His complexion was sallow, and if I had to guess, I'd say his people came from somewhere west of the Danube. He was only average in height, maybe five ten, but he was heavily muscled and compactly built. He gave the impression that if he fell, he'd bounce. And I noticed that he wasn't wearing a helmet.

"It's been too cold for me," I explained. "Haven't been riding that much."

"Would have seen you if you'd been in the Park," he said, looking at me closely. "What's the matter? You look all pushed outta shape."

"Aw, some asshole just tried to run me off the road."

He nodded knowingly. "One of those, huh," he said. "When I catch one of those bastards, they're eating through a straw for a month." He reached into his chest pocket and came out with the kind of retractable blade used to open cartons in supermarkets. "If I can't punch 'em out, they're gonna need a new paint job after fuckin' with me," he said, a wicked glint in his eye. He made a slashing gesture with the blade and accompanied it with a sound effect.

"It was a green Datsun 280Z," I said. "Have you seen it?"

"No, I'd only notice 'im if he messed with me. Mercedes are the best, though." He grinned and repeated the slashing gesture. "Love to get those guys. A friend of mine likes to punch out their windows with a chain when they mess with him. I don't ride with a chain, though. Extra weight. My name's Mike. What's yours?"

"Charlie."

He glanced over his shoulder. There was no traffic. "Okay, Charlie, whadda you say we do some laps?"

I said okay. Mike, or Mike-the-Bike, as the other riders called him, set off at a steady and contained pace, which he varied occasionally with a blistering sprint. We did ten laps, nearly forty miles on the short loop, in an hour and forty minutes.

When we weren't sprinting, we had a chance to talk. He admired my classic Lejeune, and I drooled over his feather-weight graphite. "Get yourself some skins," he advised me. "They decrease drag."

He was a street kid from the Village, I learned. He worked at whatever he could, bike messenger, bartender, construction, and film grip. He was saving up for a tryout for the Tour de France team. I also learned he rode in heats sponsored by a brewery on weekends up in Harlem.

"Any prize money?" I asked.

"Fifteen hundred, three grand a winner, sometimes. They have heats for guys your age."

"Uh-huh, old farts' races."

"I didn't say that." He grinned. "They can move, some of those old farts, you'd be surprised. Last lap, come on, let's pick it up."

We stood in the stirrups and pumped, a flying squadron of bicycles. We sprinted that way for about two hundred yards, then settled down to a lung-busting pace. Mike-the-Bike let me hang with him for a mile or so, then he pulled away effortlessly. So did most of the other riders. These were all young guys. I had to have ten years on the oldest of them. I didn't feel too bad. There were still a few guys behind me when we came full circle again.

I told Mike that I'd had enough, I was going downtown. He said he was going to do some more laps. We exchanged phone numbers and said goodnight.

It was dark now, too dark. And he was traveling too fast. It was impossible to get a license plate number. The Datsun blew by me with two short beeps as I turned west, against the traffic, on Thirty-eighth Street. The Datsun was just saying "hi" to me.

Strunk was on the answering machine, when I got back to the studio, cursing me for not being where I said I would be, and leaving a number where I could reach him after seven. "And be sure and call, Byrne. I've got some interesting shit for you," he promised.

I dialed the number and waited. "Hello," a woman's voice said, picking up on the fourth ring.

"Hello," I said. "It's Charlie Byrne. Is P. C. Strunk there?"

"Just a minute," she said and put the receiver down. "P.C.," she yelled, "it's for you. Charlie Byrne."

A medley of domestic sounds—droning television, kids, dishes and cutlery—vamped in the interval it took for Strunk to stumble to the receiver, pick it up, and breathe into it. "That you, Byrne?" he demanded in his diffident manner. He sounded as though he were talking through a mouthful of food.

"Himself," I said. "Am I interrupting dinner?"

"Just finishing up," he said. I heard him swallow, and smack his lips with satisfaction. "Gotta have you over for dinner sometime, Byrne. That woman does ribs like she was a chinaman."

I wondered if Mrs. Strunk had a name. "I'd like that, P.C. You said you had some information. Did you find Pesce on the computer?"

"No, not Pesce, wasn't that easy."

"Don't tell me Sloane Marshall was on the computer?"

"No, she wasn't on the computer either. They're clean so far as the computer's concerned. It was the kid, Shawn. He's got a sheet longer than the Thruway."

"How'd you find him? All you had was a first name."

"A pal of mine, Joe Lazarus, in the Thirty-first, the precinct where Pesce's got his laundromat, knows the kid. He's collared the kid more times than tackles get sacks. He knows the kid from when he was called—" Strunk was interrupted by an explosion, shouts, yells, and shrieks in the background noise. It sounded as though WW III had just broken out among the Strunk siblings. "Hey, you kids," Strunk bellowed, "shut up in there. Your momma's gonna put you down for the night you don't behave yourselves." The armistice was declared faster than the war. Strunk waited momentarily to see if the peace would hold. "It ain't me they're afraid of," he continued. "It's their momma. That woman's strict. Where was I?"

"Your friend knows the kid from when he was called—?"

"Oh yeah, Lazarus knows the kid from when he was called Hauser. So did the computer. Garbage in, garbage out, as they say. These are a few of the charges the kid's been up on; drugs, naturally, jacking cars, breaking and entry, possession of stolen goods, aggravated assault, rape, arson, and prostitution. Just an average clean-cut kid, huh?"

"Uh-huh, a boyscout. Hasn't been up for murder yet?"

"It's just a matter of time until he gets around to it."

"Or they get around to charging him with it."

"I got into trouble when I was a kid," Strunk said. "When I was coming up, I thought I was bad, but this guy makes me look like a pussy."

"Your friend knew him as Hauser, you said. What name does he use now?"

"Pesce."

"Pesce?"

"That's right. Pesce adopted the kid when he was seventeen."

"Huh, adopted him," I murmured.

147

"Yeah, until then, the kid had been on his own since he was twelve. Old man Hauser went out for cigarettes one night, when the kid was six, and never came back, says Lazarus. The mother works in a bar in Belmore, and she's no prize either. She's got a sheet. Drugs, and a couple of prostie busts."

"Swell, sounds like Shawn's got every reason in the world for being a screwup."

"You could look at it that way. He's just society's child. He's not to blame if he's the brain-dead sociopath that Lazarus says he is."

"Lazarus said that?"

"That's what he called him. And he says the only reason he hasn't been in trouble lately is because Pesce does his thinking for him."

"Does he have a job?"

"Yeah, he's supposed to be the manager of a health club called Muscle Mania in Long Island City. It's owned by Pesce, his daddy." Strunk chuckled. "They're body-building buddies. Isn't that cute? Shawn was Mr. Long Island City last year."

"Your friend seems to know quite a bit about them."

"He's not the only one I talked to. Some of this stuff I got from another friend in the D.A.'s office."

"Did they have anything on Pesce's background?"

"It's sketchy. What they gave me was mostly rumor and hearsay, but if only half of it's true, you're fooling around with a very spooky character."

"Oh? That was my impression, P.C."

"Between the two of them, here's what I was able to patch together. Stein had the guy pegged right."

"He's a wiseguy?"

"He's a little different, but he's a wiseguy. He and the kid are a couple of faggots, if you haven't figured that one out yet."

"I've heard that rumor. That's unusual, isn't it, a gay wiseguy."

"Shit," Strunk scoffed. "It doesn't take all kinds, we just got all kinds. We've got gay cops, don't we? Why not gay robbers?"

"Somehow it's hard to imagine him playing cards and twirling pasta with the rest of the torpedoes."

"Yeah, well, he's made his bones," said Strunk. "The word is, he's a made man, a capo in the Joey 'Panzy' Panzellone crime family. Just like his father, Big Anthony, before him."

"You mean he pulls rank? This is getting weirder by the minute."

"It may only be an honorary thing. He's definitely a loner. Surveillance has yet to pick him up on video, or wiretaps, according to my friend in the D.A.'s office. He doesn't make the scene much at the Rod and Gun Club."

"Yeah," I cracked. "Panzellone probably doesn't want him hanging around the club making the intern hoods' bones. They'd be the laughingstock of the other crime families."

"Ha, ha, Byrne," Strunk said. "You wanna hear the rest?"

"Sure," I said. I realized it was a bad joke. That this was hardly a laughing matter. But if I didn't laugh, I was going to cry. I didn't want Strunk to see me doing that. And if I didn't cry, I was going to shit. I didn't want him to see me do that either.

"Big Anthony and Panzy were tight, so the story goes, just like brothers. They became made men on the same hit, and were moving up the ranks together, that is until Big Anthony got whacked by a car bomb. One version has it"—Strunk chuckled—"that only one of them could become don, and that Panzy beat Big Anthony to the punch by rigging the bomb himself. Then, to show his heart was in the right place, Panzellone took care of the widow and the kids. He raised Little Anthony like he was his own son."

"How many kids are there?"

"Two, Little Anthony and a sister, Angela. Anyway, when Little Anthony turned out to be gay, Panzellone disowned him, sort of."

"Sort of?"

"Yeah, he's smart and slick, and he's too good an earner to kick out of the family. So they tolerate him, like a black sheep. Panzellone lets him run the laundromat, and the health club, a couple of pasta parlors, and a gay bar. He used to have a sex club, too. He was partners in that with a rogue cop, but that got shut down. The rest of his hustles the family stays out of."

"Does Stein know any of this?"

"I've informed him."

"And what's he say?"

"He admits he took the broad for some dough, and that he banged her, that's all. Oh, and he says she was a bum lay." Strunk laughed.

"A real gentleman," I said. "What did he say about Little Anthony?"

"Pesce?"

"Who else? Look, P.C., if Stein had stuck to our original agreement this would be no big deal. It probably would blow over. But Pesce and Sloane Marshall claim he took them personally for almost half a million. Actually, it was three hundred and fifty thousand."

"He took the broad for some dough, was all he said," Strunk repeated.

"He nicked Hungerford for a million three, P.C."

"How do you know that? Never mind," he said quickly. "I'll pretend I didn't hear that. I told you, Byrne, I don't want to know about any frauds you and Stein perpetrated."

"P.C., Pesce and Marshall regarded Hungerford as their personal cash cow. I'd be looking for Stein, too, if I were them. And Pesce'll find Stein. He found Hungerford. I just don't want to get stepped on in the process."

"I don't know what to tell you, Byrne."

"That's comforting."

"Stein's a hustler, thief, and con artist, but he's not really greedy."

"Really?"

"This is America, Byrne," he said pedantically. "Big is best. Records are made to be broken. Go for it, as they say. And that's what Stein did. He's like a guy who can run a mile in less than four minutes, or smack a baseball over five hundred feet. Only difference is, his best trick is fraud. He steals because that's what he's good at. Stein can't help himself. It's compulsive behavior. It's a sickness, like any other. But he's got the numbers to prove he's the best. And we just try to channel his energies for the benefit of society."

"P.C., spare me the psycho-babble. What about the money?"

"What about it?"

"Where is it? Whose is it?"

150

"It's Stein's now. He's probably got it in 'tax-frees' stashed away in safe deposit boxes around the country under the various aliases he uses."

"But that money belongs to Hungerford's investors."

"Haven't they filed criminal complaints against Hungerford?"

"Yes."

"Well, what kind of defense do you think Hungerford can make of a claim that Stein defrauded him? 'Ah, judge, I gave the money to Mr. Stein. He promised me a fantastic return trading on insider information.' How do you think that'll go down in court?"

"Lousy."

"You got that right, Byrne. Even if he does claim he gave Stein the money, Stein will say, 'No way, Your Honor, did Mr. Hungerford give me—how much was it?'"

"Hungerford's end was a million three, but counting Sloane and Pesce, it must have totaled a million six, or more."

"All right then, 'a million six. Your Honor, what's more, the money he did give me was lost on a legitimate deal that went sour.' Then, too, there's the fact that, instead of facing the music, Hungerford split on the investors. That'll look nice in court."

"I see what you mean, P.C. So Stein's not greedy, just lucky, and the best. And the 'ducks' are screwed."

"'Ducks'?"

"That's what Pesce calls the investors."

"I like that. I'll have to pass that on to Stein. But to answer your question, yes, it looks like the 'ducks' are screwed. Hey, Byrne?"

"What?"

"Ya havin' any fun?"

"Nothing but, P.C."

"Good."

"P.C., you still on the phone?" called his wife. "It's time to put the children down."

"I'm coming, baby," Strunk bellowed.

"I'll let you go, P.C.," I said.

"It's that woman, Byrne," he said. "I gotta go." He hung up.

Chapter 13

Tito read the *Daily News,* I read *The New York Times.*
Both papers had the story the next morning. The *Times*
account, under the head "Swindler Asks Mercy Because Of
Mistress" gave this account:

A lawyer for a Long Island public relations executive who pleaded guilty to stealing more than $12
million from 200 people by means of a fraud scheme,
asked the judge yesterday for leniency on the grounds
that his client had difficulty supporting a mistress.

"Unfortunately, he met this woman," Leonard Baskin told Judge Harold A. Flaxner of Criminal Court in
Manhattan, "and it became impossible to support two
households, so this Ponzi scheme developed."

The executive, Richard Andrew Hungerford, forty-
three years old, of Sagaponack, L.I., as part of a
plea-bargain arrangement, pleaded guilty at the arraignment to stealing the money over a five-year
period by promising investors a return as high as fifty
percent.

Assistant District Attorney Martin Cerni told the
judge that one of the victims was a woman who lost
her entire savings, including the benefits from her
husband's life insurance.

The defendant's lawyer, Leonard Baskin, asked for
mercy, saying his client's remorse for his actions was
such that he had become a born-again Christian.

Judge Flaxner released Mr. Hungerford on
$500,000 bail until sentencing in sixty days.

The *Daily News* reported the story in much punchier prose. Headline: "Ponzi Schemer Pleads Guilty to $12 Million Fraud."

Nowhere did the numbers jibe, I noticed. Linhardt had said fifteen million. The *Times* said twelve million. Hungerford claimed he only needed seven to get even and get out. And if Stein were talking, which he wasn't, he'd lowball it. Probably no one really knew the exact amount. But another thing I noticed was that Hungerford had no trouble making bail.

As I was pondering these matters, the phone rang. I picked it up and said hello.

"Hello, Charlie, Sloane Marshall."

The mistress. What a surprise. "Yes, Sloane," I said cautiously.

"I called to apologize . . . for yesterday. It's . . . well, it's just that I've been under such stress lately, and well—"

"I understand," I lied.

"That was such an ugly scene, and—"

"It's quite all right, you don't need to say a thing."

"Anthony behaved so badly."

"Forget about it, Sloane. I have." I lied, the hard, speculative look in Pesce's eye still vivid in my mind.

"I can't forget about it, Charlie. Anthony can be quite nasty when he feels he's been taken advantage of . . . and well, I wanted to apologize, and make it up to you . . . if I can."

She could be quite nasty, too, I remembered. "Consider it forgotten, Sloane. Apology accepted. Okay?"

"No, it's not okay," she insisted. "And that spokesperson job? I got it. It was your pictures that did the trick."

"I'm happy to hear that. Congratulations."

"Yes, isn't that wonderful. Are you free tonight? I want to take you to dinner."

"Ah, yes, I am," I said. She caught me flatfooted with that one.

"Good. It's a date then."

"Wait a minute," I said. "Only if Anthony Pesce's leashed, muzzled, and caged."

She laughed melodiously, as though I'd said the most hilarious thing in the world. "Oh, you don't have to worry about Anthony, Charlie. Actually, he's really very sweet, once you get to know him."

Oh sure, and so was Joe Stalin. How much more did I really need to know about Little Anthony Pesce, I wondered? "May I ask you a question, Sloane?"

"If you like," she said slowly.

"What's Anthony to you anyway?"

"Oh." She laughed. "Do you mean is he a boyfriend? Heavens no. Anthony's nothing more than a dear old friend."

"I see," I said, feeling as much in the dark as before.

"Pick me up at seven?"

"Fine." I thought again about yesterday and wondered what I was letting myself in for.

Expensive habits die hard. Sloane was willing to spring for a four-star French restaurant. But I'm still uncomfortable when a woman is picking up the tab, and since she was between men at the moment, I assured her that that wasn't necessary. I try to be a cheap date, and never order from the top of the menu when it's the woman's treat. A couple of drinks and a plate of pasta doesn't buy much more than light conversation—so much for role reversal. The more things change, the more they stay the same. A Frenchman said that, I believe, and it probably sounds better in French.

We ended up in the Village, at Bradley's on University Place. The food is passable, the drinks are good. If conversation falters, the music is live and worth listening to. And best of all, the prices are reasonable. The crowd is mostly middle-aged rebels who have mislaid their causes.

Rules were made to be broken, we agreed, so we dined on fish in a cream sauce, and drank red wine. She beamed at me from across the table, amber blond, languid as honey, her mouth full of food. It was easy to understand, gazing at her in the soft light, how Hungerford could fall so hard for her. A man could dream a lifetime and never know a woman like her.

She dabbed at her lips with the napkin. "You have no idea, Charlie," she sighed. "My life has been the pits lately."

"It hasn't been all bad," I said. "You've got a new job."

"That's true, and thank God. But what I mean is since

this awful thing with Richard, I get calls all hours of the day and night. Horrible calls. People threatening . . . saying terrible things and then hanging up."

"I can imagine."

"I've been like a crazy person."

"Like yesterday," I said helpfully, as I was supposed to say.

"I made such a fool of myself," she said, flushing slightly. "Can you forgive me?"

"Of course. It was understandable. You were upset."

She touched the back of my hand. "I was so nervous about calling you," she confessed. "It took all day for me to screw up enough courage." She slid her hand around, underneath mine, and our fingers touched each other's palms.

"You needn't have been," I said politely.

She bowed her head, and looked up at me. "I know that now," she said. "There are some things I've wanted to say to you. To explain. I'm sure you've heard the talk going around . . . about Richard and me. That he was keeping me?" She paused for a reaction.

"I have heard some talk," I said. I doubted she read the newspapers.

She withdrew her hand. "Well, it's all a pack of lies. It's simply not true," she said. "You know how people love to talk."

"Yes, I know."

She lowered her gaze to her wine glass. "Richard is an attractive man, and very persuasive. I thought I was in love with him." She raised her eyes to mine. "But I have my own career, as you know, Charlie. I've always taken care of myself."

"I'm sure."

"The gossip . . . it's just not fair. I've never been kept. I've always worked. I've always been independent. I just want you to know that. But then, women are always getting it for this," she said with a rueful grin.

"It isn't fair," I conceded.

"I was duped by Richard, too, just like the others."

"Ginny Rowen tells me—"

"Are you still seeing her?"

"Occasionally."

155

"Mmm." She smiled. "Your duty punch?"

"Hardly!" I laughed. "Anyway, she says it was you who introduced her to Richard."

"I introduced a lot of people to Richard. And why not? He was making money, or I thought he was. Anyway, no one was obliged to invest, certainly not her."

"Certainly not," I said. "Did Richard pay a commission for referrals?"

"Charlie, one doesn't do these things for nothing."

"I didn't know," I said innocently.

"Of course he did. It was modest enough, though. One or two percent of the amount invested. Nothing really. And he cheated me besides, I'm sure of it."

She was a smooth and polished high-gloss article when she had her control. I saw no point in asking how she happened to come by a co-op on Park Avenue. I was sure she'd have a plausible answer of some kind. "How did you meet Richard?" I asked.

"He hired me as a spokesperson for a tradeshow."

"And it was love at first sight?"

"No." She smiled. "I didn't care much for him at all when we first met. He's not an easy person to get to know. He can be very arrogant, in an offhanded sort of way. But we were thrown together on the job, and, eventually, something clicked."

"He wasn't married?"

She gave me a false smile. "All the best men are married."

"To all the best women."

"I deserved that!" She laughed, half seductively, half self-deprecatingly. "What about you, Charlie? Is there a Mrs. Byrne and a station wagon full of kids somewhere while you fool around in the city?"

"Nope."

"You're not gay, are you?"

"No, just content."

"You're a bastard then. Most men are, one way or another."

"I don't think so. My mother had a license."

"Okay, I'll reserve judgment on that one, then. Are you a sleaze?"

"I have my quotient, I suppose."

"An honest man. And you don't smoke, I notice."

"Nope."

"Or drink?"

"Some." I toasted her with the wine glass.

"You sound too good to be true, Charlie Byrne. What are you on?"

"Eastern Standard Time, I hope."

She laughed a full-throated laugh.

She didn't seem to mind talking about Richard; in fact, she seemed anxious to explain herself. I'd heard Richard's version of the story. If she would continue to talk as freely as she had, chances were I'd hear her version. It would be interesting to compare the two. "How did Richard happen to get into the money management business?" I asked, attempting to steer the conversation in that direction without seeming to pry.

"He'd been playing the stock market when I met him," she said, her face solemn, her voice easy and relaxed, "and doing quite well at it. He wanted to impress me, I suppose, so he persuaded me to give him some money to invest. I gave him the money and he got me a very nice return on it."

"And you were impressed?" I asked, rhetorically.

"I certainly was, and you would have been, too."

"So you were his first client?"

"Indeed I was."

"And when did you first notice that there were problems?"

"You mean, when did I first notice Richard was in trouble?"

"Yes."

"I didn't. I never had the slightest idea that there was ever anything wrong. Oh, sure, I'd noticed that Richard had grown remote . . . and irritable recently, but I thought that had to do with the two of us. That we just weren't getting along. I had no idea it was because of financial problems. There was nothing unusual in his being out of town on business for a week at a time even. I hadn't a clue that he'd skipped."

"What about October nineteenth, 'Black Monday'?" I asked. "Surely you wondered how the market had affected him that day?"

"Of course I did, and I asked him whether or not he had taken a beating in the market."

"What did he say?"

"He said he was okay. He said he was out the week before. I realize now that he was lying. But Richard can look you right in the eye when he's telling a lie. He's a very good liar."

"Well, how did you learn there was trouble then?"

"When I started getting the phone calls."

"Oh, yes, the phone calls."

"Yes, the phone calls," she repeated with a strained smile. "And there's hate mail, too. They call me names like 'bitch' and 'cunt' and worse, and then hang up. Their grubby letters are riddled with atrocious spelling. They threaten me with everything from disfigurement, torching my summer house, and death. Real nice, huh?"

"It must be very unpleasant," I said sympathetically, thinking about Little Anthony's implied threats yesterday.

"I wouldn't wish it on my worst enemy," she said.

"It's to be expected though," I said mildly.

"Why?" she demanded. "I didn't skip with the money."

"I know, but after all those investor parties, and the like, it's reasonable that people would assume you were associated with Richard."

"They can assume whatever they like," she said hotly. "They had no complaints when they were lapping up the booze and stuffing their faces with roast beef."

I didn't want her getting testy on me, so I changed tacks. "Did you see today's papers?" I asked.

"I don't read the papers."

"Richard pleaded guilty at his arraignment yesterday."

She compressed her lips into a thin red line. "Oh?" she murmured.

"Yes. He's out on bail. He's due back in court in June to be sentenced."

She focused her gaze on the middle distance and raked her hair with lacquered nails.

"It was a plea bargain arrangement," I rambled on, hoping she'd respond. "They'll go easy on him, I'm sure. Three years in Allenwood. Time off for good behavior. A fine, and a promise of restitution, if possible."

"Restitution? Ha, that's a laugh. I feel sorry for Richard. I really do. But he's a waste. I feel sorrier for myself and all the other people he's swindled."

It was interesting the way she distanced herself from

Hungerford, and any wrongdoing. In her version of the story she was merely another victim. I might have expected as much. Why wouldn't she be as smooth and plausible a liar as Hungerford when she was calm and collected?

"You're right, of course. It's too bad about Richard. But it's the investors who deserve the sympathy."

She brightened and signaled the waitress for the check. "I want us to be friends, Charlie," she said, riffling through the credit cards in her wallet.

"So do I."

She laid a prosaic American Express Gold Card on the check like she was playing an ace on top of a king. "I want to have some fun for a change," she said, her eyes glittering. "Let's have some fun, Charlie."

"Sure." I smiled. "What have you got in mind?"

"Wanna go dancing?"

I wanted to go dancing about as much as I wanted to do Chinese algebra. But we ended up in a loft off the Bowery on Houston Street anyway. It was called 'the club,' lower case, and catered to a sexually ambidextrous crowd who had to dance. Boys boogied with boys, girls boogied with girls, and boys and girls together were okay, too. These were aggressively tolerant people. The bathrooms were reserved for the abuse of controlled substances, and for raw sex.

Sloane dragged me straight to the dance floor. "I love to dance," she said, swaying fluidly to the music. It didn't seem to bother her that my efforts were as stolid as a bear's. The heavy, throbbing beat loosened me up eventually, though, and I began to move my booty.

Sloane was too good for me. As soon as I thought I was holding my own with her, Sloane would show me a new move, and the gap in our dancing talents would yawn again. She beamed at me. She was having fun.

After the second number, which was a lifetime for me, we took a break and elbowed our way to the bar. Beer, wine, and designer water were all they offered. Seven bucks a pop. She had a glass of wine, I had a beer. We drank them quickly, without conversation, which was impossible anyway.

"You go dancing often, do you, Charlie?" she yelled in my ear.

"All the time!"

She laughed, returned the empty glass to the bar, and took my hand. "Come on, we're just getting warmed up."

We pushed our way toward the dance floor. "Sloane," a voice called. A woman rushed Sloane, they embraced and she kissed Sloane on the lips. I recognized her as one of the beautiful people from the party.

"I've been so worried about you. How you been, baby? You look wonderful."

Sloane said, "Hi, Ronnie." And tossed me an apologetic what-can-you-do look.

Handsome described Ronnie better than beautiful. The beautiful one, her clone, lurked behind her.

"Doesn't Sloane look wonderful tonight, Dusty?" Ronnie asked her clone.

"Fabulous," said Dusty, his Adam's apple bobbing.

It was a cinch Ronnie didn't write grubby letters, or make crank calls. I glanced at Dusty. His frozen smile masked annoyance with Ronnie. What sort of perverse sexual jealousy was this? I wondered.

"Do you mind?" Sloane asked with a lame smile.

I grinned and nodded okay.

"Never mind him, baby," said Ronnie, nudging Sloane to the dance floor.

They beamed at each other a moment, then picked up the beat and went into motion. Ronnie, elegant, and as slim as monofilament, her dark hair cropped short, her long legs sheathed in loose black silk pants, her broad shoulders and flat chest in a white silk shirtwaist, played the man. Sloane, in a loose-fitting tunic the color of her hair, and belted at the hips, that flowed with the curves and movement of her body, was surely a handsome woman. I stared at them. They danced so well together. Hell, they even looked great together.

"Wanna give it a try, handsome?" Dusty asked, his eyebrow arched.

"I like to watch," I said.

"See ya then," he said and moved off.

I pushed my way back to the bar. The bartender, a rough-trade cutie in a black nylon tank top and faded jeans, rippled his biceps and served me up another seven-buck bottle of beer. I leaned on the bar and glanced at my watch. It was going on one-thirty and this party was just getting

160

started. Nursing my beer, I wondered if these people had anything heavier on their agendas tomorrow than a visit to the gym, getting a razor cut, and scoring some coke.

Sloane materialized out of the haze. "Wanna go?"

"Yeah, it's past my bedtime."

She slid across the seat to me, the hem of her tunic riding up her leg, and pulled me to her. "I don't want to be alone tonight," she said. She was flushed and hot from dancing. Her smell filled the backseat of the cab. She put her lips on mine. I saw the green Datsun 280Z through the rear window.

"Not tonight, Sloane, I've got a headache."

She frowned.

"Look, it's late, I'm tired," I pleaded. "Besides, I never even kiss on the first date."

"You don't?" she pouted.

"Well, hardly ever."

"That's better." She smiled. "You're afraid of me, aren't you?"

"A little."

"You don't have to be," she said, the tunic rising even higher.

"Anyone you know drive a green Datsun 280Z?" I asked, glancing out the window again. He was still there.

She straightened up and looked out the window. "Anthony's friend, Shawn, drives a green Datsun."

The Datsun turned right off Park. Maybe he saw us looking back at him. "That car's been following us since we left the club," I said.

"Shawn could have been at the club. I know he goes there. But why would he follow us?"

"That's what I was wondering," I said. The cab pulled up in front of her building.

"Merde," she muttered. "Driver, don't stop. Keep going."

"What is it?" I said, peering past her to the street.

"That fool's haunting me," she said.

"What fool?" I caught a glimpse of a heavyset man, hands jammed deep in his pockets. He seemed to be arguing with the doorman. It was the lawyer, Philolius.

"Take me to your place, Charlie."

Somewhere, in the back of my mind, all evening long, I'd

half entertained the idea that our date was a setup. But Philolius did seem to catch her off guard. "Make a left, driver," I said, "give us Fifth and Thirty-eighth." I preferred my place to her place. "Who was that guy?" I asked, pretending I hadn't seen him.

"I told you about him, didn't I? Phil Philolius, one of the investors?"

"The lawyer."

"Yes."

"Yes. He's been after me, and now that Richard's out of the picture . . . well, you know how it is," she said impatiently.

"How juvenile waiting outside your door that way."

"Isn't it," she giggled.

When the cab dropped us, I scanned the intersection in all directions. There was no sign of the Datsun.

Her eyes came up from under to meet mine, and she toyed with the buttons of my shirt. She pushed me playfully against the wall of the elevator, rubbing against me, kissing me hotly. Her hand dropped to my belt buckle, then brushed my crotch. She gave me a melodious laugh, and a quick squeeze.

"Not tired anymore, Charlie?"

"Second wind."

"Mmm, how nice."

We spilled out of the elevator, and I grabbed for her ass. She dodged me with a merry laugh.

"I want a shower and a brandy, in that order," she announced, on the way through the door. She headed for the bathroom.

I poured two large brandies, and two tall glasses of ice water, and toted them upstairs to the bedroom. I remembered that she liked him, so I put the Wes Montgomery tape on the stereo. I barely had time to slip into a robe and light a candle, when she appeared, lugging her bag. She wore a bath towel and heels.

"I'd like a shower myself," I said. "Don't go away."

"I'm not going anywhere," she said, and let the towel drop.

I took my own sweet time admiring her. She was a credit to her gender. She met my gaze with a steady gaze of her own, casually caressing her breast. "I won't be long," I promised.

"I hope not," she said. She sat down on the edge of the bed and rummaged through her bag, which was at her feet. I noticed how her breasts brushed against her knees before tearing my eyes from her and heading for the shower.

When I returned she was lying on her back, her skin and hair golden in the candlelight. She was a real blonde.

The room reeked of pot.

She gestured to a small marble pipe and a Dunhill lighter. "Why don't you have a hit?" she said.

I joined her on the bed and lit the pipe. I inhaled and immediately coughed. It was strong dope. I took another hit, exhaled slowly, and passed the pipe to her. "Do you like coke?" I asked.

"Are you offering?" She propped herself up on her elbow, brushed her hair from her forehead, and took the pipe.

"Just curious."

She exchanged the pipe for the brandy and sipped. "I don't like coke," she said. "It gets me too crazy."

"Yeah," I agreed, but I would have guessed otherwise.

She passed the glass to me when she was through. "This is just fine." She smiled with heavy eyelids. She moved casually behind me and slipped my robe off my shoulders. I felt her breasts pressed against my back. She reached around me and pressed the palms of her hands against my chest. "Mmm, nice," she murmured. I liked the feel of her warm hands on my skin.

I turned to her and we moved into each other's arms for a long embrace. Our hands and mouths began a languid exploration of the strange, and new, topography of each other. And when the pot hit me, I wanted it to go on forever. But she seemed to have other ideas. There was an almost sudden and unexpected urgency in her movement. Her breathing became labored and more rapid.

She grabbed for me. "Fuck me, now," she said. Clumsily, she put me inside her. She tossed her head from side to side, and made panting and mewing sounds that grew louder as she quickened the pace. Her hands fluttered frenetically across my back and shoulders as she heaved spasmodically on the bed.

"Come, baby, come," she urged.

So I did.

No one could live up to her advertisements, nor was I convinced she had had as much fun as she pretended to have. But she made no complaints. I don't know whether it was the dope, the booze, the sex, or fatigue, but she even seemed to glow when we kissed goodnight. We rolled in opposite directions to sleep. As brief as it was, though, I enjoyed it. At your cervix, Madame.

It was clear, with our first stirrings that morning, that there would be no reprise of last night. I offered to take her out for breakfast, but she said she didn't have time. We had coffee and juice in the studio.

At the elevator, she gave me a cheerful goodbye kiss and said, "I had a marvelous time last night, Charlie."

And I said, "So did I."

Chapter 14

Today we were going on location. We were shooting interiors for a condo prospectus. Tito wouldn't be in for another hour, so I had some time to kill. It took five minutes to double-check the equipment Tito had packed the night before. Everything we needed was there. Satisfied that he was as thorough as ever, I went out for the *Times*.

The weather was perfect. The sky was clear and powder blue. A stiff breeze snapped the pendants on the marquee of the Greek coffee shop. It was a good day to go on location. But it was an even better day to fly a kite, or fish for trout.

Back in the studio, I drank coffee and buried my nose in the newspaper while I waited for Tito.

Sloane was smart not to waste time on the newspapers. The world was in a sorry state. The dollar was in free fall.

Trade wars were imminent. The municipal scandals continued to plague City Hall. The tenant in the White House finally had a "Gate" he could call his own. And all the groups that had never seen eye to eye in the past were no closer to seeing eye to eye in the foreseeable future. And the sports pages, where you might expect some relief, weren't much better. Junky jocks were detoxing by the roster, and debate raged whether or not whole leagues should be required to pee in bottles.

I don't know how I missed the item, but I did. I would find out about it soon enough, though.

When Tito and I got back from the location, it was just after five. We were unpacking the gear when the doorbell rang, and I answered it.

"Charles Byrne?"

"Yes," I said.

He flopped open a wallet and flashed a potsy. "Detective Edward Hannibal," he said.

"Come in," I said, and felt my sphincter tighten.

He stepped by me lightly, a ruddy and rough-complexioned middleweight in his late forties, neatly dressed in a dark blazer and flannel slacks. There was something vaguely familiar about him.

"Remember me, Mr. Byrne?"

"I was just trying to place you. You took our statements after the car bombing, right?"

He rewarded me with a swift smile. "That's right," he said, sizing me up with a disarming expression and a steady gaze. He seemed like the kind of guy who was quick with a joke, and quicker still to get one.

"How about something to drink?" I asked.

"I'm off the hard stuff," he said with a Boston accent.

"Seltzer then?"

"That's fine."

I poured him a seltzer, and fixed myself a bourbon on the rocks—I had a feeling I was going to need one—and we moved to the lounge. I gestured to the couch and he eased himself down. From the inside pocket of his blazer he pulled out a notebook and a ballpoint pen.

"Well, how can I help you?" I asked.

He considered the question a moment with the same

disarming expression on his face, but his eyes were as cool as icewater. "Have you seen the newspapers today?" he asked finally.

"The *Times,* this morning."

"Perhaps you saw it then?"

We'd be at it forever at this rate. "Saw what?" I asked.

"They pulled a stiff out of the Ramble in Central Park Tuesday morning."

"That's news?"

"This one's name was Warren Ulrick."

"That's news." Warren, the putzy actor, as Stein had called him.

"Did you know him?"

"If I didn't, would I have the pleasure of your company?"

"Your name was in his address book." He smiled.

"I hope mine wasn't the only name."

"No, but 'B' for Byrne puts you right up there at the head of the list," he said with his swift smile. "It's donkey work, but we've got to check out the names one at a time."

"It was in the *Times,* you said?"

"Yes."

"Excuse me a moment."

He nodded.

I got the paper. It was easy to miss, a single column, three inches deep in section B. "Body of Actor/Singer Found in Central Park" read the headline. A professional dog walker, it went on to say, discovered the body of actor/singer Warren Ulrick, in the area of Central Park known as the Ramble. There was no mention of the cause of death, merely that the dead man had been identified by papers found on the body. Then they listed his modest credits, and the fact that he was survived by a mother in Sarasota, Florida, and a married sister, in Cleveland, his home town.

"How was he killed?" I asked.

"We're not releasing that information at this time," said the detective impassively.

"The Ramble's a well-known pickup spot. Was it a fag bashing?"

"Might have been. Might have been rough trade. He may not have been killed there. He may have just been dumped there, for all we know."

"I wouldn't have thought he was gay," I said, and remem-

166

bered my bourbon and took a swallow. Whatever Warren Ulrick's sexual slant, his death wasn't a case of fag bashing. That much was sure.

The cop scribbled on his notepad and, without looking up, said, "You are, of course, under no obligation to answer them, but I'd like to ask you a few questions, Mr. Byrne."

"As long as you're not reading me my 'Miranda,'" I replied affably, and hoped I wouldn't regret this later.

He flashed a swift, thin smile. "What was your relationship to the dead man?" he asked.

"Relationship?"

"Yes, you reacted quite strongly to the news he'd been killed," he said, his eyes narrow, his face grave.

"It startled me. It was only a little while ago that I photographed him."

"Please understand, Mr. Byrne," he said mildly, "I have to ask these questions."

"I understand, but we didn't have any relationship," I said. "We did a job together, once. Business, that's all."

"A photographic job?" He looked at me and smiled, but his eyes didn't.

"Yes, I hired him as a model."

"I see," he said, and dropped his eyes to his pad and scribbled. "And did you have any other dealings with him?"

"No, it was strictly a one-shot."

"Would you mind telling me how you spent Monday, April second?"

"We're talking murder here, not just killed, aren't we?"

"Not just killed?"

"Yeah, as in 'accidentally.' You know, being in the wrong place at the wrong time."

"For now, all we're trying to do is eliminate as many names as possible in the deceased's address book," he said with a disarming glance. "You're right, though, there's a difference between killed and murder."

"Just so I know what we're talking about. You want all day?"

"That would be best."

"Well, I was here in my studio most of the day, working. My assistant was with me. Later I went for a bike ride in Central Park."

That perked him up. "What time were you in the Park?"

"From approximately seven-thirty until ten, ten-thirty."

"Got any backup? Anyone see you there?"

"I did laps with another guy. Want his name and number?"

"If you don't mind," he said, pen poised.

I gave him Mike-the-Bike's name and number. He noted it duly, finished his seltzer and got to his feet.

"Thanks for your cooperation, Mr. Byrne, and the seltzer." He paused, slowly returning the pen and pad to his inside pocket. "Strange bumping into you again under these circumstances," he said with a sly glance.

"It's quite a coincidence. Has there been any progress on the car bombing case?" I asked.

"Not much, sorry to say. It was a pipe bomb, either wired to the car's ignition, or triggered by a remote, and that's as much as we know at this time."

"It's been a while now. That isn't much, is it?"

"I'm afraid not," he admitted. "Tell me, Mr. Byrne," he said, "was there any connection between Warren Ulrick and the professor and his wife that you are aware of? Did they know one another?"

"You're asking the wrong guy. I didn't know any of them that well."

Hannibal hesitated a moment, his expression bland, his eyes shrewd. "The reason I ask," he continued casually, "is yours isn't the only name in Ulrick's address book linking him to the professor and his wife."

"Oh?"

"Nope," he said, the initiative his again. "Don't worry, Mr. Byrne, we'll solve the car bombing case."

"You think so?"

"Sure, and you wanna know how?"

"How?" I asked, the perfect straight man. I had a pretty good idea whose names would be in Warren's address book, but there was no way I could ask without making this canny cop more suspicious than he already was. And he'd never play all his cards at once anyway.

"The car bombing will get solved accidentally, heh, heh, heh." He laughed like he'd just delivered the punchline, or solved a case.

"Accidentally?" I asked as expected.

"Yes, it'll get solved right along with another case we're working on," he beamed.

"Huh," I said. "I suppose that happens."

"Yeah, all the time. Anyway, thanks again for your cooperation, Mr. Byrne," he said, tossing me the swift smile. "Now how do I get out of here?"

I showed him to the door and wished him good luck, wondering how much I had cooperated with him.

Tito gave me a baleful glance as I was going for the phone. "Don't you have something to do?" I snapped at him, instantly regretting it.

He looked hurt. "Yes," he said and turned from me.

I called Strunk first and told him about Detective Hannibal's visit. He didn't say much, only that he'd get back to me as soon as he found out what had happened to Warren Ulrick. Then I called Ginny. There was no reason for Pesce to think she knew anything about Stein; there was no reason for them to bother her. But after what Hungerford had said about his cute fifteen-year-old daughter and Shawn, I wasn't so sure. Who really knew what those guys thought? They knew we were friends, that was enough to make her vulnerable. They'd pull any and all levers to get at Stein. Suddenly, I was anxious to hear the sound of her voice.

I didn't get her, though. What I got was a tape recording of her voice, like a clone in ether, saying: "This is Ginny Rowen, I'm not in right now, but if *blah, blah, blah* . . ."

I put the time and date of my call on her answering machine, and asked if we could get together later on tonight.

Tito was still puttering around with the equipment and film from the shooting. "It's been a long day, Tito," I said. "Why don't you go home? I'll take care of the film."

"I still have things to do," he said stubbornly.

"Look, I'm sorry for barking at you," I said. "Why don't you let me finish up here?"

He smiled shyly. "It's all right, Charlie. But what's happening? We used to be a photo studio, now it's crooks and cops every day," he said quietly.

"I know, it's a drag," I confessed. "But, as you know, I've got myself in a jam because of this Ginny Rowen thing."

"Is there anything that I can do?"

"Not unless you wanna loan me half a million bucks." I smiled. "You did enough the other day."

He looked at me in alarm. "You in the hole for half a million?"

"No, nothing like that. That was a bad joke."

"Oh, yeah, well, I wasn't joking about the Ithaca 12-gauge, Charlie. I can get you one downtown, off the street," he volunteered. I didn't doubt him. He wasn't afraid to mix it up. He dealt drugs before cleaning up his act and coming to work for me. And even though he wasn't a very big guy, it would be a mistake to underestimate him. He was a guy you'd rather have on your side.

"I might take you up on that offer," I said. "Come on, I meant it, I'll finish up here. You go on home."

The Cheshire grin bloomed on his face until he looked like a Mexican bandit. "Hokay, boss, I jus like my yob, ees all."

"Yeah, you eye-talians, you're stand-up guys," I said. "Now get outta here."

"Hokay," he laughed. It didn't take him long to get his coat and get out the door.

I hit the bourbon again as soon as he was gone. A solid three fingers this time. Then I took the glass, climbed the stairs, and flopped at my desk. My desk is a nice place to sit and think. It's a nice place to sit and drink, too.

There is a kind of life after death, if only in the memory of the living. I wondered who remembered Warren Ulrick, and who, besides his mother and sister, grieved for him. And I wondered how they remembered him. Because I remembered him as vain and venal, a fatuous asshole. These aren't capital offenses, however, and he had as much right to live as anyone. Whoever remembered him, I hoped, remembered him as kind, generous, and even valiant. He didn't deserve to die for Ginny Rowen's measly fifty grand. He especially didn't deserve to die because I wanted to play Lochinvar.

The ringing phone interrupted my morbid musings.

"Strunk," he announced in his bluff baritone.

"What did you find out, P.C.?" I said.

"He died of a cerebral hematoma induced by a blow, or blows, to the head, the coroner's report says. And that's the good news."

"Good news? What do you mean that's the good news?"

"His spleen was ruptured, his kidneys were black and

170

blue. He had a herniated large intestine, and the abdominal cavity was a bucket of blood. Oh, and the small bones of his left foot were crushed."

"The bad news, huh? Christ," I groaned.

"How did you guess? He died slow, Byrne."

"I figured that out, P.C."

"They worked him over to get him to talk, and when he didn't talk, they beat him to death, is how it looks," said Strunk. "But who knows, maybe they just beat him to death for the hell of it. Whichever it was, it seems certain it was done somewhere else and he was dumped in the Park later."

But Warren must have talked. It was just that he didn't have much to say. He told them I cast him for the job, and that I was part of the charade staged for Sloane's benefit. He told them I was there when he dickered with Stein over his fee, and again when he was paid. He had that much to talk about, but he couldn't talk about the subject that interested them the most, Henry Stein. No matter how bad his karma, I thought, Warren didn't deserve to die that way.

"I owe you a Szechuan, P.C."

"You bet your white ass you owe me," Strunk said. "And, Byrne—"

"What?"

"Remember, I'm a cop, too."

"How could I forget. Thanks again, P.C."

"You're welcome," he said and hung up.

I dialed Ginny's number and the machine answered. This time I didn't leave a message. It seemed unlikely we'd be getting together tonight. The best I could hope for was to hear her voice, her real voice.

I went downstairs and freshened up the bourbon. After that, because I had nowhere better to be, and because I had to be somewhere, I returned to my desk. While I still had half a brain left, I could put this time to good use and catch up on the paperwork. Write a few checks, maybe, and whittle down accounts payable. Or type up a bill or two. If I felt really ambitious, I could do the sales tax. Not exactly out of sight, out of mind, but it would kill time and leave me something to show for it.

That was my intent. What I did was collapse in my chair, stare at the wall, and brood. I didn't have half a brain left. I had a sodden brain. Gimme a break. The paperwork was going to have to wait. I put on my own machine. I was calling time out.

Little Anthony, aka Mr. Fish, wouldn't be calling time out, though. And he wasn't going to wait. When he really wanted Hungerford, he got him. And now he'd nabbed Warren Ulrick. Mr. Fish got what he wanted, that much was clear, and what he wanted was Stein. I was the man in the middle; my ass was between him and Stein. If I let him, he'd go through me like I was petty cash.

There was no wind, but when I got to my feet, I swayed. I had a snootful of bourbon, self-loathing, and self-pity.

The message on my machine that morning was brief: "Sorry I missed you last night, Charlie. I'm running around, try and call you later." I was relieved to learn Ginny had made it through the night, even if she'd done it without any help from me.

The Szechuan *joint du jour's* name was Szechuan Fire. It was in the basement of a disreputable-looking brownstone on Mott Street. Late last night, I had called Strunk at home and demanded that he set up this meeting. It seemed like a good idea then, but now that I had arrived, I wasn't sure what I hoped to accomplish.

When I stepped inside, I was disappointed not to find a bunch of guys wasted on opium. It was merely another in the long succession of working-class Chinese restaurants to which Strunk seemed addicted. There was the usual beaded curtain divider separating kitchen from dining area. The tables were chrome and formica. The stuffing was coming out of the vinyl backing of the chairs. The paint curled and flaked off the ceiling. The specials were probably lo mein and lead poisoning.

Strunk was sitting in the rear of the restaurant, his back to the wall. He looked like Samson in the Temple—all he had to do was push and the building would tumble down. He waved a pink palm at me as I entered. I threaded my way to him through the empty tables and chairs. When you lunch with Strunk, you catch the first seating.

"How are you?" I said.

"Fine," he said and glowered at me.

"Nice place, P.C. How's the food?"

"There's not a dime's worth of difference between these places," he said with startling candor. "You all right? You sounded lousy last night."

"I'm okay." I pulled out a chair, inspecting it before sitting down. "I went a few pops over the line last night, is all. But the stomach's strong enough to handle the unknown. Where's Stein?"

Strunk nodded at the door. Stein approached, grinning.

"The search for the ultimate in Szechuan cuisine goes on, huh, Strunk?" he said. "How are you, Charlie?"

"I'm okay."

"That good, huh?" He lifted his eyebrows, gave me a mild smile, and sat down.

The waiter appeared immediately, laden with bowls of food all looking suspiciously the same. "I ordered," explained Strunk.

"You're the gourmet," Stein said amiably.

We gave the waiter an order for three beers, and Strunk took the liberty of serving us.

"Well, together again," Stein grinned, shifting his gaze from me to Strunk, and back again. "Well, to what do we owe this reunion? Got another Ponzi for me, Charlie?" he smiled.

"You wish," I said sourly. "I would think one Ponzi was enough. That you'd never need to work again."

He looked offended, but not *very* offended. "Money isn't everything, you know," he said.

"Oh, no?"

"No, I'm too young to collect Social Security. And I like to keep busy." He gave the plate of gruel Strunk placed before him a worried glance. "Ah, Charlie, a word of caution before we begin."

"Yeah, don't go back for seconds."

He laughed. "That, too. But what I was going to say was, our friend, Strunk here, is sworn to uphold the law. Be careful what you say."

"He's reminded me of that frequently."

Strunk blissfully stuffed his face, and beamed at his prize pupils.

"Hungerford pleaded guilty," I said.

"That was smart," said Stein. "Although I don't see what else he could do. He'll do two or three years in a gentleman's

173

jail, and he'll be out. He won't have to worry about picking up the soap in the shower."

"He made bail," I said.

"Did he?" Stein's eyebrows rose. "He must have had a hidy-hole. He must have socked a few dollars away for the proverbial rainy day."

"Yeah, but maybe he'd be better off if he hadn't made bail," I said.

Strunk listened and shoveled, his eyes shifting back and forth between us, as if he was at a tennis match.

"Hungerford's not due back in court until June," I continued. "I've got a hundred dollars that says, as long as he lives, he'll never see the inside of another courtroom."

Stein didn't need it spelled out for him. He didn't take the bet. He lifted a forkful of noodles to his mouth, his head bent thoughtfully over his plate.

I still had the floor. "Did Strunk tell you about the stiff they pulled outta Central Park Tuesday?" I asked.

Stein glanced at Strunk. "No, he didn't."

"It was Warren Ulrick."

"Warren?" he murmured, with a grave face.

"Yes, Warren."

"They puréed the guy," Strunk offered.

"I'm sorry to hear that," said Stein calmly, lifting another forkful of food. "But how did they find him?"

"That's the fifty-thousand-dollar question, Henry," I said. "Warren was a bit player, using an assumed name. Only Sloane actually met the guy. Even so, they found him."

"Who's *they?*" Stein asked.

I glanced from him to Strunk. "Didn't you tell him, P.C.?"

"I haven't told him anything," said Strunk.

"Well, what are you waiting for?" I said. "Tell Henry what you told me about Little Anthony Pesce and his playmate, Shawn."

Strunk paused and gazed balefully at the diminutive Stein. Then he launched into a monotone recitation of Shawn and Pesce's criminal résumés. Stein listened impassively.

"That's what we're up against, Henry," I said when Strunk finished.

"What about Sloane?" Stein asked. "Anyone know what Pesce is to her?"

"An old friend, she tells me," I said.

"She's got some strange friends," Stein said.

"Henry, Warren talked," I said, "and I don't blame him. I'd talk, too, if I was tortured the way he was."

"What did he have to talk about?" said Stein.

"Not much," I said. "But he could have told them that we were working together. That I helped you scam Sloane. And he could have *told them,* if they wanted to find Henry Stein, they should ask me."

Stein gave me a bleak smile. "And you would tell them where to find me, Charlie?" he asked with a sly smile.

I looked him in the eye. "If they were giving me the business, Henry, the way they did Warren Ulrick, and I knew where to find you, you're damn right I would. You should have stuck to the bargain."

"I see," he said. "Well, we can't let that happen." He produced his billfold and handed me his card. "You're an honest man, Charlie," he said with that bemused grin. "I should be Diogenes. Here's my address, in case they snatch you. Drop in whenever you're in the neighborhood."

He made an unlikely Diogenes, but maybe con men do search for honest men. I handed the card to Strunk. He confirmed with a solemn nod that it was indeed Stein's address. I pocketed the card without giving it a further glance.

"Of course, if they snatch you, Charlie, it won't much matter what you have to give them," he said with a strained smile.

"I realize that, Henry."

"I've dealt with wiseguys before. As long as the family's safe, I can deal with Pesce," he mused with a grave face. "Marion and the kids can visit relatives out of state until this thing blows over."

I believed him when he said he had dealt with wiseguys before. He had Pesce made for a wiseguy from the get-go. I had to hand it to the little man, he was a gutsy guy. He lived by his wits, cool and cynically detached. If something went wrong, he'd hang tough and leave a rich widow. He might not be able to hide from Mr. Fish, but it wouldn't do Mr.

Fish much good to catch him either. He'd get nothing from Henry Stein. Even though Stein was a thief, bigtime, and a snitch, I found him irresistible. Living is a murky business at best.

"Let me give you a description of Little Anthony's playmate, Shawn," I said. "He's a good-looking, big blond kid. He wears his hair flat on top, long on the sides. He sports a pair of gold hoops in one ear. He drives a dark green Datsun 280Z. You won't have any trouble recognizing him, he's bigger than an NFL linebacker."

"He doesn't sound like the type who could get lost in a crowd. I'll keep an eye out for him," Stein promised.

"Do it, Henry. The guy's a sociopath. He carries a gravity blade and a long-barreled .22 automatic, but he could kill you bare-handed," I said.

"Like Warren?" said Stein.

"Like Warren," I said.

Strunk looked unhappy. "You said you believed he was carrying. How do you know what the guy carries?"

I told them about my rumble with Shawn at the laundromat.

Strunk was not amused. "That was a stupid thing you did, Byrne. You should have called the cops. That's what they're there for."

"There was a warrant out on Hungerford," I said lamely. "If I had called the cops, they'd have arrested him. After what Stein and I had done to the guy, I felt I owed him a break."

Stein had that bemused grin on his face again.

"That's exactly the kind of shit I don't want to hear," said Strunk. "You didn't owe Hungerford a thing. He's a crook. You must think you're still a CIA cowboy, Byrne."

"You're right, P.C. But I did get a chance to hear Hungerford's version of the story."

"Oh, yeah?" said Strunk.

Stein's broad dome knitted with interest.

"Yeah. He admitted to me it was a Ponzi."

"Amazing," Strunk scoffed.

Stein was bemused, but alert, especially when I got to the part where Sloane began steering friends to Hungerford."

"And one of these friends was Pesce," said Stein.

"Of course," I said. "Hungerford and Sloane were in

176

business. He paid her a commission for steering her friends to him."

"Of course," said Stein. "But a wiseguy like Anthony Pesce wasn't going to be content with what Hungerford was paying the other investors. He was going to want a special rate. And soon, between the demands of the broad, and the arm twisting he was getting from the wiseguy, poor Hungerford found himself drifting into the hole."

"You've heard this story, Henry?" I asked.

"How many times have I heard this story?" he said.

"It's a common tale?"

"Uh-huh."

"Shall I continue?"

"Please."

"Well, then he started fooling with stocks he knew nothing about, trying to play catch-up. And most of these investments went south on him. He managed all the while to keep up a good front, though. Sloane and Pesce never suspected how desperate the situation was. But then came October nineteenth, Black Monday, and—"

Stein cut me off. "Don't listen to a word of this, P.C.," he grinned. He switched his gaze to me. His eyes glittered. "Hungerford now sees me as his last chance to get even. He plunges, and he loses. So he splits, and the rest is history."

"More or less," I conceded. "No one likes a know-it-all, Henry."

"When Hungerford split," said Stein, "that was the first sign of trouble Sloane and Pesce had?"

"There wasn't a hint of trouble until Hungerford disappeared," I said. "Hungerford kept up the front right to the very end."

"Are there any other wiseguys in the picture besides the kid, Shawn?" asked Stein, stonyfaced.

"I doubt the mob's involved in this one, Henry," said Strunk. "This guy, Pesce, is a black sheep. My guess is that the Hungerford scam was his own private hustle."

"When Pesce had Hungerford snatched upstate, he used a cop and a fireman for muscle," I said. "And it was just he and Shawn running the show at the laundromat, and again when they visited my place with Sloane."

"So it looks like there's only the two of them then," Stein mused with a mirthless grin.

177

"That's what I think," I said.

Stein's plate was clean, I noticed, as was Strunk's, and the serving bowls. It wasn't bad grub, but I was still picking at my food. I pushed my plate away. I wasn't hungry.

Strunk eyed my plate. "Didn't your mama make you clean your plate when you were a pup?" he said.

"Only when there was food on it. You want mine, P.C.?"

He regarded me with disdain.

"I thought it was better than usual, P.C.," said Stein, hailing the waiter. "One check, please," he said. "This one's on me, fellas."

"What did it come to, Henry? I wouldn't want it getting around I'm on the pad with you," Strunk cracked.

She called later that afternoon. I was at my desk, phoning clients, halfheartedly attempting to drum up business. Between calls, I fingered Stein's card and thought about his parting shot after lunch. I picked it up on the second ring, said hello, and there she was.

"Where have you been, lover? I've missed you. Why haven't you called?" Sloane complained in a silken voice, her intonation mock-plaintive. "Am I going to see you again?"

Heady stuff—if you like domination.

She succeeded in making me feel guilty and horny in the same breath. "Of course," I answered quickly. She'd had a lot of practice at this kind of stuff. Who knows how many guys it worked on before? I could think of a couple right off the bat, and even though I ought to know better, it wasn't entirely wasted on me. "I've missed you, too. I really want to see you, Sloane," I found myself explaining. "But I've got to go on location for the next few days. I'll call the minute I get back."

"Promise?"

"That's a promise."

"All right, then," she agreed hastily. "Charlie—?"

"Yes?"

"I really want you tonight," she said, her voice husky.

Uh-huh. "I want you, too, baby," I lied.

She was working on me, hard. The question was why? Sloane had that gift for making men think they wanted her, had to have her, or that they could have her, which is not

178

always the same thing. Men like Hungerford and Philolius, tangled in the wanting and the having, forgot to ask themselves what Sloane wanted. And she counted on that. When it came time to find out what Sloane wanted, it was too late. They'd been had and that was not a mistake I intended to make. There's nothing for nothing in Sloane's world.

There were a couple of answers to the question of what Sloane wanted from me, and none of them had anything to do with my services as a stud. Like Stein, I took her because I could have her. And because she was the consolation prize for Ginny. The problem was, what to do with her after I had her? The answer? Go on location. Most people take a sick day when they feel like copping out. Photographers go on location.

I didn't know how long, and I wasn't taking a camera. But it was no lie, I was going on location. I'd made up my mind after lunch with Stein and Strunk. When I quoted Joe Louis, Little Anthony's favorite philosopher, to Stein, "he can run, but he sure can't hide," Stein had replied with a dry smile, "Sure you can. But who wants to be looking over their shoulder forever?" Pesce said the same thing about Hungerford. I didn't know what Stein intended to do about them, but I didn't intend to be a sitting duck for Pesce and Shawn. *I* wasn't going to look over my shoulder forever.

I sent Tito home early, went to Avis, and rented a two-tone brown Dodge Dart, and aimed it at the Fifty-ninth Street Bridge. It was too early for rush-hour traffic and I made good time, hitting Long Island City by four o'clock.

There was no sign of Pesce or Shawn at the laundromat, only a handful of neighborhood people doing their wash. I nosed the Dart out into traffic and drove to the health club.

It was in the basement of a commercial building at Twenty-fifth Avenue and Fiftieth Street. A small black awning, over what had once been a service entrance, bore the legend "Muscle Mania" in pink, sans serif type. Parked smack dab in front of the place was the Datsun 280Z. The nearest place I could find to park was around the block.

I walked back to the corner, and parked myself in the pizza parlor across the street. From there I kept an eye on the gym through the big plate-glass window while I munched a slice and washed it down with a Coke.

Muscle Mania's clientele seemed very young. No one

older than thirty-five, I'd guess. That made me feel good. The men had that puffed-up, inflated look that bodybuilders have. For some reason they made me think of the balloons in the Macy's Turkey Day parade. The women seemed to be mostly soubrette types, dressed in leotards, Reeboks, and bulky sweaters. They were cute, bouncing along on the balls of their feet. How much could one of these little girls press? Or is it pump? I wondered. I had no idea, but they were very appealing. I could have cleaned and jerked every one of them.

I finished the slice and the Coke. The idea of going back for seconds came under the heading of wretched excess, so I was forced to move on. I ducked into the drugstore across the avenue for a moment and purchased a pair of sunglasses, aviator style, what I imagined a bodybuilder would wear. Looking as if I was, as they say, "happening" in my new shades, I headed for Muscle Mania. A long hallway, lit by neon and done in pink and charcoal, brought me to the head of a flight of stairs leading to the basement. A mural-size blowup of Shawn, greased and pumped up in a jockstrap, posed against the skyline of Manhattan, was on display at the head of the stairs. I studied it: a low-angle shot—the colossus effect—making him larger than even the Twin Towers. The skewed perspective, unfortunately, also made his head appear too small for his bulky body. Not that this was necessarily a distortion in Shawn's case; it's a whole lot easier to pump iron than brains. I had to hand it to the kid, though. If beef was your thing, the kid was a hunk.

Tacked to the wall next to the blowup of Shawn was the headsheet of a modeling agency. The Muscle Mania Model Works was the unlikely name of the agency. I'd never heard of them, not that that meant anything. Nevertheless, there they were, the dudes and dolls of Muscle Mania, busting out of their spandex, in poses that looked as painful as they were awe-inspiring. While I was occupied scrutinizing the assorted pecs, delts, and lats, a couple on their way out tossed me a skeptical glance.

An airlock of swing doors delivered me into what seemed the inner sanctum, a single large room. On my right was a counter where you signed in, picked up your locker key, bought vitamins and steroids, posing briefs, body oils, depilatories, and the other sundries of the beefcake game. A bulletin board kept track of the club's standings in various competitions, offered used weights and muscle-manufacturing machines for sale, and advertised photographers specializing in bodybuilder's glossies and portfolios. A market for my own wares that I had neglected, and would probably continue to neglect. There was also a machine where one could test one's body-fat-to-muscle ratio.

On my left were a couple of sheetrocked cubicles that served as offices. One had Shawn's name on the door. Straight ahead, open to public view, was the gym itself, and all the paraphernalia and gizmos one could wish for in pursuit of a better bod. Floor-to-ceiling mirrors covered all the available wall space. The lockers and showers were out of sight somewhere. I wondered if they were co-ed. I wondered if this crowd would even notice.

There seemed to be as many people milling about the foyer as actually working out. It was a busy place. And I could see over the heads of these people, most of them anyway, men included. I decided bodybuilding was a short person's form of compensating.

A couple rode side by side on exercise bikes, chatting away happily. A tiny girl, lying invitingly on her back, legs spread, hoisted a barbell in each hand in rapid motion, grimacing as she did so. No pain, no gain. I noticed another pony flexing her calves, thighs, and buttocks for an attentive guy. I tried hard not to gawk as I felt a stirring in the groin.

Shawn was working out, too. Right in plain view, which was where I wanted him. There was nothing short about him, I was reminded again, except in the head. He was also horizontal, on a floormat. He wore shorts and sneakers, no socks. His toes were hooked under a bar as he did high-speed sit-ups. Sweat glistened on him, and his stomach muscles, when contracted, looked like a stack of sandbags. I was tempted to stroll over and bounce a barbell off his head, as I suspected he might have done to Warren Ulrick's foot. He'd never even see me coming. I was well out of his field of vision. Not that it mattered. He was so enthralled with the sit-ups, I doubt that if I hit him in the gourd with a sledgehammer it would get his attention.

"Can I help you?" said the girl at the counter. She was as bright as a button with biceps the size of apricots, and tits that were not much bigger.

181

"You may, and you can," I replied, mindful I was in Queens. "Tell me honestly now, do you think I'm too old to develop a bod like, oh, shall we say, that fellow over there?" I pointed to the blur of perpetual motion that was Shawn.

Sensing a possible membership sale, she answered diplomatically: "You're never too old to improve yourself."

"You are so right. But if I exercised for a thousand years, I'd never look like that hunk, I'm afraid." I broke my wrist and pointed at Shawn again. Shawn continued to rise and fall as mindlessly as an elevator.

A film came over the girl's eyes. "That's Shawn, he's a special—"

"He's gorgeous," I interrupted her.

"I was gonna say, Shawn's a special case. He's an athlete. He competes," she said loftily. Her eyes narrowed. "Are you interested in an exercise class, sir?"

"Well, actually I'm more interested in—I hope this is the correct term for it—pumping a dumbbell?"

That did it for Miss Biceps. Chilling me with a frosty glare, she turned on her heel. I watched as she whispered in the ear of a guy with biceps the size of cantaloupes. He scowled back at me. I smiled diffidently at him. Then he started in my direction, fire in his eyes. I entertained, momentarily, the notion of testing with my fist the ratio of bone to glass in his jaw, and decided better. Short of that, it seemed as propitious a time as any to spin. Which I did. Shawn, I noticed in a backward glance, was still whacking away at the old sit-ups.

I returned to the car, found a spot closer to the club, and parked. Shawn emerged about an hour later draped in earth-colored threads, and carrying a canvas totebag containing his soiled jockstraps, I supposed.

I tailed the Datsun to a townhouse complex in Long Beach. The name on the mailbox said Pesce. I wondered if Shawn's dad was home. It was hard to imagine wiseguys keeping regular hours, and it was even harder to imagine that these birds had roosted for the night.

There was someone else I wanted to look in on while I had the car. I debated whether I should wait or not.

I stuck it out, and was glad I did. My watch read ten o'clock when *père et fils* exited the townhouse and climbed into the Datsun. I tailed them through light traffic out to the

Long Island Expressway. When they turned east, I didn't bother to tail them any further. I was going east myself, so it seemed we were of similar minds.

The lights were still on, the curtains drawn, when I parked the Dart across the street from 578 Midas Drive, Sagaponack, just after midnight. It had been a long time since the Coke and slice of pizza, and my stomach grumbled in Serbo-Croatian.

First, one shadow played across the curtains, disappeared, then a moment later came back again. Another shadow, a smaller one, repeated the pattern. Then the glare of headlights caromed off my rearview mirror, and I had to slide down in the seat until the car cruised by. I cranked myself back up in time to see the green Datsun Z roll up the block and make a leisurely left turn at the corner.

I started the car and turned the headlights on the silver BMW in Hungerford's driveway. I noted the license plate number, and just barely had time to repark when the Datsun swung around the corner for a second casual pass. The silhouettes of a man, presumably Hungerford, and a woman, presumably his wife, reappeared from opposite sides of the window frame. The Datsun paused to watch the shadow show. The figures merged, seemingly engaged in a struggle. The smaller silhouette broke free and smacked the large silhouette in the face. The large silhouette, in turn, belted the smaller one and it sank out of frame. The large silhouette then moved out of frame. Several seconds later, the lights went out and the Hungerfords had presumably retired for the night. The Datsun rolled on.

I tried to get comfortable in the front seat of the Dart. It was going to be one long miserable night. I cursed my low-rent mentality. I was cold, hungry, and cramped and the stakeout had just begun. Why hadn't I had the foresight to spring for a medium-size, instead of a compact? Why hadn't I had the foresight to bring a bottle to pee in?

What was I doing camped out in a toy car, freezing my ass off playing gumshoe, I asked myself?

I was here because I'd let Ginny Rowen suck me up the exhaust pipe with a hard-luck story about her financial planner.

I was here because I wanted to play Lochinvar.

And I did. I protected Ginny from a Ponzi scam. Which was another reason why I was here.

But those reasons were all smoke now. I was here because Warren Ulrick was dead. I was here because Pesce meant business. I was here because I had to be here. I didn't want to be looking over my shoulder all the time. I wanted to save my life. And finally, I guess, I was here because everybody's got to be someplace.

Kicking around the cosmic question—"Why am I here?"—was a yawn and I finally dozed off.

Dawn ambushed me in mid-dream. Ginny and I were out bike riding. Then we were at the laundromat. It was just starting to get good. We were tearing the clothes off each other and stuffing them into a washing machine when the first rays of daylight snuffed the dream. I awoke resentfully, in an evil mood. I was as twisted as a pretzel in the front seat of a Dodge Dart, at five o'clock in the morning, when I should be home in bed. Then I remembered why I was here. I jerked myself up in the seat. The BMW was still sitting in the driveway. And the Datsun was back, parked down the block, discreetly out of sight of the house.

"Pesce and Shawn, those faggots, probably had a circle jerk, and some shuteye in a nice warm motel before going out on the morning shift," I complained out loud, picking the sleepers from my eyes.

I snuck a glance at Hungerford's single-level contemporary. A modest house by any standards, and a modest neighborhood as well, I noticed. No doubt about it, Hungerford lived better in town.

And then, all at once, there he was.

I laughed a little as Pesce and Shawn slid down in their seats, disappearing.

I made myself small, too, continuing to keep an eye on Hungerford.

He was dressed in a gray business suit and a poplin raincoat. It was overcast. He carried a leather attaché case. He was followed to the door by a gray-haired, faded-looking woman in a housecoat. She appeared far too frail to have put up the tussle the smaller silhouette put up last night. She watched impassively as he got into his BMW. The light was blue to begin with, so it was difficult to be certain, but I

thought her cheek appeared discolored. The morning still-
ness was broken when Hungerford put the key in the
ignition. He backed out of the driveway and onto the street.
He drove off without so much as a wave to the woman. She
waited until he was out of sight, then she went back inside,
slamming the door after her.

The Datsun came to life. I hesitated before starting the
Dart, and it hesitated before it caught, coughing like a
chronic smoker climbing out of bed. We formed a stately
procession to the Long Island Expressway, where
Hungerford turned west toward New York, and so did we
all.

The morning rush-hour traffic made it easier keeping tabs
on both cars without drawing attention to myself. I was
grateful for that, but I would have been even more grateful
for a hot cup of coffee. Instead, I had to settle for drive-time
radio to wake me up. I couldn't hack that for long, though,
so I shut the radio off and concentrated on my driving.

Hungerford bore right on an off ramp and we were
traveling north on the Van Wyck Expressway. We were on
our way to Kennedy Airport, I realized.

The Datsun was nowhere in sight when I parked fifty
yards or so from the BMW in the airport lot. I saw
Hungerford dash for the Eastern Airlines Terminal.

I decided to chance it.

I slapped on the sunglasses and followed. The Datsun sat
on the off ramp to the terminal, Shawn at the wheel, my
peripheral vision informed me. I hustled after Hungerford.
He went directly to the gate, presented a boarding pass and
entered the aircraft. Nice timing. Only a black family called
it closer, arriving after him. Eastern flight 209 to Jamaica, it
said above the gate.

I hung back. Pesce had to be somewhere in the vicinity.
Sure enough, no sooner did the gate close than Pesce was
there. I stayed put. I saw the purser palm the bill. He ran a
finger down his clipboard, and spoke to Pesce. Pesce nodded
and left.

I went to try my luck. Twenty bucks ought to do it, I
thought. I folded the bill and held it between my index and
middle fingers. "Hey, pal, wait a second."

He turned, clipboard tucked under arm. He was an

average-looking guy, medium height, medium build, early thirties, the way airline personnel tend to look, average. An average, bribable man.

I reached out. "How ya doing?" I said. He felt the bill in the palm of his extended hand. The lights went on in his average brown eyes. "The big man, gray suit, overcoat and attaché case, got on just before the black family—got a name for him?" I asked.

He glanced at the denomination of the bill. He didn't need to consult the manifest a second time. "H. Andrew Richards," he said.

"Thanks."

"Well, thank you," he grinned.

I had a feeling Pesce had scored for a ten-spot.

Was this a business trip, a few days at most, or had he flown the coop for good, I wondered. He carried no luggage, only the attaché case. What did that mean? Not much, probably.

I went to the reservation counter of Eastern, and checked the return flights from Jamaica for that evening, and the following day. I was sure Pesce had done the same thing. The Datsun was gone when I made my way back to the Dart.

"You look like something the cat dragged in," Tito observed cheerfully, as we stepped into the elevator in the lobby that Friday morning. "Been out partying all night?"

"Sure," I said.

"That nightlife's no life for the working man." He smiled.

"Yeah, I feel like something the cat dragged in."

Tito brewed up a pot of strong coffee and I waited avidly for the first mug. We examined some test exposures from the previous day and I made a few suggestions. Then I got on the horn to Strunk.

"He's traveling under the name of H. Andrew Richards, P.C.," I said.

"They always do that."

"Do what?"

"Pick an alias that's a family name, or a variation of their own name. Original, huh?"

"Easier to remember, I suppose. Why do people play their birthday when they play Lotto?"

"How hard can it be to remember your alias?"

186

"You've got a point there. Can your office get the passenger lists for these flights, P.C.?"

"Let's have 'em."

I read off Eastern's flights from Jamaica.

"I'll see what I can do."

"Also, if it's possible, P.C.," I said, "can you check the offshore banks in the area for an account in Hungerford's name, or in the name of his alias, and any other variations you can come up with?"

"A tall order, Byrne."

"I realize that."

"I can do it, though. It's possible we'll turn up something. But there isn't much time. I'll have to get right on it."

"I can't ask for more than that, P.C."

"Later, Byrne," he said and hung up.

After the night I'd had, I had to crash for a couple of hours. Tito woke me up at noon. Strunk was on the line.

"I have a return on H. Andrew Richards, Eastern flight 213. Arrives Kennedy, 7 P.M. Saturday," he said.

"That's great, P.C. Were you able to find where his account was?"

"Not so good in that department. There was nothing under his name, his alias, the one we know of, or any variations we could come up with."

I was thinking aloud. "He's going for the money, the stash, I know it. There's got to be an account—"

"Something familiar," Strunk suggested, helpfully. "His kid's name, maybe? The wife?"

"You can scratch that," I said.

"The family dog?"

"Don't know if he has a dog."

"His mother-in-law?"

"No, but keep going. What else can you think of?"

"How about where he lives? Good Christ, Byrne!" he exploded in frustration. "What is this shit anyway? What kind of game are we playing here?"

"Did you say where he lives?" I latched right on to that idea. "I think you hit it, P.C. See what you can find under Midas, Midas Ltd., Midas Holdings, Midas Inc., anything with the name Midas in it."

"Like in touch, and muffler?"

"Yes. He lives on Midas Drive."

"It's worth a shot. I'll run it down and get back to you."

It was another couple of hours before he called back. "I've got a Midas Universal, S.A., out of Panama, in a Cayman Island bank," he said.

"Damn," I muttered.

"Wait a minute, Byrne, that could be him," said Strunk. "If he's slick and making the right moves, he just might register a corporate name in one country and then bank under that name in another country. It would give him one more layer of protection."

"Well, if it *is* him, there's gonna be a substantial withdrawal, and pronto."

"I can check that out."

"You can?"

"Easy, as long as we've got the name of the account and the bank. They balk at first. Give you a lot of horseshit about confidentiality, but as soon as I tell 'em we're going through all their transactions for the last six months with a fine-tooth comb, they become very gregarious. Amazing what a little intimidation will do!" He chuckled.

"You can do that?"

"We're the law, Byrne, we can do anything. Well, almost anything. Banks all have something to hide. What my office can't do, the SEC can. They don't want either one of us nosing around their business if they can help it."

I was sitting down to an omelette and a Heineken on Saturday at one o'clock in the afternoon, when Strunk called back.

"Midas Universal, S.A., out of Panama, had a four-hundred-and-ninety-thousand-dollar withdrawal Friday afternoon, Byrne. Account closed," he said, laconically.

At 6:45 P.M. I was at Kennedy watching Eastern flight 213 passengers disembark. No Hungerford. I checked information. I was told 213 was the last flight from Jamaica today. Had I heard Strunk right? Yes, that was the flight. Had Hungerford changed his itinerary? Possibly. He was trickier than I imagined. A hidy-hole with half a million stashed in it. A Panamanian corporation with a secret Cayman Island account. Hungerford had a devious mind.

I'd kept an eye peeled for Pesce, but evidently he wasn't

wasting any time on flight 213 because he was nowhere to be seen. I wondered if the party was out at Sagaponack. My heart sank at the idea of having to hump out there again.

On the off chance that Hungerford's return wasn't scheduled until Sunday, I detoured through the parking lot. The BMW was still parked there.

And so was Hungerford. He was in the driver's seat, his head thrown back against the headrest, like he was asleep. Or so I thought, until I saw his eyes were open. I walked around the car and looked in from the passenger side. There was a clean puncture in his right temple. A purplish bead of blood glittered in the garish light of the sodium vapor lamps. The car was locked. His hands were at his sides. The right hand clutched a .22 pistol. I looked for a bundle big enough to be half a million bucks, but all I saw was Hungerford, profoundly still, asleep with his eyes wide open, and the gun. Whoever did it wanted it to look like a suicide. That didn't seem to me to be wiseguy style.

I went back to the terminal and dialed 911. I told them where they could find the body and hung up.

Chapter 15

Heitor Villa-Lobos transposed a photograph of the Manhattan skyline to the music staff, substituting notes for buildings, and composed a symphony. That was in the Forties, a lifetime ago. Another time, another city. As the last feeble light of day bleakly filtered through the gaps in the new and incandescent skyline that loomed before me, I wondered how Manhattan would sound to Villa-Lobos tonight.

To me, Manhattan sounded like the goofy do-wop music on the car radio. I had the heater on full blast, but my bones could still feel a cold, damp night hunkering down on the city.

I couldn't shake from my mind the image of Hungerford, entombed in the BMW, as though doomed to an eternity of Interstates.

No one ought to die for money.

But they do, and all the time.

Money is a killer.

It killed the professor and his wife.

It killed Warren Ulrick.

And it had killed Hungerford in the end.

Hungerford had been playing slo-pitch until he met Sloane. From then on it was hardball. And that was way out of his league. Somewhere between the on-deck circle and the batter's box, he had given some thought to the late innings. The hidy-hole, the Midas Universal account demonstrated that. Then they started throwing at his head. There was nowhere to hide. He had to run. He got around the bases, but he got tagged out trying to steal home.

As another sage of sport once said, "It ain't over until it's over." And this ballgame was going into extra innings. Pesce may or may not have killed Hungerford. My guess was someone beat him to it. But assuming for the moment that it was Pesce, he'd never be satisfied with Hungerford's half a million. Hungerford was just a piece of unfinished business to Pesce. Pride and honor had to be considered when dealing with a wiseguy. Pesce wanted Stein more than ever. Stein was the final out. But I was the guy at bat.

They played "My Boyfriend's Back" on the radio. I wasn't feeling so young anymore, but the night was still young. Saturday night. I didn't want to be alone tonight. I thought about calling Ginny. "Forget about it," I said out loud.

But there it was again, that same feeling. Like after the car bombing. The nearness, the immutability of death. Hungerford's corpse winking at me, mocking me. And I felt that urgency, that need to reaffirm that I was still among the quick. Death was nothing but an old lewd slut, and I was ashamed of the power she had over me. But I wanted to get laid.

I called Ginny the minute I got back in the studio.

"Charlie, what a nice surprise," she chirped.

"Yeah, listen, Ginny, are you free tonight?"

"You might have called a little earlier, turkey."

"I know, but I didn't know whether I'd be free."

"Really. I'm flattered."

"No, no, that isn't what I meant. I was on a job. I didn't expect to wrap it as soon as I did. How about tomorrow night then, whadda you say?"

"Tomorrow night? Hmm, let me see . . . you sound desperate, Charlie." She giggled.

"I am."

"Well, I'm not free . . ."

"You're not?"

"But I'm reasonable."

"Funny girl. I'll see you tomorrow then."

"Goodnight, Charlie."

Nice try, pal. Should I have played for her sympathy, told her about Hungerford, and that I was the one who found him? It wouldn't have worked. That would only have made her uptight, like after the car bombing. I was glad I hadn't told her. But I was going to have to be careful how and when I broke the news.

I entertained the idea, only momentarily, of doing some bar crawling and seeing what I could pick up, but I dropped it as too depressing. There was the consolation that tomorrow night I could celebrate the life force, which was more than poor Hungerford could do.

Meanwhile, there was always the Lejeune.

Madison Avenue was dead on Saturday night. And who needed that? So I rode up Sixth Avenue instead. It was about nine o'clock, and the strip from Forty-second to Fifty-ninth Streets was alive with people. All kinds of people. Some of them even loners, like me. They were doing ordinary things, like jogging which, like sex, seemed to be something city people did around the clock, bike riding, and going for the Sunday *Times*. Couples were on their way to clubs and movies. Others were peddling—things like junk jewelry, cheap watches, handbags, remaindered books, mechanical toys, novelties, drugs, and themselves.

The heavy traffic and crowded streets made the going slow. My leg muscles knotted in protest against the damp, numbing weather, and riding the bike was laborious, like bucking a powerful and constant headwind. I shifted to a lower gear to increase the torque and make my legs work

191

faster. It helped me generate some heat. When I entered the park, I shifted back to a higher gear and picked up speed. The leg muscles were gradually loosening up, and the snap and elasticity were returning.

I was pleased to find Mike, and a gang of hardcore, all-weather bikers lounging on the benches in their usual spot behind Tavern On The Green. I pulled over and joined them.

"How you doing, pal?" Mike greeted me, impassively.

"I'm doing all right. How about you?"

"I'm okay."

There was a dispute raging among them about Greg LeMond's comeback chances. The majority opinion seemed to like his chances. Mike kept his opinion to himself.

"Like to give it a shot yourself, huh?" I said.

"What do you think?" he said. His gaze was fixed on a stretch limo dropping off a party at the restaurant. The women were in gowns, the men in tuxedos. They were probably about seventy yards away, but they might as well have been on the far side of the moon. That was the look in Mike's eye. Money makes the world go round, even on a bicycle.

"How do you think you'd do?" I asked.

"I could make a team," he said solemnly, a simple statement of fact.

I believed him. "All you need's a sponsor, huh?"

"Yeah," he said laconically, not much interested in this line of patter. "Had a visit from a cop the other day. At home. He asked about you."

"Hannibal?"

"I think that was his name."

"What did you tell him?"

"I told him the truth."

"I would have done the same thing."

He smiled faintly. "The stiff they pulled out of the Ramble last week?"

"What about him?"

"Did you know the guy?"

"I knew him."

"That's what the cop was all about, wasn't it?"

"You tell me."

192

"Yeah, that's what I thought." He gave me a curious glance. "The green Datsun was here again, tonight," he said.

"What time was that?"

"Earlier, around eight o'clock. It was the same Datsun that was hassling you the day before the stiff turned up."

"Yeah, I know."

He paused, giving me a hard look. He seemed to be making up his mind about me. "It's too cold to sit around here all night," he said finally. "Let's go for a ride."

When he stood up, everyone stood up. I didn't count, but there must have been more than twenty of us. A guy on a Cannonade went out in front, and played rabbit.

It was understood. This was a heat.

Be prepared for more than ten laps, something told me. I hung next to Mike, in the middle of the pack, where the better riders slipstreamed behind the leaders.

The sensation was as close to flying as you could hope to come without wings and feathers. More than twenty bodies hurtling through space at the same velocity, in the same direction, and then changing direction in unison, a lean right, a lean left, rising and falling with the contours of the earth. Instinctually, like a single being, we moved in complex patterns. We were a whole, a flock of swifts. There was communion in being part of this.

We did ten laps grouped nearly in the positions in which we had started. Then the better riders asserted themselves almost reluctantly, and the rabbits fell off the pace. Now they were sprinting.

Mike refused the lead, playing possum. I managed to stay with him for one more lap, then I fell off the pace, hopelessly. Mike must have lapped me twice. But I toughed it out, lungs screaming, a stitch in my side, drenched in sweat, and finished the twenty laps.

Later, Mike and I rode downtown together. I glowed with a natural high, confident I could improve on my performance. I peeled off at Thirty-eighth Street. Showered, skipped supper, and went straight to bed. I felt clean and healthy and lonely. Virtue is a solitary vice. I masturbated and fell asleep, the .32 on my night table.

The next voice I heard was my own. The phone rang in what seemed the middle of the night. The answering machine picked up the call. I lay on my back and listened to my voice recite its message to the caller. At the sound of the beep, a tenor voice with a Boston accent spoke. "Hello, Mr. Byrne. This is Detective Hannibal. Please give me a call." He left a phone number and hung up.

I sat up. The illuminated face of the clock-radio read seven-thirty. Seven-thirty A.M. o'clock, Sunday fucking morning. I flopped back on the bed and stared at the ceiling. The room was still dark. I couldn't see a thing. I wondered about this cop. Was he a lonesome guy? Was he always on the case? Didn't he have a family? The phone rang again. I didn't budge. It was Strunk. Call him, he said, and left a number. I continued my blind inspection of the ceiling. The phone rang a third time. I stayed put. It was Stein this time. He wanted a call.

Grudgingly, I dragged myself out of bed. I shambled downstairs and put on the coffee. I'd be damned if I'd talk to anyone before I had a cup of coffee. While the coffee brewed, I took a shower. On the way to the bathroom, I flicked off the answering machine. This was not smart. But it was barely the crack of dawn, and it's a rare day I'm even half smart any sooner than noon. The phone rang for the fourth time as I was shaving, and working on a second cup of coffee, and getting smart.

"Give it a rest," I grumbled. I reached the phone after a dozen rings and juggled the receiver, switching hands too late to avoid the side of my face still lathered. "Hullo," I said.

"Charlie?"

"Yeah."

"It's me, Sloane."

"Sloane, yeah," I mumbled dumbly.

"Charlie, I've got to see you."

"Ah—"

"Now."

"Sloane, I—"

"I can't talk. There's a coffee shop on the corner of Eighty-sixth and Third. Meet me there. Half an hour." She hung up.

"Sloane, Sloane," I called after her in frustration, waggling the receiver button hopelessly. What was that all about? Had she just learned that Hungerford was dead? It was a long way till noon, and two cups of coffee hadn't even made me half smart yet. The exchange had been so brief you could read almost anything into it. Did she sound frightened? Was that a cry for help? Or was I being summoned? Or was it all of these? All my befuddled brain knew for sure was she sounded urgent.

I topped off my coffee, and returned Strunk's call. He told me Hungerford was dead. I told him I knew that. He asked if I had done it.

"What for?" I said.

"The money."

"Forget about it."

"Forget about half a million?"

"P.C., he wasn't on flight 213."

"Uh-huh."

"Gotta run, P.C. Call you later."

"Goodbye, Byrne," he said.

I dialed Hannibal. "Detective Hannibal?" I said when someone picked up the receiver.

"This is Hannibal."

"Charlie Byrne. You called."

"Yes, Mr. Byrne. Have you heard about Richard Hungerford?"

"Yes."

"Your friends seem to be thinning out lately, Mr. Byrne."

"I was stunned to hear about him, naturally, Detective, but I'd hardly say we were friends. We were barely acquaintances."

"Acquaintances, then," he said reasonably. "In any event, I'd like to ask you a few questions about the deceased."

"Shoot."

"Not on the phone, Mr. Bryne."

I sighed. "Where?"

"Midtown North, three hundred and six West Fifty-fourth."

"When?"

"Now's a good time."

That's what he thought. "All right," I said. "I'll be there within the hour."

"I've got coffee and danish," he said.

I poured my fourth cup of coffee and went upstairs to dress. I chose jeans, Nikes, and a crewneck Shetland sweater as the uniform of the day. Then I called Sloane. But there was no answer, not even a machine. Everyone had a machine, didn't they? She must have gone out and left hers off. I'd tried, I could tell her. What else was I supposed to do? I was being hassled by the cops. Why should I feel I had to make excuses to her? Sloane didn't play straight with anyone. And it wasn't as though I was unhappy about standing her up. I smelled a setup. That was all on the one side, the flip side was that I was dying to know what she wanted.

I stuck my head out the window for a weather check. It was still damp and chilly. The sky was the color of lead and seemed close enough to touch. I pulled on my suede jacket, cap, and yellow scarf, and locked up.

It's weird, I'll grant you, being the only person living in a twelve-story commercial building in midtown Manhattan. As one guest over her orange juice had put it, the "splendid isolation," is definitely not for everyone. After business hours, and on weekends, I'm locked in by two pairs of plate-glass doors, half an inch thick, which bolt into the marble floor. This is ordinarily a very good thing, given the tolerance for street crime these days, and I'm not complaining, mind you. But it does get to be a drag coming and going after hours. You've got to squat to unlock, and then squat again to relock each door separately. If it's weird, even a bit eerie, living in such "splendid isolation," well, it's my life. My studio is my aerie, or at least that's the way I like to think of it.

My key was in the lock of the street door. I was squatting. He stepped up and put the barrel of the .22 pistol to my head. I felt a cold spot where the steel touched my temple. "Hi, guy," he said.

All I could think, absurdly enough, was hawks don't squat, ducks squat. Then he clipped me. And that was the last thought to flap through my brain for a long time.

How much later it was, when consciousness returned with a twitch and a spasm, I didn't know. Instinct warned me not to open my eyes. It would hurt. Light was painful, as painful as the mega-decibel rock-and-roll assaulting my eardrums. I was aware of being upright, almost, of straddling something, my back at forty-five degrees. I smelled stale sweat. I opened

196

my eyes cautiously. They snapped shut again tighter than a spooked clam. Light hurt all right, and so did my head.

I wasn't sleeping, I knew that, but I was having a nightmare.

The afterimage of Shawn was seared in my mind. He was seated opposite me, in shorts and tank top, automatically giving bench press to a humongous barbell.

It was Shawn all right, I could hear him grunting in time with the music as he lifted. I flexed my legs, then my arms. I could twitch, but I couldn't move. My hands were duct-taped to the crossbar of a weight that pinned me to the bench. My feet were taped to weights as well. I sensed that my position mirrored Shawn in attitude, if not in energy.

I tensed the muscles in my legs again, testing them. They seemed to respond normally. I repeated the pattern with my arms and chest. They, too, responded normally. Apparently nothing was broken. I pushed tentatively against the barbell. Excruciating pain crackled like sheet lightning through my skull. I clung unwillingly to the barbell, eyes shut, motionless, waiting for the pain to recede to a dull ache. I probably had a mild concussion, I thought, remembering the clip on the head Shawn had given me. Aside from that, I was in fair enough shape. It's doubtful, though, that I was ever in good enough shape to heft the barbell I was taped to.

I let my eyes open slowly, accepting the pain with the light. Shawn, oblivious in his dedication, continued pumping iron. I watched for several moments. He showed no sign of stopping.

"Got an aspirin?" I asked. It was a lame question. When they were through with me a headache would be the least of my problems. But I felt intuitively the need to say something.

"I'm busy," he grunted, without a glance.

Did that mean I might get some aspirin? I decided against getting my hopes up. I looked around me and waited. I had no other choice. We seemed to be alone. I pushed against the barbell again. The pain didn't seem as bad. And the barbell did budge slightly. It must have weighed two or three hundred pounds, I guessed. I entertained the notion, momentarily, of heaving it at Shawn, assuming I could. But I couldn't risk the weights on my feet pulling me up short, leaving me in a more awkward position than I was already in.

I hadn't been counting, but he must have set a record for whatever the hell it was that he was doing. He eased the barbell onto its rest and snatched up a towel. Muscles rippling, he began wiping off his face, chest, and arms.

"You're in great shape," I said, hoping to establish some kind of rapport.

"Think so?" He smiled, pleased with the compliment.

"Yeah, but I don't have to tell you that."

"I like to take care of myself."

"And by the looks of it, you're doing a good job. Do you compete? You ought to."

"Yeah, I compete," he admitted.

"Uh-huh, I thought so." I nodded at him. "A good-looking guy like you, with that body, you'd be hard to beat. And you're young, just a kid."

He flushed with pleasure. It seemed probable I could establish some kind of rapport with the kid. I had nothing to lose. "I photographed Arnold Schwarzenegger once, you know," I lied.

"Really?" he said, wide-eyed.

"Really."

"What was he like?"

"A nice guy, a real nice guy."

"My friends tell me I look a lot like him."

I gave him the once-over, pretending to make the comparison. He tossed his head obligingly and presented his profile. Then he turned back and smiled at me shyly.

"I can see a resemblance. But you're better-looking," I said, and hoped the kid didn't think I was making a pass at him. Although, on second thought, what was the harm in that? "You must have won something, if you compete. Something local, maybe?"

"Mr. Long Island City," he said modestly.

I tried to look suitably impressed and keep a clamp on my lip. "Keep up the good work, kid, and who knows, next year you could be Mr. Queens," I wanted to say.

"It's a start. You're on your way," I said. "Ah, any chance I could get a couple of aspirin?"

"Got a headache, huh?"

Now how did he know that? "Uh-huh."

"Sure, I'll get you some aspirin."

He went to the counter where the vitamins and the steroids were stocked. Then he went to the watercooler and filled a paper cup with water. He hand-fed me two aspirin and held the paper cup to my lips for me to drink.

"Thanks," I said. It was a relief to know that I wasn't going to die from a migraine. But now what? On the subject of bodybuilding, I was a lightweight. I couldn't hope to engage a pinhead on the topic for very long.

Luckily, the kid bailed me out.

"When you photographed Arnold Schwarzenegger, ah . . ."

"Yes?" I said eagerly.

"What kinda picture was it?"

"What kind of picture?"

"Yeah, was it a portrait . . . or did he actually pump up?"

"Oh, I see what you mean. He pumped up."

"Yeah?"

"Yeah, it was a series of photos actually. He went through his whole routine for me, the same one he uses in competition."

"That's neat."

"Yeah, it was like having a front-row-center seat."

"He's like God."

"He's unbelievable, a real showman. He knows how to get his business across to the judges."

"That's so important."

"I guess it is. He told me he worked with his music and mirrors as much as he did with his weights." I couldn't believe this conversation, but we seemed to be getting along famously.

"I know exactly what he means. I've been working my buns off on my routine. I even got a choreographer. Hey, wanna see my routine?"

Now there was an idea. What did I have to lose? "Sure, I'd love to," I said, "if it's not too much trouble." How long could I hope to keep this balloon in the air? And was this the last thing I'd see before I died? I wondered.

"No trouble, handsome." He pinched my cheek. "You're kinda cute, ya know. You gotta nice body. You oughta lift. Don't go away, I'll be right back."

"Take your time, I'm not going anywhere."

He giggled and disappeared behind a mirrored door.

I waited and worried that Shawn and I were getting on too well.

Shawn reappeared, oiled and in posing briefs, tits and buns jiggling. The music changed from rock to disco. He cleared himself a small stage a few feet in front of me. He tapped time with his foot, waiting, then on the beat he struck a pose. Arms up and flexed, he stood facing me. He swung from this pose into Atlas with the world on his shoulders. Compliments of his choreographer, he moved from this pose, with a small dance step, into a pose designed to show off his dorsal development.

I had to yell to be heard over the blare of the stereo. "Marvelous . . . looking good . . . fantastic . . . that's really hot," I yelled with each change of pose.

Watching him do his routine reminded me of Sloane. There was no doubt that my cheers turned him on. With each encouragement, he'd hold the pose a little longer, until he quivered. Whether they wear a jockstrap or a G-string, an exhibitionist is an exhibitionist.

He faced me now, full frontal, as they say, and grinning, winking his pecs in double and triple time. All he needed were tassels.

"The phone," I yelled. It must have been ringing for a while before I finally heard it.

"Shit!" he said, deflating. "Well, you get the idea." He dashed for the phone.

"That was great, kid, just great," I yelled at his back. "Thanks for sharing that with me." I worked my hands furiously on the bar, trying to stretch the duct tape, trying to create a little play.

Shawn rejected the cassette on the stereo and grabbed the phone. My poor head went right on throbbing to the beat. He glanced my way, his lips moved, and he nodded his head, but I couldn't hear what was said, and he didn't waste any time on the phone.

"That was Fat Tony." He giggled impishly at his own temerity. "He'll be here in a few minutes. We're gonna have some fun then"—he grinned malevolently, his eyes shone knowingly—"know what I mean?"

I think I did.

He casually swung a leg over the bench, straddling it and

my legs. He made a fist, and I stiffened in anticipation. He cocked his arm and unloaded. I tried to brace myself, but the bench held me in a firm position for the blow. I took it in the solar plexus, and nearly passed out.

Then the gravity blade was in his hand, its point under my chin. His face was too close to mine. With steady pressure on the blade, he forced me to lift my face to his. "I like you, you're one cool dude," he grinned. "You took Arnie Schwarzenegger's picture, didn't you, dude?"

"Lots of people have taken his picture," I said.

"I know," he said, and gave me a humorless laugh, shaking his head in wonder. "Man, you can sure talk some shit, pal."

He smacked me across the face with the flat of the blade. I rolled my head with the motion of his hand. My cheek felt a rush of warmth, then it tickled. He threw the blade between my legs. It made impact with a dull sound, and stuck in the bench, vibrating momentarily.

He wrapped his big hands around the crossbar, working them to get a good grip.

"Lift!" he ordered me.

I shook my head weakly. "I can't," I protested.

"Pussy," he said, with a contemptuous laugh.

He set his feet, twisting first one, then the other, on the concrete floor, like a batter digging in at the plate. Then he jerked the barbell from its rest to his chest. My arms followed loosely, coming alive like a puppet on a string. He flexed his knees, setting to lift, crossbar under his chin.

"Hup!" he shouted, expelling air. The cords in his neck bulged, his face reddened.

I uncoiled from the bench, arms rigid. The momentum was mine. I heaved against him, aiming the crossbar for his jaw. He threw his head back to avoid it, and his legs buckled. There was a flicker of shock and fear in his eyes before he toppled over backward. I rode him down to the floor. His head struck the concrete with a solid and satisfying sound. He didn't move after that.

The impetus of the barbell had pulled me forward. I was on all fours, my groin in Shawn's unconscious face, gnawing feverishly with my teeth on the duct tape binding my right hand. The sweat poured off me while I worked. I had only one thought in mind, please don't let Fat Tony find me like this. The tape gave gradually. There was more and more play with each pull. Then there was a tear, and another tear. I could slide my hands together on the bar. Suddenly my right hand came free. I turned for the gravity blade, but it was beyond my reach. Frantic, I clawed my left hand free of the barbell. I reached for the blade again. I got it this time and cut the weights from my feet.

I climbed unsteadily to my feet, clutching the blade. If I met Pesce on my way out I didn't want to be empty-handed. I reeled, like a drunk, through the gym, catching a glimpse of myself in a mirror. My cheek was bleeding. I rubbed it with my hand. It wasn't deep, only a nick, long but shallow. The blood made it look worse than it was. I found my cap and jacket in the reception area. There were clean towels on the countertop. I helped myself to one and fled.

Chapter 16

Outside, on the street, I inhaled deeply and winced, waiting patiently for the pain that exploded in my chest to subside. The fresh air was cool and sweet after the gamy atmosphere of the gym.

I checked my ribs. There was nothing broken, although it felt as though I had been kicked by a mule. I tested my skull and found a gummy spot where Shawn had clipped me. I examined my fingertips. They felt tacky, but there was no blood. I dabbed at my face with the towel. My cheek continued to bleed, but it was like a razor cut, more annoying than serious.

I must have looked fairly disreputable, like someone in a drug or alcohol stupor, propped up against the building, fumbling with myself, because a dowdy woman, dressed in her Sunday best, fixed me with a baleful glare as she mother-henned her brood of brats around me.

I glanced at my watch. It was only eleven o'clock, still morning. Have a nice day, pal. I needed to regroup.

I dragged myself to a neighborhood bar, and climbed upon a stool at the end of a scarred and stained oak bar. Except for the short and stocky, sixty-year-old bartender, the joint was empty. He cast a skeptical glance in my direction and kept at what he had been doing when I came in, which appeared to be setting up for business with the Sunday afternoon regulars. I put an elbow on the bar and held the towel to my cheek. My gaze wandered through the tubing of the neon taproom sign and out the window. One lone bus breezed by, but otherwise the street was emptier than an Edward Hopper painting and as desolate as my mood.

He must have decided I wasn't going to go away if he ignored me, because he finally approached, drying his hands on his apron. "Help ya, bud?" he said.

"A cup of coffee . . . and a bourbon," I said.

He went away, returning with a cup of coffee in one hand, a bottle of bourbon in the other. He slid the cup across the bar to me, spoon in the saucer. From under the bar he brought up a shotglass and poured.

"How ya take it?" he asked. The bar sugar bowl was poised in his hand.

I waved him off. "Black's fine," I said.

He put the bowl back under the bar. "Hope ya don't want nothin' ta eat. Kitchen's closed. Da cook, he don't come in 'til noon."

What was the matter with this guy anyway? I wondered. Wasn't it obvious that I was postoperative? That I was recovering from abdominal surgery? Hadn't I just had a fist removed from my intestines? Food? The thought of it made me want to puke. "It's all right," I said. "I'm on a caffeine and alcohol diet."

He gazed at me impassively and unamused, waiting. I got his drift. I reached for my wallet, pulled out a ten and put it on the bar. He nodded, wrapped one meaty paw around the neck of the bourbon bottle, and picked up the bill with the other. He went to the cash register, rang it up, and returned to shove a five and three singles across the bar at me. I let them lie there. I might want a refill.

I sipped the bourbon. It was cheap, and possibly watered. I sipped the coffee, it was half chicory and bitter, but it was hot. They both burned going down, giving me reason to believe I was doing something good for myself. My head ached and my guts hurt, but I was improving. They ached and hurt less than they had half an hour ago. I was going to live.

The question was, how long? The next time Pesce and his pal got their mitts on me I wouldn't be so lucky.

There was a definite tremor in my hand as I helped myself to another, more liberal dose, first a slug of bourbon, then a swallow of coffee, of my medicine. Feeling steadier now, I asked the bartender for change of a single. In the rear of the joint I found a pair of wall phones separating the "lads" from the "lassies" rooms. I dropped a quarter in the slot of the nearest one and dialed.

"Detective Hannibal?"

"This is Hannibal."

"Charlie Byrne, Detective."

"What happened to you, Byrne? I've been waiting."

"Sorry, Detective, but I don't think I can make it today. I'm not feeling so hot."

"A little sudden, Byrne."

"Yeah, I know."

"Nothing serious, I hope?"

"No, it's nothing serious. Look, you sure we can't do this by phone?"

"I'm sure."

"Well, when then?"

"As soon as is convenient for you, Byrne."

It would never be convenient, but it could be soon. "How about tomorrow, ten A.M.?" I said arbitrarily.

"How about at your studio?"

"If that's convenient for you."

"That'll be fine. See you then, Byrne."

They would solve the professor's murder accidentally, when they were working on another case, I remembered him saying. From my perspective, it was beginning to look like he had more than a fair shot at fulfilling that prediction. Counting the professor's wife, he had four unsolved homicides that were linked. All he had to do was his donkey work, it seemed to me. Mine wasn't the only list of friends thinning out lately.

Proximity to the "lads" room gave me an urge. I bellied up to the porcelain with a mixture of curiosity and dread. My relief was double when I saw a clear, yellow stream, but then it had only been the one punch, and that wasn't in the kidneys.

I returned to the phones, dropped another quarter in the slot, and dialed Stein. He picked up on the fourth ring.

"Henry, it's Charlie. You called."

"Yeah. Hungerford bought it, did you hear?"

"I phoned it in."

"They're calling it an 'apparent suicide.' How did it look to you?"

"'Apparent' is the operative word. He was shot in the right temple, probably by the gun he had in his right hand, a .22 caliber automatic."

"The passenger side, huh?"

"Yeah, he knew his killer, or killers. They tidied up before they left. And you were right about the hidy-hole. He had just returned from the Bahamas carrying half a million dollars in cool cash."

"Did you whack him, Charlie?"

"Yeah, Henry, I whacked him. I was a little short on my IRA and Keogh money."

Stein chuckled.

"I wasn't the only one on Hungerford's case," I said.

"No?"

"No. Mr. Fish and the lovely Shawn were tailing him too."

"But if they whacked him, why would they bother making it look like suicide?" Stein asked. "That doesn't sound like their style."

"I agree. But it's on the record that Pesce and Hungerford had dealings. Maybe they thought whacking him gangland style would be like leaving a calling card. This way it seems Hungerford was despondent over his troubles and decided to end it all. There's no reason to think that there was robbery involved, and they walk off with the money, no questions asked, case closed."

"Sounds good, Charlie. But take it from me, if Pesce did

it, he wouldn't bother making it look like suicide," said Stein. "But her nibs? Now that's another story."

"I knew you were going to say that, Henry."

"Then you must have had the same idea."

"I have," I admitted. "But if Pesce didn't whack Hungerford, I doubt he's gonna think of Sloane first, when he hears about it."

Stein gave me a hollow laugh. "He's gonna think you were the one who whacked him and took the money. I expect you'll be hearing from Mr. Fish momentarily."

"I've got news for you, Henry, I already have." I told him all about my aerobics class at Muscle Mania with Mr. Shawn.

He was quiet when I finished, then he said: "Well, my friend, we'll have to think of something, won't we?"

"Yeah, Henry, I'll think of something, my health."

"Good idea," he said cheerfully. "And while you're at it, Charlie, keep a tight behind."

"Goodbye, Henry."

"Stay in touch."

"I'm gonna try."

I went back to the bar and finished the bourbon. I took a swallow of coffee. The coffee had grown cold. I ordered a refill on both. In rapid succession, I administered several more doses of the good medicine.

I thought about Stein. Stein was interested in his own self-preservation, that came first. And I hardly blamed him. It was one thing we had in common. He didn't call this morning to tell me Hungerford had bought it. That was just a pretext. He figured I was Pesce's next piece of business. He was keeping tabs on me. He was curious about the condition of my health. What had he meant when he said, "We'll have to think of something"? My money said he had already thought of something. But he wasn't giving anything away, not that schemer.

I motioned to the bartender and asked him to break the five-dollar bill. He did it out of his pocket. I pushed two bucks back at him. "T'anks," he said.

I went to the phones again, dialed Sloane, and got her machine. While I waited through her recorded greeting and instructions, I tried to picture her sitting in the coffee shop, still waiting for me. Say what?

"Sloane, this is Charlie," I said to her machine. "I'm sorry about this morning. I was on my way to meet you when I was run over by a fruit truck. I'm all right, though. I'll call you later." I wondered if she'd find that humorous.

What next? I had no agenda, hidden or otherwise. Until my date with Ginny, I was at loose ends. I could visit Sloane—sooner or later, I would have to, anyway. But if she wasn't home, why waste the trip? Now that I had his address, I could pay Stein a visit. In spite of the invitation, I wasn't sure how welcome I'd be. He didn't need me to babysit him, and then I'd only have to turn around and come back to the city later. I rejected that idea. What made the most sense, as much as I hated to admit it, was to tail the muscle boys again. If it didn't exactly steal a march on them, it couldn't hurt to know where they were and what they were up to.

I did none of the above. Instead I beat it back to the studio, my aerie. Whether I liked it or not, it seemed to be dwindling down to the waiting game. Waiting for Mr. Fish. Why not wait in comfort? And more important, why not wait where the gun was?

The cab dropped me at the corner, and I walked the fifty yards or so west to my building. This time I was more cautious before squatting. I made damn sure the street was empty. Even so the flesh on the back of my neck crawled as I unlocked the door, and I didn't feel safe until I had both sets of glass doors locked. Upstairs, once again secure, I played back the answering machine before I took off my jacket and cap.

"Charlie, what the hell happened to you? I waited over an hour for you. I've got to talk to you. It's important. Where are you anyway?" The machine clipped short, with an angry hang-up, Sloane's dulcet voice.

I dialed her number and got a busy signal. Someone was home. Didn't she have call-waiting? Moments later, I tried again without connecting. No answer, and no machine either. Had she gotten my message?

And was her call for real? Because if it was, it meant she hadn't set me up for Shawn. And it meant I was becoming paranoid.

I tried her once more and got no answer. If she was so hot

to hear from me, how come her machine wasn't on? Could it be that when she picked up my message, she realized there had been a glitch? Had I accidentally tipped her that Shawn muffed the job? Was she devious enough to cover her tracks by leaving that message on my machine? She was good, real good—indignation had dripped from her voice. Could she be a better actress than I'd given her credit for? The paranoid in me answered these questions, yes, yes, yes, and yes.

The night was cold, and I wore an overcoat. The deep pockets easily concealed the .32 revolver. After locking up with the utmost discretion, I walked to Twenty-third Street and Lexington, where I stomped around in the cold waiting impatiently for Ginny under the marquee of the Gramercy Theater.

Maybe it was crazy, going out on a movie date when there were a pair of wiseguys out there looking to feed my nuts to me, but I liked the idea. I liked it for its ordinariness. I thought I did, anyway. Where the hell was Ginny? Jesus, I hoped Pesce hadn't snatched her. He'd like to use her to get at me. I sighed with relief when I spotted her slamming a cab door across the street. I wanted her with me. She was safer with me. So far, so good—life must go on, even under siege. So we went to the movies.

I sat through the film in a daze, my mind unable to concentrate. The movie seemed to be about a married man who has a fling with a wacky career woman who càn't, or won't, take no for an answer. If she can't have him, no one's going to have him. An apocryphal tale, the point of which seemed to be that there was no such thing as safe sex.

After the movie we went to Caliban's on Third Avenue. The ambience—exposed brick walls, an L-shaped, burnt umber bar, a proper brass footrail, and sepia-toned lighting —was spare, but warm, elegant even, in an uncluttered way. It's more of a saloon than a restaurant, although there is a small dining room in the rear, and the food is decent. The bar was being propped up by three or four regulars, and besides ourselves, there was only one other couple having dinner, but then it was Sunday night.

My system was hollering for protein, and I ordered a bruised sirloin steak. Ginny had chicken breasts with a lemon sauce. As we ate, I reluctantly told her about Hungerford. She absorbed the news calmly enough, if somewhat grim-faced. "The poor man," she murmured, her green eyes dark and downcast, her mouth a thin line.

"Yeah," I agreed, "but he hurt a lot of little people with what he did."

"I suppose something like this was bound to happen," she said evenly.

"He was in way over his head . . . and with a rougher crowd than he knew." I was glad to see she was taking the news so well.

She continued to eat, listening to me ramble on about tailing Hungerford, the bank account in the Bahamas, and the half a million dollars he was carrying when he died. She was hungry and cleaned her plate. Over coffee and brandy, she drew a comparison between Hungerford and Sloane, and the movie we had just seen. Life imitates art, or is it the other way around? It was an apt comparison though. One way or another, Sloane had been the death of Hungerford.

We paid the bill and left the restaurant. On the street, waiting to hail a cab, I found myself looking over my shoulder from time to time, and touching the pocket of my overcoat where the .32 lay buried. It didn't take that long—only a short eternity—until we finally caught a cab and piled in. With some relief, I gave the driver Ginny's address. When she snuggled up to me with a glance, slipped her arm through mine, and took my hand in both of hers, I wondered how obvious it was that I was spooked.

We rode in silence through deserted streets, turning south on Seventh Avenue. I was staring out the window when the cab stopped for a light before making the right on Ginny's block.

He'd stick out in a parade of mummers. He couldn't be inconspicuous if he tried. It was Golden Boy, his complexion sallow, his hair almost green in the garish, blue light of the Korean convenience store. He was dressed down tonight in faded, tailored jeans, white sneakers, and a pink-and-black sateen Muscle Mania team jacket, standing under the urethane awning, head tilted back, guzzling a carton of orange juice. A Korean woman, seated on a milk crate arranging fruit, looked up at him with a mixture of awe and loathing.

"Shawn!" Ginny exclaimed when she spotted him.

"Yeah," I said. I held her, shielding our faces from him. The cab turned the corner. "Driver, forget about this stop," I said. "Give me Thirty-eighth and Fifth. Go up Sixth Avenue, okay?"

"You're the boss," the old guy behind the wheel said. Unperturbed, he breezed past Ginny's brownstone. "Ya want I should turn on Seventh?"

"That'll be fine," I said. I looked, but didn't see the Datsun. It was enough to have seen Shawn.

"Charlie, what's the matter with my place?" said Ginny.

"I'd rather not go there with him hanging around."

"This is crazy! You mean because of him, I can't go to my own apartment?"

"It isn't safe, Ginny."

"Why? Just because Shawn's in the neighborhood?"

"It's no coincidence he's hanging around your neighborhood. The guy's not just out cruising." I told her about my morning workout at Muscle Mania.

She slumped back in the seat, hugging herself, her eyes fixed on the street ahead. "What about the police? What about 911?" she protested.

"You want to take your chances with them? They don't protect you, they just clean up the mess."

"God! How long is this going to go on? I can't be living in constant fear of my life."

"I know," I said mildly.

She pulled at her hair with an anxious hand. "I've got a life to live," she said sullenly.

"Is there any place you could go for a few days? Preferably out of town."

She groaned at that suggestion.

"Think about it," I said. The cab made a right on Thirty-eighth Street. "Go slow, driver," I said. He obliged. We rolled leisurely up the block to Fifth Avenue. I studied both sides of the street. There wasn't a soul in sight. The block appeared desolate. We left the cab at Fifth and walked back to the studio. I gripped the revolver deep in my pocket.

I had no problem with the big glass doors this trip. I handled them quickly and smoothly. Ginny watched the procedure with curiosity, stepping lightly through each set

210

of doors in turn and into the foyer. "Are we safe now?" she asked, as I straightened up from locking the last door.

"I think so," I said, pressing the elevator button. The doors of both the elevators flew open, saluting us. I ushered her into the one on our left.

We faced each other, backs against opposite, narrow walls. She gazed at me with an earnest face, the slight overbite lending her sober expression a faintly comical aspect. She ran her tongue pensively across her teeth. "Friends?" she asked, favoring me with a small version of the lopsided grin.

If that was the way she wanted it. "Sure, friends," I said.

"Good." She moved to me. "Still want me . . . like you did last night?"

"Yeah." It was obvious to both of us when our bodies touched.

She rubbed against me. "Ah-ha, you are glad to see me," she grinned. "Lucky me. And lucky you."

"Hmm, I know."

"I mean lucky you I'm not like Sloane."

"How's that?"

"I'm not trouble, like she is. I like men," she gloated.

I returned the grin she gave me without flinching. She pulled my face to hers. Our mouths met and we kissed, our tongues playing tag like a couple of seals in the surf, until the door of the elevator opened on my floor.

"I've got a little surprise for you tonight, Charlie," she said, as I turned the key in the lock.

"Do you?"

"Yes," she promised, with a wicked smile. "You're in for a treat. I want you to take me upstairs, now." She took my hand and led the way.

"What could it be?" I said, following.

She smiled enigmatically.

We undressed one another hurriedly. The surprise turned out to be a black garter belt, attached to the sheer stockings and the heels she was wearing. I reached for her panties, but she pushed me away. I fell back on the bed, propping myself up on my elbows, my eyes riveted on her. She stepped nonchalantly out of her panties and took a stance.

"Well," she demanded, "does this do anything for you?"

"You must be blind."

She giggled. "Aren't guys supposed to be crazy about girls in garter belts?"

"I'm crazy about you. Can't you see?"

Her mood changed to serious. She stepped back and pirouetted, as a runway model might do, letting me have the full effect of her slim body and coltish legs in the gear. I wanted her at that moment, and I lunged.

She sidestepped me easily.

"Not so fast," she said, shoving me roughly back on the bed. "I want to do it to you. My treat." She was astride my chest in one silky motion, hair and breasts in my face. Her lips found mine, then they moved to my chest, and stomach. She worked herself to the edge of the bed and, kneeling, took my cock in her mouth. When I glanced down, she stared back at me.

Heels and all, she climbed back on the bed when she was finished with me, and spread her legs. "Do me now," she said. "And take your time."

"Yes, Ms. Rowen," I mumbled.

"I shaved my legs specially for you," she cackled softly, and squirmed against my face.

Afterwards, before we fell asleep, I asked again if there wasn't some place she could go for the next few days. She thought for a moment, then replied, "I suppose I could go to Florida. I've got some work there that I could do."

Ah, the architect, I thought. "I'll make a reservation on Eastern for you first thing in the morning," I said. "Don't go home, not even to pack. You can buy what you need down there."

"Yes, Mr. Byrne," she murmured sleepily.

"You'll leave from here. We'll phone for a cab to take you straight to the airport."

She tried, in the morning, to give me an argument about going. She was worried about me, she said. She didn't want to leave me alone. I told her that Detective Hannibal would be here in an hour, and Tito sooner than that. I'd be all right. The best thing she could do, if she really wanted to help, was stay out of harm's way. I could look out for myself, but not for both of us. She gave me a skeptical glance, but she let me hustle her into the waiting cab. Call me, I said. She'd call me tonight, she said. I watched the cab pull away, then I walked over to Madison Avenue and picked up the *Times* and a pint of half-and-half.

Upstairs again, I scooped up the mail from outside my door. I had my key in the lock when the second elevator arrived and deposited Pesce and Shawn on the floor.

"Good morning, Charlie," Pesce said amiably.

I was disgusted with myself. That was twice now I'd been caught flatfooted by them. "What do you want, Anthony?"

Shawn moved to block the stairwell. I was doing a swell job of looking out for myself so far.

"Not a morning person, huh?" Pesce grinned. "Actually, I want to apologize for the—er, misunderstanding yesterday."

"What misunderstanding? I don't remember any misunderstanding."

"Maybe not, but then you ran off before we had a chance to talk. Before I got there, in fact."

"Cut the bullshit, Anthony. What do you want?"

"To apologize . . . for Shawn." He smiled.

"Okay, apology accepted."

"Aren't you gonna ask us in?"

"No."

"I apologized, didn't I? Don't be rude."

Shawn grinned and breathed through his mouth.

"You want to talk?" I asked.

"Yes, as a matter of fact." He made a sweeping gesture with his hand. "But not out here, like this. This is not the place to talk."

"I'll be the judge of that. What have we got to talk about?"

"Aw, ya see, Tony," said Shawn. "What did I tell you. He's a wiseguy."

"Shawn's impetuous," Pesce said, gazing fondly on his adopted son momentarily.

And eager to play catch-up, I was thinking. "I know," I said. "Isn't he a little young for you, Tony?"

Shawn smirked.

"I like 'em young. Don't you, Charlie? Now be nice, and invite us in."

"Fuck off."

Shawn advanced. Pesce restrained him with a touch of his hand. "There's no need for that kind of language. Invite us in."

"I said, fuck off." The last thing I wanted was for Shawn to get his hands on me. A body punch would be useless, but a shot to the head might slow him down. He went out easy enough yesterday.

"Charlie, Charlie," intoned Pesce, "I'm losing patience with you. Be a good fellow. Invite us in, or Shawn is going to rip your fucking face off."

Shawn beamed at the prospect.

I had two pretty good reasons already for letting them in. That made three. "Well, why didn't you say so?" I turned the key and stood aside. "Come on in."

They exchanged smiles and entered.

It was almost nine-thirty, and Tito was overdue. That was reason number one. Reason number two for my change of heart was the ten o'clock appointment with Detective Hannibal. I hoped he was punctual. If I still had a face when he arrived, it would give me great pleasure to introduce him to the steroid queens.

"I wouldn't say no to a cup of that marvelous coffee of yours," said Pesce.

"By all means," I said politely. "How about you, Shawn?"

He shook his head.

I poured two mugs, and handed one of them to Pesce. We adjourned to the lounge. Shawn remained standing, engrossed in the sudden discovery of a hangnail. Pesce made himself comfortable on the couch. He took a long, slow sip of coffee. "Ah, very good," he said.

"It's El Pico," I said. "Glad you like it. Now, what would you like to talk about?"

"You've got something that belongs to me," Pesce said, after a dramatic pause.

Shawn gazed impassively at me.

"Oh? And what might that be?" I asked.

"Five hundred thousand dollars," Pesce said, leveling his sardonic eyes on me.

"How do you figure that?"

"I figure that was what Hungerford was carrying when he got back from his trip to the Bahamas."

214

"But Hungerford's dead."

"I know that."

"And you think I killed him?"

"Who else?"

"Who else? How about you guys?"

Pesce smiled and placed his palm on his chest. *"Moi?* I'm afraid you'll have to do better than that, Charlie."

"What makes you think it was me?"

He and Shawn exchanged glances. "Did you spend a comfortable night in the front seat of that compact?"

"Okay, you spotted me, what's that prove? You guys were tailing him too. You probably even knew that he switched planes, and landed sooner than expected."

Pesce sipped his coffee, then put the half-filled mug down on the table. He stood up and smoothed the lapels of his jacket. "All I know is Hungerford's dead, and you've got the money," he said. "All you need to know is you've got twenty-four hours to come up with five hundred thousand dollars."

I jumped to my feet. Shawn shoved me back in the chair. Where the hell were Tito and that cop? "Hey, wait a minute, fellas," I said, "let's talk about this."

"What is there to say, Charlie, except that you've got twenty-four hours to come up with the money. That's all," said Pesce. "Oh, there is one more thing . . . but never mind. It will keep."

He was playing with me, he thought, but I wanted to keep him talking if I could. "Tell me, what is it? I wanna know."

"I said, it will keep."

"Listen, Tony, what if I didn't do it? What if I haven't got the money? Have you thought of that?"

"Frankly, no," Pesce replied. "Nor do I want to."

"That would be ugly," Shawn added solemnly. They gazed at me without pity, like I was so low on the food chain I didn't matter.

"Besides," said Pesce, "if you didn't kill Hungerford, and you don't have the money, then Henry Stein killed him, and he's got the money. Unfortunately for you, from my point of view, it's all the same."

The sound of Tito's key in the lock startled them. "Expecting someone?" demanded Shawn.

"My assistant."

"The little Rican? No sweat," he said.

But there were two voices when the door opened.

"Good morning, Mr. Byrne," said the detective, appearing from behind Tito. His eyes darted from Shawn to Pesce to me. "I'm early. Hope I'm not interrupting anything?"

I got to my feet with a smile and took the hand he offered. "You're not interrupting a thing," I said. "In fact your timing couldn't be better. These are a couple of gentlemen you ought to meet, and they were just about to leave."

Shawn glanced at Pesce, but Pesce was busy studying Hannibal.

Tito grinned furiously, like a Mexican bandit.

With a gesture toward Pesce, I began the introductions. "This is Anthony Pesce," I said. "And this is, er . . . his son, Shawn." I beamed at Shawn. "It is Shawn Pesce, isn't it?" I asked innocently.

"Stuff it, asshole," he said.

Pesce silenced Shawn with a look. He knew a cop when he saw one.

Hannibal smiled pleasantly and studied the contrasting Mediterranean sleekness of the father, and the Nordic bulk of the son.

"Never mind," I said, with a sly glance at the father, "Pesce, or Hauser, it's not important. What's important is that Mr. Pesce, and his, er, son, were also friends of the late Richard Hungerford."

"Is that so?" said Hannibal.

"Yes," I beamed.

"Who's this guy?" said Shawn, glowering at the cop.

"Be quiet," snapped Pesce.

Shawn gave Pesce a sullen look.

"I was just coming to that," I said. "Anthony, I'd like you to meet Detective Edward Hannibal, NYPD, homicide. He's investigating the deaths of Warren Ulrick, Richard Hungerford, and Professor Louis Leveau, and his wife, Marie."

I wish I could say that the law put the visegrips on Pesce, but that's not the way it was. The wiseguy's brush with the law was a bust in the instant gratification department. Pesce was more than adequate to the occasion. Affable and relaxed, he urbanely pumped the hand of the cop, and assured him that he'd be delighted to assist him in every way possible.

"Feel free to call anytime," he said grandly, and he passed his card to Hannibal.

"Thanks, I will," said Hannibal, with a glance at the card. He tucked it into his notebook.

Pesce pivoted in triumph from the cop to me. "And I'll expect my pictures tomorrow morning, then, Charlie," he said with a significant wink. "Come, Shawn."

Shawn backed off, then turned and followed his father. Tito grinned and showed them to the door. I grinned too. A tip of the hat to Pesce for grace under pressure.

I offered Hannibal coffee, tea, milk, and club soda, and got four refusals. A hard man to bribe. Why did I have the feeling I was about to get the blocks put to me?

"Did you have a pleasant weekend, Byrne?" he asked, after settling on the couch.

I preferred Mr. Byrne. "Why don't you call me Charlie," I said.

"If you like."

"I wouldn't characterize the weekend as pleasant."

"How, then? Interesting?"

"Yeah, that, and busy. You said you have a few questions?"

"Yes."

"Before you start, Detective, you said you'd solve the professor's murder when you were working on another case, remember?"

"It happens that way sometimes."

"Yeah, well, those were prophetic words, Detective," I said. I had to go on the offensive. Before he read me my Miranda, I wanted to get in a few allegations of my own. "You just shook hands with the professor's killers, and for that matter, Warren Ulrick's killers."

He raised his eyebrows in mild astonishment and smiled disarmingly. "Really? They seemed like such nice guys. Why would they want to kill all those people?" He watched me with cold, piercing eyes.

I waded into the deep water. "The professor suspected Hungerford was running a Ponzi scheme. He told me this at a party at Hungerford and his girlfriend's just before he died. He was unhappy. He was worried about his money, and intended to go public with his suspicions. Pesce killed him to prevent this."

"Why would Pesce care if Hungerford was running a Ponzi scheme?"

"Because he, and the girlfriend, Sloane Marshall, were steering investors to Hungerford for a commission."

"But if they thought Hungerford was legitimate, there was nothing wrong with that."

"Maybe, but Pesce was an investor too, and he wasn't in it for the interest. It was vigorish he wanted. He was bleeding the guy. He and the girlfriend had a good thing in Hungerford, and they were making the most of it."

"Why did they kill Ulrick?"

This was a tricky question. "I'm not sure, but I'd guess they thought Ulrick and Hungerford had scammed them somehow." That answer had a grain of truth in it. It sounded plausible. And I left Stein and myself out of it. So far so good.

"And Hungerford?" he asked, with a flinty smile. "Got an opinion on who killed him?"

If Pesce hadn't killed him, and apparently he hadn't, he had tossed me a screwball. It was getting messy. There were too many killers. "Not yet," I said.

"I see," he said dryly, then he launched into a line of donkey questions. The facts, just gimme the facts: "Where were you Saturday evening at seven o'clock?"—"Then where did you go?"—"What did you do there?"—"Anyone who can testify they saw you there?"

I answered all but one question truthfully. I had been closer to Hungerford's corpse Saturday night than I could afford to admit. I told Hannibal that I was scouting a location at that time.

Eyes glued studiously to his notebook, he scribbled away. I didn't volunteer but rather "cooperated." And I managed not to mention Stein. More for my own protection than his. I also didn't mention that the pictures Pesce expected in the morning were all of Benjamin Franklin. Cops aren't interested in opinions, threats, or allegations. Only the facts. I can understand that, and to my best recollection, I left it at that.

He glanced up at me, signifying the interview was coming

to a conclusion. "Let me read what I've got back to you," he said.

"Go ahead."

I listened carefully while he ran quickly through the list of questions and answers. "Did I get it right?" he asked, impaling me with his cold eyes.

"Yes, you got it right."

He got to his feet. "Well, I'm glad we finally got together, Charlie. You've been very helpful."

"Be sure and take Anthony Pesce up on his generous offer," I said.

"I will, don't worry," he said.

But I did worry.

Chapter 17

As soon as the cop left, I beat it over to Sloane's place. I caught her without her makeup on, but she looked fine anyway, younger, girlish even. "My God," she protested, "I've only just learned about Richard. I needed to talk to someone and I called you." She smoked and paced as she spoke.

"And I got back to you."

"Sure you did," she fumed, heavy on the indignation. "We had a date, remember."

"I just told you what happened," I said.

"Why would Shawn do a thing like that?" she said, blowing smoke. She was wearing a black sweatsuit, and cushy black Reeboks, over the ankle, and fashionably untied.

"Only one reason I can think of."

She swung around, facing me. Her breasts, loose under

the sweatshirt, moved in unison, a beat behind her, as though they were live things. "Oh, and what's that?" she snapped.

"Anthony told him to do it."

She inhaled fiercely. Two quick strides brought her to the coffee table. She stabbed the ashtray with the cigarette butt, and resumed her pacing, arms folded, hugging herself. She looked as good going as coming, better in fact; there was no bluff and bluster going away, only a sweet promise of carnality, her ass moving nicely under the clingy fabric. "Why would Anthony want to have you roughed up?" she asked, as though it were as natural as breathing for Anthony to have people roughed up.

"Because Anthony thinks I killed Richard and stole half a million bucks from him."

Her eyes narrowed, her brow furrowed, her feral teeth flashed stormily. "And you think that I set you up. You think that my call was a setup, is that it?" She wasn't beautiful when she was angry.

"I didn't say that, but you can see how the thought might have crossed my mind. You call. I rush out to meet you. Go to black. When I wake up I find I've joined a health club, and the lovely Mr. Shawn is fixing to work me over. What would you think if you were me?"

She hesitated a moment. "I see how you could think that. It's understandable, I suppose," she said reasonably.

"What are those guys to you anyway?"

She sat down next to me on the sofa. Calmer now, she dropped her chin and gazed up at me with liquid eyes. "They're nothing to me, really. Anthony's an old friend, that's all."

"What's that mean, 'old friend'?" There seemed to be a lot of this friendship stuff going around lately, like the Taiwan flu.

"Just that, he's a dear old friend."

"Is that 'old friend,' as in former lover?"

"Hardly." She smiled. "Charlie, you must believe me when I tell you that I called only because I needed you then. I had no one else to turn to. And I was hurt when you stood me up. I couldn't understand why you would do that." She hesitated, lowering her eyes. "But I understand now."

"Sure," I said. "It was just a misunderstanding." I wasn't buying a word she said.

She raised her eyes innocently to mine. "Why would Anthony think you killed Richard?"

I stared at her blank face. "What you mean is, did I kill Richard, right?"

She averted her eyes, but not before I caught a trace of a smile. Her phone rang, and she jumped to answer it. I stood up, meaning to leave as soon as she was off the phone.

This was the third time that I'd been here, the night of the big party, the night I picked her up for dinner, and now. Either she was in the midst of redecorating, or, now that she and Richard no longer entertained, the place was getting a lived-in look. There was a quirkier, chaotic appearance about the apartment now. The Bloomingdale room set perfection was a thing of the past.

The nude effigy had been deposed. It leaned facing the wall, at the start of a long wait until it became old enough to be new again. Its place had been usurped by a painting of what looked like the leftovers of a psychopathic artist's meager lunch. It had been gouged out of black, chrome yellow, orange, and vermilion with a mad palette knife.

Sloane stood beneath the painting, at a glass table resting on chrome sawhorses, which served as a makeshift desk. She held up her end of a cryptic phone conversation with repetitions of yes and no, never referring to the party by name, and tossing me a helpless look indicating they wouldn't stop talking. Near the table were a couple of Channel Thirteen tote bags, and one of those luggage caddies. Just the thing for hauling half a million bucks, I thought.

I browsed the book rack beside the desk, waiting for her to wrap up the call. I wondered if it was Little Anthony on the line, as I scanned paperbacks by Follett, Krantz, Updike, Steel, Saunders, and Atwood. Their spines were uncracked, but then she probably didn't have much time for reading. There were scripts, too, mimeographed and bound by Studio Duplicating Service, and a collection of slim volumes from Samuel French, plays by William Inge and Tennessee Williams. Good parts for bitches in these plays, I thought. There were also some reference books, dictionaries in French, Italian, and English. And a copy of *The Player's Guide.*

A paper bookmark with the legend "Booksmith, best in paperback and hardcover" protruded from the book. I glanced at Sloane. Her eyes darted away immediately. She had been watching me. Curious, I reached for the book, and it fell open to the page marked.

"Yes, yes, that'll be fine. I said, I'll see you then," she said, irritably to whoever it was on the line, and promptly hung up on them.

I looked down at the open book. Warren Ulrick's picture smiled back at me from the page in a small, two-inch cut next to a brief bio. I closed the book, and casually placed it back on the shelf.

Sloane was braced, and waiting.

Of course, it could only have been her, I'd realized that all along. But now I knew how they found him. I tried to remain calm, and show no anger, no excitement. Let her guess, let her worry, did I catch it, or not? I couldn't see anything to be gained by confronting her.

"You asked why Anthony would think I killed Richard?"

"Yes," she said uncertainly.

"My guess is, for no other reason than he knows *he* didn't kill Richard, and if it wasn't him, than it had to be either Stein or me."

"Yes, Stein," she said hopefully. "He could have done it."

"I don't think so. And I may not be able to convince Anthony, but you can believe it, neither did I."

"I never thought you did."

"Then where does that leave us?"

Her features were composed, the anxiety of a moment ago past. But she enunciated each word, in that soporific voice of hers, as though she'd just popped a downer. "I don't know, where?" she asked.

"Yeah, where?" I repeated, as though puzzled myself. "Over a hundred people had a motive to kill Richard."

"Yes, that's true, I suppose," she agreed, quickly.

"Anyway, I've got to get going," I said. "I'm glad I had a chance to clear up our little misunderstanding."

She brightened considerably. "Me too, Charlie," she said, edging toward the door. "I had no idea what could have happened to you the other day."

"Let's forget about the other day, okay?"

"That's fine with me," she said, guiding me to the door.

"And, Sloane," I said, pausing at the door, "will you put in a good word for me with Anthony?"

She smiled faintly. "I'll try," she said. "If I speak to him." As an afterthought, she pulled me to her and kissed me. I couldn't tell whether she intended it as a demonstration of concern or affection, but I felt as though I had been marked for killing.

I hopped a cab on Park Avenue, anxious to get back to the studio, and on the phone to Stein. Sloane, I imagined, was already on the phone to the Fish.

I didn't have a clue what I was going to do when the time ran out and Pesce didn't have his portraits of Ben Franklin. Hang tough, I guessed, and see what developed. But then I talked it over with Stein. He wanted to take the initiative. He had a plan.

"What have you got to lose, Charlie?" he asked, after sketching out his plan.

"Just my ass."

"There you go. That's the right attitude."

"What I don't get is, how come you're so hot to risk yours, Henry?"

"I'm not," he replied cheerfully. "But what am I gonna do, let you twist in the wind? Besides, I like to meet trouble head on."

His plan was that I should arrange a meeting with Pesce, who would naturally be delighted to see Stein. He'd demand that Stein hand over the money swindled from Hungerford. We'd grease Pesce with a hundred grand or so, pleading we needed time to raise the rest of the cash. Meanwhile, Stein would be wearing a wire in hopes of getting Pesce to incriminate himself, particularly regarding the matter of Warren Ulrick's murder. We'd accomplish two things with Stein's plan. One, we'd buy time to plan our next move. And two, if the wire idea proved fruitful, we'd have something to use on Pesce and Shawn.

My fervent hope was to keep as much space between the Fish and myself as I could manage, but I hadn't been able to manage at all so far. Since that wasn't much of a plan, I let Stein convince me that his was the better way to go. One thing was sure, when it came to dealing with the Fish, I didn't mind having Stein's company.

At seven o'clock the next morning, Stein and I were sitting in his Volvo station wagon outside of Muscle Mania, with two Halliburton aluminum suitcases full of money. And Stein was wearing a wire for our scheduled power breakfast with the firm of Pesce & Son.

"Ready?" Stein asked, his broad mouth set between a grin and a grimace.

"Let's go," I said. We climbed out of the car. I attempted to appease a coffee-acid stomach with the wistful notion that Little Anthony would soon be incriminating himself pell-mell on Henry's tape recorder. That was the plan, wasn't it? My stomach didn't seem to find that notion especially soothing. I hoped that wasn't a gut reaction to our strategy.

"Here, take one of these," said Stein, bouncing ebulliently on the balls of his feet, and handing one of the suitcases to me. He wheeled and strolled off cockily for the entrance of the gym.

As I trailed him, I wondered what Stein was so pumped up about. Obviously, he didn't realize that if I was supposed to play the muscle of this team, we were still a man and a half short. We were wading, with our eyes wide open, into the big muddy, and the little fool was saying, "Push on." I wished I had thought to bring the damn .32 along. A recurring thought, lately. Hell, I wished I had thought to bring a SWAT team along.

He was wearing a towel over his shoulder and a pair of trunks when he came to the door to let us in. He glistened with the dew of a dawn workout. It was the first time that Stein had laid eyes on the kid, and he gazed at Shawn momentarily with his usual expression of bemusement. Then he rocked on his heels, and reached up and tapped the kid playfully on the biceps with his fist. "Lookin' good, babe," he grinned, continuing to size him up with shrewd eyes.

Shawn, temporarily disarmed by Stein's hubris, gave me an uncertain glance. I returned it with a half smile. Languidly, he gestured, with the barrel of the .22 automatic, in the direction of a mirrored panel in the rear of the gym.

Evidently, Stein had not succeeded in totally disarming him.

It was almost reassuring, though, to see the gun right out in front like that. You should expect to find guns around large amounts of cash. They go together like linguini and clam sauce. But then, dressed as he was, Shawn would have difficulty hiding his comb on his person, let alone a .22 automatic pistol.

With Stein in the lead, Shawn marched us single file to the rear of the gym. "Push," he ordered, when Stein came up against the panel. It swung open to his touch, and we made our way through a narrow passage to the light of an open door.

Pesce, poring over business papers, waited for us there. He looked up at us with hooded eyes. Shuffling the papers, he put them aside. "Come in," he said, and stood up politely as we entered the room. Although he was in his shirt-sleeves, his tie was in place and he was nattily dressed, as always. He might have been an accountant or a lawyer. The remains of half a grapefruit, a glass, and a bottle of designer water sat in front of him on the table. Was this the new Mafia?

I glanced around me, at a room about fifteen by twenty. It featured an oval table that seated ten. In one corner was a Mr. Coffee machine perched on top of a small refrigerator. In another, a TV monitor with a ¾-inch tapedeck. A couple of peepholes for projecting and the place could be an advertising agency conference room. There were a pair of air ducts on the wall, and Johnny Mathis, singing "Chances Are," was being piped in from somewhere.

"Great place for a card game, Tony," said Stein, beaming and rocking on his heels.

Pesce patronized him with an indulgent smile, and turned to me. "I can offer you coffee, not quite as good as yours, Charlie, orange juice, Perrier . . ."

"I'll have a Beck's, if you've got it," said Stein.

"As you wish," said Pesce. He looked inquiringly at me.
"Coffee," I said.

"Please be seated," he said, pointing across the table.

Stein and I sidestepped around the table and took our seats. Stein was on my right. Shawn seated himself opposite me, blocking the doorway. He pulled the towel from his shoulders, folded it neatly, and placed it on the table, then laid the pistol on top of it, folded his arms across his chest, and studied us impassively.

Pesce served us himself. He placed a mug of coffee in front of me, flipped the beer bottle on end, glass over neck, and poured for Stein. Then he resumed his place opposite Stein. There was a round of polite smiles, then we settled down and the meeting came to order.

Pesce's face went dead, devoid of expression. "Well," he intoned, his dark eyes moving slowly from Stein to me, "I believe you have something for me."

"Yeah, we have something for you, Tony," said Stein, doing a bad imitation of a hood. I glanced at him curiously. "We have money for you. That's what you want, isn't it?"

Pesce examined him like he was looking at a bug. "Yes, that's what I want. You're very bright. What money is this that you've brought me?"

"What money?" said Stein.

"Yes, what money? Is this the money you swindled from us, or is this the money Charlie stole from Hungerford?"

"Anthony," I said, "I told you, I didn't kill Hungerford, and I don't have that money."

He waved a hand in the air, as though erasing my words. "Charlie, Charlie, Charlie, I don't want to hear that," said Pesce. And it crossed my mind, inappropriately, that he, too, was doing a bad imitation. Of whom, I wondered?

"I'm sure you don't, and you're gonna want to hear who did kill Hungerford even less," I said.

"All right," he sighed impatiently, "who do you think killed Hungerford?"

"Your friend, Sloane Marshall."

He didn't show a flicker of emotion, other than a slight narrowing of the eyes.

"Sloane?" snickered Shawn in disbelief.

"That's right," I said.

Pesce sighed again, lifting exasperated eyes to the ceiling. "You're reaching now, Charlie, and you know it," he said.

"Why? What's wrong with that?"

"She's my sister, that's what's wrong with that."

"Sloane Marshall?" Strunk had said there was a sister, I recalled.

"That's just a stage name, a professional name, if you will. Her real name is Angela Pesce. Nice try." He smiled.

Angela Pesce, of course! It rang true, like a silver coin on marble. I might have made the connection sooner if Sloane was anyone other than Sloane. I'd made the same mistake everyone probably made. I assumed any relationship Sloane had with a man had to have a sexual basis. I glanced at Stein. His mobile features were a mixture of mild astonishment and bemusement. He answered my glance with a shrug. Pesce and Shawn grinned smugly at us.

"I don't understand—why the mystery, Tony?" said Stein.

"There was no mystery," said Pesce. "We just keep our lives separate. We like it better that way."

Sloane liked it better that way, I thought. No connection to the mob. "But, Anthony, this doesn't change anything," I said. "I'm telling you, she did it. Hungerford was crazy about her. He was still carrying a torch for her. Wasn't that true?"

"What if it was?" he said impassively.

"So he called her. Before he left for the Bahamas. He wanted her back desperately. But the only way he could get her back was if he had money, lots of it. Right?"

"Go on," he said, with a faint smile.

"He told her he had money. Plenty of it. In the Bahamas. Enough money to last the two of them for the rest of their lives. He asked her to run away with him, and she agreed. He said he'd call, and tell her where to meet him. He was going for the money, he told her. He must have known we were following him, because he changed flights to shake us." I paused for emphasis. Shawn and Stein gazed at me in rapt attention. The godfather glowered at me silently from under hooded eyes. I went on. "He called her from the Bahamas and told her what flight he would be on. She was at the gate to meet him. But Sloane never had any intention of running away with him. We all know that this was a case of unrequited love. He was crazy for her, she could take him or leave him.

"The rest was easy. They walk to his car, get in, Sloane pulls a .22 automatic out of her handbag, and pops him. Then she tidies up a bit, and puts the gun in his hand to make it look like a suicide. She hauls a suitcase full of cash out of there on one of those little caddies, and hails a cab back to the city." I paused again.

227

It was very quiet in the room. I could see Shawn was a believer, and Pesce was more than entertaining the notion. The fit was too good. I went for the closing. "It was considerate of her to make it look like suicide, though. If she'd hit him mob style, that would have cast suspicion on you. But she is your sister, after all, even if she doesn't mind doublecrossing you when it comes to a buck."

Shawn's jaw was slack, his eyes darted anxiously to Pesce. Pesce stared silently at me with mordant eyes. It was hard to read him, but I'd put a worm of doubt in his ear. He knew little sister Angie better than anyone. I'd given him something to think about.

"I was there, I found him, Anthony," I said. "Take it from me, only someone who knew him very well could have gotten close enough to pull it off. The cops, with no reason to suspect robbery as a motive, would find suicide plausible, given Hungerford's troubles.

"Sloane couldn't kill a man," Pesce said defensively.

"You don't think so, huh?" I said. "Didn't she order the killing of the professor and his wife? It doesn't seem like much of a jump from that to doing it yourself. I know one thing, you'd never catch me in a parking lot at night with half a million in cash and an appointment with Sloane."

Shawn giggled.

I was talking trash. It was pure speculation on my part, but they didn't know that. And saying it aloud gave it weight and credence. I was guessing, but judging from Pesce's somber presence, I was guessing good.

Sammy Davis was singing "The Candyman Can" on the Muzak, and I marveled at the patina of health *père et fils* exuded: Shawn nearly naked, monumental in scale, glistening; Pesce, in a crisp white shirt, smaller, but radiating energy and power. Their hair and nails were impeccably groomed. Their teeth were bonded. They sported tans that seemed to have been appliquéed. These were details only the excess of disposable income bought. Runty Stein and paunchy me were by comparison a shabby twosome.

"The professor had had enough of Hungerford," I said, filling the void, and hoping one of them would say something incriminating. "He wanted out. He told me so himself. If he didn't get his money back, he was gonna file a complaint with the D.A.'s office. Hungerford had had enough of him, too, but he couldn't pay him off because you guys were bleeding him dry. So he bitched to Sloane about it, and that's when you got the call." I gave Shawn a nod. "Homeboy, here, wired their car while they were at the party, and waited. When they got into the car, he triggered the bomb with a radio remote control, probably from a model airplane kit . . . and boom! That problem was blown away. It was back to business as usual."

A startled Shawn began to speak. Pesce silenced him with a touch. "They want us to talk," he said. He gave me a brief, twisted smile, then he switched his gaze to Stein. "One of them's wearing a wire."

"Hey, Tony, it's no problem," Shawn giggled. "They won't be wearing it when they leave here."

What was I doing here? Why had I listened to Stein? I wondered. I could have handled the situation just as badly on my own.

"Let's hear all of it, Charlie," said Pesce. "What else have you got?"

"Whatever you say. Well, it's obvious if meathead, here"—I nodded again in Shawn's direction . . .

"You're gonna beg me to kill you, pal," Shawn snarled.

"Be quiet," Pesce said to him. He nodded for me to continue.

"As I was saying, if Shawn beat the pudding out of Warren Ulrick, which, of course, is what had happened, the only one who could have fingered him for you guys was Sloane. She was the only one who knew what he looked like. The guy was a prime ham. And she smelled it. She figured out he could be an actor, and checked him out in her copy of *The Player's Guide*. Lo and behold, there he was. Easy meat."

Stein appeared uninterested, totally unconcerned. He was drumming his fingers softly on the desk in boredom, a look of perpetual bemusement on his face. I wondered if the guy had icewater for blood. And I had a sinking feeling that I'd unwittingly let him get me in over my head one more time.

"That's very good, Charlie," Pesce said. He glanced from me to Stein. "Are you rolling tape?"

"Yeah, we're rolling," grinned Stein.

"Good, because I want to be sure you get this down," said

Pesce. He threw up his hands in mock surrender. "We want to confess, don't we, Shawn?"

Shawn emitted a scary titter.

"We did it, Shawn and I. We killed the professor and the actor, just as you said. Did you get that?" he said.

It was a ghastly stab of blitheness, but it seemed to amuse Shawn, who was foolishly grinning from ear to ear.

Stein shook his head in doubt. "I got it, Tony. But you guys are something else," he said. "You're a pair of what proctologists look into."

Stein had spoiled his fun. Pesce's face was as cold and hard as concrete. "All right, funny little man, it's show time. Let's see what you've brought me."

We exchanged glances. Stein nodded at me solemnly. "Go ahead, Charlie," he said.

Shawn's hand, I noticed, rested lightly on the grip of the pistol. Without breaking eye contact with him, I moved deliberately, in measured increments, and reached for the suitcase at my feet. I lifted it slowly off the floor and placed it on the table. The locks snapped open with a touch of the hand. I raised the lid and stared a moment. It was an icon of crime, a classic image. Neat rows of hundred-dollar bills bound in stacks of fifties. "I'm waiting," I heard Pesce say. Stein nudged me. I turned the case around to face them, and gently pushed it across the table.

I kept my eyes fixed on Pesce and Shawn, but I was aware of Stein swinging the other case onto the table. I heard the sound of the hasps' release. I watched as Pesce plunged his hands into the suitcase I had passed them. The question was in both their eyes. Was it all money, top to bottom? Shawn gawked at the money. Pesce, satisfied, straightened up. Arms bent at the elbows, fingers curled in, he gestured in universal sign language: "Gimme-gimme, me mine." "Keep 'em coming, funny little man, keep 'em coming," said Pesce.

"Keep 'em coming to poppa," twittered Shawn.

My eyes were on the pistol. I didn't see what started it. I heard Pesce yell: "You little sonofabitch." And all hell broke loose. Murder in his eye, Pesce was coming over the table. I lunged for the aluminum case. Stein was outside my field of vision. Shawn was leveling the gun in Stein's direction when I hit him with the case. He bobbed to his left to avoid me.

There was a blast, an explosion. Shawn yelped in shock and pain, twisting toward Pesce. The pistol fired with a dull report, and Pesce fell. I jumped Shawn, managing to get both hands on the gun.

"Give it up!" Stein commanded.

The gun came loose in my hand, and it was over—the whole thing taking less than ten seconds, the time it takes to run a down in football. Pesce was slumped on the table, the crisp white shirt flecked with red. Shawn's big body hovered over him, trembling. "Tony, oh God no, Tony," he sobbed. "It was an accident. I didn't mean it, Tony."

I glanced up at Stein. He was backed against the wall, his face grim, a .357 magnum in his hand. My ears were ringing with the sound of the big gun and James Taylor singing, "You've Got a Friend."

Chapter 18

Stein and I scrambled frantically to retrieve the scattered packs of bills, and stuff them back into the Halliburton case. Pesce, time running out on him, stared eerily, following us with vacant eyes, his head cushioned on Shawn's massive chest in a grotesque parody of a Pietà. The slug from the kid's .22 was lodged somewhere in his brain. He bled from the back of the head and the nose. Shawn was covered with blood, Pesce's and his own. Stein had grazed him with the .357, opening a nasty gash on his left shoulder. There was a hole in the wall behind them where that bullet had lodged.

"Come on," said Stein, hurriedly packing the cannon away in its foam-lined case. "Let's get the hell outta here."

"For God's sake, call an ambulance," pleaded Shawn.

"Sure, kid, sure," said Stein, tugging at my sleeve and pulling me from the room. I needed no encouragement to get out of there.

We drove back to Manhattan in oppressive silence under a leaden sky that hung so low it seemed to want to crush us. "I want a drink," Stein said finally. "How about you?" We were on the ramp leading to the Fifty-ninth Street Bridge.

I didn't know what I wanted, heroin, maybe, but a drink would do until I could think of something better. "Yeah, sure, a drink," I said numbly. "I could use a drink."

"Know a place?"

"Nothing open this early."

"I mean like where the nightshift goes to unwind, an after-hours place," he said hopefully.

I wondered if he wanted to party. "There's one in Clinton . . . hell, come up to the studio, I'll fix you up."

That idea was fine with Stein. He parked the Volvo in a lot on Thirty-seventh Street, and we dodged a sprinkle of fat raindrops as we toted the Halliburton cases back to my place. Was I carrying the gun or the money? I wondered idly. I had a feeling it was the gun. Whichever it was, there would be no confusion in Stein's mind.

While Stein called the precinct house in Long Island City and anonymously tipped them that there had been a shooting at Muscle Mania and that someone might need an ambulance, I brewed a large full-strength pot of El Pico.

"I promised the kid," Stein said, when he hung up.

"Just didn't say when, huh?" I filled two mugs with half-and-half, coffee and bourbon, and passed one to him.

He gave me a tentative smile. "Well, to your health," he said, raising the mug and sipping.

I nodded sternly and drank. Although I searched Stein's face for a trace of the conniver, I could find none. Instead, he met my gaze with one of curious amiability. What's in a face anyway? I wondered. I shifted my gaze. The caffeine and alcohol hit my bloodstream with the jolt of a one-two combination.

"All right, let's have it," he said. "What's on your mind?"

"You know, I keep forgetting what a manipulator you are, Stein."

His eyebrows lifted in mild astonishment.

"Don't give me that," I mimicked him. "That's twice now

232

you've fucked me. You used me as your stalking horse. You went out there intending to whack them. The payoff and the tape recorder were just some more of your bullshit."

"Don't stop," he said. "Get it off your chest."

"Don't worry, I will. You were gonna have to deal with Pesce, sooner or later. And sooner was better, so beat him to the punch, right? And I was the chump to set him up for you. It was nothing more than a hit, Stein."

"Is that it? Are you done?" he said solemnly.

"Yeah, I'm done."

"Feel any better?"

"No." I felt like a fool.

He regarded me thoughtfully a moment, then he said, "So I planned it. And I used you. Would you have gone along with me if I told you up front what I had in mind?"

"No."

"I thought not." He placed the mug on the countertop, reached around his waist, underneath his shirt, and pulled out a tiny cassette recorder. "See, I was wearing a wire. Wanna hear it?"

"What's on it? Me shooting off my mouth."

"Pesce confessed," he grinned. "Remember?"

"That tape incriminates us as much as it does them."

"Yeah, I suppose so," he agreed. "Charlie, let me explain why I did it."

"Go ahead."

"Okay, in no particular order, here are the reasons why. I did it because once a guy like Pesce gets it into his head you owe him money, you never get done owing him money. I did it before they could do it to you or me. I did it because they're bigger than me. I did it because they asked for it. I did it because I don't run from anyone. I did it because I do my own dirty work. I did it because there's no other way to deal with a problem like this. And last but not least, I did it because I don't like living alone. Want any more reasons?"

"Maybe if you had run it by me like that beforehand, I would have gone along with you."

He shrugged. "I doubt it. You're too nice a guy. You ever kill a man, Charlie?"

"No."

"I didn't think so, and I didn't want to be responsible for you losing your cherry."

"So you let me walk in there empty-handed. What were you thinking, it was gonna be like shooting fish in a barrel? Just whip out that cannon and blaze away. What kind of plan was that?"

"Well, if you had proposed a better plan, I'd have gone with it. Mine was far from perfect," he admitted with uncharacteristic modesty. "And remember, Shawn had a pistol. Fish in a barrel don't shoot back."

"It's a wonder I'm not shitting a .357 magnum slug."

He chuckled softly. "I would have blown a hole through Pesce as big as your fist, if you hadn't bumped me when you went for the kid."

"Maybe." I wasn't aware I had bumped him.

"No maybes about it," he said. "If your ass hadn't been in my line of fire I would have had the kid, too. After Pesce took it from that peashooter it was too late, though." He paused for a quick swallow of bourbon and coffee. "It would have been an execution then," he added.

It was a pretty nice distinction he was making, but it explained the lousy goon imitation, the attitude. He was goading them. He wanted them to go for him. He went out there to kill them, but drew the line at cold blood.

"Now what, Mad Dog?" I said.

The appellation drew a tart smile. "Back at the gym, you mean?"

"Yeah."

"It's a cinch Pesce's not going anywhere. And if the cops get there quick enough, they ought to find the gun. I hope they do, that'll give Shawn some explaining to do."

"What about Pesce? He wasn't dead."

"But he was definitely on the critical list, and not likely to improve. You never can tell about those peashooters, though. Look at that guy, Brady, the President's press secretary, takes one right in the head and goes on living."

I was skeptical. "He looked bad to me."

"I hope so," Stein said fervently.

"The .22 automatic seems to be a popular piece. Shawn's been packing one since the day we met, and Hungerford was shot with one."

"The wiseguys like them. They've got a lot of impact at close range, and they're easy to silence. That makes them good for hits. Myself, I like firepower."

234

"I noticed."

"Anyway, one thing's sure," Stein finished, "even if Pesce survives, his career in crime is finished. He'll be lucky if he can learn to tie his shoelaces again." He drained the mug. "That was good, Charlie. Can I make a long-distance call?"

"You know where the phone is."

I finished off my mug. It wasn't every day I saw a man shot in the head before breakfast. I felt I was entitled to more of the same and refilled our mugs. I placed Stein's at his elbow. He rewarded me with a broad grin. I drifted over to the windows to avoid hearing his conversation. There wasn't much of a north light today, and the light that did filter in was bleak and gray; $f/1.4$ at a full second on tri-X, I estimated, looking out on the pedestrians below hustling along Thirty-ninth Street in the rain. Stein's voice was a muted background sound. Now and then I'd catch the word "honey."

"What a crummy day," Stein observed, joining me at the window. "I'm gonna need fortification if I'm going out in that." He took a healthy swallow. "Ahh," he shivered, and raised the mug again, finishing it in a single draught. He smacked his lips and bounced on the balls of his feet. "When it comes right down to it, they're the ones we do it for, Charlie."

"Who?"

"The women."

"Aha."

"Yeah, it's not normal for a man to live alone. What you need's a wife, Charlie."

"I'm auditioning, Henry."

"Just remember, looks aren't everything," he beamed. "And with that thought I'll leave you."

I trailed him to the door and out to the elevators. He made a doughty little figure with a Halliburton case in each hand. A half-pint Willy Loman of flimflam, I thought.

It was just after nine when Stein left, and Tito hadn't arrived yet. I dashed off a note saying I'd be out on errands for a couple of hours, and locked up. I jumped into a cab at Madison and Thirty-eighth.

The idea was to surprise her nibs and show up unannounced. That was the only way I could expect to find

Sloane in. I bought a bouquet of flowers, red and yellow tulips, as a prop for the old trade delivery dodge, and gained access to the building through the service entrance. Minutes later I was knocking at her door.

"Delivery, flowers," I called through the door, careful to screen my face from the peephole with the floral wrapping paper.

When I heard her throw the lock, I pushed my way in.

"Charlie!" she cried, in a voice wavering between anger and relief. "My God, you scared me. I thought I was being attacked. What's going on? What are you doing here at this ungodly hour?"

She didn't look at all bad, tousled slightly and glowing, in a terrycloth robe and a pair of mules, fresh from bed. But I've never seen her look bad, ungodly hour or no.

She gave me half a smile and nodded at the flowers. "Are those for me?" she asked.

"Uh-huh." I handed her the bouquet, wishing I'd thought to ask the florist what was appropriate for a death in the family. Lilies, perhaps?

"You're sweet, Charlie." She smiled, accepting the flowers. "But you shouldn't have." She laughed, low and throaty. "People say that, 'Oh, you shouldn't have,' but they don't really mean it, though, do they?" She bent over to place the bouquet on the coffee table, distracting me with an up-from-under look, her breasts playing peek-a-boo in the vee of her robe. "Although, on second thought, you should bring me flowers," she said. "You haven't been very nice to me lately."

"Let's cut the crap, Sloane."

Her face clouded over, her eyes grew stormy. "This is not a friendly call, is it?"

"No."

"Well, I don't need abuse. If you can't be civil you can leave. In fact, why don't you leave? I really don't have anything to say to you." She moved to show me the door.

"You're wrong there. We've got a lot to talk about." I grabbed her by the shoulders and tossed her upright onto the couch. There was a flash of skin—she was naked under the robe.

"I don't go in for rough stuff," she warned me with sullen eyes, adjusting the robe without modesty.

236

"Not much you don't."

"Just say what you came to say. Then get out."

"All right, I'll give it to you straight. You set me up. Your phone call . . ."

"Jesus, are you still ragging on that? We went through all that yesterday."

"Not quite. We didn't go through how you fingered Warren Ulrick and got him killed. And how you ordered the professor and his wife rubbed out, like you would order a pizza to go."

She started to rise. "I'm not listening to this."

"Yes you are. Sit down." I shoved her back on the couch, rougher this time. She glared at me. "The professor and his wife got themselves in trouble. They're none of my business. Warren Ulrick is, though. He's dead because of me. I got him in trouble. But you, precious, were the only one who could identify him to the killers. You were the only one who knew what he looked like. When I was here yesterday, I discovered how you did it. It was *The Player's Guide.* You matched his face to his real name and you had him. You were even careless enough to have marked the place."

Her face was pale. "Is my copy of *The Player's Guide* the only one with his picture in it?"

"No, but you're the only one with the motive and a copy of *The Guide.*"

"It proves nothing."

"Only to me, darling."

"Why are you doing this?" she moaned. "I thought we were friends."

"You wanna know why? I'll tell you. There's a cop with four unsolved murders who's beginning to wonder why whenever a body drops, I'm the one standing closest to it."

"Does he think you killed Richard?"

"You'd like that, wouldn't you?"

"Charlie, I only asked. I don't know why you're behaving this way toward me."

"You don't, huh? Well, maybe I'm pissed because a friend set me up to be worked over by a three-hundred-pound dumbbell."

"Could happen again," she said with a grin.

"I don't think so, Angie, baby."

She went off like a Roman candle. "You motherfucker,

237

Byrne," she spit. Her eyes bulged, the cords in her neck stood out.

"You figured I was tailor-made to take the fall for Richard with big brother, didn't you, Angela?"

She flung the tulips in my face. "Because you're a dead man, Byrne," she said.

"Maybe, but what's Anthony gonna say when he hears how little sister screwed him out of half a million in cash?" I gathered up the flowers, careful to keep an eye on her nibs.

"Why should he believe anything you say?"

"Because, when he's hurting me, I'm gonna talk. It'll be no time to lie. And you'll be all I'll have to talk about."

"And you think Tony'd believe I killed Richard?" She sounded less sure of herself than she intended.

"When he couldn't squeeze the money out of me, he'd be convinced. After all, didn't you and Richard stay in touch? Didn't he tell you he had money? Didn't he beg you to run away with him?"

"How do you know that?" she cried.

"Richard was a sucker for you, Angie. Even after Anthony and Stein, he still wanted you."

She hugged herself, bare knees showing. It had a calming influence on her to be reminded of her slaves.

"Why else would he keep calling?"

She didn't answer.

"The reason you were willing to take his calls was because you believed him. You believed he had money. You were waiting by your phone for his call from the Bahamas. When he landed at Kennedy, Saturday night, you were there to meet him." I paused. She sat tense and expectant. I caught the movement out of the corner of my eye and looked up.

The dyke from the disco, Ronnie, legs that went to her armpits, long and white under a black silk pajama top, stood in the bedroom doorway casually puffing on a cigarette. My gaze switched back to Sloane. She returned it with a rueful half grin.

"Hi, what's all the noise out here?" said Ronnie.

I ignored her. "You walked to his car," I said, picking up where I left off. "The two of you got in the car. You pulled the .22 automatic from your bag and shot him once in the head. Then you wiped your prints off the gun, placed it in Richard's hand, and waltzed off with the cash."

Ronnie strolled over, flicked her ashes in a tray on the table, and plunked herself down next to Sloane. "Did you do what the man says, sugar?" she asked.

Sloane smiled momentarily at her friend, then turned back to me. "Is that what you think happened?" she asked, her eyes meeting mine.

I shrugged. "It doesn't matter what I think happened, it's what Anthony thinks that counts."

"How much cash was that?" said Ronnie.

"Half a million," I said.

"That's an awful lot of money, honey, half a million," said Ronnie. "What did you do with all that money?"

"Yeah, it is." I smiled.

Sloane laughed her patented, throaty laugh.

"Wait a minute," said Ronnie. "When did you say all this happened?"

"Saturday night," I said.

Ronnie crossed her legs, man style. She wasn't wearing underpants, and didn't care if I knew it. "Couldn't have been Saturday night, pal." She laughed, shaking her head.

"Why not?"

"Remember?" She laughed, stroking Sloane's thigh. "I had to beat those dykes off you with a stick." She leveled her eyes on me, her face serious. "I never let her out of my sight Saturday night, pal. That's prime time."

"I bet," I said.

"The mortgage," she said. She turned to Sloane with a pout. "Does this mean you don't have the money, sugar? Oh well, never mind, I love you anyway."

I nodded at Ronnie. "The alibi, huh?" I said. "Might work with the cops, but she won't help much with Anthony." I had the sudden urge to decamp. It was creepy enough breaking in on her, but with Ronnie in the picture, I felt about as welcome as eczema at a nudist camp. Pity, this might have been fun under different circumstances.

They stood up, sensing perhaps I was anxious to leave. Ronnie's eyes gleamed in triumph.

"Yes, my alibi," Sloane smirked. "Although I don't think I'll need one. I haven't done anything wrong." She scooped up the flowers from the table. "Don't forget these." She gazed at me with mixed emotions, defiance, tinged with regret, I thought.

"They're yours," I said. "I brought them for you. You're right, I haven't been very nice to you lately." An image of Anthony cradled in Shawn's arms played on the small screen of my mind.

"In that case, thank you." She passed them to Ronnie, who hovered nearby. We moved to the door. "I wish you had called first." She smiled weakly.

"Yeah," I grinned.

"I could put in a word for you with Tony," she offered mildly.

"I think it's too late for that," I said.

She looked puzzled as she closed the door quietly after me.

It was too early for the Metro edition, but the Final edition of the *Post* had the story complete with photos of Pesce's crumpled form. That was fast. Radio had the story every hour on the hour. I flicked on the TV: Gang Rubout in Queens, film at five, they promised. I read, listened, and watched it all avidly. "A tipster phoned the police," went the story, "that there had been a shooting in a Queens health spa. Arriving at the scene, police found the body of Anthony Pesce, an alleged rising star in the Joey 'Panzy' Panzellone crime family." There was no mention of Shawn or the gun.

Bruce Linhardt, my pal from the laundromat, called later that day. "Have you heard about Hungerford and Pesce?" he wanted to know.

"Yes, I have."

He snorted in disgust. He sounded disappointed he didn't have the hot skinny for me. "Sonsabitches deserved it, both of 'em," he exploded.

"I have no qualms about Pesce, but I'm not so sure Hungerford deserved to die."

"Not so sure?" he scoffed. "The guy stole people's life savings. They oughta give whoever killed him a medal."

"Whoever killed him did a whole lot better than a medal. They got a half a million bucks for their trouble."

"No kidding. Jeez, I would have done it for nothing. So would a lot of other people. Hey, ya don't think Sloane did it, do ya?"

"As a matter of fact, I do."

"What about Pesce? He coulda done it?"

"Yeah, but he didn't."

"You like Sloane, huh?"

"That's what I said, but there were nearly two hundred investors, remember? Any one of them could have done it."

"I guess," he said gloomily. "Life's not fair, is it?"

"No, it's not. But how do you mean?"

"Sloane could get away with murder and pick up all the marbles too."

"I guess she could."

"Hey, why not. She's gotta have a few bucks salted away from this thing already. If, like you say, she snuffed Hungerford, there's half a million more. There's the co-op, a summer house, and now, the latest I hear, she's gonna marry the lawyer."

"Philolius?"

"Yeah, Phil Philolius, the slob with all the jewelry."

"Where did you hear that?"

"From Philolius's wife. I call 'em once in a while, like I'm callin' you. They're on my list of investors. Last time I called 'em, I got her, and she unloaded on me. Phil's been boffing Sloane, she bitches, and he wants a divorce so he can marry her. What's she gonna do? She's got a family. She's gonna make the dopey bastard pay. She was a crazy woman."

"I can't say I blame her," I mused. So Bruce had some hot skinny for me after all.

Linhardt laughed. "She sez ta me, 'Whatta you guys see in that bimbo? She's nothing but a forty-year-old mattress.'"

"Ouch," I winced. "Listen, Bruce, I gotta go, but thanks for keeping me posted."

"Anytime. Well, that's about it then, I guess," he said.

"It seems to wrap it up," I concurred.

Glamorous investor parties, models and Mafia guys, fraud and sex and murder, heady stuff, and Bruce Linhardt, a workaday daddy from Queens, had had a ringside seat through all of it. He had hobnobbed with all the main players. It wasn't a cheap ticket—it had cost him some—but it had proved worth the price of admission. Instead of interest, the big bamboozle delivered vicarious thrills at an outrageous rate. The reluctance of his hangup was palpable. Its inevitable conclusion saddened him.

Chapter 19

Nah, he'd never buy the "I was riding my bike" alibi twice, I thought, when Hannibal showed up in my place early the following morning, unannounced. I ran through the coffee, tea, and club soda routine again while searching for something more original in the alibi department. He surprised me and accepted coffee. A hopeful sign. He seemed less testy, less dogged than the other day.

"What's happening?" I asked cautiously, drawing up a director's chair.

"It's all happening," he grinned, making himself comfortable. "Hear about Pesce?"

"Of course."

"Wasn't that something? I never had a chance to talk to him."

"It was sudden," I said guardedly.

"Sure was. You know, in the Department, the right hand often doesn't know what the left hand's doing."

"I can imagine."

"Two different precincts can be working on the same or related cases and not know it."

"Doesn't the computer help?"

"That's what I mean, it doesn't always show up on computer. When something like this happens, however, the publicity blows it wide open. There's a cop in the Thirty-first named Lazarus who knows these guys, Pesce and his pal, Shawn. What's more there's a state investigator, Strunk, says he knows you—he's with the Securities Bureau and he's been making inquiries recently."

"Strunk? How did he get into it?"

"Hungerford was moving money internationally."

"I see."

Hannibal laughed. "Did you know Pesce and his buddy are gay?"

"I knew that."

"Gay wiseguys," he said, shaking his head. "Nowadays, it's happened before you can invent it. Anyway, as soon as he heard about the shooting, Lazarus hustled out and tossed Pesce's condo. What do you think he came up with?"

"I have no idea. What?"

"A radio remote control for a model airplane, and demolition percussion caps."

"One case will solve another. You said it would happen this way."

"Did I say that?" he grinned. "Well, Forensic has yet to match the stuff with the debris from the Subaru wreck—looks promising, though."

"Anything on Warren Ulrick yet?"

"Not so far."

"And what about Shawn? Any sign of him?"

"Not yet. But he'll turn up, and when he does we'll get a few more pieces to the puzzle," he replied cheerfully.

"He's a monster, you know."

"I know. Met him here the other day, remember?"

"That's right."

"But I don't care if he's Godzilla, we'll collar him."

"He drives a green Datsun 280Z, if that'll help you," I said. I even remembered the license plate number.

He whipped out his notebook and jotted the number down. "Sure it'll help," he said. "Anything to make him for the Ulrick job."

"They said on the news that Pesce was a mob hit."

"Maybe. According to Lazarus, Pesce was a made man. And the gun was a .22 caliber. But the gay angle, and the fact the kid's missing, has us thinking it might have been a lover's quarrel. The kid was a male hustler, rough trade, before he hooked up with Pesce, Lazarus says, and anything could set him off, and wham, you've got a homicide. Happens all the time."

"Well, that leaves the Hungerford case," I said, wondering exactly what pieces to the puzzle they would find when they picked up Shawn.

"Lots of suspects," he said, cool eyes sparkling.

"Oh?" My gut went into free fall.

"Yeah, we haven't ruled out Pesce and the kid, but at the moment, we're leaning toward the wife on that one."

I was stunned. "The wife? You're putting me on."

"Not at all." He grinned.

"But what about Sloane Marshall?"

"She's a possibility, too."

"But why the wife? Who thought of that one?"

"A cop, me." He smiled. "That's the way a cop thinks."

I itched to tell Hannibal about *The Player's Guide,* but there seemed to be no way of doing that without incriminating Stein and myself. "I guess it makes sense," I murmured. Up till now, I liked the way cops thought.

"Damn straight it makes sense," said Hannibal. "I've seen plenty of these cases, where the wife pops her old man before she's dumped for a younger woman. This was a woman scorned. She's very bitter, and she's not the least bit shy about it. Don't know as I blame her. Hungerford sounds like a dirtbag. She thought—correctly—he was fixing to split with the money and the girlfriend, and there was no way she was gonna let that happen. If there was any money left after the swindle collapsed, she figured she had as much right to it as anyone. So she was right there waiting when he got off the plane from the Islands. The way he was shot indicated he knew his murderer."

"It seems to me, aside from the jealousy factor, you could run the same scenario for Sloane Marshall."

"Yeah, but don't you see, it's jealousy plus money that makes this the more attractive package."

"But what about the weapon? Was it coincidence that it was a .22 pistol?"

"Plenty of 'em on the street."

"Would the wife be satisfied with one slug in the temple, or would she empty the gun in the son-of-a-bitch?" I asked.

"Good point, that's the way a cop thinks." He gazed at me momentarily with piercing eyes. "What have you got against the Marshall woman?" he asked.

"Nothing," I said. "But she was Pesce's sister. They were bilking Hungerford."

"Good points all. As I've said, we've got plenty of suspects."

"Then you haven't charged the wife?"

"No. Have you ever met the woman?"

"No, I haven't."

"Well, she's not much to look at, but she's a cool head. She claims she was at the mall, shopping, when her husband's plane landed. She can't prove she was, naturally. No one saw her there. The problem is, we can't prove she was at Kennedy, and for the very same reason. No one saw her there." He drained his coffee cup and got to his feet slowly. "Well, Charlie, as the poet said, the best-laid plans of mice and men, eh?"

I accompanied the detective to the door with an enormous sense of relief. It was messy, but it was working out. And for the moment, Hannibal wasn't giving me any heat. Stein would appreciate these developments, I thought.

Section C of Friday's *Times* carried an article claiming Thai food was the new star cuisine. Strunk probably didn't read the *Times* because at noon, the gang of three, Strunk, Stein, and myself, put on the nosebags in yet another dingehole. This one went by the improbable monicker of Foo King's.

"Hey, Strunk," said Stein, winking at me, "hear the one about the chinaman who called his doctor up in the middle of the night?"

Strunk looked up from his plate and shook his head no. "No, but you're gonna tell me, aren't you," he said, returning to his forage.

"Okay," grinned Stein. "The chinaman says, 'Doctor, doctor, come right away.' And the doctor says, 'Who is this?' The chinaman says, 'I'm Foo King.' 'So am I,' says the doctor . . ."

" 'Take two aspirins and call me in the morning,' very funny, Henry," said Strunk, chewing. "You just make that up? That's a terrible joke."

"So's this food," said Stein.

Strunk mopped his plate with the end of an eggroll and dispatched same with the speed of sound. He wiped his mouth with a paper napkin. "Excellent," he beamed. "You fellows enjoy yours?"

"Delicious, P.C.," said Stein with a sour face.

"Yeah, delicious," I said amiably. I marveled at Strunk's girth. He seemed to be expanding by forkfuls. He must be meeting all the snitches in Chinese restaurants nowadays, I thought.

"Spoke with your pal Hannibal yesterday," Strunk said blandly.

"Oh yeah."

"Yeah. Lazarus put him on to me."

"And what did he want?" I asked, exchanging a wary glance with Stein.

Strunk regarded me momentarily with a mixture of skepticism and determination. I was reminded by his expression that he was a cop first and a friend second. "Not much," he said finally. "He just wanted to know what I knew about you."

He was going to make me play Twenty Questions. "What did you tell him?"

"I told him you were a spook and a womanizer," he beamed.

"I knew I could count on you for a reference, P.C."

"Anytime."

"What did you really tell him?"

"Interested, huh?"

"Gimme a break, P.C., what did you tell the guy?"

"I told him that you were tailing Hungerford, and that I helped you with the banks and the airlines."

"Jesus, P.C., he probably thinks I nailed Hungerford."

"Chill out, Byrne. You have friends in law enforcement." He grinned broadly. "I told him you got crossed on the scheduling, and got there too late to whack him."

"Gee, thanks, P.C."

"Don't thank me, Byrne. I told him you're on our side."

"Ah, the real mob." I grinned back at Strunk.

"Believe it," he said straightfaced. "Anyway, Hannibal thinks the wife beat you all to the punch."

"Yeah, I know. That's what he told me."

"And did he tell you about the remote control equipment and the percussion caps?"

"Yes, he did."

"Then you know they think the kid shot Pesce."

"That's what Hannibal said."

"I spoke with Lazarus. A lover's spat is what they think it was. Although there is one curious thing," said Strunk, shifting his gaze to Stein. "They pried a .357 magnum slug from the wall."

"A fresh one?" asked Stein innocently.

"It was a fresh one," said Strunk.

"So you think there was another person in the room, is that it?" said Stein.

"It's not what I think," said Strunk. "It's what Hannibal thinks." His sly brown eyes regarded Stein. "But I know you're partial to cannons, Henry."

"When I hit 'em, I like 'em to go down and stay down," he said with a shrug.

"Yes, I know," said Strunk. "Naturally, when Hannibal mentioned the slug in the wall, I thought of you. You realize, if there was another person in the room when Pesce was shot, they'll find out who or whom when they collar the kid."

I resisted the temptation to check Stein's reaction, holding my gaze on Strunk instead. "What did Hannibal say about the Ulrick murder?" I asked.

"Ulrick? . . . Oh yeah, the shill you used to set Hungerford up. As I said, when they collar the kid they'll probably get the answers to a lot of questions."

"Ulrick's body was dumped in the Ramble, in Central Park," I said. "I can place Shawn there that day and so can another witness, a friend of mine. He tried to run us off the road with his car while we were bike riding."

"Did you get the license plate number?"

"I gave Hannibal the make, model, and plate number."

"Again, if they get the car when they collar the kid, maybe they'll find a trace of blood or hair or something that can be matched up in the lab to Ulrick."

"Hannibal said the same thing. *I know how Pesce and Shawn found Ulrick,*" I said, and switched my gaze from Strunk to Stein.

Stein looked quizzical and bemused, but didn't speak.

"Did you tell Hannibal?" asked Strunk.

"No."

"Why not?"

"Because I don't see how it would help our side."

"I told you, Byrne, you've got friends in law enforcement." His eyes were as hard and black as anthracite.

247

"You maybe, P.C., but I'm not counting on the other guy. Let's see what happens when they get the kid."

Strunk nodded gravely.

"I've got some disheartening news for you, Henry."

"What's that?" he asked.

"Her nibs is engaged to be married."

"Sloane?"

"Who else? One of the investors called today with that item."

"Really." He mugged mild surprise by lifting his eyebrows. "Who's the lucky guy?"

"A lawyer, Phil Philolius."

"Way to go, Sloane," Stein grinned. "A lawyer, huh? She can always use one of those, if he's any good."

"He was an investor. That's how they met, I guess."

"Oh-oh, can't be that smart, then."

"I wouldn't think so."

"Well, a good lawyer's hard to find." He laughed.

Chapter 20

⎯⎯⎯⎯⎯⎯⎯⎯⎯⎯

The daylight hours were stretching out now and a pale blue light still lingered in the sky when Mike-the-Bike and I were coming home from the park that evening about seven-thirty. We were traveling at a brisk clip, with Mike several bike lengths in the lead as we approached the Forty-second Street Library.

I heard the motor accelerate, whining in protest. I heard tires squeal when he came around the corner. And I heard the horn blast. But I never saw him coming.

We were in front of the library steps, right between the carved stone lions, at Forty-first and Fifth. The car bumper touched the rear wheel and the Lejeune shuddered. The bike veered left. I lurched forward, out of the saddle, and was airborne. The bike followed after me. Asphalt rushed past me in a gray blur. Then there was a blur of blue sky. The Lejeune and I parted company in midsomersault. The Datsun blew by me.

I landed on my hands and knees, facing down Fifth Avenue. That was pure luck, it had nothing to do with me.

I heard Mike shout.

I turned.

The Datsun rocketed into reverse, motor revving at a feverish pitch. The car slammed back into first. He came at me again, burning rubber.

I made a dive for the curb and the lamppost, the only possible cover, and heard that sound, a sharp pop, like a firecracker. I grabbed for my shoulder, where it burned.

The rest happened with surreal clarity. There was Mike, clinging to the driver's side of the Z with one hand, a glint of refracted light in the other hand. The car slowed and weaved. There was a flurry of one arm sparring as Shawn beat at him with the long-barreled pistol. I was on my feet and running when Mike's head and shoulders were swallowed up by the Datsun. Riderless, his bike jumped the curb.

Mike hit the ground and rolled, ejected from the Datsun like burnt toast.

The Datsun lurched forward and careened madly down the avenue.

Mike, his eyes wild, bounced to his feet. The retractable blade showed red in his hand. "Crazy bastard tried to kill us," he gasped.

We ran after the car to Thirty-seventh Street, but it's all downhill from there. We froze, watching with horror as the Datsun weaved erratically down the avenue. It veered left suddenly, jumping the curb, and plowed lackadaisically into a plate glass window.

"Get your bike. Let's go," said Mike.

I glanced at his hand.

He raised the hand mechanically and we gazed, transfixed, at the blood.

"I must have hit his carotid artery," he said, and turned

and walked to the curb. He calmly dropped the blade down the sewer grate, then wiped his hand with a brown bag from the trashbasket and tossed that after it.

We climbed back on the bikes and coasted downhill to Thirtieth Street, where a small crowd of rubberneckers had already formed. We pushed our way through the crowd. The Datsun had gone through the Rajah Ranee, an establishment that dealt in oriental carpets. Shawn looked dead, slumped over the dash, the windshield splattered with his blood. I noticed that the front left wheel still spun slowly, and that there were no bloodstains on the display carpet.

Tito stopped me at the door with a warning finger to the lips and a nod toward the client lounge. It was early afternoon and I'd just returned from a three-hour client lunch, feeling dull and listless.

Not knowing what to expect, I peeked around the corner and saw a pair of black Reeboks—very trendy—attached to a pair of manufactured faded jeans. A further peek revealed Ginny Rowen, sitting among the marks of her trade, a cluster of shopping bags, flipping through a copy of *Vanity Fair*.

She shot up from her seat as I bounded in to greet her. "Charlie," she beamed.

"Ginny, good to see you. You look great. Florida must have agreed with you."

"You should have seen me a week ago, Charlie. My tan's almost gone now."

Yeah, I thought, but she still had that sexy overbite and the fine-boned grace. And that smashing combination of green eyes and auburn hair. Maybe she wasn't a real beauty, like Sloane, but she was a very nice package. She'd get by. There'd always be a place at the table for a woman with looks like hers.

"Well," I beamed, "you've been pretty scarce lately." In fact, she'd been so scarce, I hadn't seen her since putting her in the cab for the airport. And it was nearly two weeks since I'd called her in Florida with the all-clear.

"Oh, you know how it is," she said, "busy, busy, busy."

"Oh, sure."

"Well, what's the news from the underworld?" She flashed her lopsided grin.

"You knew about Pesce, right?"

"Yes."

"But have you heard about Shawn?"

"No, have the cops picked him up?"

"Better yet. He was involved in a car accident and it proved fatal." The cops knew it was no accident, of course, but it seemed easier to leave it like that with her.

"No kidding?"

"No kidding. Too bad, huh? Another promising career in crime nipped in the bud."

"And what about Sloane?" she said. "Any news of her?"

"Remember Bruce Linhardt?"

"Our friends from the laundromat, Bruce and Barbara. Yes, I remember them."

"Well, Bruce called the other day to say Sloane's getting married."

"Who's the lucky guy?"

"Phil Philolius, the lawyer."

"Oh, no!" She giggled and puffed up her cheeks. "Not the fat guy with the dumpy wife and all that gold jewelry?"

"You got it."

"Ha, way to go, Sloane! She'll make him a wonderful wife, don't you think?"

"They'll be a fun couple, for sure."

She grew serious, giving me a meaningful look. "I guess I was really lucky, wasn't I?"

"How do you mean?"

"I was the only one to get their money back, wasn't I?"

"Yes, you were."

"Thanks to you, Charlie."

"Yeah, well, Sloane and Pesce played rough. You were lucky you didn't get killed," I said, only half joking.

"Like the professor and his wife, you mean?"

"Uh-huh."

She brightened. "But I was lucky, I had you to protect me."

I grinned. "And now it's time to get on with our lives again, isn't it?" I said.

"Yes," she said, and lowered her eyes, messing with her hair in that schoolgirl habit of hers. "Ah . . . Charlie," she said solemnly, "can I ask a favor of you?"

"What's that?"

She ran her tongue across her teeth speculatively. "Ah, I'm a little tight for cash at the moment," she murmured. "I could use a small loan."

"How much did you have in mind?" I asked anxiously.

"Say, five hundred dollars. It'll only be for a month or so and I'll pay you right back, I promise."

"I guess I can manage that. But why are you so tight, may I ask?"

She gazed at me gravely for a second or two, then her face crinkled up in merriment. "I know exactly what you'll say when I tell you." She laughed.

"Ah-ha, you're a prophet."

"Don't be a smartass, Charlie Byrne."

"Go ahead and try me then."

"The reason I'm tight for cash at the moment is my friend Todd, he's an architect . . ."

"Yes," I said attentively.

"And well, he's putting together a syndicate of investors to develop a piece of property he owns in Florida."

"Uh-huh, and that's where the fifty grand is parked at the moment?"

"That and whatever else I could scrape up. Charlie, I couldn't pass this one up. Beachfront condos in Florida . . ."

"Beachfront condos in Florida, huh," I repeated. "What'll they think of next?"

Grinning, she pointed a finger at me, "See, I knew it. But seriously, this is a great deal, Todd says, double your money in three years. And he's offering the best return to the first investors. If you've got any money, Charlie, now's the time. I can get you in on a good thing."

"I think this is where I came in," I smiled.

"You're such a skeptic. This is a golden opportunity."

"Double your money in three years? Sounds too good to be true, and it probably is."

She pointed her finger again. "See, I knew it," she said, "I knew that's what you'd say."

"Then I'm right, you are a prophet. Tell me, what do you see for tonight? Sushi at Akasaka, perhaps?"

"I'd love to, really, but not tonight. Can we make it for next week, say Wednesday?"

"Sure, it's a date," I said.

"I've got to dash, Charlie."

"All right, I'll get that check."

She gave me a quick kiss on the lips when I handed her the check. "You're a living doll," she said.

"You're not so bad yourself."

I helped her to the elevators, toting one of her bags. As I trailed her through the door, I thought, she doesn't walk like one, and she doesn't quack like one, and she certainly doesn't look like one. She could never be a duck.

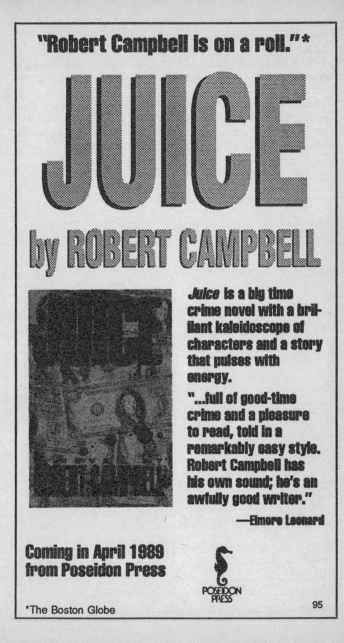